Robert Goddard

CLOSED CIRCLE

LONDON NEW YORK SYDNEY TORONTO

This edition published 1993 by
BCA
by arrangement with Bantam Press
a division of Transworld Publishers Ltd

CN 2410

Printed in Great Britain by
Mackays of Chatham Plc, Chatham, Kent.

CLOSED CIRCLE

CLOSED CIRCLE

CHAPTER

ONE

Chance had been our ally too often. We had grown complacent, over-confident of its loyalty. And so the moment when it first chose to betray us was also the moment when we were least likely to suspect that it might.

Max and I were leaning against the railings on the empty starboard promenade of the lounge deck, smoking cigarettes and gazing ahead at the widening river as the liner eased away from the shore. On the port side, a crush of passengers were still waving goodbye to the friends and family they were leaving behind in Quebec, but of wistful farewells we had no need. In Max's hand, folded open at an inside page, rested a two-day-old copy of the *Wall Street Journal*, and in the emboldened head-line of one of the columns blared silently the reason why we had eyes only for the seaway. BABCOCK FRAUD CASE TO GO TO TRIAL IN FALL. I watched Max scan the words once more and clench his jaw muscles in frustration or shame or relief or whatever he truly felt. Then he took a long pull on his cigarette and said, 'Well, that tears it, doesn't it?'

'We knew it was coming,' I said, by way of consolation. But in the look that passed between us there was an admission that foreknowledge only compounded the offence. 'He'll have a good lawyer,' I added with a shrug.

'He'll need one. They both will.'

'And there's nothing we could have done, except . . .'

'Go down with them?'

'Exactly.'

'Which isn't our style?'

'No. It isn't.'

For an instant, I expected him to deplore what we had done. Not simply our desertion of the Babcocks, but all the other immoralities and illegalities which lay scattered across our pasts. It was a rare sentiment in either of us, though perhaps not as rare as we cared to pretend. And, in this case, it remained unspoken. Max crushed the last inch of his cigarette against the guard-rail and turned towards me with that crooked smile I knew so well. 'It's bad luck on Dick. But we're well out of it, I reckon, don't you?'

'Assuredly.'

'Even if it means going back to Blighty.' He sighed and pushed himself upright. 'I'm for a bath before dinner. Meet for cocktails at seven?'

'Good idea.'

'And don't worry.' He slapped the newspaper against my shoulder. 'I won't bring this with me. What do you say to a ban on the subject – at least until we reach England?'

'I agree. Whole-heartedly.'

'Good. See you later, then.'

He moved past me, grinning with a sort of stubborn jauntiness, and headed for the companion-way. I finished my cigarette, watching the tugs fall away behind us in the rippling shadows of the funnels. Then I too decided to make for my cabin.

As I turned from the rail, I saw ahead of me a bulky figure – female and tweed-clad – descending the companion-way from the sports deck, an unlikely eyrie, I remember thinking, for one so stout and venerable, the creak of whose stays I almost believed I could hear above the rumble of the engines. Her ankles were swollen and her feet squeezed into what looked like an excruciatingly under-sized pair of high-heeled shoes on which she teetered top-heavily. The roll of the ship was modest, but still I would have bet against her completing the descent without mishap. And I would have won. A breath of Laurentian air twitched at the brim of her Alpine hat, she raised a hand from the rail to prevent it blowing off and a misplaced foot hovered ominously in mid-air.

'Oh . . . Oh my goodness . . .'

8

'It's all right,' I said, gripping her firmly by the elbow. 'I've got you.' I smiled as reassuringly as I could and did not release her until we were both standing square upon the deck, she staring up at me from a foot below, pale blue eyes wide and bosom heaving in alarm, perfume and naphthalene neutralizing each other bizarrely in the air around us.

'Dear me, dear me. Thank you so much, young man.' She was English, sixty or sixty-five I would have judged, with the butter-ball build of a dowager, all quivering jowl and pigeon chest. A triple necklace of pearls caught my eye, as did a flower-bouquet brooch on her left lapel in which rubies and sapphires glittered abundantly. 'What would have happened if you'd not been passing by I dread to think,' she said as she recovered her breath.

'Glad to have been of assistance, Miss . . .'

'Charnwood. Vita Charnwood. And how nice of you *not* to call me madam.' Thus was my guess of lifelong spinsterhood confirmed. 'Do I detect the accent of my own homeland?'

'England? Yes, though corrupted by many years on this side of the Atlantic.'

'In Canada?'

'No. The United States, actually, but . . .'

'Like me, you've been lured north by Canadian Pacific's promise that nearly a third of the crossing will be in the calm waters of the Gulf of St Lawrence? I quite understand. I too am a martyr to sea-sickness, Mr . . .'

'Horton.' I plucked off my hat and shook her hand, surprised to find that her grip was considerably stronger than her stumble on the companion-way had implied. 'Guy Horton.'

'Yes, Mr Horton, a martyr. There is no other word. Our voyage out was purgatorial.' *Our* voyage, I noticed. So, she was not alone. 'We must hope for better from this route, must we not?'

'Indeed.' I smiled, content to let her assume I had chosen to sail from Quebec rather than New York for the same reason she had. The truth would have been altogether too alarming for an owner of natural pearls and genuine rubies. And I was not in the habit of telling the truth except when strictly necessary.

'The only disadvantage is that there is nobody to see one off. Hence, I suppose, your presence on this side of the vessel. I happened to see you talking to another gentleman by the rail while I was craning out above you admiring the view.'

'That was Max. We're old friends.'

'And both going home after lengthy absences?'

'Yes. It must be . . . oh, seven years or more.' It was, in fact, nearer nine since either of us had lived in England, nine years which had, on the whole, treated us generously. The last two had been the least generous, but even so not as parsimonious as they might have been. To stand, well-dressed and sleekly groomed, on the first-class deck of the ocean's newest liner, while ashore depression sinks towards slump, is no mean achievement, even if riches do not await at the end of the voyage. Besides, there was always the hope of discovering riches *en route* to lift the spirits if they were in danger of sagging.

'You will notice many changes in England, Mr Horton. They will not all be to your taste. Seven years ago, everything was so much . . . jollier.' A thought seemed suddenly to occur to her. She planted an imperious forefinger on my sleeve. 'You must come to a little party I am holding tomorrow night – before the Atlantic does its worst. My niece and I would be delighted to see you. And your friend too.'

'Well, I . . .' Briefly and discouragingly, I imagined the niece, as thin as her aunt was fat, moth-balled and bespectacled. And then a shaft of sunlight struck the brooch below me. 'I'd be charmed to attend. As would Max, I'm sure.'

'Diana and I will expect you at six o'clock in our suite, Mr Horton. The gathering will not be a large one. But you will enjoy the company, I feel sure.'

'So do I, Miss Charnwood. So do I.'

Those of us who live by our wits can never afford to relax completely. Since abandoning the humdrum world of fixed hours and monthly salary ten years before, I had ceased to relish total idleness, tinged as it always was with a suspicion that I was wasting *my* time rather than somebody else's. Where was the profit in it, I would inevitably wonder, where the opportunity?

Knowing Max to be of like mind, I sauntered up from my cabin to meet him that evening feeling distinctly pleased with myself. Miss Charnwood's party might yet prove the dreariest of non-events, but, then again, it might not. Unpredictability had been the key to many of our successes and I was not about to lose faith in it. Stepping out onto the promenade, I filled my lungs with the sun-cleansed air of New World confidence, then went in to infect my friend.

10

It was an infection of which he was badly in need. He had installed himself in one of the farthest reaches of the orientally styled lounge and was regarding his fellow-passengers with what amounted to morose indifference as they gazed in wonder at the ebony pillars and exotic décor. Dick's arrest had struck him hard, harder, it seemed to me, than it should. The Wall Street Crash had obliged the Babcocks to sail too close to the wind – and we had sailed with them. The outcome could have been a great deal worse – especially if Max had not insisted on storing our nest egg in a Toronto bank. Yet he seemed unable to derive any comfort from his own prudence.

Perhaps age was the problem. Max was only a few months older than me, but in recent years his hair had thinned and his waist had thickened, so that he could have been taken for ten years my senior. He drank little more than me, but seemed to carry it less well than once he had. There was a vagueness sometimes to his thoughts and words, a vacuity to his gaze. He frequently complained of migraines and I could not help suspecting some connection with the head-wound he had suffered in Macedonia. I did not voice my suspicion, of course, so whether he feared the same himself I had no way of knowing. Whatever the cause, he was not quite the devil-may-care Max with whom I had first crossed the Atlantic seven years before.

No doubt he could have said something similar about me. And yet, studying my reflection in a mirror on my way through the ship, I would have begged to differ. My hair was still dark and vigorous, my face unmarked, my figure slender and elegantly tailored. There was no sign of physical decline, no hint of inner doubt. I was what the world and I had made of me between us: vain and egotistical no doubt, but then what handsome realist is not?

'You look a trifle down, old man,' I remarked, joining Max on his sofa.

He smiled ruefully. 'I'll snap out of it.'

'I know. I've devised the perfect restorative. Or perhaps I should say I've been presented with it.' The arrival of a steward imposed at this point a dramatic pause while I chose a cocktail and Max ordered what I estimated to be his third scotch and soda. When I told him my news, his initial reaction was one of unconcealed disappointment.

'Some frowsty old dame and her plain Jane niece? Sounds ghastly to me.'

'Perhaps. But Miss Charnwood's clearly not short of money.'

'Who *is* aboard this—' He broke off and stared at me, his eyebrows meeting in a frown. 'What did you say her name was?'

'Charnwood. Miss Vita Charnwood.'

'And the niece?'

'Um . . .' I struggled to remember.

'Diana?'

'Yes. That's it. How did—'

'Hah!' He slapped my knee and grinned broadly. 'You're right, Guy. Lady Luck has smiled on us once more.'

The steward loomed up with our drinks before he could continue. When we were alone again, I was made to wait till we had toasted our good fortune before Max consented to explain.

'Haven't you ever heard of Diana Charnwood?'

'Not that I can recall.'

'You should read the gossip columns. I've told you so often enough.'

'But you do it for me, Max. So, who *is* Diana Charnwood?'

'Daughter of Fabian Charnwood, head of Charnwood Investments. Presumably, you *do* know that name?'

I did indeed. Charnwood Investments was known to any student of the financial world as an influential holder of stakes in a score or more of major companies, so discreet in its exercise of power that it enjoyed a reputation far exceeding its size, so diverse in its holdings that it seemed to be riding out the Depression with ease. A chance encounter with its founder's sister was therefore a gift from the gods – one it had simply not occurred to me to think they might be generous enough to bestow.

'Diana is not just Charnwood's daughter. She's his only child.'

'Unmarried?'

'Notoriously so. There was an engagement about five years ago to the younger son of a marquess, but it ended at the graveside, not the altar.'

'Suicide. I *do* remember. Lord Peter Gressingham. Shot himself after she'd jilted him.'

'That was never confirmed. The inquest jury preferred to believe it was an accident. Either way, his former fiancée must count as one of the most eligible heiresses a chap could wish to meet.'

'And dangerous, if Lord Peter's example is anything to go by.'

'The fellow obviously let his heart rule his head. We wouldn't make that mistake, would we? We never have and we never will.'

12

I knew at once what Max was thinking of. Le Touquet, 1924. My brief but highly remunerative engagement to Caroline, only daughter of Sir Antony Toogood, sewing-machine magnate and doting father. It had been, in many respects, our finest coup. We had both set our caps at her, but even then I was Max's superior when it came to wooing. I had won poor Caroline's heart within a fortnight, and broken it within another, bought off by Sir Antony for a price I had not thought he would go to. There was a perfection to it, a simplicity which surpassed anything we had subsequently done. We had turned a handsome profit for nil outlay and nobody had lost what they could not easily replace – Sir Antony by cutting his salesmen's commission for a month and Caroline by finding a husband who really could make her happy.

'The man who wheedles his way into Diana Charnwood's affections wheedles his way into a fortune,' said Max. 'One way or another.'

'This isn't Le Touquet.'

'No? In principle, I should have said it was.'

'I mean it isn't the same situation. From what you tell me, Diana Charnwood is no blushing ingénue. In short, she isn't Caroline Toogood.'

'We don't know what she is – until we find out. And this party gives us the chance to do so. You're not suggesting we just let it slip away, are you?'

'Of course not.' Strangely, Max's enthusiasm now eclipsed my own.

'Good man.' He downed some more scotch with obvious relish. Unpredictability had revived him as I had hoped. In fact, my hopes had been altogether exceeded. 'What say we play to the same rules as in Le Touquet?'

'There's no need for that, surely? We weren't so trusting then.'

He smiled mockingly. 'And we are now?'

'Well, we've come a long way since on share and share alike. It's never had to be written down.'

'You can't share a wife, Guy.' Seeing my eyebrows shoot up, he added: 'Or a fiancée. It worked for us then, didn't it?'

'Yes, but—'

'So it could be just the good luck charm we need this time as well.' He raised a finger to summon the steward, ordered two sheets of writing paper to the fellow's well-disguised surprise, then lounged back, beaming from ear to ear. 'She'll be a tough nut to

13

crack, I don't deny. Maybe too tough. Certainly her reputation's no encouragement. It suggests she has a heart about as yielding as a diamond. But even diamonds can be cut if you have the knack of it – and the proper equipment. I'd say we have both, wouldn't you?'

'I'd say our record spoke for itself.' We exchanged a smile of mutual remembrance, acknowledging all the things we had done that it was infinitely better *not* to speak of. When the steward returned with the paper, Max whipped out his fountain-pen and, leaning forward to reach the angular table beside us, began to write on one of the sheets, handing the other to me.

I hesitated for a moment, staring at the embossed letterhead, then letting my eye wander across the watermarked space below. Max had spoken of the promissory notes we were about to exchange as good luck charms, but in my mind they were already beginning to seem more like omens of ill fortune. Whether this was because following in our own footsteps of seven years before struck me as tempting providence or because I was in the grip of some more general foreboding I cannot say. Whatever the cause, I had still not written a word when Max tossed his sheet into my lap and announced: 'That covers it, I reckon.'

> I hereby undertake to share equally with my good friend Guy Randolph Horton all financial proceeds, however they may accrue, of any engagement to marry and/or actual marriage I contract with Miss Diana Charnwood if and whenever it may occur.
>
> M. A. Wingate
> 19th July 1931

Such a document had no legal weight, of course. Neither of us could be bound by what we wrote. It amounted to something only if our friendship amounted to more than an alliance of financial convenience. And that, I suppose, is why I was so reluctant to commit the words to paper. These were hard times, as we and all the world knew. There was no telling what adversity might persuade us we needed to sacrifice in order to prosper. We had not scrupled to leave Dick to his fate. If it came to the point, would we be any more loyal to each other? It was a question I preferred not to answer, but, in his eagerness for written undertakings, perhaps Max had already delivered his verdict.

14

'This may be a waste of effort,' I protested in vain. 'Miss Charnwood may be impervious to our charms.'

'Then you can toss your copy over the side. And I'll do the same with mine – assuming I ever lay hands on it.' Our eyes met. 'What's holding you up?'

'Nothing.' And, so saying, I began to write.

Max and I dined at separate tables that evening, thus doubling our chances of striking up other promising acquaintances among our well-heeled fellow-passengers. Those whose company I was obliged to endure through so many gourmet courses that I lost count included a Newfoundland wood-pulp millionaire and his mountainous wife, an actress of the unrestrained school and her lugubrious husband, a Polish countess of enigmatic mien, the ship's surgeon, who nearly had to spring into action when milady wood-pulp suffered a choking fit, and the reticent but watchful Mr Faraday.

Faraday worried me more in retrospect than at the time, when, lulled by good wine and egregious service, I failed to notice that he was playing much the same game as me: listening to the revealing babble of others while disclosing virtually nothing of himself. He was about fifty years of age, short and slightly built, with close-cropped black hair and moustache, a mobile mouth that seemed to be savouring some delicacy even when it was empty, the faintest of quivers to his head as he concentrated on what was being said and, most disturbing of all, an unblinking gaze of moist and feline intensity. His manners were impeccable, his remarks unobjectionable and yet I did not like Mr Faraday. More precisely, I did not understand him. Worse still, I had the disquieting impression that he might understand me all too well. I resolved to avoid him for the rest of the voyage.

Of Miss Charnwood, aunt or niece, I saw no sign. They either dined later than us or in their suite. Perhaps the diamond-hearted Diana had decided to make her social début when she could be assured of being the centre of attention. Or perhaps she did not care for the seating lottery of the restaurant, a prejudice I was inclined to share even though I could not afford to indulge it.

Yet my hopes of seeing her before the party and so taking the measure of our task were not to be dashed. All next day, the *Empress of Britain* cruised serenely out across the Gulf of St Lawrence, white-hulled and resplendent beneath a cloudless sky.

15

And out into the air came its passengers, to sit beneath plaid rugs and play at quoits, to walk off breakfast and squint at the horizon, or, in some cases, to observe without being observed.

For this purpose, Max and I spent much of the day wandering the ship, steamer-capped and mufflered, apparently idle but actually intent upon our particular occupation. It was while nearing the stern end of the sports deck promenade shortly before noon that I noticed below us on the lounge deck, waddling out to sniff the ozone, none other than Miss Vita Charnwood, unmistakable in brogues and tweed. But, on this occasion, she was not alone. Beside her, walking with considerably more grace, was a slim young woman in fur-trimmed coat and cloche hat.

'The Charnwoods,' I whispered to Max. We stopped in the shadow of a lifeboat and peered down at them. 'Do you recognize her?'

'From a few old magazine photographs?' exclaimed Max. 'Not at this range. Why don't I step down and take a closer look while you stay here? It's the only chance I'll have of a dekko before we meet them tonight. And you've already met the aunt.'

'Good idea.'

So Max headed for the nearest companion-way while I remained where I was. The Charnwoods were halfway round a circuit of the stern rail when he appeared below me. By following the same route in the opposite direction, he was able to engineer a good view of them, especially since they paused at one point to speak to somebody. At length, they passed out of my sight back into the lounges, leaving Max leaning against the rail. Waiting only to be sure I would not encounter them on my way, I went down to join him.

He had lit a cigarette by the time I reached him and seemed to be lost in thought, eyes fixed on the blue ensign fluttering above us in the breeze. 'Well?' I demanded, when it became obvious that he was about to volunteer nothing.

'Sorry,' he murmured, smiling faintly and looking at me like a man waking from a dream. 'It's her all right. The photographs don't do her justice.'

'Quite a looker, then?'

'You could say so, yes.'

'But what would *you* say? All *I* could see was the brim of her hat.'

'Yes. I suppose it was.' His gaze drifted past me once more. 'As a matter of fact, old man, I'd say she was probably the most beautiful woman I've ever seen.'

The curse of a classical education is that mythological parallels occur unbidden to the mind when dealing with everyday realities. As soon as Max had praised Diana Charnwood's beauty, the fate of Actaeon when he spied on another Diana insinuated itself into my thoughts. Yet the goddess, I reminded myself, had been bathing, the heiress merely promenading. And Max had always understood that the pursuit of wealth is more rewarding than the pursuit of beauty. I felt sure I could rely upon him not to forget this simple truth.

There was no denying, however, that his tantalizing glimpse of what lay beneath the cloche hat had made him even more determined to exploit our opportunity. We had agreed to present ourselves at the Charnwood suite a quarter of an hour after the party was due to commence, in order to avert any suspicion of over-eagerness. But when I came to leave my cabin at ten past six, I found a note had been slipped beneath my door. It was from Max.

Decided to go on ahead. See you there.
M.

I could not help smiling at his cunning. The embarrassment of introducing himself was nothing compared with the disadvantage of arriving in my incontestably handsome shadow. But the night was scarcely born. I had no reason to expect I would continue to be outmanoeuvred.

The Charnwood suite was one of the largest on the ship and I found it already comfortably full, golden shafts of sunlight from the port-side windows lancing through a gabbling press of party-goers. Running a gauntlet of champagne- and canapé-wielding stewards, I came upon the elder Miss Charnwood, looking even vaster in low-cut pink satin than she had in straining tweed.

'Mr Horton!' she proclaimed. 'You were able to join us after all, then. I'm so glad.'

'There was never any doubt of it, Miss Charnwood.'

'But your friend, Mr Wingate, implied you might be detained elsewhere.'

'Really?'

17

'Perhaps I misunderstood. No matter. Diana will be *so* pleased to meet you. She's . . . oh . . . on the balcony at present, I think. Let me first introduce you to some of our guests.' She flapped one hand towards a bearded man of about her own age and some timid creature I took to be his wife. 'We first encountered Mr and Mrs Preece here at Niagara Falls. Then again at our hotel in Quebec. Mr Preece is something of an expert on Esperanto. He's just been telling me all about it.'

I had no intention of allowing Preece to tell me anything, let alone all, about Esperanto and I slipped away from him a matter of seconds after Miss Charnwood had done the same. The balcony was, needless to say, my destination.

It was there, where sea breezes offered relief from the noise and heat within, that Diana had taken up her station, surrounded by admirers both young and old. There they were, Max among them, shoulders squared to exclude newcomers, tense with the effort of capping each other's remarks, taut with ill-suppressed rivalry. The scene was not a new one. I had witnessed it before, at parties in New York graced by the presence of a Hollywood starlet. And I knew better than to join the ruck. To be late on such occasions is to be lost. Better to hover hopefully, perhaps even mysteriously. Which is what I endeavoured to do, retreating to the other end of the balcony, where I could sip my champagne and examine the object of so much attention.

She *was* beautiful. There was no pretending otherwise. Her dark brown hair was drawn back in a chignon, leaving her face clear and open. Normally, however pleasing a face may be, there is some flaw, some thinness of lip or fullness of jaw, to preclude the suggestion of perfection. But not in this case. The eyes as they sparkled in the sunlight, the mouth as it opened in an easy smile, the neck as it stretched in languid gesture: all conspired to stray beyond the limits of visual appeal into the realm of immediate fascination.

She wore an ultramarine dress of quiet elegance, a topaz pendant and a slim gold bracelet on her left wrist. But really these adornments were irrelevant, as her ease with herself suggested she realized. She was polite and amiable, yet also remote, glancing just often enough out to sea to imply that the company, however witty, however flattering, would always fall short of what she deserved. Whether Max was faring better than the others I could not tell, but there was no disputing that he was faring better than me.

I was just debating whether to make some effort to supplant him when the odious Faraday appeared on the balcony and instantly caught my eye.

'I hadn't realized you were acquainted with the Charnwoods, Mr Horton,' he remarked with a smile.

'Nor I you, Mr Faraday.'

'Oh, I rendered the elder Miss Charnwood some small service while she was in Quebec.'

'What manner of service?'

He tapped the side of his nose and smiled more broadly. 'You're enjoying the party?'

'Of course. And you?'

'Why, yes. I find it most . . . instructive.'

'Mr Horton?' Suddenly, Diana was standing next to us, smiling straight at me. She had broken free of her retinue, who were straggling the length of the balcony, uncertain at what pace it was seemly to follow.

'Er . . . yes.' I shook her hand, noticing the sinuousness of her fingers. 'Delighted to meet you.'

'I recognized you from my aunt's description.' At closer quarters, the remoteness in her bearing seemed to vanish, the warmth of her gaze to become irresistible. 'And from your friend's.' She glanced back at Max, whose grin was for my benefit: a mixture of the sheepish and the superior. 'You know Mr Faraday?'

'Only very slightly.'

'Then you know him as well as anyone can.' She glanced at him as she said it, but if the remark was intended to be provocative, it did not succeed. His only response was a faint twitch of the eyebrows. 'I'm so grateful to you for coming to Aunt Vita's aid yesterday,' she added, looking back at me.

'It was nothing, really. Do you share her preference for this route?'

'Yes. But not for the same reason.' Growing suddenly solemn, she said, 'Excuse me,' and moved swiftly away into the cabin.

Seeing me frown at her abruptness, Faraday sidled closer and said: 'An ill-chosen question, I'm afraid, Mr Horton.'

'It seemed harmless enough.'

'Her mother died on the *Lusitania*. Didn't you know?'

'No,' I snapped. 'I did not. Obviously.' Then, deciding to glean as much as I could, I added more moderately: 'You seem remarkably well-informed about the family.'

19

'Not really. Merely better informed than you.'

Refusing to be riled, I smiled and asked as casually as I could contrive, 'Was Miss Charnwood rescued from the *Lusitania*? Or was she not aboard?'

'The latter. Her mother had travelled alone to visit her family in Pittsburgh. She was a McGowan, you know.' Diana's connection with the famous Pennsylvania steel dynasty made her an even more desirable catch. I sensed Faraday judging my reaction to this revelation and endeavoured to ensure there was none for him to judge. 'Well,' he said after a pause, 'I really must circulate.' And, with a condescending little bow, he was gone.

'What do you make of him?' asked Max, who had remained on the balcony and now stepped across to join me by the rail.

'Even more treacherous than you, I'd say.'

He smirked. 'No good blaming *me* for *your* poor tactics, old man.'

'A word to the wise. Her mother went down on the *Lusitania*. And *she* was a McGowan.'

'I know.'

'You do?'

'Gossip columns. Remember?' His smirk began to verge on the intolerable. 'You'll be glad to know I'm doing rather well.'

'Really?'

'I think she may have her eye on me.'

'If you say so.'

'I do. Perhaps I'm the type she's always been wanting to meet.' My expression must have made my incredulity obvious. His smirk evaporated. 'You've always thought me a dull dog when it comes to the fairer sex, haven't you, Guy? Well, maybe you're about to discover that not all women want their men to look like hand-me-down Valentinos.'

'Oh, for God's sake.' I slapped the rail in irritation. 'She *is* beautiful. I agree. Memorably so. Desirable from every point of view. But she's also very much the mistress of her own destiny. I don't think you – or I – have the slightest chance of winning her heart.'

Max's gaze narrowed. 'We'll have to see about that, won't we?' And, turning on his heel, he left me to my champagne and dented pride.

Max turned out to be a good judge of his own success. When the party fizzled out, he was near the centre of the favoured group that accompanied Diana and her aunt to dinner. So, to my horror, was Faraday, although his attentions, in so far as one could tell, seemed to be focused on Vita. Perhaps he knew his limitations even if Max did not know his.

I had certainly been given a salutary lesson in mine and consoled myself by buttering up the Atkinson-Whites, an innocent Home Counties couple eager for advice on what to do with a recent and substantial inheritance. This struck me as a problem which it would have been churlish of me not to assist them in solving and they seemed grateful to know that I would be in touch soon after we reached England.

As to Max, the first opportunity I had of gauging his progress in a more dispassionate light came the following morning, after a game of real tennis. He had won most of our matches over the years at the Tuxedo Club in New York, but the unfamiliarity of a floating court was not the reason why I recorded a rare victory on this occasion. The truth is that jealousy makes a fine coach.

Max took defeat in his stride, as, in the circumstances, he could afford to. 'The high seas agree with your game, Guy,' he remarked in the changing-room afterwards. 'Or perhaps something disagrees with mine.'

'Smugness, you mean?' I retorted. 'I've certainly never seen you lose so many points with a smile.'

'I've plenty to smile about, as it happens. A chase to beat any you made out there.'

'It goes well, then?'

'Uncommonly well. She likes me. Call it my good fortune or her good taste. Either way—' He tossed a damp towel at me to silence my guffaw. 'Either way, old man, why should you complain? You'll share whatever I earn from this venture.'

'You think we will earn something?'

'It's too soon to say. But I'm . . . quietiy confident.'

Confident? Yes, he was. But that was not all. Nor was money what he was necessarily confident of obtaining. Reluctant though I was to believe it, Max was beginning to look and sound happier than he had in years, to look and sound, indeed, like a man falling in love. After our shower, we stopped for a drink in the trellis-and-wicker café adjoining the tennis court. There I had the chance to study him at leisure, staring dreamily through the smoke from his cigarette, failing to finish sentences, losing track of whatever we were discussing. The signs were clear and I did not ignore them.

21

But there was no reason to be alarmed. Infatuation might lend conviction to his performance. I knew him too well to believe it could ever rival the governing motive of our lives.

Besides, as Max had pointed out, I had no grounds for complaint. While he went off to meet Diana for lunch, I adjourned to the ship's library and looked up her father's entry in *Who's Who*.

> CHARNWOOD, Fabian Melville, MA; JP, Surrey; Proprietor, Charnwood Investments; *b* 17 May 1870; *o s* of Andrew Charnwood; *m* 1901, Maud (*d* 1915), *d* of Zachary McGowan, Pittsburgh, USA; one *d. Educ*: Christ's Hospital; Sidney Sussex College, Cambridge. BA 1892; MA 1897. Entered 1893 his father's firm, Moss Charnwood Ltd, rifle and small arms manufacturers, London; Director, 1901; Chairman, 1906. Resigned to establish Charnwood Investments, 1907. *Address*: Amber Court, Dorking, Surrey. *T*: Bookham 258. *Clubs*: Ambassador, Gresham, St James'.

It was, by the standards of the publication, a brief and uninformative biography. But I found this strangely reassuring, for reticence is often the surest symptom of wealth. And wealth was our target as well as our ambition. While Max aspired to the daughter, we could both aim at the father. Fabian Melville Charnwood was in our sights.

CHAPTER

TWO

The voyage proceeded smoothly and so, somewhat against my expectations, did Max's courtship of Diana Charnwood. They lunched and dined together, usually without even Vita for company, the oceanic phase of the trip having had its predicted effect on her constitution. They waltzed by night and promenaded by day. They displayed on every occasion that exclusive delight in each other which to the cynical observer is an unmistakable sign of the psychiatric disorder commonly called love.

Like any man of reasonable intelligence, I had long since realized that love amounts to no more than physical desire draped for decency's sake in some skimpy shreds of philosophy. I had convinced a good many women over the years that they loved me, but I had never for one second believed that I loved them. And the same went for Max. Or so, until now, I had supposed.

But, as day followed day and my only glimpses of Max were in moonstruck contemplation of the beauteous Diana, I was forced to revise my opinion. Thirty-four was late in life for such foolishness, worryingly so in view of the tendency for childhood ailments to be more serious when contracted by adults. Yet I was not worried. In the unlikely event of them marrying, Max would do well by me. The contract he had signed – and our long association – guaranteed that. In the far more likely event of Diana's father trying to buy him off, Max could be relied upon to see reason. As for Diana, I hoped this was no mere shipboard romance. All I could do to sustain it was to let it flourish unhindered. Accordingly, I gave the pair a wide berth. And the little I saw of them suggested I was wise to do so.

Happily, I saw even less of Faraday, whom I imagined to be busy dancing attendance upon the prostrated Vita. Certainly he was not among the nightbirds whose company I kept. They were generally rich insomniacs who played poker even less well than they slept. By the time the last evening of the voyage approached, I was beginning to wish we were on a round-the-world cruise. But all good things must come to an end and I had no wish for my luck to be one of them. So, on balance, I was quite pleased to be nearly home – even if England did not seem very homely, either in recollection or anticipation.

After letting Atkinson-White beat me at squash – a far from simple task – I took a lengthy bath, then dressed early for dinner and ascended to the principal lounge, a Ritzy cavern of marble and plaster, where I thought to consume a restful Manhattan in a bay-window armchair, gazing out at the limitless blue of sea and sky. But there was nothing restful about being surprised after only a few minutes by the soft-footed arrival of Mr Faraday.

'May I join you, Mr Horton?' The fellow's politeness was one of his keenest weapons. 'Our paths don't seem to have crossed of late.'

'It's a big ship,' I countered.

'But not big enough to prevent certain . . . social developments . . . becoming apparent in the course of a few days.' He lowered himself effortlessly into the armchair next to mine. 'Wouldn't you say?'

'I'm not sure I know what you mean.'

'Diana Charnwood's latest conquest, for instance. You of all people must be aware of that.'

'Must I?'

'Well, you and Mr Wingate are old friends, aren't you? School-friends, I believe.' He broke off as the steward brought him a drink. It looked disgustingly like *crème de menthe*. The shock of realizing he knew more about me than I knew about him fused horribly with the suspicion that he might have ordered his drink while spying on me from the far side of the lounge. Then shock and suspicion grew infinitely worse. 'Winchester, wasn't it?' he enquired with a grin.

'Max and I were at Winchester together, yes. But—'

'And in Macedonia during the war, with the King's Royal Rifle Corps?'

I paused and lit a cigarette to compose my thoughts. 'Do you mind explaining how you come to know all this, Mr Faraday?'

'I listen and observe.' He sipped at his *crème de menthe*. 'In this case, I listen to what Diana tells her aunt about the new man in her life. And I observe the ties he wears during their promenades on deck – old school *and* regimental.'

'How perspicacious of you.' I was relieved to know he had to engage in some limited form of deduction. Nevertheless, a possibility I had not previously considered was now lodged in my thoughts: the possibility that Max's tongue might grow dangerously loose under Diana's influence. 'You are Miss Vita's confidant, I take it?'

'She looks to me for occasional advice. Nothing more.'

'On any particular subject?'

'Her niece's welfare is naturally close to her heart. And her brother is not here to consult. In truth, I merely act as a sounding-board for her own thoughts.'

'And what are her thoughts about the budding romance?'

'You think it *is* budding?'

'I thought you did.'

He chuckled. 'Perhaps we can agree they seem to be attracted to each other. I confess myself somewhat surprised. As to Mr Charnwood's reaction . . .'

'You're acquainted with him?'

'I've had certain business dealings with him. Sufficient to make me doubt that he would wholly approve of Diana associating with . . . such a man.'

'Isn't she old enough not to need his approval?'

'Her age is neither here nor there. She has always abided by her father's wishes.' He glanced away for a moment, then said: 'So her aunt tells me.'

'Then what is Miss Vita's problem? Why not simply await her brother's verdict?'

'Because—' Faraday broke off to swallow some more *crème de menthe*. 'She might be able to influence him . . . in Mr Wingate's favour. If she knew more about Mr Wingate, that is. Winchester and the Rifle Corps take us only so far. What of the last . . . twelve or thirteen years, for instance?'

'They featured nothing in the least discreditable to Max.'

'But what *did* they feature?'

I smiled, as much at his effrontery as at his evidently low estimate of my intelligence. 'I think I'd better leave Max to speak for himself, don't you?'

'You could speak for *yourself*, though. After all, you and he have long been business associates. What applies to you applies to him.'

I leaned forward to stab out my cigarette and asked quietly, 'What precisely is your interest in this matter, Mr Faraday?'

'I'm simply trying to help.'

'Help whom? Vita? Diana? Fabian Charnwood? Or yourself?'

For answer he merely grinned.

'Well, whoever it is, I don't think you're making a good job of it. Now, excuse me, will you?' I rose and hurried out, overwhelmed by a powerful need of the open air.

The cards did not favour me that night. So I told myself, anyway, although it was also true that Faraday's words lingered in my mind, sapping my powers of concentration. And a distracted man makes a poor poker player. There was nothing for it but to quit early.

The following morning found me up and restless at dawn, eager for the end of our voyage. I decided to take a swim before breakfast and descended to the pool hoping to find it deserted at such an hour. And so it seemed to be, just the stone turtle who kept permanent guard over the deep end waiting to greet me. But solitude, as so often aboard ship, proved illusory. While I was hanging my robe and towel in one of the cubicles, I heard a door further down the row open and close, followed by a splash as somebody dived into the pool.

It was a woman, swimming fast and vigorously. As I stepped out of the cubicle, I moved instinctively behind a pillar and watched her reach the end nearest me, then turn and complete another length. It was only then, as she pushed herself away from the edge and slowed into a backstroke, that I could be certain who she was: Diana Charnwood. As soon as I emerged from behind the pillar, she saw me and stopped, treading water in the centre of the pool.

'Most impressive,' I said, raising my hand and smiling.

'Mr Horton,' she replied breathlessly. 'I didn't . . . I thought I was alone.'

'So did I.'

'I come here most mornings . . . at this time.'

'Then you could reasonably expect to be alone. I'm sorry to have disturbed you.'

'Don't be silly. Aren't you going to join me?' Her smile seemed genuinely inviting. With as much athleticism as I could muster, I dived in, swam past her once, then joined her beneath the turtle, where she had moved to rest against the rail. Even in a bathing cap, with her face wet and bare of make-up, her uncommon beauty was apparent.

'I don't suppose you've succeeded in luring Max down here,' I remarked.

'No. He says he can't swim.'

'Quite true, I'm afraid. You'll have to teach him.'

'I'd like to if . . .' She blushed slightly. 'You and Max are close friends, Guy, I know. May I call you Guy? Max has told me such a lot about you it's hard to think of you as Mr Horton. And please call me Diana. Max and I. . .well, we. . . It sounds silly, schoolgirlish almost, but I've never met anyone quite so. . . I like him a lot. He's able to make me happy. Some men I've known seem to have found that difficult. Even impossible.'

'Surely not.'

'It's true. But. . . Look, what I want to say is this. I think Max and I are actually rather good for each other. But I've no intention of trying to change what he is. Too many people have tried to change what *I* am for me to make the same mistake. So, there's no question of my coming between Max and his friends. Especially his best and oldest friend of all.'

'I never thought there was.'

'Good.'

'I wish I could say the same for Mr Faraday.' She frowned. 'He's been quizzing me about Max. On your aunt's behalf, I gather.'

'On nobody's behalf but his own.' Her tone had suddenly altered. 'What Aunt Vita sees in the horrible iittle man I don't . . . I advise you to ignore Mr Faraday, Guy. As I do. And as I wish Aunt Vita would.'

'I'll do my best.'

'How about doing your best over a couple of lengths? A race will give me an appetite for breakfast.'

And so it may have done. But, in my case, another kind of appetite was sharpened at the end of our race – which we agreed to pronounce a tie – when she climbed from the pool, costume plastered to her skin, and walked slowly round to her cubicle. It

27

had been easy – and safe – to admire her facial beauty. But now, confronted with the physical reality of her seemingly perfect body, it was even easier – and far less safe – to acknowledge the stirrings of sexual desire. How I wished then that I rather than Max had taken her fancy. Profit was one thing, but Max seemed likely to have more than his share of pleasure as well. While all I could do was watch – and imagine.

A pall of cloud over the ship heralded England in all its summer glumness. With the Cornish coast looming grey and sodden off the port bow, I headed for my cabin to pack. But hardly had I commenced the task when a visitor arrived. It was Max.

'I thought we should have a word, old man,' he announced.

'It would make a pleasant change, Max, certainly.'

'I've been rather preoccupied of late.'

'Oh, I *quite* understand. Diana explained everything to me this morning.'

'So she told me.'

'Your campaign seems to have been a resounding success.'

'So far, yes. And remember – it's *our* campaign.'

'I haven't forgotten. It's just that I'm finding it difficult to believe. I mean, how far is this romance going to go? Should I be preparing a best man's speech?'

'Very funny, Guy.' But he was not laughing. There was an earnestness about him which suggested matrimony might not be so very far from his thoughts. 'Wouldn't a dowry be just as acceptable as a bribe?'

'It would. Especially for you, I imagine.'

Pursing his lips, he moved away across the cabin, stopping by the window to gaze out at the unwelcoming shores of home. 'She's no fool, Guy. You said so yourself. I have to tread carefully.'

'Of course.'

'There's her father to consider. He'll need delicate handling.' He took out a cigarette and propped it between his lips, but seemed disinclined to light it. 'Very delicate handling.' Then he removed the cigarette and turned to look at me. 'She's invited me down to their house in Surrey next week. To stay for a few days.'

'Sounds promising.'

'The invitation's extended to you as well.'

'That's kind of her.'

'Yes. But then she is. Very. The snag is. . . Well, we want this to go smoothly, don't we? And. . .that being the case. . .'

'Spit it out, Max, for God's sake.'

'I don't want you there.'

'What?'

'I want you to decline the invitation.'

'Why?'

'Because . . .' He put the cigarette back in his mouth and began patting his pockets in search of a lighter. Exasperated, I offered him mine. He accepted with a flickering smile of embarrassment and inhaled the smoke gratefully. 'You'd feel the same in my position, Guy.'

'Would I?'

'You know you would.'

He was right, but I was not about to admit it. He knew, and so did I, that I would not be content to play gooseberry during a long week-end in the country. And, even if I were, it would only set back our cause. Yet I could not rid my mind of the memory of Diana as I had seen her that morning. Not promenading, of course, but bathing. 'I'll decline,' I said with a grudging nod. 'As politely as I can.'

'Thanks, old man.'

'What about Faraday? Will he be there?'

'I hope not. With any luck, we'll soon have seen the last of Mr Faraday. I met him over breakfast this morning and he said he'd be leaving on the tender at Plymouth in order to catch a fast train to London. Important business to attend to, apparently.'

'But whose business? He seems uncommonly interested in ours.'

'Don't worry about him. He's no threat. In fact, don't worry about anything.' He was suddenly cheerful now I had agreed to give him a clear run, optimistic to a degree I only wished I could share. 'I didn't want to scuttle back to England, Guy. You know that. But now. . . Well, I think it may have been the best move we ever made.'

Faraday did leave at Plymouth. I watched him go, unsure whether to be pleased we were rid of him or perturbed by the urgency of his departure. Then, summoning a brave face, I lunched with Max and Diana and explained why my own *important business* meant I could not join them in Surrey. Vita was still feeling queasy and, to aid her recovery, Diana had persuaded her to stay in

29

Southampton that night, at the South Western Hotel adjoining the docks. Max, it briskly transpired, had volunteered to stay with them. I, needless to say, could not spare the time for such dallying.

Which was ironic, in view of the fact that absolutely nothing awaited me in London except an empty flat near Berkeley Square. It belonged to Max's father, but was now seldom used by him. For a pair of returning exiles, it offered an adequate bolt-hole and Max had cabled ahead to say we would make use of it. I had not anticipated arriving there as now I would: alone.

We reached Southampton late in the afternoon. Viewing our stately progress up the Solent from the aft rail, I could not keep at bay the melancholy thoughts of many a traveller concerning the certainties he has left behind and the uncertainties he has yet to confront. Until 1922, this orderly land of jetties and fields had been my home. But 1922 was a long time ago. I had visited it only twice since then, most recently for my mother's funeral, which fog in mid-Atlantic had caused me to arrive twelve hours too late for. I could hardly claim to know it any more, but I supposed it would admit to knowing me.

And so to the gloomy chaos of disembarkation. The pampered ease of a first-class cabin was exchanged for the weary discomfort of the passport queue and the customs shed. Eventually, we reached the waiting boat-train. There, on the crowded platform, as porters scurried back and forth with huge numbers of trunks and portmanteaux, I said goodbye to Max, whose eagerness for me to be gone was transparent, and to Diana, who at any rate pretended she was sorry I could not remain. As for Vita, whom dry land was already reviving, the news that I would not be joining them in Surrey seemed genuinely to disappoint her. Affecting a different kind of regret from the one I actually felt, I took my leave of them all and, as the train moved out, headed straight for the restaurant car.

Only to find myself sharing a table with a bibulous prophet of doom called Millington, whose acquaintance I had mercifully not made aboard ship. As soon as he heard how long I had been out of England, he launched himself on a colourful recital of the nation's woes. 'Nearly three million unemployed. Closures and bankruptcies wherever you look. Gold flowing out of the Bank of England like blood from a severed artery. The Chancellor of the Exchequer no more able to balance the budget than he is a needle on its point. But what can you expect from a Labour government? Funk and folly's their recipe for everything. We'll end up like the Germans did, mark my words. Pushing barrow-loads of sovereigns down the street to buy a loaf of bread. A fine country brought to its knees by sheer bloody incompetence.' He broke off to order another bottle of champagne, then glanced out of the window at the passing scene. 'All I can foresee is total unmitigated catastrophe.'

We were passing through Winchester at the time and all I could see, in my mind's eye, was the thirteen-year-old boy I had once been arriving for his first day at College, which was also the first day I met Max Wingate. There, on the station platform that was now but a fleeting blur, we had stepped down, overloaded with luggage and home-sickness, hot and nervous in the September sun. And, on discovering we were both scholars, had inaugurated our friendship with a solemn handshake. '*Pleased to meet you,*' Max had said. And I had said the same.

'If I were you,' Millington remarked, leaning towards me across the table, 'I should clear straight off back to America. There's nothing here for an enterprising chap like you.'

I smiled and said nothing, but silently agreed.

The flat in Hay Hill was small but comfortable, attended to by the redoubtable Mrs Dodd, who ran a tobacconist's shop with her husband in Oxford Street. From them I obtained the key, settled in as best I could and awaited Max's arrival. In the event, the whole of a desolate week-end had passed before he put in an appearance, having telephoned me on Saturday from Southampton to say he was popping up to Gloucestershire first to see his parents. When he burst through the door on Sunday night with a merry laugh and a spring in his step, the contrast with my own mood was all too apparent.

'Down in the dumps, old man?'

'Somewhat.'

'Well, why not look up your folks while I prosecute our ambitions in Surrey?' He rubbed his hands in glee at the prospect before him. 'You've nothing else to do, have you?'

'Because,' I replied with heavy emphasis, 'my family don't know I'm in England, a state of affairs I'm very happy with, and because, as a matter of fact, I have plenty to do – once this rotten week-end's out of the way.'

'No need to get shirty about it. Do as you please.'

'Thanks. I believe I will.'

Max set off for Surrey on Tuesday, bright-eyed and confident. I wished him luck, though no more sincerely than I wished it for myself. Millington's analysis of England in the summer of 1931 seemed only too accurate to me as I wandered London's streets in weather more suited to February than July, read gloom-laden newspaper articles about the state of the economy and generally did my best to work up a fine sense of self-pity.

Tea with the Atkinson-Whites in Windsor on the afternoon of Max's departure supplied some welcome solace. Cheered by their willingness to follow my financial advice, I arranged to have lunch the following day with 'Trojan' Doyle. He had been a year below me at Winchester and was still making, as he had been in 1922, a comfortable living out of managing other people's money. Negotiating a share of the commission he would charge the Atkinson-Whites was unlikely to make me rich, but would at least keep me busy until Max brought home the bacon. Besides, Trojan – who had earned his sobriquet by continually mispronouncing the name of the Latin poet Horace – kept his ear to the ground in City circles. I wanted to know what he could tell me about Charnwood Investments. So, as soon as we had reached agreement where the Atkinson-Whites were concerned, I changed the subject.

'Charnwood Investments, Trojan. Ever had occasion to give it the once-over?'

'Can't say I have. Fabian Charnwood plays his cards close to his chest. Always has.'

'But doing well?'

'Better than most.' Trojan's eyebrows, which had developed into a pair of tangled hedges over the years, bunched together in a frown. 'What's your interest?'

'I might – just might – do some business with him, that's all.'

'I wouldn't if I were you. A slippery customer.'

'More slippery than you?'

He grinned. 'A sea-serpent to my eel. Simply no comparison. His father was in munitions before the war.' I let the slight inaccuracy pass, calculating that the more ignorant he thought me, the more informative he might be. 'Charnwood started with the firm as a salesman, flogging howitzers to Balkan hotheads. Ended up on the board. Became chairman when his father died. Then, within a year, he sold up. Lock, stock and barrel.' He laughed at the aptness of the phrase. 'That must be nearly twenty-five years ago. Since then, he's contented himself with investing in all manner of enterprises, here and overseas. Armaments, of course, but also shipbuilding, aircraft production, banking, gold mines, telephones, newspapers. He chooses well – and profitably. And he takes risks. He's said to be active in all the currency and futures markets. Well, they're no place for the faint-hearted. Never have been. But he goes from strength to strength. His judgement can't be faulted.'

'But something else can?'

'Did I say so?'

'No. But your expression implied it.'

He shrugged. 'I told you he plays his cards close to his chest. Well, that's the point. Altogether too close. Too mysterious. And mystery is worrying. Some find it fascinating, I suppose. Plenty of people – big companies, not just individuals – have backed Charnwood's investments. And they've done well out of them. But he's too unfathomable for my taste. And for yours, I should guess. Which reminds me . . . Didn't I hear you and Max Wingate were in business in America with Richard Babcock, the banker's son?'

'Did you?'

'Yes. And now I read he and his father, Hiram Babcock – the chairman, or should I say ex-chairman, of the Housatonic Bank – have been arrested for fraud, embezzlement and God knows what else. You must have still been in New York when that happened. What can you tell me about it?'

'Nothing.' I summoned my most disingenuous smile. 'Nothing at all.'

'Come off it.'

'It's true. The Babcock affair is a closed book to me.' And so it was, along with a great many other affairs I preferred to forget. But Fabian Charnwood was different. He was a closed book only because he had not yet been opened.

Doyle's parting remark after lunch was a recommendation to back Poor Lad in the Stewards' Cup at Goodwood that afternoon. Naturally, I did nothing about it, only to learn from the evening paper that the wretched horse had romped home at nine to one. I hoped Max was having better luck in Surrey – or making more of whatever came his way – and a telephone call from him the following evening suggested he was.

'I'm in a call-box near the house, old man. Ostensibly taking a stroll before dinner. Actually, I thought you'd like to know the state of play.'

'I would. Very much.'

'Everything's going famously. Diana and I seem to be made for each other. Likes, dislikes, sense of humour, approach to life – we see eye to eye on everything. I was afraid it might be different on her home ground, but I needn't have worried. She's a lovely girl, she really is. I wish I'd met her years ago.'

'Sounds like you might be popping the question any day.'

'I might at that. But don't rush me.'

'What about her father? Have you met him yet?'

'We dine with him nightly. Seems a perfect gent. I think he's taken a shine to me.'

'Really?'

'It's not so strange. I *am* a charming fellow, after all. And at the moment I can do no wrong. Diana's been showing me round the neighbourhood in her sports car and you could wish for no more fetching chauffeuse, believe you me. We took Vita to Goodwood yesterday and had a couple of big wins.'

'Including Poor Lad in the Stewards' Cup?'

'Yes. Did you back it too?'

Before I could reply, the pips intervened.

'I'll be staying until after the week-end,' Max bellowed in their wake. 'See you on Tuesday.'

'Good luck,' I managed to respond through gritted teeth. There was every reason to be exultant at how well he was doing, but such is human nature that I could not help resenting it. After he had rung off, there really seemed to be nothing for it but to become horribly drunk. And to dream of Diana Charnwood riding naked on horseback.

I was roused on Friday morning, head splitting, by a hammering at the door. Blundering down, I found a uniformed messenger standing outside. No sooner had I confirmed my identity than he thrust a letter into my hand and bustled off. I tore the envelope open and found myself squinting in puzzlement at a wholly unexpected invitation, written on the headed notepaper of Charnwood Investments, Cornhill, London EC2.

31st July 1931

Dear Mr Horton,
I should esteem it a favour if you would join me for
luncheon at the Ambassador Club, 26 Conduit Street, this
afternoon at one o'clock.
                              Yours truly,
                         Fabian Charnwood.

After throwing on some clothes and forcing down a cup of strong
black coffee, I re-read the letter, but was none the wiser about
Charnwood's intentions. What he wanted with me as opposed to
Max I could not imagine, but fortunately I did not have long to
wait in order to find out.

The Ambassador Club had not existed in 1922, so far as I could
recall. From what circles it drew its membership I did not know.
The Gresham was synonymous with banking and the St James'
with diplomacy. I might not have felt at home in either of them,
but at least I would have understood why Fabian Charnwood
should. Perhaps that was why he had chosen to meet me instead
in the mirror-walled dining-room of the Ambassador, where Doric
columns, multifarious reflections and roseate light from a tinted
glass roof created a thoroughly bemusing environment.

In that sense it was also highly appropriate, since Fabian
Charnwood was a thoroughly bemusing man. The frock-coat, wing-
collar, carnation button-hole and stiff-backed bearing all confirmed
Max's description of him as '*a perfect gent*', but he was far from
being the stout red-faced sexagenerian I had expected. There was
something almost athletic in his build. His hair, though white, was
as plentiful as mine, his features regular and singularly unlined,
his gaze uncomfortably direct. He spoke quietly but firmly, as if
used to being obeyed without question and came to the point as
soon as we had settled ourselves at a corner table and ordered
our meals, with which, I noticed, he specified wine for me and
Malvern water for himself.

'I'm obliged to you for coming at such short notice, Mr Horton.
I wish to discuss the blossoming romance between my daughter
Diana and your friend, Max Wingate.'

'What can we possibly discuss on that score, Mr Charnwood?'

'We can discuss how it's to be brought to an end.'

'I beg your pardon?'

'Mr Wingate has been a guest in my house for the past three days. I have been left in no doubt as to how matters stand between him and Diana. She has told me she loves him. I think it only a question of time before he proclaims his love for her and asks me for her hand in marriage. Don't you?'

'Well . . . I . . . I'm pleased for Max if . . .'

'Spare me your pleasure, Mr Horton. There's none to be felt by a father whose daughter is entangled with such a man.'

'Damn it,' I said, simulating outrage on my friend's behalf, 'if that's the way—'

'Spare me your play-acting too. It really isn't necessary. I know exactly what you're up to. Both of you. You are a pair of unprincipled adventurers who understand the value of nothing except money.' A silence fell while his mineral water and my aperitif arrived, but his eyes never left me. When the waiter had retreated, he said: 'Happily, I have no difficulty with people such as you. We agree a price and we have done with it.'

'Your frankness, Mr Charnwood . . . er . . .' I struggled to frame a response, disarmed by the blatancy of his approach. 'It takes me somewhat aback.'

'My frankness is the product of my knowledge. That is naturally not confined to what Mr Wingate has told Diana about himself, which is true as far as it goes but goes hardly anywhere. You were contemporaries at Winchester, I believe, and served together during the war in the King's Royal Rifle Corps. In 1919, Mr Wingate went up to Oxford, while you took up a junior position with the firm for which your father worked: the Goddess Foundation Garment Company in Letchworth. Mr Wingate described you as "a corsetry clerk", unflattering but presumably accurate.'

'Very amusing,' I said levelly.

'Your friend's joke, Mr Horton, not mine. Besides, you cannot help coming from a poorer background than him. I do not blame you for that. I do not even blame you for throwing it all up two years later to join Mr Wingate in business. He has told my daughter he left Oxford of his own accord, but you and I know he was actually sent down for acting as an agent for an illegal lottery. A humble start to a career of fraud and trickery, in which you have been his loyal partner.'

'Who dug this rubbish up for you?' I countered. 'Faraday?'

He frowned at me. 'Who is Faraday?'

'Your spy on the *Empress of Britain*.'

'I do not employ spies, on land or sea. My information has been given to me by a fellow-member of this club whose name will be familiar to you: Sir Antony Toogood.'

'Toogood? I'm not sure I . . .'

'You met him at Le Touquet in 1924, when his daughter was the object of your attentions just as mine is now the object of Mr Wingate's.' He smiled. 'Perhaps you think it unfortunate that I should be acquainted with Sir Antony. You should not, for two reasons.'

Soup arrived. I had little stomach for it, but gulped some wine and waited for Charnwood to continue between spoonfuls of vichyssoise.

'Firstly, because it saves time for both of us. It means I know who I am dealing with and what they want. Sir Antony was most illuminating about the activities you and Mr Wingate engaged in between 1921 and 1924. You began as minor figures in Horatio Bottomley's empire of corruption, touring the country to post illegal lottery material for him and, of course, those vital winning entries from fictitious members of the public. You operated accommodation addresses for him in Paris, Geneva and Lausanne in connection with his fraudulent overseas bond clubs. After Bottomley's imprisonment, you remained on the continent and turned freelance. You carried out specious enquiries on behalf of English relatives seeking news of their loved ones who had been posted missing during the war and who you implied might still be alive. You blackmailed ex-servicemen on behalf of their former French and Belgian mistresses and alleged offspring. You returned to this country solely for the purpose of libelling an unsavoury individual named Smallbone and splitting the resulting damages with him. And then you descended upon Le Touquet in search of a rich man's daughter. Who, should you be interested, is now happily married to a gentleman farmer in Shropshire and the mother of two children with a third on the way.'

It sounded even worse in Charnwood's rounded phrases than I remembered. There was nothing I could do but smile weakly. 'Well, motherhood will have suited Caroline. She certainly had the hips for it.'

He did not laugh. I had indeed the greatest difficulty imagining him ever doing so. 'Secondly,' he implacably resumed, 'the ethos of the Ambassador Club is one for which you should have some sympathy. Were the grouse season not imminent, I would probably be able to point to a lively cross-section of the peerage at adjoining tables. Not to mention the baronetage and knightage. Politicians of all parties. Traders in every commodity. Exponents of almost every way of life. Eclecticism is the club's watchword. What binds us together is an understanding that everything and everyone has a price. I take it you agree?'

'Yes,' I murmured. 'I suppose I do.'

'So I thought. To business, then.' He finished his soup. 'A peerage fetches thirty thousand pounds these days, a knighthood ten thousand. On that sort of sliding scale, I estimate the value of Mr Wingate abandoning my daughter at no more than fifteen hundred. But I am prepared to offer a bonus for early settlement. Shall we say two thousand?'

I gaped at him, unable to disguise my astonishment. A moment before he had been anatomizing the long-ago frauds and shady practices by which Max and I had endeavoured to make the kind of living we thought we were owed for wasting more than three years of our youth in a mosquito-ridden wilderness called Macedonia. He had done so calmly and mercilessly. Now, without altering his tone in any way, he had virtually admitted that the club of which he was a member was no better than a mart at which honours and sundry other favours were bought and sold at fixed prices. 'That being so,' I said slowly, 'you and your friends, Mr Charnwood, are no better than me and mine.'

'Perhaps so.' Our soup dishes were removed, our glasses recharged. 'But I never said we were, did I?'

'No. Not exactly. But—'

'And I haven't asked what you've been doing in America for the past seven years, have I? Nor why you've suddenly returned home.'

'No. You haven't.'

'So, can we agree on two thousand pounds?'

'Well, I'd have to consult Max, of course, but . . .'

'Consult him as soon as he returns to London. I believe we are to have the pleasure of his company throughout this week-end. I shall say nothing to him about our conversation, of course. That I shall leave to you. The money is payable on condition that he breaks with my daughter cleanly and irrevocably. And without telling her the real reason why. He may invent whatever lie he pleases.'

'Aren't you worried how Diana may react?'

'She is resilient. I would be a great deal more worried if the illusion of happiness Mr Wingate has planted in her mind persisted for any length of time. My sister should have prevented it taking root in the first place, but she is incurably soft-hearted. I am not.'

'Obviously.'

'Are we agreed then, Mr Horton?'

Two thousand pounds was a fair price, indeed a generous one. There was nothing to be gained by haggling. 'I believe we are, yes.'

'Good.'

'But I do have one question.' The arrival of our main courses interrupted me and I wondered if, after all, I should put such a point to him. The last thing I wanted to do at this stage was antagonize him. But, in the end, I reckoned he would take it in good part. 'If honours are so readily available, why is a man of your means and connections still plain *Mr* Charnwood?'

'Because I do not want what is readily available.'

'What *do* you want, then?'

A faraway look entered his eyes. When he replied, it was wistfully, with no hint of dissimulation. 'The past over again.' He smiled at me. 'Can you arrange that, Mr Horton? I would pay you every penny I possessed if you could.'

I shook my head. 'Nobody can. Not even. . . Not even God.' The profundity sounded strange and unfamiliar on my lips. I doubt I had spoken of the Almighty, other than profanely, in more than ten years. To find myself doing so now, in such a setting, was bizarre, as Charnwood seemed to acknowledge.

'A strange thought, eh? If you could change one thing, just one, that the past has placed beyond your reach, what would it be?'

Unaccountably, I heard myself reply honestly and instinctively. 'I would give my brother Felix back his sanity. He lost it . . .' My words failed as I realized how revealing my answer was. It was the first time I had mentioned Felix's name to a stranger since leaving Letchworth. 'He lost it in the war,' I concluded.

'Ah, the war,' said Charnwood reflectively. 'Always there is the war.'

'What would you change?'

'I would prevent my wife boarding the *Lusitania* in New York on the first of May 1915. The war again, you see?' We eyed each other warily, suspicious of the intimate direction our exchanges had taken. Both of us, I think, were happy to draw back. 'The present is so much simpler, Mr Horton. Take your money and leave my daughter alone. It's all you have to do. It's all either of us can reasonably ask. Don't you agree?'

'Yes. I do.'

'Then enjoy your meal. And drink your wine.' He raised his glass and stretched across the table to touch it against mine. 'May you spend your ill-gotten gains wisely.'

CHAPTER

THREE

A wet bank holiday week-end in London would ordinarily have depressed me beyond measure, but the excellent news I had for Max served to keep my spirits up. On Tuesday, I introduced Atkinson-White to Trojan over lunch at Trojan's club. Our discussions went well and I returned to Hay Hill afterwards in a mood of brandy-mellowed self-satisfaction. On entering the flat, I found Max patrolling the hearth-rug, a cigar in one hand, a glass of champagne in the other. The smirk on his face suggested he had good cause for celebration, which puzzled me somewhat, since I had not yet told him what it was.

'Guy,' he proclaimed, clapping me on the shoulder. 'You're just in time. Help yourself to some bubbly.'

The 'bubbly' turned out to be a rather splendid Pol Roger, propped idly in an ice-bucket on the table. 'Has Charnwood spoken to you?' I asked as I poured myself a glass. 'I didn't think he intended to.'

'In the circumstances, it's for me to speak to him. Which I shall do, next week-end.' He frowned at me. 'I take it you've guessed my news?'

'Not exactly.'

'Diana's agreed to marry me.' A huge grin spread across his face. 'You can drink to our future happiness.' He drained his glass and started towards the ice-bucket, then realized that no champagne had passed my lips. 'What's wrong?'

41

'Nothing. It's just . . .' A pleasing thought came to my mind. 'Actually, this makes it better still. An engagement means we may be able to negotiate a supplement.'

'A supplement to what?'

'I had lunch with Charnwood on Friday. He's prepared to pay us two thousand pounds. I thought it was as high as he'd go, but if you're—'

'Two thousand pounds?' Max stepped closer and stared at me. 'What does he want for his money?'

'Our departure from his daughter's life. *Your* departure, I should say.'

'You can't be serious.'

'It's what we planned, isn't it? It's Le Touquet all over again. And it's more than we extracted from Toogood. Of course I'm serious.'

'Did you agree?'

'Naturally. But not so explicitly that I can't ask for another few hundred. He may cut up rough, but it's worth—'

'You agreed? Without consulting me?'

'What was the point? It's just the sort of deal we were hoping for. Better, I'd say. So, let *me* propose a toast. To our continuing prosperity.'

Suddenly, Max snatched the glass from my hand and slammed it down beside the ice-bucket so violently that the stem snapped, spilling a fizzing pool across the table. But he paid it no heed. His face was darkening ominously, his mouth quivering angrily. 'You shouldn't have done this, Guy. Damn it all, you had no *right* to do it.'

'What the devil's the matter with you?' Looking into his eyes, I began to see what the answer might be, but I did not want to believe it. 'I've done well by both of us. Two thousand pounds is one hell of a lot of big wins at Goodwood.'

'She's agreed to marry me!' he shouted, lunging away across the room. He stopped by the mantelpiece and leaned against it, running his fingers through his hair and grimacing like a man distracted. 'We're pledged to each other.'

'Then break your pledge. It wouldn't be the first time. But I can't recall another occasion as profitable as this.'

'*Profitable?*' He glared back at me. 'What profit is there for me in abandoning the girl I . . .' His voice faltered as he realized what he was about to admit. Then he seemed to cast aside all pretence,

42

standing upright and turning to confront me. 'I love her, Guy. And she loves me.'

'What?'

'You heard. And you're going to have to accept it. Just as Charnwood is. Diana and I will be married. There will be no accommodations, no hole-in-the-corner deals. I will not be bought off.'

'I don't believe it.'

'You must. For once in my life, I'm not for sale.'

'But . . . you promised. We signed a contract.'

'And I'll honour it. You'll have your share of the marriage settlement.'

'There'll be no settlement. For God's sake, Max, there'll be no marriage. Charnwood won't allow it. And if you persist in this madness, we won't even have two thousand pounds to remember him by.'

'I don't want his money. I want his daughter.'

'Then have her. Before you cut and run. But cut and run you must.'

A look came into his eyes such as I had seen many times, but never before directed at me. It was one of utter contempt. 'You don't understand the meaning of the word *love*, do you, Guy? I don't blame you. Neither did I, till I met Diana. I ought to ram what you've just said about her back down your throat. And I will, if you dare to repeat it. I'll let it pass this once, for old time's sake. But, if you set any store by our friendship, don't ever take her name in vain again. If you do, it'll be the end between us. For good and all.'

He was deadly serious. There was no longer any room for doubt. He was in love with Diana Charnwood. Or, as I saw it, he was sufficiently obsessed with her to glorify his emotions with such a description. But the definition was less important than the effect. And the effect, in my judgement, could only be disastrous – for both of us. 'Let's take this calmly,' I said, as much for my own benefit as Max's. 'There's no reason for us to fall out.'

'I agree. As long as you don't interfere in my plans.'

'I won't. But Charnwood will. He knows a lot about us. And he has the resources to find out more. He won't hesitate to tell Diana what sort of lives we've led.'

'Let him. She knows I'm no angel. And she knows her father won't approve of her choice of husband. Not initially, anyway.

That's why we've agreed she'll spend the next few days winning him over. She can twist him round her little finger. I've seen her do it. By the time I go down there next week-end, he'll already be as good as convinced. Once I explain the misapprehension you and he were labouring under . . .'

'He'll shake you by the hand and give his consent. Is that how you see it?'

'Yes. It is. And why not? Beneath the bluster, he only wants Diana to be happy. Well, so do I.'

'Max, it's not as simple as—'

'It's as simple as this!' He pointed his finger at me imperiously. 'We love each other and we mean to be married. Do you understand?'

'Yes. I rather think I do.'

'Good. In a few days, Charnwood will as well. Until then, I don't want to hear another word on the subject.'

An uneasy truce prevailed between Max and me for the rest of that week. There was clearly nothing I could do to make him see reason. I could only hope Charnwood would succeed where I had failed – and adhere to the terms we had agreed. But unpleasant doubts about the whole enterprise had been sown in my mind. The money was there for the taking. My every instinct told me not to delay in accepting it. Yet delay was the only policy Max would permit. And any protest by me seemed likely to provoke a permanent rupture between us.

The atmosphere in the flat became, not surprisingly, intolerable. Eager to escape it, I embarked on a journey which it had been in my mind to undertake since my meeting with Charnwood. For he had prompted me to speak of my brother Felix. And I knew I could confide in Felix with absolute confidence – for the simple reason that he would not remember a single thing I said. He would probably not even remember my visit. And, if he did, nobody would believe him. Not my father or my sister, anyway. However low their opinion of me might be, I was certain it would not have sunk to the point where they could be persuaded I had returned to England after seven years without troubling to tell them.

So it was that on Friday morning I walked to St Pancras and caught a train out into the Hertfordshire countryside south of St Albans. My destination was Napsbury Hospital, where

Felix had been admitted in 1917, supposedly suffering from neurasthenia, a diagnosis later amended to embrace whichever neurosis his doctors had last chanced upon in the writings of Sigmund Freud. I had always thought bad luck was what Felix really suffered from, the bad luck to have enlisted in the Hertfordshire Regiment and to have served on the Western Front, where, by losing his sanity, he was only responding logically to the madness of his situation. Conversely, I had had the good luck to enlist in the King's Royal Rifle Corps, which happened to be based in Winchester and to have close links with the College OTC. I had served in the safe if disagreeable backwater of Macedonia, where one was more likely to die of malaria than enemy action and where, as if to prove the point, Max had been shot by one of our own men. I had returned cynical, selfish and intact, whereas Felix had returned like a parcel crushed in the post – the fastening un-ravelled, the contents either missing or mangled, the blame shrugged off with official disdain.

I walked the quarter of a mile from Napsbury station to the hospital wondering whether I had been wise to come. I had not seen Felix for four years. Judging by his deterioration during previous such intervals, it was impossible to feel optimistic about what I would find. None the less, I pressed on, bracing myself for the gloom which always seemed to pervade the sprawl of red-brick ward-blocks and out-buildings. Recent storms had added a sodden and wind-lashed despondency to the scene, but the day was dry and along the paths that wound between the fir trees one or two patients were to be seen, fitfully a-tremble and aimlessly wandering.

I entered Felix's ward full of foreboding and noticed the nurse's surprised expression when I said who I wanted to see. He was fetched from a crowded sitting-room where a wireless was playing loudly and emerged looking faintly resentful. He was as thin as ever, but more stooped and tremulous than I recalled, a strange mixture of the dashing young soldier and the querulous old invalid. But he recognized me at once. He had always done so, even when hopelessly vague about the identity of others. He recognized me and threaded his arm through mine.

'Come to. . . Come to take me for a walk, Gewgaw?' He had dubbed me 'Gewgaw' when I won my scholarship to Winchester, infuriating me with his explanation that Dr Johnson's definition of a gewgaw – 'splendidly trifling, showy without value' – fitted me

45

exactly. I resented it no more, merely marvelled that he still remembered.

'A walk sounds like a good idea,' I replied, catching the nurse's nod of approval. We headed slowly towards the exit. 'How have you been, Felix?'

'I caught a cold.'

'Rather like the government.'

He frowned at me, then said: 'Is Mr Asquith ill?'

Not having the heart to tell him Asquith was long since dead and gone, I mumbled, 'Not exactly,' and led him out into the grounds. 'What shall we talk about?' I ventured, as we inched our way along a tree-shaded path.

'Any . . . Anything.'

'I'm sorry not to have seen much of you lately.'

'I expect . . . you've been busy.'

'Yes. I have.' I smiled. 'Buying and selling parts of the Florida Everglades as building land. Striking deals between Canadian brewers and New England speak-easys. Sitting on the board of half a dozen high-sounding investment trusts. Riding the boom – and the bust. Oh yes, I've been very busy. Lately, I've even tried my hand at match-making. And match-breaking.'

He stared at me uncomprehendingly. 'They won't give me any matches.'

'I expect they're worried about fires.'

'They want to keep me . . . in the dark.'

'The staff, you mean?'

'No. The enemy.'

Thinking he meant the Germans, I said, 'The war's over, Felix.'

'That's what they want you . . . to believe. But it isn't. The squirrels know. They see them.' A squirrel was at that moment scurrying across the path ahead of us. 'They see them in the trees.'

'Who do they see?'

'The enemy . . . following me . . . waiting for . . . their chance.'

I looked around. 'Nobody's following us.'

He smiled at me, indulgently as it seemed, scarcely expecting me to understand. 'You can't see them. They won't let you. Only . . . a glimpse. Now and then . . . when the light fades . . . and they grow careless. That's when I see them . . . from the corner of my eye. But I can never . . . never catch a clear sight.' We came to a dead stop. 'Can you?'

I shrugged, not knowing what to say.

'You have my eyes, Gewgaw. Maybe . . . one day . . . you'll catch a clear sight of them. Then we'll know . . . who they really are. Won't we?'

Still I said nothing, struck as I had been before by the oddly disturbing nature of Felix's delusions. In a world that thought itself so wise yet behaved so stupidly, it was possible sometimes to believe that only the mad saw matters as they truly were, that only people like my brother were prepared to admit what they saw from the corner of their eye.

'You'll tell me . . . if you do, won't you?' he persisted. 'You'll come . . . and tell me?'

'Oh yes, Felix.' I practised my sane unseeing smile. 'I'll be sure to.'

Max had left for Dorking by the time I returned from Napsbury. I did not know when to expect him back and so should not have been surprised – though I was – when he appeared early on Monday morning. I was digesting my breakfast and smoking a reflective cigarette at the time, while reading an apocalyptic editorial about what everybody now seemed to agree was a full-scale economic crisis. But it was immediately obvious to me that Max's thunderous expression owed nothing to the run on the pound.

'Don't say it,' was his cryptic greeting. 'Just don't say it.'

'Don't say what, Max?'

'That you told me so. You were right, God damn it. Charnwood won't budge an inch.' He helped himself to coffee from the still warm pot on the table and ran his hand ruefully over his unshaven chin. 'I practically pleaded with the man. Begged him to give me a chance. I was *abject*.'

The philosophical tone to his remarks gave me cause for hope. 'He refused to give his consent?' I asked as sympathetically as I could. 'It doesn't surprise me.'

'He said I wasn't worthy of his daughter, wasn't fit to marry her.' He slumped down in the armchair opposite mine, coffee-cup cradled in his hand. 'I love her, for God's sake. And she loves me. But he doesn't seem to care.'

'I'm sorry, Max, really I am, but it's only what I warned you to expect.'

'He took me out into the garden. Walked me round explaining

47

why he'd planted roses here and rhododendrons there. And then he explained why he'd never allow his daughter to marry a man like me. Why the only thing he was prepared to give me was money. And not even that if I didn't abandon Diana sooner rather than later.'

I could not suppress an apprehensive intake of breath at this confirmation of my worst fears. Max heard it and shot a forbidding glare at me before continuing.

'You may as well know I tried to persuade Diana to elope with me. After what Charnwood had said, there seemed to be nothing else for it. If I'd succeeded, he'd probably have cut her off without a penny. But you'll be glad to hear she refused. God knows why, but she needs him to approve of what she does. He realizes that, of course. It's why he's so confident of her obedience – and of my compliance with his terms.'

'So you *will* comply?'

He stared at me, then slowly shook his head, as if despairing of my ability to understand. 'I can't comply, Guy. I love her. Without her . . . two thousand pounds would mean nothing.'

I grimaced. 'I never thought I'd hear you say such a thing.'

'Neither did I. But it's true.'

'If Diana won't disobey him, and you won't withdraw, what will you do?'

'Change his mind.'

'How?'

'It's why I caught the early train. Diana has an idea she wants to discuss with you.'

'With *me*?'

'Yes. She's accompanying Vita on some hat-buying expedition to Harrods today. She can easily slip away for a while and meet you outside. She suggests the door at the corner of Hans Road and Basil Street around noon. Can you be there?'

'I can, but—'

'Diana will explain everything. It's our only chance, Guy, hers and mine. Say you'll at least listen to what she has to say.'

I could, and perhaps I should, have refused. But already I had begun to hedge my bets. It was obvious Max was not going to give up until our chances of being handsomely bought off were scuppered. And elopement, followed by disinheritance, was to be avoided at all costs. If I could play some part in persuading Charnwood to accept Max as his son-in-law, however, something

48

lucrative might yet be salvaged from the situation. 'Very well,' I said after a moment's thought. 'I'll see her.'

There was some pretence of summer in the weather that morning. Waiting in the sunshine at the back of Harrods, it was almost possible to imagine I was feeling hot. I had seen a dozen ladies built and dressed very like Vita go in or out, and a badger-legged old soldier with a chestful of medals and a begging-tin complete two circuits of the building, when Diana Charnwood emerged to remind me that true beauty is a very rare commodity but was in her embodied.

'Thank you for coming, Guy,' she said, with a smile I could well imagine melting Max's heart. 'I knew we could depend on you.' She clutched my hand for a second and for about the same length of time I too thought of myself as dependable. 'Shall we walk?'

'By all means.' We set off along Basil Street. 'Max said you were anxious for a word.'

'He's told you what happened this week-end?'

'Yes. I'm sorry if—'

'My father's attitude isn't your fault. And don't apologize for striking a bargain with him you weren't in a position to honour.' Seeing my jaw drop, she smiled and said: 'Max has been completely honest with me. He's kept nothing back.' This I found hard to believe. Certainly, I did not want to believe it. But clearly Max had been more candid than I would have wished. At every step, I seemed to find the ground cut from beneath me by his new-found capacity for love. 'There can be no secrets between a man and the woman who is to be his wife, Guy. Surely you see that?'

'But are you to be his wife, Diana? I gather your father won't hear of it.'

'He doesn't understand how love can transform a person's character. Or perhaps he's forgotten. It's sixteen years since Mama died and. . . But you don't want to hear my family history. Papa knows I love Max, but he can't bring himself to believe Max loves me for my own sake.' We turned into Hans Crescent. 'We have to convince him he's wrong.'

'We?'

'I mean you, of course. If you will.'

'How can I do such a thing?'

'By explaining that Max has confounded all your expectations.'

'He certainly has.'

49

'By explaining, as his friend, that what he feels for me has changed him, that what you and Papa agreed is simply . . . irrelevant.' With a toss of the head, she lightly disposed, as only an heiress could, of the small matter of two thousand pounds. Her hair, where the sunlight struck it beneath the brim of her straw hat, was a golden brown flecked with something close to red. Her eyes sparkled with confidence as she looked up at me. And trust seemed magically to be offered, there on the pavement, outside the world's greatest emporium, wherein almost everything else was available – and none of it was free. 'He'll believe you, Guy, because you and he speak the same language.'

'Which isn't the language of love?'

She blushed and looked away. 'I don't mean to offend you. I don't even mean to inconvenience you, as apparently I have done by falling in love with your friend.'

'It's not a question of—'

The old soldier loomed suddenly up in front of us, rattling his tin. Diana gave him half a crown, shaming me into fishing a few pennies from my pocket. I disguised them beneath my hand as I dropped them into the tin. She looked back at him over her shoulder as we proceeded. 'Another victim,' she murmured. 'There are so many. We owe them at least a job, don't you think?'

'Since you ask, no, I don't.'

To my surprise, she smiled at me. 'So like Max, with this show of heartlessness. But it's not what you really feel, is it?'

'Isn't it?'

'How did Max come to be shot in Macedonia? He says it was an accident.'

'So it was, after a fashion.'

'What fashion?'

We reached the Brompton Road and began to traverse the main façade of the shop. I debated whether to tell her, then decided I might as well. If Max could be candid, so could I. 'A private called Hopkins went berserk. Driven mad by mosquitoes and boredom. Max and I tried to disarm him and he fired his rifle. The bullet struck Max a glancing blow on the head. It wasn't intentional. Hopkins wouldn't have hurt a fly. That's why we both said the rifle had gone off accidentally. Saved Hopkins from the firing squad, though not a lengthy stay in the glass-house. Max reckoned it was the least he could do in the circumstances. The wound got him sent home and invalided out before the war was over. The rest of us were stuck there till long after the Armistice.'

'You make a joke of it, but you didn't need to do it, did you? You didn't need to take pity on Private Hopkins.'

'I suppose not, but—'

'And Max still suffers from headaches because of that, doesn't he? He's been in pain lately, I know. I've seen it in his face. Arguing with my father's probably made it worse.'

'All right.' I pulled up. 'I'll speak to your father.' It was still, I firmly told myself, the only practical course to follow. Let Max and Diana believe I was acting altruistically if they wished. The truth was otherwise. And any comparison with a show of humanity in Macedonia thirteen years before was false. 'I'll try to change his mind for you. For both of you.'

'It's all I ask. Oh, bless you, Guy.' She suddenly leant up to kiss me. The touch of her lips against mine was as disarming as it was delightful. But it did not fool me. Not for a moment. 'You're a true friend.'

'Diana—'

'I must go now. Aunt Vita will be expecting me. See Papa as soon as you can. And remember, Max and I are relying on you. Our hopes will be with you.'

'Yes, but—'

It was too late. Already, she had turned and slipped away through the door held open for her, her patterned dress vanishing in the shadowy interior of the shop. I sighed and started along the road towards the Bunch of Grapes, where Max was waiting for me. According to Diana, their hopes went with me. In which case they were in good keeping – so far as I was concerned.

The offices of Charnwood Investments occupied the top floor of an imposing building otherwise given over to an insurance company halfway along Cornhill's southern side. Charnwood's harpyian secretary consented to allot me twenty minutes in the great man's hectic schedule at three o'clock the following afternoon and I took good care to ensure I was not late.

Charnwood was drinking tea when I arrived, with lemon. There was no sign of milk or sugar, far less a biscuit, and he did not offer me a cup. There was a noticeably brisker air to him than I recalled, a hint of impatience as he waved me to a chair and addressed the matter between us without preamble.

'I take it Mr Wingate has seen reason and sent you here to conclude our agreement.'

'I'm afraid not. He—'

'Wearied me with protestations of love for my daughter last week-end. Surely he is not still persisting in his claim to have no financial motive?'

'He is. And I believe him.'

'You surprise me, Mr Horton.'

'Max has surprised me. But there's no doubt he loves Diana quite genuinely – and she him. He may have begun as a fortune-hunter, but your daughter has transformed him into an adoring suitor.'

Charnwood let out a mirthless laugh. 'What poppycock!'

'So I thought at first. But they've convinced me otherwise.'

'And now *you* hope to convince *me*?'

'Yes.'

'Is two thousand not enough for you? Are you holding out for more, perhaps? I should not, if I were you. The time is not ripe. Haven't you read the newspapers? The party leaders are being recalled from their holidays. The bankers are in emergency session. Rumours are abroad in Threadneedle Street that the Bank of England will soon be unable to meet its commitments. What will your two thousand pounds be worth then? My advice to you is to take it while you still can and convert it into dollars at the earliest possible opportunity.'

'If only I could. Unhappily, Max is no longer interested in money.'

'But you are?'

'Of course.'

'Very well.' Charnwood rose from his chair and moved to the window behind him, where he gazed out towards the Royal Exchange and drummed the fingers of one hand on the cast-iron radiator beneath the sill. 'Tell the *reformed* Mr Wingate that I have as much faith in his honesty as I have in the gold standard: precisely none. I shall instruct my daughter to consider their engagement ended. I shall forbid her to have any further dealings with him. *And* I shall take whatever steps may be necessary to ensure that she obeys me.'

This sounded as bad as it possibly could. Desperately, I tried to temporize. 'Mr Charnwood, perhaps I haven't explained clearly enough—'

'Oh, but you have!' He swung round from the window. 'You want to be sensible but your friend doesn't. Isn't that how it is?'

'I suppose so, yes.'

'And you calculate that your only hope of reward is to act as broker for his marriage to my daughter.'

'Well, I—'

'But you're making a mistake. You're failing to see matters from your own point of view. Look here.' He plucked a silver five-shilling piece from his waistcoat pocket and laid it on the desk before me. 'What shape is this coin?'

'What *shape*?'

'Yes.'

'Well, it's a circle.'

'Quite so. But now?' He gathered it up in his hand, then held it out towards me, flat between his forefinger and thumb. All I could see from my position was its milled rim. 'What shape now, Mr Horton?'

'Er . . .'

'Forget it's a coin. Simply describe what you see.'

I shrugged. 'A straight line.'

'Exactly.' Smiling, he balanced the coin on the polished surface of the desk, flicked it into a spin and watched it rotating with evident satisfaction. 'So, a circle and a straight line may be the same thing, depending on your point of view.'

'I don't quite—'

'My daughter and your friend are looking to you for help. Well, so am I.'

'*You* are?'

'Diana's . . . infatuation . . . may prove stronger than her devotion to me. She and Mr Wingate may seek to present me with a *fait accompli*, hoping my objections will be overcome once they are married. They would be wrong, of course. I would cut them off . . .' The coin rattled to rest on the desk. 'Without so much as a five-shilling piece between them.' He looked straight at me. 'Be under no illusion, Mr Horton. I would pauperize my daughter – and your friend with her – if I had to.'

'I'm not sure such a prospect would deter them.'

'Neither am I. Which is why I'm looking to you for help. I shall take Diana abroad at the end of the month, safely out of Mr Wingate's reach. Until then, there exists this danger I have spoken of. If I had warning of their plans, prior notice so to speak, I could pre-empt them, of course. As their confidant, you could give me such warning.'

'I could?'

'And, if you did, there would be a reward. Your share of what you would have been paid already but for your friend's obstinacy.' He picked up the coin from the desk and slipped it back into his waistcoat pocket. 'One thousand pounds, Mr Horton. A fair price?'

'It sounds more like thirty pieces of silver.'

'It's four thousand pieces, actually. And you don't strike me as the remorseful type. Besides, penury would soon shatter your friend's illusion of love. And my daughter's. You'd be doing them both a favour. Their circle would be your straight line. With a thousand pounds at the end of it.'

He understood me as well as I understood myself, perhaps better. What he had said made perfect sense. Even that last little concession to my vestigial conscience was finely judged. I rose slowly from my chair. 'I'll think about it,' I said softly. 'Very seriously.'

Max was downcast at the news of Charnwood's intransigence. But he derived some comfort from what, with my encouragement, he perceived to be a change of heart on my part. 'You don't think I should give up, then?' he asked.

'It's a difficult decision,' I replied, with a frown of resignation. 'But sometimes love must be given its head. Clearly, this is one of those times.' Not, of course, if I had anything to do with it. But poor besotted Max was in no state to hear the truth. I had no choice but to lie, as much for his benefit as for mine. One of us had to think of pounds, shillings and pence even if the other was temporarily blinded to their importance. Our only remaining hope of profit from this enterprise lay in what Charnwood had offered me for betraying Max and Diana's plans. It was therefore incumbent upon me to ensure they had some plans to betray. One day, I did not doubt, my friend would thank me for what I was doing. But that day seemed likely to be a long way off. Meanwhile, there was nothing for it but bare-faced duplicity. 'Just don't let Diana slip away from you now I've made this sacrifice,' I said with a smile. 'She's too good to lose.'

'Don't think I don't know it.' He chewed pensively at his thumbnail. 'But she wants to please him so much. I . . . I just don't know what she'll do.'

'When will you next see her?'

'Tomorrow, near Dorking. We agreed to meet for tea at Burford Bridge. It's an hotel at the foot of Box Hill – a safe distance from the house.' He thought for a moment, then said: 'Why don't you come with me? You can make her understand just how unreasonable her father's being.'

'Well, if I can help . . .'

'I'd appreciate it. I really would.'

'Then say no more. I'll be there.'

We caught an afternoon train from Victoria and were walking down the lane from Box Hill station towards the river Mole by three o'clock. Ahead of us, where the main road from London crossed the river, stood the hotel, rambling and substantial in its leafy setting beneath the downs.

Max was nervous lest Diana would not be there. I think he was afraid Charnwood might have imprisoned her at Amber Court. But he need not have been, for she was already installed in a quiet corner of the hotel lounge, tea and cakes arranged on a table before her. She looked sombre and somehow more beautiful because of it, the delicate forget-me-not pattern on her dress emphasizing her vulnerability. If she was surprised to see me, she covered it well. Perhaps, I thought, she had guessed Max might bring me.

We ordered more tea and sat down together. At once Diana lowered her voice and said: 'I'm grateful for what you tried to do, Guy, but you've only succeeded in hardening my father's heart.'

'I'm sorry,' I replied, endeavouring to look suitably crestfallen. 'Really I am.'

'He's forbidden me to see any more of you, Max,' she said, taking his hand discreetly in hers. 'Simply by being here, I'm going against his wishes. He says we're to spend next month abroad. In Italy. Out of harm's way. Meanwhile, I'm not even allowed to visit London. And my dear little Imp's been locked in its garage, the keys confiscated. I've never known him to behave like this before. It's as if he's suddenly become some . . .' Tears glistened in her eyes and she reached for a handkerchief. 'Some kind of ogre.'

'Don't distress yourself, darling,' said Max, patting her hand. 'He won't stop us marrying. He can't.'

'Can't he?'

The question was left hanging in the air as our tea arrived. After the waitress had spent an age arranging cups and saucers amidst many an echoing clatter and finally withdrawn, I decided to contribute my four penn'orth to the anguished discussion. 'I believe pride is what's stopping your father admitting he's wrong, Diana.'

'Surely he wouldn't let that stand in the way of my happiness?'

'He can't help himself.'

'Then what's to be done?'

'You must take matters out of his hands.'

'You mean . . .' She bit her lip and frowned. 'But I'd so hoped to have his blessing.'

'And you will have . . . after the event.'

'Steady on, old man,' said Max, clearly worried that I was rushing our fences. 'What Guy means, darling, is—'

'I know what he means. And he's right. I thought it myself last night, while I was tossing and turning in bed, wondering what to do for the best. It's the only way, isn't it?'

'I think it is,' I said. 'I truly do.'

And so it was agreed. The two young lovers – or not so young in Max's case – adjourned to the hotel garden, there to stroll hand in hand among the borders and hatch the romantic scheme I had conceived for them. I remained in the lounge, smoking a cigarette and idly turning the pages of *Country Life*. I was not told the details of what they had agreed until Max and I had boarded the train back to London, but he did not hesitate once we were under way to take me into their confidence. Diana was to give her father the impression that she would, however reluctantly, comply with his wishes, while Max – with my assistance – would make the necessary arrangements for a register office wedding at the end of the following week. At two o'clock in the morning of the relevant day, Diana would steal from the house and meet Max halfway up a wooded path leading to the Dorking road. He would have a car waiting on the road and would whisk her away to London, where the ceremony would take place a few hours later, with my good self serving as best man. Diana would meanwhile have left a note for her father explaining her action and hoping to find him reconciled to it upon their return from a honeymoon in Paris.

So far, so touchingly simple. Max and I spent most of the next day browbeating various jacks-in-office into supplying a marriage licence without notice and fixing a date and time for a wedding at Marylebone Register Office: Saturday the twenty-second of August at ten o'clock. We then gladdened the heart of a car dealer in Tottenham Court Road by buying a nearly new Talbot Saloon from him for three hundred pounds and dined at the Ritz on the strength of Max's certainty that an idyllically contented future was about to be his. All he had to do now was await the joyous day with as much patience as he could muster.

And I had little choice but to wait with him, knowing it would never dawn. For the expression of dog-like devotion I had seen on his face as he held Diana's hand that afternoon at Burford Bridge had convinced me Charnwood was right. I really would be doing Max a favour by sparing him the creeping realization that love in a garret is very soon hatred in a ditch. I would be saving him and Diana from a grievous disillusionment. And I would be ensuring Max had his share of Charnwood's thousand pounds to console him for his loss, this last being the most compelling argument of all for biding my time and pretending I had not already decided what to do.

But I had. And two days almost to the hour before the wedding was due to take place, I did it. There were no difficulties gaining admittance this time. The secretary had been told to expect me. Nor were there any sleights-of-hand with five-shilling pieces. Charnwood merely heard me out in silence, then wrote out a cheque for a thousand pounds and slid it across the desk to me.

'I'm obliged to you, Mr Horton. You may rest assured Mr Wingate will be given no cause to suspect you were the source of my information.' We rose and shook hands. 'It's been a pleasure doing business with such a straightforward man as yourself. It makes life so . . . simple.'

Simple for Charnwood perhaps, I reflected as I pocketed the cheque. But, thus far, I had found simplicity to be in desperately short supply.

CHAPTER

FOUR

I did not know how Charnwood intended to prevent the elopement and I did not want to know. Ignorance was, in my case, a guarantee against detection. I took the further precaution of opening a new bank account in my own name, into which I paid his cheque, Max and I having transferred our Canadian deposits to a joint account in London. I had every intention of pooling the money with our other resources in due course, but a good deal of dust would have to settle before I could.

It was then only a question of awaiting developments. As Friday evening drew closer, Max and I both grew nervous, though for different reasons. He was eager to start for Dorking and proposed, to my dismay, that I accompany him. I resisted the idea at first, but could not afford to make him suspicious by behaving as if I knew something was amiss. Faced with his desire for company during the midnight vigil on the downs that lay ahead, I reluctantly consented.

We dined at an hotel near Leatherhead, but still reached Dorking with more than four hours to while away before the rendezvous. Driving out aimlessly along the Guildford road, we stopped at a wayside inn and installed ourselves in the saloon bar. Several large whiskies later, Max's confidence was at a high and garrulous pitch, whereas mine was rapidly ebbing. How was he going to react to whatever form Charnwood's intervention took? What would he do when he realized Diana could not be his? And what, more to the point, would I do? The uncertainties multiplied in my head as alcohol leached away my ability to resolve them.

Fortunately, Max was too intoxicated with his own optimism to notice any trepidity on my part. One of the other customers, by the look and sound of him an opinionated commercial traveller, had been flirting with the barmaid all the time we had been there. He had eventually persuaded her to call him by his Christian name, which he had claimed, somewhat implausibly, to be Hildebrand. The barmaid had laughed uproariously at this, but Max had taken it for an omen.

'Remember the "*dwarfish Hildebrand*", Guy?'

'In *The Eve of St Agnes*, by Keats. I remember. What about him?'

'He was Porphyro's sworn enemy, wasn't he? But he couldn't prevent Porphyro stealing off into the night with his beloved. Well, Charnwood won't prevent me stealing off with my beloved either.'

'Let's hope not.'

'Don't worry. Nothing can go wrong.'

But it already had, as I was hard put not to tell him. Our glasses were empty and, as I went up to have them refilled, the un-dwarfish Hildebrand was entertaining the barmaid with a conjuring trick that involved plucking a red silk handkerchief from the front of her low-cut blouse. How I wished I could practise some similar magic for Max's benefit and call up a happy ending to our night's work. But I had ensured it could not end happily. So there was nothing for it but to blame my sentimental regrets on the whisky – and to order some more.

We lingered at the inn as long as we could, but were eventually obliged to leave. Max had shown me the positions of Amber Court and the meeting-place on a map, but the reality of narrow lanes winding up thickly wooded hillsides beneath a starless sky was infinitely less clear-cut. Moths swirled in the headlamp beams and a fine drizzle smeared the windscreen. When we reached the point where the footpath from the house met the road, Max nosed the car in beneath the trees and turned off the engine and lights.

It was nearly midnight, dark and silent enough to remind me of all the reasons why I distrusted the countryside. Not completely dark, of course. As my eyes adjusted, I could make out the gap in the trees where the path began. Nor yet completely silent. My ears began to detect faint rustlings and stirrings in the undergrowth.

An owl hooted somewhere. A fox barked. Then Max struck a match and offered me a cigarette.

'You reckon I'm mad to do this, don't you, Guy?' he asked with a chuckle.

'I never said so.'

'No. But you came close. In your shoes, I might have come closer. So, don't think I'm not grateful, because I am.'

His gratitude was like a blow to the solar plexus. It was the last thing I needed. 'What time is it?' I hastily enquired.

He struck another match and looked at his watch. 'Four minutes past midnight. Less than two hours to go. A mere bagatelle compared with those stints we used to do at Lake Doiran. Sometimes, I thought we'd be there for ever, you know. But we weren't, were we? We came through. And now Macedonia's just a memory. Like this will be, one day. Except this'll be a happy memory. For both of us, I promise. Charnwood will come round once Diana and I are married. You see if he doesn't. He dotes on her really. And when it comes to spending my new father-in-law's inexhaustible wealth, you can be sure I won't forget my best friend. Or my best man, as you'll soon have the pleasure of being. *Amor vincit omnia*. Old Carter dinned that phrase into my head twenty years ago and I never once believed it – till now.'

There was more, much more, in a similar vein as the time ticked slowly by. I was torn between wishing it would accelerate, so that we might have done with whatever the next few hours held, and wanting them never to elapse. Max had set so much store by what I knew he could not have that I alternately craved and dreaded the moment of his enlightenment. Meanwhile, there was nothing I could say or do to moderate his hopes. As they soared, so were they bound to fall. And, as they soared, so my fears increased.

At a quarter to two, Max set off for the meeting-place: a stile where the path crossed the boundary of Charnwood's property, marked by a fence erected in the farther outskirts of the wood. He anticipated being back within half an hour, Diana by his side, and responded jauntily to my parting words.

'Good luck, Max.'

'Thanks, old man, but I won't need it.' Then he patted my shoulder through the open window of the car, set off along the track, paused to flash his torch back in farewell, and was gone.

Leaving me to debate with myself what would happen and how

I should react. When he realized Diana was not coming, would he come back or proceed to the house to seek an explanation? If the latter, what would he find? Was she still there? Or had Charnwood spirited her away? How had he prevented her from going through with the elopement? Was it perhaps possible he had not succeeded? No. On this point I was certain. Charnwood would have found some way to come between Max and his beloved.

Two o'clock came and went. Then the half-hour Max had set himself expired. There was no sign of him, no sight or sound, nothing in the blanketing darkness to reveal what he had done. By half past two, I felt sure he must have realized he was waiting in vain. If so, he was obviously not returning to the car. I forced myself to calculate what I should do if I knew only as much as I had claimed. And the answer was plain: *go after him*. I thought it through again and the answer was the same. It was vital I behave like the innocent I was not. Bowing to the logic of my own argument, I climbed from the car and started down the track.

Max had bought a brand-new torch a few days previously. Mine, found in a cupboard at the flat, was a much inferior model with a sloppy switch and a beam that began to fade almost immediately. I should have fitted new batteries, but of course I had not bothered to and now I regretted it, as, by the faltering light it cast, I advanced along a narrow but distinct path between gnarled old oak and beech trees, the leaf litter of countless autumns swamping my feet at every stride. After what seemed like ten minutes' walking, I considered calling out, but somehow felt forbidden to. By day, I might have been gambolling in a sunlit glade. By night it was a different place: silent, watchful and forearmed against my dull urban senses.

Then the path divided. It was a contingency I had not anticipated. Neither way seemed better trodden than the other and, even if I had been in the mood to play the tracker, I had not the skills for such a role. Nor could I call to mind the footpath routes marked on the map, which I had stupidly left in the car. I wondered if I should go back for it, then reflected that I was scarcely better at map-reading than tracking. I could simply have given up there and then, of course, but the situation seemed to demand rather more in the way of persistence. The left-hand way looked slightly broader and straighter. I decided to try it.

I soon began to suspect I had made a mistake. I had gone far enough to reach the stile, but there was no sign of one. Then the trees thinned and, almost before I had realized it, I was out of the wood and several yards into a field, an open gateway behind me. I cast about in dismay and was about to double back when, topping some unseen crest, I saw the lights of a house about a quarter of a mile way down the slope. The number and spacing of the illuminated windows suggested a substantial dwelling. It had to be Amber Court. The open gate implied there were no livestock in the field. On the face of it, there was nothing to prevent me walking straight down to the house. Max had said the path crossed a meadow beyond the wood, separated from the gardens by a ha-ha. If I stuck close to the edge of the wood, I must inevitably arrive at the same point. Yet it might still be best to go back to the fork in the path. At all costs, I had to avoid betraying myself. And I had to find Max. After some agonizing, I decided to retrace my steps.

I re-entered the wood, moving as quickly as the inky blackness permitted, anxious to minimize my use of the torch in case I needed it for something more important than dodging tree-roots. Suddenly, away to my left, there was a shout. '*Who's there?*' It was a woman's voice, raised in alarm, perhaps Diana's, perhaps not. Either way, it was not aimed at me. There was a crashing in the undergrowth from the same direction, somebody bursting through leaves and branches. Then the sound was on the path ahead. No, on the other path, reaching and passing the fork as I listened, the sound of somebody running headlong towards the road. '*Who's there?*' came the shout again. '*Stop, I say!*' It was Vita, not Diana, her voice cracking as she shrieked out the command. But the command was not heeded.

Anxiety flooded over me. What the devil was going on? I ran ahead, shining my torch at my feet to avoid tripping, and regained the main path. Whoever had raced by was now out of earshot. But where was Vita? What was she doing in the wood? '*Oh, no!*' came a cry from behind me. This time, surely, it was Diana's voice. '*Oh, dear Lord, no!*' Then silence. I hesitated for a moment, but the appeal for help in her words seemed irresistible. I started along the path, flashing the torch at intervals. Almost immediately, I reached the stile and scrambled over. A torchbeam glimmered ahead.

'Hello? Is that you, Diana?'

'Guy?' I could not see her, but judged her to be about twenty yards away.

'Yes. It's me.'

'Where are you?'

'Here.'

Suddenly, I rounded a bend and found them. Vita was standing directly in front of me, wearing a shapeless felt hat, long raincoat and Wellington boots. She was holding the torch, shining it down to where Diana knelt at the side of the path, bare-headed but likewise booted and gaberdined. In front of her, supine in a patch of ferns, lay a figure in a black overcoat, tweed trousers and stout shoes. The soles of the shoes were muddy, but the uppers were newly polished, gleaming in the torchlight. I could not see who it was from where I stood. The head was obscured in a way I could not at first comprehend. I stepped closer. And then I saw. It was Charnwood. The whole right side of his head had been smashed into a blood-choked crater of bone and brain.

'Oh my God,' I said, starting back instinctively.

'Papa,' Diana murmured, reaching out to touch his chin. 'My poor dear Papa.'

'What are you doing here, Mr Horton?' asked Vita grimly.

'I was with. . . That is . . .'

Diana looked up at me. 'You were with Max, weren't you?'

'Yes. But—'

'Where is he?'

'I don't know.'

'We heard somebody running. Was it Max?'

'It might have been. I . . .' I heard it at the same moment they did. A car starting and accelerating away along the Dorking road, the sound carrying clearly through the trees. It was the Talbot, the note of its engine familiar and unmistakable. 'I don't understand,' I said. 'This doesn't make any sense.'

'My brother has been murdered,' said Vita. 'He came here to meet your friend after Diana had repented of her misguided plan to elope.' Diana began to sob, slowly and insistently, but Vita took no notice. 'When he did not return, we came in search of him. And this is what we found. My brother, bludgeoned to death.'

'You surely don't mean—'

'Your friend has fled, Mr Horton. He has fled the scene of his crime.'

'No. That's not possible. Max wouldn't murder anyone.'

'In a fit of rage, realizing he could not have his way—'

'No, God damn it, no! There must be some mistake!'

63

'I wish there were, Guy,' Diana murmured in the hush that followed. 'With all my heart, I wish there were.'

I knelt beside her, averting my eyes from the sprawled body, the blood-spattered coat, the gory remnant of his face, the hideous gaping wound. 'You can't stay here,' I said. 'You should go back to the house.' I took her gently by the hand.

'Yes. Of course.' She let me raise her to her feet. 'Back to the house. But Papa—'

'You can't help him now.'

'Mr Horton's right,' said Vita. 'Let him take you back. I'll wait here . . . with Fabian.'

'It might be best if *you* escorted Diana, Miss Charnwood. This is . . . no place for a lady.'

'He's my brother,' she said, jaw jutting protectively. 'I won't leave him.'

It was useless to protest. 'Very well,' I said.

'Call the police as soon as you reach the house.'

Out of loyalty to Max, I wanted to object. But what could I reasonably say when the evidence of his guilt seemed so stark and incontrovertible? Already, I had ceased to wonder *if* he had killed Charnwood and begun to wonder *why*. But I knew why. We all did.

'There must be no delay,' said Vita emphatically. 'I want him found.'

Diana and I said not a word to each other as we made our way out of the wood and down across the meadow to the garden-gate. She leant heavily on my arm as we went, breathing deeply to hold back the tears. I could think of no comforting words to offer, no explanation or apology I might venture. For my part, the meaning of what had occurred grew worse with every additional realization. There must have been an argument, I reasoned, one beyond peaceful resolution. Perhaps Charnwood had infuriated Max with a show of arrogance, even of contempt. Perhaps a weapon had come all too readily to Max's hand: a heavy stone, a lump of wood, maybe the torch he had been carrying. Whatever the weapon, it had been used in a frenzy, a spasm of murderous violence for which, in some measure, *I* was responsible. It could not be changed now. It could not be averted. The act was irretrievable. One human was dead. But a dozen others had to live with the consequences.

I was aware of Amber Court as we approached it merely as a

random scatter of illuminated windows against a dark mass of chimneys and gables. We entered beneath a high stone porch. Diana composed herself briefly in the panelled hallway, then went to alert the live-in staff: a cook, two maids and a chauffeur. She returned after a few minutes, led me into the drawing-room and proceeded at once to telephone the police. Some vagary of the line obliged her to shout to make herself understood and the words echoed around the room. '*My father has been murdered. Please come at once.*' My gaze wandered to a portrait above the fireplace: an elegant dark-haired woman in a cream dress of Edwardian style. Her eyes were Diana's, set in another face.

'My mother,' Diana said quietly, looking at me as she put the receiver down. 'Painted thirty years ago.' A tremor ran through her as she spoke. She hugged herself and closed her eyes.

'You should drink some brandy. I'll pour you a glass.'

'I don't want any.' But after she had sat on a sofa near the hearth, she accepted the brandy, with a trembling hand. 'Thank you,' she murmured.

'Sip it,' I cautioned, lowering myself on to the sofa beside her. 'It'll . . . lessen the shock.'

'Nothing can do that.'

'No. Of course not. But. . . What exactly happened?' I needed to know as much as she knew, more importantly *how* much. 'What made you decide not to go through with the elopement?'

She looked at me and, for an instant, I expected her to throw the question back in my face, but all she did was shake her head in sorrow. 'Papa found out what we were planning. He confronted me immediately after dinner and—'

'Dinner last night?'

'Yes. He called me into his study and told me he knew about the wedding. He wouldn't say how he'd found out. Perhaps he just guessed what our intentions were and checked with every registrar's office between here and London till he found the right one. It doesn't really matter now, does it?'

I hesitated for a moment, then replied: 'I suppose not.'

'I admitted it. All of it. What else could I do? At first, I was angry – angry that he'd been spying on me. We had the most awful argument.' She put her hand to her forehead, pained, it seemed, by the recollection. 'But when I saw how disappointed he was in me – how stricken at the thought of my stealing away like a thief in the night – I realized I simply couldn't do it. Not with Mama

dead and no son – or other daughter – for him to put his trust in.'
She swallowed hard. 'Max was asking me to betray Papa's trust,
you see. In the end, that's what stopped me.'

'And your father went to meet Max in your place?'

'Yes.' She glanced down, then raised the hem of her dress and
stared at several dark bloodstains hiding among the polka-dots.
'Why did he do it, Guy? Why did he do such a dreadful thing?'

'I don't know. I was waiting in the car. I followed when he didn't
return and took the wrong path. Until I came upon you, I had no
idea . . . no inkling . . .'

'Oh, God.' Suddenly, she took my hand, then, turning, sank her
head on my shoulder. I thought she would cry, but instead, after
a few seconds, she pulled herself upright and took a long slow
breath. Her eyes were moist, but there were no tears coursing
down her cheeks. 'Papa would want me to be strong,' she said.
'For his sake, I must be.'

'Diana . . . if Max did this . . .'

'Can you doubt it?'

'I don't know. But. . . If he did, he won't run far. That was just
panic. When he realizes what he's done . . . the enormity of it, I
mean . . .'

'You think he'll give himself up?'

'I'm sure of it. He wouldn't have wanted . . . not for all the world
. . . to hurt you like this.'

'But he has.'

'He still loves you.'

'Yes.' She looked away. 'That only makes it worse.'

The police arrived in two detachments: a sergeant and some
constables from Dorking, plain clothes detectives from Guildford.
Diana insisted on leading them up to where Vita was waiting with
the body, rejecting my offer to do so on the sensible grounds that
I was unfamiliar with the route. She was tight-lipped and logical
now, tearfulness and confusion set aside in her determination to
behave as her father would have wished.

The officer in charge, a stout gravel-faced chief inspector called
Hornby, left me with firm instructions to wait where I was. One
of the maids lit the fire in the drawing-room and brought me some
coffee. She professed herself stunned by the news. It was an
understandable reaction, but not one I could afford to give way
to. Smoking one cigarette after another and pacing up and down

beneath the late Mrs Charnwood's portrait, I began to consider what I should tell the police when the time came, as soon it would. The truth – or only part of it? How much was essential, how little sufficient? If there had been any way of helping Max, I would willingly have explored it. But there seemed to be none. He had gone too far towards confirming his own guilt for my efforts to be of the slightest use.

At length, the sergeant returned with Vita and Diana. They joined me in the drawing-room, both of them pale and grim and silent. More coffee was served. The fire was stoked. The room remained stubbornly chill. Scarcely a word was spoken, cowed as we all were by grief or guilt or both. The night dragged its way towards dawn.

Then the sergeant reappeared to report that the removal of the body was imminent. We repaired unquestioningly to the porch, there to witness the covered stretcher being loaded into an ambulance. Drizzle had begun once more to fall, imparting a strange ethereality to the lamps and torches which lit the last departure of the master of Amber Court. The doors slammed behind him, the ambulance moved off and the police ushered us back in. The dead had been attended to. Now the living were to be called to account.

Chief Inspector Hornby spent the better part of an hour closeted with Vita and Diana in the drawing-room. I was banished to the library, where a goggle-eyed constable kept me mute company, mute, that is, apart from clearing his throat every couple of minutes. There was one early interruption, when a sergeant hurried in to ask me the make, colour and registration number of the car. After that, I was left with nothing to do but survey Charnwood's collection of books. Doing so, I noticed how many of them were devoted to the Great War: political and strategic studies, regimental and campaign histories, atlases, memoirs, biographies, seemingly everything published on the subject in the English language. '*Always*,' he had said, '*there is the war.*' And this accumulation of scholarship seemed to prove his point, albeit posthumously.

I took down *Harmsworth's Atlas of the Great War* and began to turn its pages, looking for those illustrating the Salonika campaign. Half-forgotten names leapt out at me when I found the right map: Monastir, the Vardar river, Lake Ostrovo, the Moglena mountains,

67

the Cresna Pass. Max and I had stood by each other in all those dismal places and it seemed wrong for our alliance to be broken now, so suddenly and foolishly. But how could it not be? He had fled and I had remained, powerless to make good what he had done.

'Mr Horton!' barked Hornby, his words shattering my thoughts as he entered the room. 'Time we had a chat, I think.'

I sat down then and told him what I judged he would believe was the whole story. Max and Diana had fallen in love aboard ship; Charnwood had forbidden their marriage; they had agreed to elope; I had accompanied my friend to the rendezvous; he had vanished; and I had found Diana and her aunt with Charnwood's body. Of money-making plans and mercenary negotiations I said nothing. Of my role as Charnwood's informant I let fall no hint.

'You agree with the ladies, then,' said Hornby when I had finished. 'A crime of thwarted passion.' He looked to me like a man who suffered from a good deal of thwarted passion himself, but I knew it was important not to be riled by his alternately polite and insinuating manner.

'I've described what happened. It's not for me to interpret events.'

'You must have an opinion, sir. Do you think your friend murdered Mr Charnwood?'

'I don't know.'

'But what do you *think*?'

'I *think* I'd like to give him the benefit of the doubt.'

'Somebody beat Mr Charnwood to death. It was as savage an attack as I've come across in many a year. Done in an uncontrollable fury, I should say.'

'Max is not given to uncontrollable furies.'

'What about these headaches Miss Diana mentioned him suffering from? Worse lately, she reckoned. Much worse. Could it have been the strain telling – the anger boiling up inside him?'

'I'm unaware of any recent deterioration in his health. He suffered a head injury during the war. But that was thirteen years ago.'

'And since then the two of you have been . . . in business together?'

'Yes. Mostly abroad.'

'What type of business exactly?'

'Finance.'

'That isn't very exact.'

'Any investment we considered likely to yield a profit,' I said levelly. '*If* it's relevant.'

'Oh, it may be.' He smiled. 'And it may not.' He stared at the atlas I had been examining, then asked: 'Where do you think Mr Wingate will go?'

'A police station, as soon as he's recovered from the shock, to offer a full explanation.'

'I wish I could share your confidence, sir, but my experience suggests otherwise. What about this flat in London you share with him?'

'Perhaps. It belongs to his father.'

'Ah yes. Mr Aubrey Wingate.' He glanced at his pocket-book. 'A retired wine merchant, I believe. Resident in Gloucestershire. Do you happen to know his address?'

'Jaybourne House, near Chipping Campden.'

'Thank you.' He noted it down. 'We'll be in touch with him, of course. Is Mr Wingate . . . close to his parents?'

'Not especially.'

'Then London's a more likely hiding-place. Is there anything he'd need to go back to the flat for? Money? Clothes? Documents?'

'Not that I know of.'

'But you *would* know if anything was missing, wouldn't you? The Metropolitan Police will have the flat under surveillance by now, but he may have beaten them to it. I'd like you to accompany me there straightaway – if you've no objection.'

I had several, but none likely to impress Chief Inspector Hornby. 'Very well,' I said with a shrug.

'Good.' He began to rise, but stopped when I made no corresponding move. 'No reason for delay is there, sir?'

'Of course not.'

'I can't accomplish much more here until daybreak, you see. Then we can commence a search for the murder weapon, *if* Mr Wingate – sorry, whoever the murderer was – discarded it. Did Mr Wingate remove anything from the car, by the way? A tyre lever, perhaps? The starting handle? A monkey-wrench?'

'Only a torch.'

'Metal case?'

'Yes.'

'Heavy?'

69

'Moderately.'

'That may have been it, then.' This time he did rise. As I stood up, I noticed him looking at my shoes. 'We'll need to take a cast of those soles, sir. Try to sort out the boots from the brogues. There should be some good footprints at the scene, given the wet weather we've been having. It may not suit the farmers, but it's a blessing for . . .' His words tailed off into a sheepish grin. 'Well, it won't take long. Then we can be off.'

'I'd like to see Miss Charnwood before I leave.'

'You're out of luck there, sir, whichever one you mean. They've both gone to bed, though whether they'll sleep much . . .' He shook his head. 'They'll have a lot on their plates tomorrow. Later today, I should say. Full statements. Formal identification of the corpse. And a mob of reporters at the door, I don't doubt. Not to mention all the to-ing and fro-ing there'd have been even if Mr Charnwood had died of natural causes. It seemed to me they should get what rest they could.'

'Very considerate of you, Chief Inspector.' I could not help suspecting some ploy to keep Diana and me apart, but its purpose, if there was one, eluded me. I felt too tired to protest, too weary of thinking without understanding to resist in any way. 'Shall we go, then?'

'Certainly, sir.' He headed towards the door, then pulled up and turned round to face me, tugging at his ear-lobe and frowning distractedly. 'One last point before we take those casts. After you'd come upon the ladies with Mr Charnwood's body, you escorted Miss Diana back here, leaving Miss Vita at the scene. Why?'

'Because Diana was extremely—'

'But why leave Miss Vita there, alone in a dark wood with no company but her brother's blood-boltered corpse?'

'She insisted on staying with him.'

'And you let her?'

'Well . . . yes.'

'You weren't afraid the murderer might strike again?'

'Of course not. He'd gone. We heard the car speeding off along—' I stopped, realizing what he had made me admit: that I had never once doubted who the murderer was. I had claimed the benefit of the doubt for Max. And now I had thrown it away.

*　　*　　*

I knew before we even entered the flat that Max had been there. I had to turn the key completely in the door before the latch slid back. But I was in the habit when leaving of pulling it shut without troubling to operate the dead-lock – and I had been last to leave when we set off for Dorking. So it was no surprise to find some of his clothes missing, along with half the roll of bank-notes we kept in a tea-caddy in the kitchen and referred to as our contingency fund – without ever envisaging such a dire contingency as this.

My lack of surprise made it easier to assure Hornby nothing had been disturbed. It was a small enough favour to do Max, meaning the police would not know whether he was wearing herring-bone or chalk-stripe, nor how much money he might have in his pocket. But I was glad to do it, relieved indeed to find one lie I could tell for his sake.

Hornby prowled and poked about, asked a few desultory questions and generally expressed disappointment at the paucity of clues.

'Are these really *all* Mr Wingate's possessions, sir?'

'He's always tended to travel light, Chief Inspector. So have I.'

'And where do you think he's travelled now?'

'I couldn't say.'

'We'll have the ports watched, you know. And this flat – for some time to come.'

'I'm sure you will.'

'What I'm saying, sir, is that we're bound to catch him in the end. If you've any idea where he may be, or if he contacts you, by letter or telephone—'

'I'll let you know immediately. Is that what you want me to say?'

'Yes, sir, it is. But it's also what I want you to *mean*.'

Hornby left soon afterwards, as the London sky was lightening. I had undertaken to report to Dorking Police Station that afternoon to make a formal statement. In the interim, while Hornby and his crew scoured the woods for evidence, there was nothing for me to do but brood upon the intractability of Max's plight. Whether or not I aided the police in their search, I did not doubt how it would end: in Max's arrest. And what then? His trial. His conviction. His execution. It was as hard to imagine any other sequence of events as it was to believe that my friend was truly set on such a course.

71

Mrs Dodd arrived at ten o'clock, flustered by being interrogated on the doorstep by a plain clothes policeman. Fluster turned to dismay when I told her what had happened. She insisted on cooking me some breakfast and speculating on how Max's parents would take the news, which I had no difficulty in guessing without her assistance. I had met Mr and Mrs Wingate on several occasions and knew them to be kindly but correct. This turn of events was certain to distress and scandalize them. Sooner or later, I was going to have to account to them for my part in it and it was not a prospect I was relishing.

It was nearly noon when Mrs Dodd left. I should perhaps have telephoned the Wingates then, but the person I most wanted to talk to at that moment, aside from Max, was Diana. Surrendering to the impulse, I put a call through to Amber Court. But Diana, the maid informed me, was unavailable. With some misgivings, I agreed to speak to Vita instead.

'My niece is resting, Mr Horton, and cannot possibly be disturbed. The poor girl is beside herself. The police are still searching the grounds and we're besieged by pressmen. The situation is quite frightful – and deeply distressing.'

'I can imagine how you feel.'

'Can you? Diana's father has been brutally murdered by a man with whom she thought herself to be in love. Can you really imagine how she feels? How I feel?'

'Well. . . Of course, I realize what a terrible shock this has been. . . Perhaps it would help if I could talk to Diana.'

'I doubt it.'

'I have to be in Dorking this afternoon to make a statement at the police station. Could I call at Amber Court afterwards?' There was a pause, during which Vita seemed to be weighing my suggestion in the balance. 'Miss Charnwood?'

'I think not, Mr Horton.' My suggestion, then, had been found wanting. 'You are closely associated in Diana's mind with Mr Wingate. Any communication with you is therefore bound to upset her. In the circumstances, I think it would be best if you left her alone. In fact, I rather think I must insist on you doing so. Now – and for the foreseeable future.'

'But—'

'Good day, Mr Horton.'

* * *

72

The harshness in Vita's voice fed on my self-pity till, by the time I set off for Dorking, my concern for Max had turned to resentment. Why on earth had he done such a thing? Murder was so pointless, so profitless. And it implicated me in a scandal of which I wanted no part.

My reception at the police station did nothing to alter my mood. In Hornby's absence, a sweaty young detective sergeant took my statement. The nib of his pen caused him frequent difficulty and this, combined with the painful slowness of his writing, ensured I was there for nearly two hours before the little I had to say was recorded to his satisfaction. I was actually on my way out of the building when something happened to imply a purpose behind his dilatoriness: Hornby burst through the door in mud-caked boots and thorn-hatched tweeds, grinning broadly. Sighting me, his grin did not so much vanish as coagulate.

'Still here, Mr Horton? I thought you'd have been gone by now.'

'So did I.'

'Ah well, the mills of God, you know.'

'What have they to do with it?'

'*Thou shalt not kill.* It's one of the Ten Commandments. I'm surprised a well-educated fellow like you doesn't know that.' He grew suddenly sombre. 'We found a heavy wedge-shaped flint earlier this afternoon in the trees near where Mr Charnwood was killed, with enough blood and fragments of bone and tissue on it to identify it as the murder weapon. There was an argument, I suppose. Mr Charnwood began to walk away. Mr Wingate picked up the flint, ran after him and, as he turned, struck him about the head, then several more times as he lay on the ground. Afterwards, he threw the rock away, ran to the road where the car was waiting, and drove off. You agree?'

'I don't know.'

Hornby stepped closer. 'Come now, Mr Horton. You *must* agree.'

'I'll believe it when I hear it from Max's own lips. Not before.'

He nodded. 'Fair enough. I'd put money on your condition being met in the very near future. Then you'll have to believe it. Won't you?'

I felt badly in need of a drink when I left the police station, but the bar of the Star and Garter Hotel turned out to be a poor choice. Charnwood's murder was the sole topic of conversation among the customers, wild theories circulating as the beer flowed. Nobody could claim to have known the victim – he kept himself too much to himself for that to be possible – but nobody, on the other hand, was lacking for an opinion about what had happened. A report of the incident on the front page of the local evening newspaper was read aloud and exhaustively debated. The significance of Charnwood's body being found by his sister and daughter, along with a man whose name meant nothing to anybody, was widely speculated upon. As to the fellow being sought by the police, Max Wingate, some said he had been a recent house-guest at Amber Court; so at least the cook was supposed to have told the butcher when he delivered the week-end joint there earlier in the day.

I fled, unable to listen to any more. But, on the train back to London, I slowly realized that I would have no choice in the matter. At least until Max was found, I would be forced to listen. Worse still, my name along with his would probably be in every national newspaper by morning. My father and sister could hardly avoid coming across the story. Even supposing they did miss it, one of their neighbours could be relied upon to draw it to their attention. My anonymity was suddenly forfeit.

By the time the train drew into Victoria station, I had decided not to go back to the flat that night. The decision meant Max could not telephone me even if he wanted to. This was a considerable sacrifice, since I badly wanted to speak to him and gauge his state of mind. But, for the present, my obligations to my father and sister had to take priority. They deserved to hear the truth – or part of it – from me before they read a garbled version of it in the Sunday papers. The prodigal son – the scapegrace brother – would have to make his overdue return.

Letchworth on a Saturday night exuded its normal level of gaiety: approximately that of a Welsh village on the sabbath. From the railway station I walked west through empty streets, past the dark and looming outline of the Goddess factory, where I had spent two miserable years trying to be the sober-suited manager of a hundred viraginous corsetières. Then I turned south along the silent half-mile of tree-screened houses at the far end of which an old man and his no longer young daughter lay unknowingly in wait. We had walked down this road together twenty-three years before to view the property generously provided by the company

74

when it moved to Letchworth. My mother and Felix had walked beside us. We had tried to keep each other's spirits up, but it had seemed so bare then, so flat and soulless. And so it still seemed to me, for all the trimmed verges and smugly angled roofs. The Garden City remained what it had always been in my mind: a wasteland.

And then I was there, beside the laurel hedge and the gravel drive I could never forget however hard I tried. *Gladsome Glade*, the sign proclaimed with obstinate absurdity. But a gladsome welcome I did not hope for.

My sister answered the bell. I saw her approaching along the hall through the frosted oval of glass, blurred into a bewildering simulacrum of my mother. When she pulled the door open, we stared at each other for a moment without speaking. What I saw was a frumpily dressed forty-year-old woman with streaks of grey in her hair and crow's feet forming at the edges of her eyes. What she saw was her six years younger brother, louchely handsome and cautiously smiling, beyond redemption but not reproach.

'Guy! So good of you to pop round.'

I felt my smile stiffen. 'Hello, Maggie. Were you expecting me?'

'Felix told us all about your visit. Dad thought he'd imagined it. I didn't.'

'Well, you always understood Felix better than the rest of us, didn't you?'

'Did I?' She considered the point for a second, then gave an exasperated little shake of the head. 'Come in, for goodness' sake.' I stepped past her into the hall and she closed the door behind me. 'I don't know what Dad's going to—' She stopped in the same instant that I looked along the hall and saw him standing in the doorway of the sitting-room, rheumy eyes fixed upon me.

'Hello, Dad,' I ventured.

His only reply was a nod. His hair was whiter than I remembered, his stoop more pronounced, his clothes more threadbare than my mother would ever have tolerated. He scratched thoughtfully at his chin without taking his eyes off me, then turned and retreated into the room.

Maggie and I exchanged an eloquent glance. Then she smiled for the first time and kissed me lightly on the cheek. 'You're looking well, Guy,' she said. 'Better than you deserve.'

'Coming home must agree with me.'

'Let's hope explaining does as well, because you've a lot of it to do.'

'Yes. I have. More than you can possibly imagine.'

CHAPTER

FIVE

My memories of family life are distant ones. From the age of thirteen, my affinity with those to whom I am related by blood began to wither, for it was then that I won a scholarship to Winchester and so divorced myself from the cares and doings of the family I left behind in Letchworth. What Winchester started the army finished and my attempt to become a dutiful son and humble clerk at the end of the war was as brief and futile as it was bound to be.

The sitting-room of *Gladsome Glade* that cool August night thus held for me no magical warmth of home. Nor did my father, a man of few words but many disapproving grimaces, attempt to induce any. He had long since despaired of me. Widowhood and retirement, indeed, appeared to have filled him with a general despair about the world. He listened to my account of what had happened with an expression in which distaste and resignation were equally matched. Only when I revealed the horror of Charnwood's death did disgust boil over inside him. He rose abruptly from his chair and stood by the piano, fiddling with his pipe and breathing agitatedly while I finished. Beside him, atop the piano, were three gilt-framed photographs: one of him and my mother on their wedding-day, one of Felix in his army uniform, one of Maggie on her twenty-first birthday. There had once been a fourth, but since my mother's death it appeared to have vanished.

'Your *friend*,' my father said at last with heavy emphasis, 'has *murdered* a man?'

'Not necessarily. Until—'

'A respectable business-man. The chairman of a successful company. And you abetted him in the mad escapade that led to this?'

'I didn't know how it would end.'

'You *didn't know*?' He gripped the stem of his pipe so ferociously between his teeth I thought it might snap. But something else snapped instead. 'This will be in the papers tomorrow, won't it? Your name – my name – will be mentioned.'

'Nobody's likely to connect—'

'They'll connect us, boy, take my word for it. I won't be able to show my face at the bowls club without somebody whispering about it behind my back. You're remembered here well enough. All too well.'

'Surely not.'

'Oh yes. People still kindly remind me of the day you walked out on a fine career.' It was easy to believe him. I had returned from a week-end with Max in London determined to quit my job and join him in an altogether more glamorous occupation. Breaking my journey at Hitchin in order to bolster my determination with several large drinks, I had reached Letchworth, the bastion of temperance, drunk enough to leave no-one, especially the managing director of the Goddess Foundation Garment Company, in any doubt about why I could stomach life and work in the Garden City no longer. How my father had endured the embarrassment my departure occasioned him I had never cared to imagine, but now he was to give me some glimmering of an idea. 'Your mother rebuked me then for saying I wished you'd never been born. But I meant it, boy, I meant it. For her sake, I pretended otherwise. But she's not here any more. So, I don't have to go on pretending, do I?'

'No,' I replied dismally, staring up at him. 'You don't.'

He grunted, tapped out his pipe noisily in a 1902 coronation saucer, then thrust his hands deep into his cardigan pockets. 'I'm away to my bed,' he said to Maggie, turning to plod towards the door.

'What about your cocoa?' she responded.

'I don't want any.'

'Shall I bring a mug up to you?'

78

'*I don't want any!*' The door slammed behind him and I looked across at my sister. She sighed.

'He was angry even before you came, Guy.'

'Why?'

'He thinks the government is leading us down the road to ruin. He predicts Goddess – and every other company in the town – will be bankrupt by Christmas and that his pension will be forfeit. All thanks to Mr MacDonald, apparently.' She shrugged. 'Now this. It's too much for him, I'm afraid.'

'I'm not pleased about it myself.'

'Of course not. It sounds dreadful.' She shook her head. 'Poor Miss Charnwood. And poor Max.'

'I thought you should be forewarned, that's all. Perhaps it would have been better if—'

'No. You were right to tell us in person. What Max did isn't your fault.'

'I'm not sure Dad would agree with you.'

'Possibly not.' She rose and stepped behind my chair, resting her hand protectively on my head. 'Why did you leave America, Guy? Didn't it turn out to be the promised land after all?'

'Not exactly. But I wish now—' I twisted round to look at her. 'We couldn't have stayed,' I murmured. 'There were . . . problems.'

'Will Dad hear about them too?'

'I hope not.'

'So do I.' She moved away, then turned to face me, pressing her hands together and tilting her head in a brisk and business-like pose I immediately recognized. 'What will you do now? Look for Max?'

'I wouldn't know where to start.'

'Have you spoken to his parents?'

'No.'

'You should see them as soon as possible. As their son's friend—'

'I know what I *should* do, Maggie, but—'

'Where do they live?'

'Gloucestershire. Near Chipping Campden.'

'Drive over there tomorrow.'

'I've no car.'

'But I have. It's a recent acquisition.' She smiled. 'So, you've no excuse now, have you?'

* * *

79

My father pointedly refrained from comment on the article headlined BUSINESS-MAN BEATEN TO DEATH – DAUGHTER'S SUITOR SOUGHT which graced his newspaper the following morning. Nor did he display any interest in the bundle of other papers which I brought back from an early foray to the newsagent, although I suspected he meant to read every word printed about Charnwood's murder as soon as I left for Gloucestershire. What the various articles amounted to was as bad as I had predicted but not quite as bad as I had feared. Max's name was prominent, but mine was also there for the eagle-eyed to spy out. And of the eagle-eyed the Letchworth Bowls Club had never been in short supply.

The only condition Maggie had imposed when making her tiny Austin Swallow available to me was that she should drive it, allegedly because I could not be trusted to keep to the left. Once we had set off, however, she admitted she was as keen to be free of our father for a few hours as I was. On the way, we discussed Felix and Letchworth politics and the state education system (in which Maggie had worked loyally with scant reward for nearly twenty years). But not until we turned into the drive of Jaybourne House, nestled in an orderly fold of the Cotswolds, and caught our first glimpse of its honey-stoned gables between the elms, did either of us mention the purpose of our journey.

'What will you tell them, Guy?'

'The same as I told you and Dad. The truth.'

'That's what it was, was it? The *whole* truth?'

'Of course.'

We pulled up in front of the house and Maggie looked straight at me, eyebrows raised. 'Mum and Dad used to blame Max for leading you astray. Do you think Mr and Mrs Wingate blame *you* for leading *him* astray?'

'Maybe.'

'If they do, this could be a difficult encounter.'

'Yes, it could. But like you said last night: I owe it to Max to face them.'

We need not have worried. The Wingates received us with sombre courtesy. Their sadness was palpable, but of bitterness there was no trace. Aubrey Wingate was a small white-haired man in his seventies, his face flushed and confused. His wife was smaller still and frailer, a cheerless smile fixed permanently to her lips. Both wore tweed and smelled faintly of the several Labradors who wandered in and out of the drawing-room as we spoke. They sipped Malmsey while I recounted the events of Friday night, frowning occasionally in pain or puzzlement but querying little and challenging less. Chief Inspector Hornby had paid them a visit and made it clear he believed what they were not yet prepared to: that Max was a murderer. From Max himself they had heard nothing.

'And until we do,' said Mr Wingate, 'we shall continue to hope he has some innocent explanation for his conduct.'

'The dear boy couldn't kill anyone,' added Mrs Wingate. 'Don't you agree, Guy?'

'Yes. Absolutely.'

'It's running away that looks so damned bad,' said Mr Wingate. 'But he'll soon see reason and give himself up. I'm sure of it.'

I nodded energetically. 'So am I.'

But both of us were exaggerating, as became clear when we left the ladies and stepped into the garden for a breath of air – and a confidential word. One of the Labradors trailed behind us as we wandered aimlessly across the lawn towards a lushly planted border. The grass was wet beneath our feet and there were spots of rain in the chilly breeze. But Aubrey Wingate did not appear to notice.

'I'm glad you're staying at the flat,' he said with gruff amiability. 'It will mean Max knows where to find you.'

'If I hear from him, I shall advise him to go to the police without delay.'

'Of course. As will I. But then?' He glanced at me doubtfully. 'What I said indoors was for Cecily's benefit. You must know as well as I do that things look black for Max. Damnably black.' He sighed. 'He came to see us a few weeks ago, just after the pair of you arrived from Canada. He announced he was in love and I believed him. I'd certainly never seen him so . . . taken . . . before. He said he meant to marry the girl and hoped to introduce her to us in the near future. No mention of her father's objections, of course. No whisper of elopement. But he was head over heels in love. That much was obvious. A man obsessed, I couldn't help thinking.'

'Love *is* a kind of obsession, sir.'

'Yes. And obsession can drive a man to murder, can't it? Do you think it drove Max to murder?'

'No. That is—' We came to a halt in front of a thick stand of dahlias. 'I hope not.'

'So do I.' Wingate's grip on his walking-stick tightened. Suddenly, he raised it to shoulder-height and slashed off the head of one of the dahlias, scattering its spiky yellow petals at our feet. 'But I fear our hopes may be in vain.'

The longer Max remained a fugitive the more his guilt would seem confirmed – to the police, to the newspapers, even to his family and friends. His father's words had made me impatient to return to London, for it was there, I felt sure, he was hiding. Our route back to Letchworth crossed the main Birmingham to London railway line at Banbury, so I asked Maggie to drop me at the station there. She agreed to do so reluctantly, suggesting I was manufacturing an excuse to avoid our father. But for once she had misjudged me. I really was thinking of Max.

But finding him was quite another matter. There was, in reality, nothing I could do to that end but go solemnly back to the cold and empty flat in Hay Hill and to wait, as the hours dragged slowly by, for the telephone to ring or the latch to yield to his key. But neither did. It was the second night since Charnwood's murder. And still Max kept his distance.

I have seldom had occasion to be grateful to politicians, but the morning of Monday the twenty-fourth of August was an exception. A crisis was in the air, with half the Cabinet threatening to resign if the Prime Minister insisted on cutting unemployment benefit, which the lucratively employed editors of Fleet Street regarded as essential to restore confidence in the pound. One consequence of this was that crime, even the murder of a prominent businessman, was given scant coverage. It became possible to believe that there were some, indeed many, for whom Charnwood's death was a matter of no importance.

I was taking some bleak comfort from such thoughts over a sparse breakfast when the post arrived, an unusual event in itself, since we generally received nothing. For a second, I wondered if it might be a letter from Max. Racing down to the door, however, I found an unpromising buff envelope lying on the mat, with my name and address type-written on it. Not until I was halfway back up the stairs did I tear it open.

As I pulled out the letter inside, an enclosure fluttered to rest on the next step. I stopped and picked it up, only to find it was Charnwood's cheque for a thousand pounds. Puzzled, I looked at the letter. It was from my bank, saying payment had been refused. The cheque was correctly dated and signed, drawn on a company account at one of Lombard Street's most reputable establishments. Yet the fact remained that it had been bounced. At first, I simply could not believe it. It was almost laughable. Dud cheques were my stock-in-trade, not Fabian Charnwood's. What could it possibly mean?

I reached the sitting-room, poured myself some more coffee and lit a cigarette. Then I sat down and re-examined both letter and cheque. But neither sense nor meaning were to be wrenched from dry banker's prose and one of the last pieces of paper Charnwood had ever put his name to. Was it some mean trick of his, perhaps? Had he directed his bank to refuse payment, calculating that I would be deterred from making a fuss by the fear of Max discovering what I had done? If so, the irony was considerable, for his death made it more difficult still for me to protest. If I did, the police might hear of it. And they might tell Diana. If my hands were to stay clean, I would have to bear the loss in silence. *Re-present to drawer*, instructed the letter. But the drawer was dead. And all I had by way of memorial was written proof of his fraudulent intent – and of mine.

I was brooding on the invidiousness of my position when the telephone rang. I bounded across the room and snatched up the receiver, hoping against hope. But the caller was not Max. It was Aubrey Wingate.

'Good morning, sir. Any news?'

'I've been thinking about the flat.' I took this to mean he had heard nothing from or about Max. 'Your occupancy of it, that is.' His tone sounded stiff and awkward, in bewildering contrast to his anxious intimacy of the day before. 'I've decided I'd prefer you to move out.'

'Move out?'

'As soon as possible.'

'But. . . Yesterday, you said you were glad I was here in case Max—'

'I've changed my mind. Your remaining there would be . . . irregular.'

'Well, of course, if—'

'I'd like you to be gone by the end of the week.' He was addressing me like some recalcitrant tenant rather than his son's best friend. The suddenness of the change left me too confused to respond. 'Preferably sooner.' He paused and cleared his throat, then added: 'I don't wish to be unreasonable, but, in the circumstances, I must insist. I'm sure you understand.'

'No. I don't. What—'

'There's no more to be said. Perhaps you'd leave your keys with Mrs Dodd.'

'But—'

'Goodbye, Mr Horton.'

Mr Horton? As the line went dead, that last phrase reverberated in my mind. Hitherto, he had always called me Guy. His abrupt descent into formality was as uncharacteristic as my eviction seemed pointless. From every side, I was assailed by incomprehensible events. The bounced cheque. The notice to quit. And Max's behaviour both on and since the night of Charnwood's murder. I had tried till now to believe some logic was at work, some sequence of cause and effect. But, if it was, it was not one I understood. Where it might next lead I had no way of predicting. But I felt uncomfortably certain that I would be carried along in its wake.

The imminence of Mrs Dodd's arrival drove me from the flat. I was in no mood for her homilies. Instead, I tried to walk off some of my frustration by marching across London to Charnwood's bank in Lombard Street. I hoped to be told the rejection of my cheque was an administrative error, but instead I was coolly advised to refer to the drawer for an explanation. The cashier did not say whether he had read in his Sunday paper how the signatory had been found battered horribly to death in a Surrey wood. Nor would he reveal on what grounds the cheque had been returned. But he did favour me with some information I already possessed: the address of Charnwood Investments.

I left the bank and headed down one of the alleys that I knew led to Cornhill. For as long as it took me to reach the George and Vulture, whose doors had just opened, I actively contemplated seeking an interview with Charnwood's company secretary and trying to persuade him I was legitimately owed a thousand pounds. So I was, but I was sure he would not agree. The slim chance he might was not worth the risk of Hornby hearing about the approach. Biting my lip, I entered the George and Vulture in search of the only solace I was likely to find.

In this at least I was not disappointed. I sat there for two increasingly bleary hours, watching the red-faced denizens of the City gobble down their steak and kidney puddings and listening while they debated what I gathered was now the actual collapse of the government. Then I wandered down to Blackfriars Bridge and trudged slowly back along the Embankment.

My route took me across Whitehall, where the crush of people in and near Downing Street was at once apparent. With nothing better to do, I stopped to see what was attracting them. A sullen-faced fellow in a threadbare trench coat and flat cap glanced round at me as I joined the throng and cocked a knowing eyebrow. 'Come to see the fun?' he asked.

'Is there any?'

'Depends what tickles you. The sight of our lords and masters scurryin' in and out'a Number Ten like rabbits from a burra' puts a smile on some people's faces.'

'But not yours?'

'Why should it? If I 'ad a job to go to, I wouldn't be standin' 'ere, would I?' A shout went up as the celebrated door opened and a stocky bowler-hatted figure emerged. It was Stanley Baldwin. 'An' it's the likes of 'im what threw us all out'a work. So don't expect me to raise a cheer.'

Baldwin marched down the centre of the street and out into Whitehall, cradling his umbrella in his arm as if it were a shot-gun and he a squire patrolling his estate. A car had been drawn up in readiness and an aide now rushed to open the door for him.

'Looks like 'e's in, dunnit?' said my companion. 'Just abaht all we bloody need.'

I watched Baldwin stoop to enter the car. As he did so, my gaze shifted aimlessly to the section of the crowd beyond him. And there, standing almost immediately opposite me, was Max. He was wearing the dark grey suit I had noticed as missing from the flat, but the black trilby looked new and was pulled well down over his forehead. He must have been watching me for some time, because our eyes met instantly. Then he flung down his cigarette and turned away, elbowing past other onlookers to reach the open pavement.

'Max!' I shouted, but he paid me no heed. I started after him, only for a policeman built like an oak tree to step into my path and lay a restraining hand on my arm.

'I don't think Mr Baldwin wants to speak to you, sir.'

'You don't understand. I was simply trying—'

'Have you been drinking?'

Baldwin's car was drawing away. Beyond it, heading in the same direction towards Trafalgar Square, was a grey-clad figure, running hard. 'Let me go!' I protested.

But the policeman's grip tightened. 'Not until I'm sure you're going to be sensible, sir. Why don't you go home and sleep it off?'

'I'm not drunk.'

'I think you are, sir. And unless you want me to decide whether you're also disorderly, I strongly recommend—'

'All right, all right.' Max was out of sight now. Once he reached Trafalgar Square, my chances of sighting him were nil. And from there he might head in any one of half a dozen directions. I shook the policeman's hand off and tried to compose myself. 'I'm sorry, Constable. I don't want to cause any trouble. I'll go home, as you suggest.'

But I did not go home, not least because, strictly speaking, I had none to go to. Instead, I wandered up Whitehall, pondering the ever greater mystery of Max's conduct. Why should he run away from me? Surely he could not have thought I would identify him to the police. If he did doubt my loyalty – for whatever reason – why had he followed me? Follow me he certainly must have, for I could not believe he was in Downing Street by chance. No fugitive would emerge from hiding simply to check on the balance of political power.

I sat on a bench in Trafalgar Square and smoked my way through the remaining cigarettes in my case while the traffic whirled remorselessly round and the pigeons rose and landed and rose again. Was Max really following me? If so, why? And what would he have concluded from my visit to the City? I thanked God I had thought better of going to Charnwood Investments. But my relief was swiftly replaced by alarm. Had Max followed me into Charnwood's bank? Had he perhaps overheard my conversation with the cashier? The possibility was too horrible to contemplate. Stifling the thought, I ground out my last cigarette and headed for Hay Hill.

* * *

86

I paid no attention to the large black car parked a few yards beyond the door of the flat, but I should have, for, as I turned my key in the lock, Chief Inspector Hornby and another plain clothes detective appeared either side of me.

'May we come in, sir?' asked Hornby. 'There's been a new development.'

'You better had, then.' I said no more. There had been so many new developments that I dreaded to imagine what else could have happened. But, as we climbed the stairs, I resolved to make no mention of seeing Max in Whitehall. At least he would not have that to blame me for.

'This is Detective Sergeant Vickers,' said Hornby, pointing to his colleague as we entered the sitting-room. 'My assistant.' And a man, to judge by his build and expression, from the same mould as his superior.

'What can I do for you, Chief Inspector?'

'You can comment on this, sir.' Vickers handed him a large envelope, from which he removed a folded sheet of paper. 'It's a letter received this morning by Mr Aubrey Wingate.' He unfolded it as he passed it to me and I recognized the hand-writing immediately.

'It's from Max.'

'So Mr Wingate confirmed. Perhaps you'd like to read it.'

I looked down at the letter resting in my hand and noticed at once the absence of either date or address. Then I read what my friend had written.

> Dear Father,
> You will know by now of what I stand accused. I want you and Mother to understand that I am innocent of Fabian Charnwood's murder. I do not know who killed him or why, but it was not me. I cannot give myself up because my friends have turned against me. Nobody will believe me except you. Do not trust Diana or Guy. They have betrayed me. I cannot write more till I have discovered the truth. But I *will* discover it.
> > Your loving son,
> > Max.

'Well, sir?'

I was scarcely aware of Hornby's question as I sank into the nearest chair and re-read the letter. Now I knew why Aubrey

Wingate had given me my marching orders: because his son had denounced me as a traitor. But it was impossible for him to have learned of my one act of treachery, unless it was from Charnwood's own lips. And he had accused Diana along with me. Surely she at least did not deserve such harsh words.

'What do you make of it, Mr Horton?' asked Vickers.

'I . . . I don't understand. What does he mean?'

'We were hoping you could tell us that, sir.'

'The letter was posted yesterday afternoon,' said Hornby. 'In Banbury.'

'Banbury?'

'Yes. Know the town, do you?' Something in Hornby's face, some narrowing of his gaze, suggested he was well aware of my recent movements – including my departure from Banbury railway station aboard the London train less than twenty-four hours before. If I was right, the police had been following me. And so had Max. This was no time to risk a lie.

'I caught a train there yesterday afternoon.'

'Really? That's a coincidence, isn't it?'

'Is it?'

'Well, if it isn't, I have to ask myself why you and Mr Wingate should both be in a town neither of you have any connection with on a Sunday afternoon. If you were *both* there, of course.'

'I've just told you I was. And the postmark proves Max was as well.'

'Not quite. It proves a letter written by him was posted there. It doesn't prove *he* posted it.'

'Then who are you—' I broke off as the drift of his reasoning became apparent. 'I've not seen Max since Friday night.'

'So you say.'

'It happens to be—' I stopped. How much *did* Hornby know? If his men had also seen Max in the crowds at Downing Street, they would surely have arrested him. Of course, it would not have been as easy for them to recognize him as it was for me. Perhaps they had missed him. But, even if they had, they could not have missed me crying out his name. 'As a matter of fact, I thought I caught a sight of him in Whitehall a few hours ago.'

'What?'

'It was . . . just a glimpse. I—'

'Were you intending to report this?'

'I'm reporting it now, aren't I?'

Hornby frowned darkly. Before he could say any more, Vickers produced a note-book and pencil. 'What exactly did you see, sir?' he asked.

As I recounted the incident and Vickers scribbled dutifully away, Hornby's gaze remained fixed on me, one eyebrow raised in dubious deliberation. It was clear he did not believe me, which was ironic, since for once I was telling him nothing but the truth. Perhaps that was what provoked me to conclude on a misleading note. 'I can't be sure it was him, of course. There were so many people milling about between us. I could easily have been mistaken.'

Hornby grunted. 'There's certainly a mistake somewhere.'

'Are you still suggesting I met Max yesterday? And posted this letter for him?'

'Are you admitting you did, sir?'

'Of course not. Damn it all, you've Max's own word for it that he regards me as a traitor.'

Hornby took the letter back from me and glanced down at it. 'Is he right to do so?'

'No.'

'Then why should he?'

'I don't know.'

'There's no reason at all?'

'None whatsoever.' With a jolt, I realized how easily I had been trapped. Hornby's theory was that Max's denunciation of me was designed to obscure my role as his ally. And now I had gone some way to proving the theory correct. 'Look, this is absurd. If I'd spoken to Max since Friday night, I'd have urged him to give himself up. He doesn't have any other choice.'

'He has the choice of running. But he needs help if he's to stand any chance of pulling it off. A quiet passage across the Channel and the money to pay for it. That sort of help.'

Had they followed me to Lombard Street and questioned the cashier? If so, they must have known I had gone away empty-handed. But my possession of a Charnwood Investments cheque would have sown a host of doubts in Hornby's mind – more than I could ever hope to allay. 'I've told you everything I know, Chief Inspector. I'm not assisting Max in any way.'

Vickers sat down in the chair opposite me and fixed me with a sceptical frown while Hornby wandered around the room, glancing at the drab hunting prints which adorned the walls. They seemed to be digesting my remarks, weighing them for sincerity and significance. At last, Vickers said: 'It's often a matter of instinct, sir.'

'What is?'

'Help. Who you give it to and who you don't. Thick as thieves, the saying goes. And it generally holds true. At *both* ends of the social scale.'

'What exactly do you mean?'

'You and Mr Wingate were at school together, weren't you?'

'What of it?'

'Winchester, wasn't it?'

'Yes.'

'Well, there you—'

'Another coincidence!' put in Hornby with sudden force. 'They do mount up, don't they?'

'I don't know what you're talking about.'

'Your car has been found. In Winchester.'

'*Winchester?*'

'Yes. In Kingsgate Street. Which, as I'm sure you're aware, runs past the College where you and your friend spent what they tell me are supposed to be the best days of your life. Well, for the likes of you two, I expect they were.'

I leaned back in the chair, overwhelmed by a surfeit of mysteries. Why had Max gone back there, of all places? Why revisit the scenes of our youth? To mourn the friendship he thought I had betrayed? Or to set it aside? 'I haven't been back to Winchester since I left it sixteen years ago,' I said, slowly and deliberately. 'As far as I know, Max hasn't either.'

'Seems he has now, sir,' said Vickers.

'The car had been parked in Kingsgate Street for some time before it attracted any attention,' said Hornby, resting his hands on the back of the sergeant's chair and gazing down at me. 'Probably since Saturday morning.'

'Are you suggesting he drove straight there from Dorking?'

'Presumably. Then back to London by train, I imagine.' He frowned. 'Unless you have some alternative to put forward.'

'Of course I haven't,' I snapped, instantly regretting my tone and fearing it would alert them to the lie I had told.

'Well, we'll know more when we go down and take a look at it tomorrow. So far, we just have what the Hampshire police have told us. One abandoned Talbot Saloon bearing the registration number you gave us.'

'With bloodstains on the steering-wheel,' added Vickers.

'Yes,' said Hornby. 'We mustn't forget those, must we?'

I studied each of them in turn, defying them as best I could with a show of impassivity. About twenty seconds must have elapsed, though it seemed more like several minutes, before Hornby spoke again.

'I think that's all for now, sir. We'll be on our way.' Vickers stood up and they both moved towards the door. I stayed where I was, too exasperated, too utterly confounded, to show them out. 'We'll keep you informed of any further developments, naturally.'

'Thank you,' I murmured.

'One last point,' said Hornby, turning back in the doorway. He was tugging at his ear-lobe and I took some comfort from having expected this to happen – the mannerism *and* the theatrical postscript; he was becoming predictable. 'Mr Aubrey Wingate tells me you may shortly be leaving here.'

'I will be, yes.'

'You'll be sure to let us have your new address, won't you?'

'Do I need to?' I raised my eyebrows, confident he would understand what I meant.

'Look on it as a matter of courtesy,' Hornby replied with a grin. 'An Old Wykehamist's strong suit, isn't it?' He paused for a second, then added: 'Along with loyalty, of course.'

Every aspect of my life seemed now to be badly awry. The police thought I was in league with a murderer. Max had renounced our friendship. My finances were dwindling. And I would shortly not even have a home-from-home to call my own.

I left the flat within an hour of Hornby's departure, nursing a hangover and more unanswered questions than my aching head could bear. A massage and a lengthy sweat at the Hammam Turkish Baths in Jermyn Street cleared my mind, but the questions remained. Where was Max? What did he hope to achieve by playing cat-and-mouse with the police? Had Charnwood told him I was his informant? Was that what he blamed me for?

I went into the bar of the Carlton Hotel and studied my smoke-wreathed reflection in one of its many mirrors over a succession of razor-edged Manhattans. The talk at nearby tables was of the newly formed National Government. Evidently, some sort of coalition had resulted from the comings and goings I had witnessed in Downing Street. But I could only think of Max's face as our eyes met across the crush of onlookers. There was stealth in his expression, and suspicion – and something horribly close to hatred. If I could only find him, I would be able to explain everything. But he did not mean me to find him. That much at least was clear.

I left and wandered up to the Plaza Cinema, where I sat through half a fatuous talky called *These Charming People* wondering all the while if Max was sitting in the dark somewhere behind me. But nobody left when I did. No shadows moved between the street-lamps as I made my way to Berkeley Square, nor hovered near as I paused beneath the trees to smoke a cigarette and watch and wait – in vain.

Morning brings resolution, albeit not of a lasting nature. Next day, I scanned the hotel columns of the paper, reckoning I could run to five guineas a week all found without exhausting my funds before some way out of my difficulties presented itself. The Eccleston Hotel, near Victoria station, seemed to fit the bill. By midday, I had booked myself in for the duration. It was not the Ritz, but a clientèle of cashiered majors and divorced gentlefolk promised at least a degree of anonymity.

I spent the afternoon trudging round the hotels of the neighbourhood, showing a photograph of Max and me to any porter or concièrge who was willing to give it a second glance. It was a snap-shot taken by Dick Babcock at the Surf and Sand Club in Palm Beach in 1925. We were both smiling, as well we might, for those had been happy days. But nobody recognized the face. I am not sure they even realized that the other face belonged to me.

I returned to the flat, defeated and dejected, to collect my belongings. Before leaving, I dutifully telephoned Dorking Police Station to report my new address. I had hoped simply to leave a message, but, to my chagrin, I was put through to Sergeant Vickers.

'Eccleston Hotel, Eccleston Square, SW1. Duly noted, sir. Is there a telephone number?'

'Victoria 8042.'

'Thank you, sir.'

'Well, if you have all that, I'll—'

'One thing before you ring off, Mr Horton. We've finished with your car. For the moment, anyway, although we must insist you notify us if you propose to sell it or take it out of the country. It may be needed as evidence, you understand. Meanwhile, you're free to collect it from the station in Winchester at any time you like.'

'From Winchester?'

'Well, we don't operate a chauffeur service, you know, sir.'

'No. Of course not.'

'Goodbye, sir.'

I put the receiver down and remembered walking out of College with Max for the very last time in July 1915, resplendent in our Rifle Corps uniform, strutting like a pair of bantam-cocks, proud of the ringing tone of our boot-studs on the cobbles. Later, we had both agreed we would probably never return, that to go back was always a mistake. But Max had gone back. And so too, it seemed, must I.

Winchester lay mellow and unaltered beneath a cloudless sky when I reached it the following morning. But for the day's sudden peak of late summer ripeness, I might have collected the Talbot from the police station and driven straight back to London. I might have, though I doubt it. In the event, it seemed impossible not to divert to the precincts of the College, to park beneath the boundary wall of the Close and to walk down Kingsgate Street, wondering what had brought Max back to this place of high walls and familiar windows – with the bloodstains I had just touched fresh on the steering-wheel of the car.

I turned in through War Memorial Gate. This had in my time commemorated the College dead of the Boer War, but I was vaguely aware that those who had fallen in the Great War were now recorded in a cloister just beyond. I had read something about an appeal to finance its construction in the pages of *The Wykehamist*, a journal which had pursued Max and me by post across many years and several continents. Needless to say, I had not contributed a penny, but clearly others had been more generous, for I found myself in a grandly conceived and ex-pensively executed quadrangle of flints and flagstones, twin-pillared stone arches running round an immaculately kept garden, with a cross at its centre, while, along the inner walls of the cloister were arrayed on plaques the names of several hundred dead Wykehamists, year by year, regiment by regiment.

I began to follow the entrance year headings towards 1910, wondering just how many of my contemporaries would be listed

93

there. But, before I had passed 1900, a figure rounded the north-west corner of the cloister: a slim elegant young woman in a black suit, her eyes shaded by the brim of a matching hat; it was Diana.

We pulled up at the sight of each other, then she raised a hand and smiled in recognition. 'Hello, Guy.'

I walked forward to join her in a sun-filled archway, struck more than ever by her exceptional beauty, which jewel-less mourning seemed only to enhance. 'This is. . . What brings you here, Diana?'

'What brings *you*?'

'I came to collect the car. The police have finished with it.'

'I suppose you could say I came for the same reason. Chief Inspector Hornby told me they'd found it here and I wanted to . . .' She shook her head. 'Well, I suppose I thought it might help me to appreciate Max's state of mind if I retraced his steps.'

'And has it?'

'No.'

'Me neither.'

She sighed and glanced up at the dazzling sky. 'You know about the letter, of course?'

'Yes.'

'He thinks we betrayed him, you and I. I suppose I did, in a sense, by yielding to Papa's wishes. But . . .' She looked directly at me. 'Betrayal is too strong a word, isn't it?'

'I think it is, yes.'

'And what does he blame *you* for?'

'I . . .' Deception is cumulative, one lie breeding a dozen others and those a dozen each in turn. Diana's question marked another stage in the ever more complicated process. 'I really have no idea. I thought I understood Max. It seems I was wrong.'

'If you don't, who can? You share so much with him. Most of both your pasts.'

'Yes. Starting here.'

'It's such a beautiful place.' She glanced around. 'Yet so empty.'

'Only for a few more weeks. Once Short-Half begins—' I smiled at her evident puzzlement. 'Sorry. That's what Wykehamists call the autumn term. Let's walk through to Meads.' I smiled again. 'The school field.'

A wrought-iron gate led us from the eastern side of the cloister directly into Meads, green and verdant beyond my recollection, the plane trees motionless as sentinels, the memories pressing in upon me of days far less idyllic than those conjured up by the scene before us.

'I wish I could have come here with Max,' said Diana softly. 'In happier circumstances.'

'I wish you could, too.'

We walked slowly on towards School Court for a few minutes in silence, then Diana said: 'Papa's to be buried on Friday. Will you come?'

'If you'd like me to. I had the impression . . . when I spoke to your aunt on the telephone . . .'

'Pay no attention to what Aunt Vita says. I would value your attendance – as a friend.'

'Then I'll be there.'

'Thank you—' She stopped and held my hand briefly in hers, gazing at me with an earnestness I found intimidating and, yes, let it be said, somehow enticing. 'I think we may both need the support of a friend in the times ahead. Max has turned his back on me. You won't do the same, will you, Guy?'

'No. Don't worry. You can rely on me.'

We spent several hours in Winchester, exploring the College and Cathedral Close and strolling by the river. Over tea at the George Hotel, Diana reminisced about her father. I found myself talking about Max and our schooldays in a similar vein, as if I no more expected to see and speak to him again than I did Fabian Charnwood. It was strange and bewildering and oddly easy. Diana's beauty, her trusting nature, seemed almost to compel confidence. I held back, of course, veiling my thoughts, but there was a contagion of frankness in the air which I had to steel myself to resist. Was this the birth of a friendship? Of course not. But, if Diana had said she hoped it was, I would not have demurred. To Max, I knew, it would have seemed altogether different – and treacherous into the bargain. '*There's no such thing as friendship between a man and a woman,*' he had often said. And he was right.

We drove out of Winchester in the declining light of late afternoon, following the same route, straight and fast to Guildford, where our paths divided. Somewhere on the Hog's Back I watched her Imp accelerate away till it was a dot in the distance. I did not follow. But the memory of her face and the recollection of her

95

voice were imprinted on my mind with disconcerting clarity. I could and did assure myself that the encounter meant nothing. But, all the same, she had left her mark upon me. And that meant rather more than nothing.

A message had been left for me at the Eccleston by none other than 'Trojan' Doyle. Hoping to hear that Atkinson-White had been raining money on him and that my share of the commission was immediately payable, I proceeded to his office in Holborn first thing the following morning. But Trojan's expression – akin to a bulldog with toothache – told me before the words were out of his mouth that the news was not good.

'Your friend Atkinson-White has contracted cold feet. He won't be entrusting his nest egg to me.'

'Why not?'

'Because you recommended me. And your name's been in the papers recently, along with Max Wingate's and the late lamented Fabian Charnwood's. Murder and mayhem tend to undermine confidence, don't you find?'

'Charnwood's murder is nothing to do with me.'

'Maybe not. But blood sticks even faster than mud in this game. Atkinson-White prefers to deal with people who go to bed at ten with a good book rather than rampaging round the woods of Surrey battering protective parents over the head.'

'Couldn't you have persuaded him to . . . think it over?'

'He had thought it over. And I can't say I blame him. What the devil have you and Wingate been playing at?'

'*We* haven't been playing at anything. It was between Max and Charnwood.'

'Come off it. You were pumping me for information about Charnwood. You said you might be doing some business with him.'

'It fell through.'

Trojan grunted. 'Count yourself lucky.'

'Why?'

'Because I've been hearing some strange rumours about Charnwood Investments. Without the man himself, it's nothing. People put money in because they trusted his judgement. Now they want their money back. And some question whether it's all there for them to retrieve.'

Could others have had the same experience as me? I had supposed till now that the dud cheque represented a personal act

96

of spite. But perhaps it was nothing of the kind. 'You assured me he was doing well,' I said, with a frown of accusation.

Trojan spread his arms wide, disclaiming responsibility. 'He *was*. But he was also highly secretive. He handled everything himself. Took all the decisions. Made all the moves. His staff were just puppets. Without him, they're helpless. Presumably, the business will be inherited by his family. But it's too soon to say what they'll make of it. And while we wait to see if they can come to grips with Charnwood's tangle of international investments, a lot of people are becoming nervous. Very nervous indeed.'

Fabian Charnwood's funeral took place in Dorking the following day and gave no hint of the worries which those who had invested in his company were allegedly harbouring. St Martin's Church was filled with an eclectic gathering of mourners, in which relatives, employees and local worthies were heavily outnumbered by what I took to be a representative sample of Charnwood's business associates: prosperous men of his own generation, many of whom looked as if they had continental origins and some of whom had the faintly familiar appearance of people I might once have seen or heard of – though where or in what circumstances I could not recall. Into which category Faraday fitted I did not know, but there he nevertheless was, bobbing and pouting in the pew immediately behind Vita and Diana.

They, for their part, bore themselves in the contrasting fashions I might have expected: Vita tearful and unsteady, forever raising a heavy veil to dry her eyes; Diana thoughtfully subdued and more concerned for her aunt's condition than her own. Lessons were read by a viscount and two baronets and rounded off by an orotund eulogy from a huge and bearded Slav whom the printed order of service credited with the rank of general in some unspecified army. He contrived to be both extravagant in his praise yet reticent about how he had met the deceased. I supposed he thought a man's funeral no place to reminisce about sealing their friendship over a contract for the supply of ten thousand rifles.

The committal at Dorking Cemetery was a brief and restrained ceremony. I kept to the rear of the mourning group, hoping to avoid Faraday. In this I was successful, but only at the expense of finding myself shoulder to shoulder with Chief Inspector Hornby, who was more poker-faced than usual but no less sharp-tongued.

'Eyeing the headstones are you, Mr Horton, in case Mr Wingate's hiding behind one?'

'You think I should be?'

'You tell me. Is he still in England?'

'How should I know?'

'The coroner may ask for your opinion on the point. I should think of a less sarcastic answer, if I were you.'

'The coroner?'

'At the inquest. We haven't fixed a date yet, but, when we do, you'll be one of the witnesses we call.'

My heart sank. Here, looming close, was another occasion when I would be hard put not to strengthen the case against Max – and to compound my treachery in his eyes.

'Look on it as an appetizer, sir. The main course will come later.' As I glanced round at him, he nodded. 'We'll bring him to trial in the end. Mark my words.'

The priest had finished and, as I peered past the hunched shoulders and bowed heads, I saw Diana step forward to scatter her handful of dust on the coffin.

'Not such a bad way to be laid to rest, is it?' murmured Hornby, almost to himself. 'There's a certain dignity about it. And it's a nice setting, with the downs on either side.' He paused, then, as the people ahead of us began shuffling towards the grave, he added: 'A pleasanter plot than the patch of prison yard they'll bury his murderer in, that's for certain.'

Mercifully, Hornby was not among those who returned to Amber Court after the funeral for tea, sandwiches and respectful small talk. Diana and Vita were surrounded by attentive sympathizers, so I drifted to the window and gazed out at the garden Charnwood had once escorted Max round while explaining his unsuitability as a son-in-law. As I sipped my tea and pondered the agonizing irreversibility of events, I failed to notice the approach of a familiar figure. When I did, it was as a suddenly coalescing reflection in the glass, followed almost immediately by the honey-rich sound of his voice in my ear.

'Who would have thought it, eh, Mr Horton? That we should meet again – in such tragic and unexpected circumstances.'

I did not trouble to disguise my pained expression, but, turning, could see no easy way to escape him. 'The circumstances are not of my making, Mr Faraday.'

'Nor of anybody present, eh? Do you know, I haven't been in this house for nearly a year. How time flies.'

'Quite.'

'And rings in its changes.' He glanced round, then lowered his voice. 'Where's Barker, I wonder.'

'Who?'

'Mr Charnwood's valet. I expected to see him here.'

'I wasn't aware he had a valet.'

'He used to have. But perhaps. . . It's my impression he was making some economies in recent months. Poor Barker may have been one of them.'

'Maybe he was.'

'You concur with my impression, then?'

'I never said so.'

'No, but . . .' He smiled and gazed slowly round the room. 'Do you think it fair to judge a man by the people who attend his funeral, Mr Horton? If so, we must accord Mr Charnwood a colourful reputation, mustn't we? Take General Vasaritch, for instance, our eloquent eulogist.' The mountainous general was at that moment not far from us, talking to, or rather bellowing at, a stout little man with a monocle and excessively greased centre-parted black hair, who was listening attentively to every word, his ear approximately level with the forked end of the general's beard. 'He hides a few secrets behind the guffaws and anecdotes, I would venture to suggest. But, like a good soldier, he understands the value of camouflage.'

'What army did he serve in?'

'I'm not entirely sure. He calls himself a Yugoslav. But what does that mean?' Faraday paused and frowned at me, then said: 'Have you found a suitable outlet for your talents since returning to these shores, by the way?'

Endeavouring to seem scornful of the question, I shrugged and replied: 'These are early days.'

'I don't mean to pry. It's simply that the man with whom General Vasaritch is conversing may have just the opening for a fellow of your particular talents. He's the proprietor of the Ambassador Club. Ah, I see you've heard of it. He's also recently acquired the Deepdene Hotel here in Dorking. On Mr Charnwood's recommendation, I believe. Would you like me to introduce you?'

I hesitated, weighing several competing considerations in my mind. Charnwood had made no bones about what sort of club the Ambassador was. Its proprietor might provide me with an entrée to a wide world of money-spinning schemes. He was therefore a man I ought logically to cultivate. But I did not trust Faraday, especially when he was offering to be helpful. On the other hand, I could not afford to be unduly suspicious. I was short of contacts in London society and would soon be short of money as well. I could not neglect the only occupation I knew for Max's sake. Indeed, I told myself he would not want me to. So, what was there to hold me back?

'I think Mr Gregory and you may find you have a great deal in common,' Faraday continued. 'A view of the world based on the same principles. It might prove a fruitful association.'

'Gregory?' The name rang several bells. And then they played an unmistakable tune. The Ambassador's proprietor had won his spurs as an honours broker for Lloyd George in the years immediately following the Great War. So, at all events, it had reliably been rumoured. Of course, the sale of honours had since become illegal. Hence the need for a more discreet setting in which to conduct such business, a gentleman's luncheon club off Bond Street being ideal. And hence, it occurred to me, the higher profit margin appropriate to an illegal trade. 'You mean Maundy Gregory?'

'The very same.'

'Then, yes, perhaps you would be so kind as to introduce us.'

'Excellent. I—'

'Excuse me, Mr Faraday.' Suddenly, Diana was between us. 'My aunt would like to speak to you. Would you mind . . . ?'

'Of course not, my dear.' There was the merest hint of irritation in his tone and in the pursing of his lips. 'I am hers to command.' He moved smartly away, raising one regretful eyebrow at me as he passed.

'Thank you for coming, Guy,' said Diana, motioning me towards the greater privacy of the bay window. 'It can't have been easy for you.'

'Don't worry about me. How are *you* bearing up?'

'Well enough, so long as I don't have to endure the company of that nauseating little man. I'm sorry he should have inflicted himself on you.'

'He was asking me what had become of somebody called Barker.'

'Barker?' She frowned. 'He was Papa's valet – until Papa decided he no longer needed one. But I really don't see . . .'

'I'm sorry. Forget I mentioned it.'

'I wish I could forget Mr Faraday altogether. Aunt Vita's enthusiasm for his advice is quite baffling.'

'What does he advise her about?'

She seemed on the point of explaining, then shook her head. 'You don't want to hear our troubles.'

'If I can help . . .'

'You can help *me* by not associating with Mr Faraday or any of his dubious acquaintances. I'd like to be able to talk to somebody untainted by the world they inhabit.'

'Well, I don't know any of these people. If that qualifies me as untainted . . .'

She pressed two fingers briefly against her forehead. 'I feel so alone, Guy. Aunt Vita means well, of course, but she doesn't understand. Papa's gone. And so has Max, to all intents and purposes. It's so hard, so very hard, to keep any kind of grip . . . when there's no-one to turn to . . . '

She seemed on the verge of tears. Moving to mask her from the rest of the room, I squeezed her hand and smiled reassuringly as she looked up at me. In her eyes were fear and hope and grief, commingled in uncertain appeal. She hardly knew what she was asking and I hardly knew what I was offering. Yet a question was silently put and an answer implicitly given. 'Whenever you can't bear to be alone, Diana . . . Whenever you need a helping hand . . .'

'Bless you, Guy.'

'I do mean it. *Whenever.*'

And so I did mean it, for the instant her gaze was fixed upon me and for the minutes after, when we stood only inches apart and I could study her flawless beauty and imagine, even then, less than an hour after her father's funeral, what it would be like to peel the black rustling fabric from her pale fluttering body.

But the charms of the flesh are less durable than the lure of riches. I had let Diana believe I despised Faraday as much as she did. Yet when, as the gathering broke up and I took my leave, he hovered beside me in the porch for the briefest of words, I did not refrain from listening.

'I spoke to Mr Gregory about you, Mr Horton. He'd like to

meet you in less restrictive circumstances. His offices are at thirty-eight Parliament Street. Why not call there after the week-end and make an appointment? I'm sure you wouldn't be wasting your time.'

I made no reply, but the address was firmly lodged in my memory when I climbed into the Talbot and drove away. I had given Max ample opportunity to explain what he wanted of me and he had spurned it. The time had come to revert to what I had always felt was my true métier: self-advancement.

CHAPTER

SIX

A miserable week-end amid the bridge sets and gossip schools of the Eccleston was sufficient to confirm me in the opinion I had formed in Dorking. There was nothing I could do for Max and nothing, apparently, that he wanted me to do. Shame and remorse for the part I had played in his downfall faded as the values which had stood both of us in good stead for the past ten years reasserted themselves. Since I could not help Max, I would concentrate on helping myself.

My first and foremost step in this direction was to seek an interview with Maundy Gregory. Evidently he valued Faraday's opinion, for I was invited to call on him within twenty-four hours of making contact. Thirty-eight Parliament Street proclaimed itself as the headquarters of the *Whitehall Gazette*, but I regarded it as certain that many more discreet and profitable activities than the publication of a society magazine took place within its walls.

Gregory's office was a baroquely furnished room cluttered with signed photographs of celebrities and enough electronic gadgets to support a spy-ring. It was the cocktail hour and he dispensed Martinis with glad-handed enthusiasm. I felt an immediate loathing for everything about him – the egg-shell charm, the wafts of cologne, the dandyish dress, the monocle, the rings, the voice; and especially the hungry fish-like eyes. But I had worked for loathsome people before without regretting it. I did not anticipate we would ever need to like each other.

'Charnwood's murder is a frightful business, Mr Horton.'

'Perfectly awful.'

'But Mr Faraday tells me you have displayed impressive powers of diplomacy in coping with its consequences.'

'I'm glad he thinks so.'

'Which means you may be suitable for the sort of work in which I always require assistance. Delicate work, you understand.' He smiled. 'But highly remunerative.'

I too smiled. 'Exactly my line of country.'

'Good.' He surveyed me for an instant, then said: 'I'm the publisher of *Burke's Landed Gentry*. You know it?'

'Of course.'

'Well, its centenary is approaching and I'm having the contents completely revised. The editor and his staff are checking every entry for accuracy.'

'A considerable task, I imagine.'

'Indeed. And also a sensitive one. You see, I look upon the publication as more than a work of reference. I look upon it as the servant of those whose lives it chronicles. The revision should be an opportunity to acknowledge merit and to encourage its proper reward. In those cases, our approach must be tactful in the extreme. There are some who deserve adornment to their title and status and who require our advice on how best to obtain it.'

'You mean there are some who might hope to be elevated to *Burke's Peerage, Baronetage and Knightage*?'

He permitted himself a chuckle. 'Succinctly put, Mr Horton. There are some who justifiably hope. And for those who are also prepared to defray the not inconsiderable expense involved in such matters, there is much we can do. Confidentially, of course. Negotiations, if they are to be taken forward, must be handled with the utmost discretion. Which is why I prefer to employ one or two hand-picked representatives for the purpose and to leave the editor and his staff entirely out of it.'

'I quite understand, Mr Gregory. I believe I could be very helpful to you in taking the necessary soundings.'

His smile broadened into a sickly beam. 'Yes, young man. I believe you could.' I did not care for the phrase *young man* as he pronounced it, but this was hardly the time to explain which of his vices I did not share. 'Supposing I were to select one or two . . . candidates . . . for you to approach, how would you set about it?'

'A preliminary letter, I should think, suggesting we meet to discuss revision of their entry in *Burke's Landed Gentry* and related matters, followed by a telephone call to arrange such a meeting.'

'Just the ticket. Take along a copy of the *Whitehall Gazette*. Last June's, for example. There's an excellent photograph in it of the Derby Dinner I hosted at the Ambassador, featuring enough dukes, marquesses and viscounts, not to mention cabinet ministers, to persuade even the most sceptical of what may be achieved on their behalf.'

I nodded eagerly. 'Then, if they seem interested, lunch . . . at the Ambassador, perhaps . . .'

'. . . Where I could exchange a few passing pleasantries with them . . .' he mused.

'. . . While I mentioned the sort of sum that might be necessary to oil the relevant wheels.'

The beam had compressed Gregory's eyes into slits. He rose from his chair, walked round to my side of the desk and patted my shoulder. Looking down at the stubby fingers, each sporting at least one glittering ring, it was all I could do not to shudder. 'I think ours will prove a fruitful association, Mr Horton. Would you care for another Martini?'

By the end of the week I had despatched two letters to specimens of the landed gentry identified by Gregory as possessing the ideal combination of spare cash and social ambition. At the beginning of the following week, I proposed to contact them by telephone. I was keen to take matters forward, since, until money changed hands, there would be no commission for Gregory – and no sub-commission for me. But I had to be patient. Such monkeys would be caught softly or not at all.

While I was kicking my heels over the intervening week-end, I received two visitors at the Eccleston. The first, hideously early on Saturday morning, was a police constable whose arrival provoked a flurry of curiosity among the other residents and knitted brows of disapproval among the staff. He served me with a *subpoena* to appear as a witness at the inquest into Charnwood's death, to be held at Dorking Magistrates' Court on Wednesday the sixteenth of September, then took his leave.

I had known it must happen, but still I felt depressed at the prospect of stating publicly what I had reluctantly concluded: that Max had murdered Charnwood. The coroner *might* let me off

105

without being explicit on the point, but at the back of my mind I feared Hornby would take steps to ensure he did not.

I was on the point of trying to walk off the gloom into which such thoughts had dragged me when my second visitor arrived. It was Diana, flushed and exhilarated after a fast drive from Dorking in her Imp. She had honoured the sunny morning with a flower-patterned dress and a skittish almost feverish air, as if rebelling against the stale confines of bereavement.

'Papa wouldn't have wanted me to mope behind the blinds at Amber Court on a day like this. I had to get away. And I thought of you, worrying about the inquest. I suppose you *have* been notified?'

'Oh yes.'

'Then come out with me and let's try to forget our troubles – if only for a few hours. It may be a vain effort, but . . .'

'It's worth trying, Diana. You don't have to convince me.'

She smiled. 'Good. Jump in and we'll go wherever the whim takes us.'

The whim took us to Hampton Court, where we strolled in the Great Fountain Garden and debated whether Henry the Eighth had loved any of his wives. To Weybridge, for lunch in a pub beside the river. And then to Sandown Park for an afternoon of enjoyably profitless betting on any horse that took Diana's fancy. For six or seven hours we entertained each other with idle chatter, excluding all mention of her father, of Max, of the state of Charnwood Investments, of the inquest at which we would both appear in eleven days' time. She seemed happy, almost carefree, and, to my dismay, I realized that I did too.

Dusk found us walking along the Bishop's Walk beside the Thames at Putney. Our parting was imminent and I detected regret on both sides. Had it not been for the metaphorical shadows that outreached by far the real ones gathering about us, I would have slipped my hand round her waist and stolen a kiss. But our different obligations to the same man held us apart. As we turned back towards Putney Bridge, I commented on the delights of the day without daring to suggest they be repeated.

'It *has* been delightful,' Diana replied. 'I've been harried by solicitors and accountants since the funeral. Papa left his affairs in some disorder, it seems. And I can't let Aunt Vita shoulder the burden alone. But I really did need to escape for a while. Thank you for rescuing me.'

106

'*You* rescued *me*, actually.'

'Did I?' She smiled. 'Well, perhaps you'll return the compliment.'

'How?'

'I have two tickets for the ballet next Tuesday. Alexandra Danilova's dancing at the Alhambra. I was planning to introduce Max to the pleasures of—' She stopped, realizing she had spoken his name aloud for the first time that day. When she resumed, her voice had dropped almost to a whisper. 'You don't have to come, Guy. You don't have to put on any kind of show for my benefit. If you'd rather we just went our separate ways . . . and tried to forget . . .'

I pulled up and, as she turned to face me, took her hands in mine. There were tears glistening in her eyes. I felt a jolt of desire more fanciful men might have thought transcended the physical. And I felt also a wrench of doubt. Perhaps it was better to sunder our links. From this point on, I would be consciously betraying Max. And I would be deceiving Diana, for the untainted status I had claimed after the funeral was forfeit now I had struck terms with Maundy Gregory. It was scarcely likely she would hear I was on his payroll, of course. Even supposing Faraday wanted to tell her, he would have to admit his own role as Gregory's recruiting agent in order to do so, which would not suit his purpose at all. Nevertheless, it was not wise, not prudent, not sensible in any way. And yet she was so beautiful. To touch more than her hand – to gain possession, however briefly, of so much beauty – was an irresistible prospect. 'I'm afraid it's too late to withdraw your invitation,' I said with a grin. 'I *will* accompany you to the ballet. Whether you want me to or not.'

And so my double – or triple – life proceeded. The recipients of my two letters agreed to see me. One of them, a Northamptonshire boot and shoe manufacturer whose ambitious wife had transplanted him to a Tudor pile in Middlesex, rose to the bait. Lunch at the Ambassador was followed by tea at Gregory's flat in Hyde Park Terrace. Discussion of a knighthood and a payment of ten thousand pounds moved forward in delicate tandem.

Meanwhile, I escorted Diana to the ballet and dined with her afterwards at Gatti's. The following Saturday, we drove to Brighton, where we toured the Royal Pavilion, lunched at the Metropole and watched the white horses rush past us on the pier.

107

The pretence that we could isolate ourselves from what had happened and what had yet to happen was intoxicating. While we were together, we existed in a bubble of Diana's desperate gaiety, sustainable just so long as I did not test whether she would yield to me or not.

Contact with my family was confined to a joint visit to Felix arranged by Maggie. She probably regretted making the effort, because poor Felix seemed quite overwhelmed by such mass attention and retreated into his shell. Our ever-sensitive father filled the void with a peroration on the wonderful example set by the King in giving up fifty thousand pounds from the Civil List to alleviate the government's financial problems – the price, I could not help calculating, of approximately five knighthoods. My father said nothing, either at the hospital or afterwards over stewed tea and stale buns in a St Albans café, about the inquest he knew to be pending. Royal examples were to be praised *ad nauseam*, his son's problems studiously ignored. Along with his daughter's, I might add, since Maggie, in common with every other teacher employed by the state, had just had her pay cut by fifteen per cent. Studying her harassed and distracted expression across the fuggy interior of the café, I silently vowed to make up the difference with whatever I earned from Gregory. At least then the honours system could be said to have done some good – however inadvertently.

I heard nothing from the Wingates or from Chief Inspector Hornby. There had been, I assumed, no more letters from Max and no sightings of him, in London or elsewhere. I thought of him often, especially at night, and sometimes varied my route back to the Eccleston to see if he was keeping watch in the square. But he never was. Once, walking along the Strand in the early hours of the morning, I saw somebody who looked rather like him about thirty yards ahead of me. This time I did not call out. Instead, I followed him for some distance, only to lose his trail in the passages under Adelphi Terrace. Picking my way past the curled forms of drunks and down-and-outs sleeping in archways under scraps of sacking, I wondered for a chilling moment if this was where Max had taken refuge. But, if so, he was beyond my help. And by the next day I had convinced myself that I was mistaken; it had probably not been him after all.

*   *   *

108

Two days before the inquest, I received a letter from Diana. We had agreed to behave in court as if we knew each other only slightly and to meet afterwards at an hotel in Reigate to discuss the outcome. But our plan, it appeared, had been overtaken by events.

Amber Court,
Dorking,
Surrey.
13th September 1931

Dear Guy,
Our secret outings have been a great source of consolation to me in recent weeks. They have given me more pleasure than I thought I would ever know again. But the problems from which I have taken refuge with you are remorseless. They cannot be wished away. Indeed, they are about to multiply. I cannot say more in a letter, but I do so want you to understand. Will you call here on Wednesday after the inquest instead of driving to Reigate? I can explain everything then. Do not worry about Aunt Vita. I have reconciled her to our friendship. Please come. It is very important.

Affectionately yours,
Diana.

I puzzled over this for several pointless hours. How could the situation have become worse than it already was? And why meet at Amber Court, with Vita on hand – reconciled or not – to hamper our freedom of speech? There was, of course, only one way to find out. But this fact made the uncertainty no easier to bear.

Dorking Magistrates' Court was filled to overflowing on the morning of the inquest. The coroner, who bore a marked resemblance to an army surgeon I had encountered in Macedonia, looked as if he preferred sparser attendances. But the ranks of the press and public were not to be denied their mouth-watering insight into a sensational murder. They had been looking forward to this day as much as I had been dreading it.

Chief Inspector Hornby greeted me with his usual brand of irksome affability, then went into whispered conference with the clerk of the court. Vita and Diana arrived to a murmurous chorus from the public gallery; I pretended not to notice. There was no sign of the Wingates, who had evidently decided not to attend. For this small mercy I was duly grateful.

Proceedings commenced promptly at ten thirty. A jury of local stalwarts was sworn in and the first of five witnesses called. This was Diana, whose softness of voice and grace of bearing made a marked impression on the coroner. She described the events of the night without flinching: her change of heart about the elopement; her father's departure to keep the appointment with Max; his failure to return; the search for him; the discovery of his body. The coroner offered her the court's sympathy and she walked back to her seat in an eloquent hush. Vita followed her into the box and confirmed what her niece had said from the point of view of a brisk and unaffected spinster equal to anything. The coroner congratulated her for waiting alone in the dark with her brother's corpse and her reply – that she had only done her duty – elicited mutters of approval on all sides.

I was called next. As soon as I admitted being Max's friend, I detected a cooling in the atmosphere around me. In his absence, I had become the surrogate villain of the piece. The coroner, meek and mild in his approach to the ladies, turned suddenly curt and severe.

'Did this escapade not strike you as grossly irresponsible, Mr Horton?'

'No, sir, it did not.'

'What did you think had happened when your friend failed to return?'

'I didn't know. That's why I went to look for him.'

'You saw him running from the scene?'

'I heard somebody running. I can't say who.'

'But they drove away in your car. Who but Mr Wingate would have known it was there? Who but Mr Wingate could it have been?'

'*I can't say.*'

'When you reached the body, Miss Vita Charnwood and Miss Diana Charnwood were already there?'

'Yes, sir.'

'And it was apparent to you that Mr Charnwood had been brutally murdered?'

'It was apparent to me that he'd met a violent death.'

'At whose hands?'

'I don't know.'

110

'Didn't you ask yourself if your friend could have done such a thing?'

'Naturally.'

'And what did you conclude?'

'That I couldn't believe he was capable of murdering anyone.'

'But was he capable of murdering Mr Charnwood?' He stared at me with flinty insistence. 'In the circumstances, Mr Horton?'

I braced myself for the hostility my reply was bound to provoke. It mattered only to Max and me what I said, since his guilt was already manifest. But it *did* matter. 'No, sir. I don't think so.'

There was a leaden pause, then the coroner said: 'Thank you, Mr Horton.' But there was no hint of gratitude in his tone. 'That will be all.'

I left the box with honour satisfied but nothing accomplished on Max's behalf. Mine had been a token protest. Whatever impact it may have had was swiftly erased by Hornby, who made it crystal clear what he believed had occurred that night.

'Mr Wingate went to meet Miss Charnwood in order to elope with her. Mr Charnwood was waiting for him with news he cannot have welcomed. Mr Charnwood was beaten to death. And Mr Wingate has been missing ever since.' It seemed to be all he could do not to add: 'Q.E.D.' He made no mention of the bloodstains on the steering-wheel of our car or the letter to Max's father. Perhaps he was saving such points for the trial on which his sights were obviously set. The coroner thanked him for his diligence and summoned the pathologist who had carried out the *post mortem*.

His evidence was gruesomely straightforward. A succession of extremely violent blows with a heavy sharp-edged object had smashed the right cheek, temporal and parietal bones of the deceased, inflicting fatal damage to the brain. His blood group matched that of blood found on a wedge-shaped flint nearby which the pathologist had no doubt was the murder weapon. Death had occurred some time between midnight and two-thirty. There were no signs of a struggle, suggesting that the first blow had been delivered unexpectedly and with considerable force. It was by some way the most savage murder he had encountered in his professional career.

The coroner then delivered a perfunctory summing-up, more or less telling the jury what their verdict should be. They obliged after such a brief retirement that there was not even time to slip outside for a cigarette. 'We find that the deceased was murdered by Max Algernon Wingate.' No ambiguity, then, no reservation. And no hope for Max, so far as I could see – if the police ever caught him.

I drove up to Box Hill afterwards and smoked the cigarette I had earlier been denied while gazing down on Dorking and the rolling farmland of the Mole Valley. The shadows of fast-moving clouds were chasing each other across the fields and the wind that propelled them was roaring past the open window of the car. For an instant I imagined the speeding shadows to be cast by the events of Max's life and mine. Each had seemed at first like an escape from its predecessor, only to reveal itself later as a blurred waymarker on our accelerating course. Hitherto, I had never thought in terms of a destination. But perhaps we really were close to one now, closer than either of us wished to believe.

An hour had passed since the inquest when I left and headed for Amber Court, long enough, I judged, for Vita and Diana to be home again, free of admirers and advisers. And so it proved. They were waiting for me in the drawing-room, still dressed as they had been in court. As the maid showed me in and they turned in their chairs to greet me, I noticed a greater similarity between them than I ever had before. Diana was young and slim and beautiful, of course, whereas Vita was none of these things. But something in their eyes illuminated a deeper resemblance: the shared instincts that made good every difference of age and temperament. Perhaps this, I thought, was what Diana had meant by reconciliation.

'Thank you for coming, Guy,' said Diana, in a tone fractionally more guarded than I had recently become used to. 'After this morning, you might have wished to drive away from Dorking and never come back.'

'If you had, it would have been partly my fault,' said Vita. 'You have balanced your obligations to your friend and your sympathy for Diana in a way which I should have praised instead of . . .' She smiled. 'Forgive a foolish old woman, Guy.' It was the first time she had addressed me as *Guy* since the murder and represented a bigger concession than any number of apologies.

'There's nothing to forgive,' I replied as warmly as I could. 'The past few weeks have been difficult for all of us.'

'Perhaps more difficult than you realize,' said Diana. 'Please sit down and I'll explain.'

112

I moved to the sofa on the opposite side of the fireplace from their armchairs. Behind them, through the bay window, I could see the clouds racing on above the swaying heads of the trees that climbed the slope towards the Dorking road. If I had gone after Max sooner. . . If I had not taken the wrong turning on the path. . . But always it was so, as the portrait of Maud Charnwood above the mantelpiece proved. A step taken or not taken was instantly irrevocable.

'Would you care for some tea?' asked Vita.

'Er. . . Well, if . . .'

'Guy doesn't want tea, Aunty,' put in Diana. 'He wants to hear what we have to tell him.' The fingers of her right hand were threaded through the fringe of her cushion, turning and twisting the silken loops this way and that. 'The whole world will know soon enough. We can't delay any longer.'

'You're right, of course. Let me—'

'No. Let *me*.' She released the fringe and laid her hand calmly in her lap. 'Charnwood Investments is insolvent,' she said, looking straight at me. 'It'll be announced tomorrow that the company's going into liquidation. A receiver will be appointed and my father's assets, such as they are, will be seized.'

'Good God!' For all that Trojan could be said to have warned me, it was still a shock. Now, at last, the bounced cheque made sense. 'I had no idea things were so—'

'Neither had we. It appears he lost a great deal of money in the Wall Street Crash and has been struggling to recover ever since. Some months ago, an Austrian bank defaulted and—'

'The Credit-Anstalt?' I remembered reading of its collapse in May.

'Yes. I believe that's the name the accountant mentioned. Anyway, Papa had some large deposits in it and in some German banks sucked down in its wake. He never breathed a word of his troubles to us. There *were* signs, but I thought nothing of them. Barker leaving, for instance. Papa said he just didn't need a valet any more and I accepted the explanation at face value. Besides, none of the economies affected me. I was completely unaware of most of them.'

'So was I,' said Vita. 'But Fabian would have wanted to shield us from any . . . unpleasantness. It was in his nature.'

'And he'd probably have succeeded in pulling it all round,' Diana resumed. 'His judgement hadn't deserted him. And his

113

clients still trusted him. He just needed time. If I'd known, I'd never have—' She paused and blinked away some tears. 'But there it is. Time ran out.'

'I'm sorry. Really I am. This must make his death all the harder to bear.'

'It does,' said Vita. 'It's as if he's to be taken from us all over again – his reputation dismantled piece by piece.' She glanced round the room. 'This house is forfeit, of course. I own half of it, but the creditors will want their share, so we'll have no choice but to sell.'

'If there's anything I can—'

'We shan't be destitute,' Vita said with sudden force. 'My father left me well provided for. And I shall ensure Diana wants for nothing.'

'Even so, if I can help in any way . . .'

'You've done enough already, Guy,' said Diana. 'From now on, we must shift for ourselves.'

'What will you do?'

'In the first instance, go abroad. To Italy, as Papa intended.'

'I have rented a villa on the Venetian Lido,' said Vita. 'We will stay there until the end of October. By then, my brother's creditors will have done their worst and we may be able to return to England.'

'Or we may prefer to remain in Italy,' said Diana, her voice assuming a distant quality. 'So much has changed. So much has ended. We must make a new beginning. But where or with whom or in what fashion . . .' She looked not at me but up at the portrait of her mother. All I did not know about her – and could not guess – seemed contained in her soulful gaze. 'I cannot say,' she murmured. 'I cannot say what our futures may hold.'

Diana walked out with me to the car when I left, perhaps as glad as I was of the chance for a few words in private. The clouds were fewer now, but the wind no slacker, tearing at the tree-tops, snatching at the hedges, scattering leaves across the gravel of the drive. The sunlight was clear and brilliant, finding and revealing every detail of Diana's beauty as she looked at me. For the first time, I felt I understood why Max had killed the man who stood between them. To be denied her might prove too much for anyone. Which was why, at the reasoning core of my being, I was relieved there were to be no more 'secret outings'. Cynicism can only

114

withstand so much joy and my reserves of it were running dangerously low.

'When do you leave for Venice?' I asked.

'Tomorrow. We would have gone sooner but for the inquest. I couldn't bear to be here when they say the terrible things they *will* say about Papa.'

'So this is goodbye, then.'

'I hope not. In fact, I'm sure not. We'll meet again.'

'At the trial, you mean?' She jerked her head away and I instantly regretted the remark. 'I'm sorry. I didn't intend that to sound . . . reproachful.'

'I know.' She composed herself with a visible effort. 'But I deserve to be reproached – for letting Papa meet Max in my place. If I'd gone myself and explained my decision to him, none of this would ever have happened.'

'You're not to blame for what Max did. And he wouldn't want you to think so.'

'No? What *does* he want, Guy? My forgiveness? He might have had that if he'd given himself up straightaway. But not now. Not after hiding for so long, without sending me word of any kind. Not after accusing me – and you – of betraying him, when he's the one who betrayed us.'

'Do you hate him?'

'No. But he killed my love for him when he murdered Papa. And nothing can bring it back.' She sighed heavily, then smiled at me. 'Why not visit us in Venice? You may find it's the change of scene *you* need as well.'

'I've tried changes of scene before – without success. No, I think I'll stick it out here this time.'

'Well, look upon it as an open invitation.'

'Thank you. I will. And now . . . I must be going.'

'Guy—'

'Yes?'

She clasped my right hand between her palms. 'Remember everything. Regret nothing. So Papa always said. Do you think it's possible?'

'I'm not sure.'

'Neither am I. But we must try, mustn't we – we who remain?' She kissed me lightly on the lips. '*Au revoir.*'

I left her standing on the lawn, the wind twitching at her hair and rippling the fabric of her skirt. I saw her last as a motionless

115

figure in black against the waving trees, bathed in light, one arm half-raised as if in benediction. I experienced a sudden desire to turn back but gritted my teeth and drove on. If I could learn anything from Max, it was not to repeat his mistake. To be tempted was one thing, to fall quite another. I would not follow her to Venice or anywhere else.

The outcome of the inquest and the insolvency of Charnwood Investments commanded less space in the newspapers than I had expected. The ever-worsening economic crisis pushed such matters into cramped paragraphs at the bottom of inside pages. And small wonder, for the men of the Atlantic Fleet had mutinied when asked to take a cut in pay, the drain of gold from the Bank of England had become a flood, the Brazilian government had defaulted on its debt and there was panic in the City.

Somewhere, in whatever hiding-place he had chosen, Max must have read of the verdict. I thought of him struggling to come to terms with the crime laid at his door. But there was nothing I could do for him. He had chosen his road and must tread it alone. I imagined the same reflections pressing in on Diana in Venice. It would have been better if they had never met. Her father would be alive and quite possibly solvent. Max would not be wanted for his murder. And she would be able to go on as before. Instead, she sat nursing her wounds in exile, while Max hid his face from view. Contrary to Charnwood's adage, there was everything to regret, as he may himself have realized a split-second after the first blow fell.

Still, at least his company's collapse attracted little attention amidst the carnage of expiring national credit. Those who had lost their money complained less volubly than Diana had feared. Her father's business reputation was dented, but his moral character unassailed. A creditors' meeting was called, but I did not attend, dud cheque clutched importunately in hand. I bore my loss in silence.

Besides, I had larger sums on my mind. The Northamptonshire knight aspirant was on the brink of parting with ten thousand pounds in exchange for a New Year honour which Gregory seemed confident he could obtain for him. Social climbing must continue whatever the state of the economic cycle. And the sherpa is worthy of his hire.

* * *

'Mr Horton?'

The man I found leaning on the railings outside the Eccleston when I returned to it early on Saturday evening spoke in a gruff but educated voice. He was short and flabby, with the pale sweaty skin of an alcoholic. His suit was old and dusty enough for its original colour to be uncertain. A mackintosh of similar vintage was draped over one arm and a battered trilby perched askew on his head. The bushy salt and pepper remnants of what had once been a fine crop of red hair – to judge by the stubbornly ginger moustache – framed a round care-worn face in which grey eyes blinked with nervous frequency.

'You *are* Mr Guy Horton?'

'Yes. What of it?'

'Could we . . . have a word?' He paused to draw on a roll-up cigarette. 'It's about the Charnwood murder. I'm a journalist and—'

'I don't want to talk about it, thank you. If you'll excuse—'

As I stepped past him, he clasped my arm with greater force than I would have thought him capable of and hissed in my ear: 'Don't you want to help your friend?'

I stopped, shook his hand off and stared at him. 'Of course I want to help him. Do you have some suggestions?'

'Not exactly. It's just – Charnwood's not the type to fall victim to a crime of passion. There's something wrong with the whole story. It doesn't fit.'

'Fit what?'

'My knowledge of the man. My experience of Fabian Charnwood.'

'You're not making any sense.'

'Let's have a drink somewhere. Then I can explain properly.'

'I don't think so.' A curtain was twitching on the first floor of the hotel. It was the room belonging to Miss Frew, most ravenous of the Eccleston's resident gossips.

'What have you got to lose?'

'Nothing. I—' Was that Miss Frew's lorgnette I could see catching the light above us? 'Oh, very well. If you insist.'

I had been using the bar of the Grosvenor as my local watering-hole, but George Duggan – as the fellow introduced himself – was not the sort of person I wished to be seen with in civilized surroundings. I piloted him instead to a pub in Warwick Street,

117

where I selected a corner table screened by a pillar and a hat-stand. Duggan downed a rum in one swallow, then began making swift inroads into a pint of beer. He described himself as a free-lance journalist with Fleet Street credentials, which sounded like the sort of smoke-screen I would have put up if claiming to be a pressman. Refusing my offer of a cigarette, he insisted on rolling another of his own. The first inhalation sparked off a racking cough, which frequently interrupted what he went on to say.

'I read the report of the inquest, Mr Horton. I'd been waiting for it ever since Charnwood's death. Thought it might reveal all. But I should have known better, shouldn't I? Not a whisper of the truth, was there?'

'*I* told the truth.'

'As far as it went, perhaps. But you know more than you let slip in court, don't you? You must do.'

'Why?'

'You refused to admit your friend murdered Charnwood. I reckon that's because you're sure he didn't. And how can you be sure? Because you've heard what really happened from his own lips. You know where he is, don't you?'

This had gone far enough. Slamming my glass down on the table, I rose from my chair. 'I've better things to do than sit here being accused of—'

'Don't fly off the handle, Mr Horton.' His wiry grip had once more closed around my arm. 'Please.' There was a hint of desperation in his voice. Against my better judgement, I gave way and sat down again.

'Two minutes, Mr Duggan. Two minutes for you to say something worth hearing.'

'All right.' He gulped some beer. 'Your friend Wingate's hiding because he doesn't think anybody will believe he's innocent. And they won't so long as they think nobody but him could have had any reason to kill Charnwood. But Charnwood was a powerful man. He had enemies. Some with good cause to want him dead.'

'Who?'

'I don't know their names. Nobody does. Not all of them. Charnwood knew, of course. He must have had them listed like a directory in his head. *Who I Made Who.* That's what he did. Made some. And broke others. Like me.' He frowned, as if in painful recollection, then rubbed at his chin. 'Maybe they found out about

118

his financial problems and were afraid of what he might reveal – if he thought he needed to. Maybe they just grew tired of depending on his discretion.'

'Are you talking about clients of his?'

'Clients? Yes, you could call them that. Clients – and co-conspirators.'

'Co-conspirators in what?'

He stared at me for a moment, flexing his lower lip abstractedly. Then he said: 'I'm saying no more until I can be sure where you and Wingate stand. If you were working for them. . . But I don't think you were.' His eyes narrowed. 'Not quite their type. And too young to have been in from the beginning. They wouldn't have used outsiders.' I was still puzzling over this remark when he leant across the table and said: 'Wingate may have seen or heard something. A glimpse. A whisper. He might think it's insignificant. A word from Charnwood before he died. A sign he made or left behind. But it could be the connection we need.'

His intensity was becoming disturbing. I shrugged and drew back. 'I don't know what you're talking about.'

'You don't have to. Just tell Wingate what I've told you. I may be able to help him. But only if he can help me.'

'I can't tell him anything. I haven't seen him since the night of the murder.'

'Pull the other one. Somebody's sheltering him. Stands to reason it has to be you.'

'Well, it isn't.'

He grunted, then drained his glass and sucked the last of the beer from his moustache. 'Have it your way, Mr Horton. Another drink?'

'No thanks. I'm leaving.'

'But you don't know how to get in touch with me.'

'Why should I want to?'

'Because I'm your friend's only chance. With my help, with what I know— ' He tapped the side of his head. 'With what's up here, he might be able to expose the whole pack of them. But, on his own, he'll do no better than I ever have. So, *if* you see him, *if* your paths just happen to cross, tell him what I said. Fair enough?'

'I suppose so.'

'I can be found at this address.' He pulled out a note-book, the covers of which were in danger of being parted from the spine by the pressure of folded scraps of paper wedged inside them.

119

Separating a nicotine-stained calling card from the chaos, he laid it on the table before me. 'By letter or telephone.'

I picked the card up and stared with some surprise at what was printed on it.

ALNWICK ADVERTISER
BONDGATE WITHIN
ALNWICK
NORTHUMBERLAND
Telephone: 88 Telegrams: Advertiser, Alnwick

'Northumberland's a long way from Fleet Street, Mr Duggan. I thought you claimed to be free-lance.'

'So I am, when I'm not knocking out six hundred words for the *Advertiser* on the price of herrings. And I *was* in Fleet Street. Foreign correspondent with *The Topical*. So don't worry. I still have my foot in the door. If Wingate has something for me, I can ensure it gets splash treatment.'

'And you came all the way from Alnwick to tell me so?'

'Yes. Because it's important. And not just to me. Fight in the war, did you?'

'As a matter of fact, I did.'

'Lose many comrades?'

'A few.'

'They're why it's important. Every Armistice Day, we promise to remember them. But what do we actually *do* for them?'

'What can we do? They're dead.'

'Exactly. Millions of them. Dead.' He stared at his empty glass. 'I need another drink.'

'I'll leave you to it.'

'Do that. But pass the message on, Mr Horton.' The note of desperation had returned to his voice. 'They may have made a mistake when they killed Charnwood. If they did, we can make them regret it.'

I nodded non-committally, slipped his card into my wallet and left. He was already at the bar when I glanced back from the door. I was inclined to attribute his wild talk to however much he had drunk before calling at the Eccleston and was most of the way back to the hotel before an odd coincidence in his remarks occurred to my mind. Both he and Charnwood had spoken about the war as if it had ended yesterday. '*Always there is the war,*'

120

Charnwood had said. And 'What do we actually do for them?'
Duggan had asked of the fallen. Why this shared preoccupation
with a conflict buried thirteen years in the past?

I diverted to the Grosvenor to consider the point over a
Manhattan. By the time I had finished it and ordered another,
along with a gin sling for the sloe-eyed vamp whose gaze met mine
in the mirror behind the bar, I had concluded that it meant nothing.
Charnwood was dead. Duggan was just a mouthy old drunk. Max
had disappeared. And for me . . . there were always consolations.

But disentanglement from the posthumous affairs of Fabian
Charnwood was not as easy as I had supposed. I had a meeting
with Maundy Gregory fixed for Monday evening, when I hoped
to be paid what I was due from our successful negotiations with
the boot and shoe magnate. Nor was I disappointed. Gregory
proved to be prompt as well as generous. But touting honours
among the landed gentry was not, it transpired, the only task he
had in mind for me.

He paid me two hundred pounds in hard cash without my
needing to ask for it, dispensed some champagne chilled in
expectation of my arrival and forced a couple of Havana cigars on
me – one to smoke, one to take away. Such a lavish reception put
me in good spirits and I smiled tolerantly as he claimed long
foreknowledge of the suspension of the gold standard announced
that morning.

'It was Charnwood who first told me it was bound to happen.
He predicted the event to the very day. "They'll have gone off
gold by the autumn." Those were his actual words. And what is
today?'

'Er . . . the twenty-first of September.'

'Which happens to be the first day of autumn.' Gregory grinned.
'Uncanny, eh? It's just a pity he's not here to see his prediction
come true.'

'Indeed.'

'Yes, Fabian Charnwood was a clever man. Very clever. You
could have learned a lot from him, dear boy.'

Irked by the term *dear boy* with which he had recently been
making free, I decided I could afford to be mildly provocative.
'Doesn't the collapse of his company suggest he wasn't quite as
clever as he needed to be?'

'It would, if one thought he truly had lost all his money – and that of his investors – in American stocks and Austrian banks. But I don't. And nor do many others who financed his speculations.'

'You were one of them?'

'I freely admit I was. And I never had any cause to regret it – until now. On which subject . . .' He paused to puff at his cigar. 'You may be able to assist me. And those who, for these purposes, I represent.' Another puff was followed by a cocking of his head and a conspiratorial narrowing of his gaze. 'You are on good terms with the younger Miss Charnwood, I'm told.'

I sipped some champagne and tried to frame a casual response. 'Really? Told by whom?'

'I have spies everywhere, dear boy. A day at the races. An evening at the ballet. Such things do not escape notice.'

'Well, I certainly escorted her a couple of times. But—'

'And now she and her aunt have fled to warmer climes. Will you be following them?'

'No. Of course not. I—'

'But you should. That's the whole point. I'd like you to. *We'd* like you to.'

'What?'

He leaned forward across the desk, his monocle swinging ahead of him on its cord, setting the lens winking in the lamplight. Lowering his voice as if afraid of being overheard, he said: 'I have agreed to do all I can to recover the money entrusted to Fabian Charnwood. None of us believe it to be lost. He was too shrewd a financier for that to be credible. He may have suffered one or two reverses, but not the wholesale failure with which his clients have been presented. No, no. We may take it as certain that he salted away the greater part of his assets – *our* assets – in a safe place. More likely, many safe places. The question is: where?'

Gregory's reasoning sounded like the kind of straw-clutching which often follows bankruptcy. But I did not propose to tell him so. I merely shrugged and spread my hands.

'The aunt and the daughter hold the key. One of them knows, possibly both. Hence their precipitate flight abroad, to avoid awkward questions. Charnwood will have let one of them in on his secret with just this contingency – his sudden death – in mind. His sister is, I suppose, the likelier of the two. But she will have confided in her niece by now, so it makes no odds. Besides, the elder Miss Charnwood has proved impervious to Faraday's charms.'

122

There could be little doubt, then, that Faraday was also a victim of Charnwood's insolvency. This conclusion planted two disturbing thoughts in my mind. Firstly, it implied that a concerted attempt to glean information on behalf of Charnwood's clients had already begun when Max and I walked unwittingly into his tangled world. Secondly, it confirmed my suspicion that Faraday had not recommended me to Gregory for altruistic reasons. Despairing of Vita, they had decided to resort to Diana. And I was to be their instrument.

'Follow them to Venice, dear boy. Invent whatever motive or pretext you like. The abject lover or the platonic friend, it makes no difference. But win the daughter's confidence and find out what she knows. Where the money is. And how we can lay our hands on it.'

My every instinct rebelled against such a notion. To deceive Diana would be to deceive Max all over again, even supposing Charnwood really had secreted his money in a Swiss bank vault or similar hiding-place. 'I can't imagine any way in which she could be persuaded to part with such information – assuming she possesses it.'

'Come, come. You are a handsome and charming young man. The beautiful Miss Charnwood will soon look for distractions in her self-imposed exile. So, all you have to do is cater for her needs. Entertain her. Satisfy her. Break down her defences in whatever way seems most appropriate. I will meet your expenses. And, should you be successful . . . well, it is fair to say that your reward would make the sums we deal with in the honours trade appear trivial by comparison.'

'Trivial, you say? Can such a large amount really be involved?'

'Oh, yes.' He grew suddenly solemn. 'The total is scarcely calculable. Numerous extremely wealthy people have an interest in this matter. Their collective loss is . . . immense. Hence the inconceivability of its truly being lost.'

I hesitated, painfully conscious that every principle of mine – every scruple – had hitherto had its price. If I refused, Gregory would probably dispense with my services altogether. In a country of three million unemployed, with winter in the wings and all too few money-making ideas in my head, a grand gesture might swiftly lead to squalor and regret. And I had never had much taste for either commodity. Venice, Diana and the promise of riches constituted an irresistible alternative. Faraday and Gregory must

123

have realized this. Indeed, they were relying on it. 'Very well,' I said at last. 'You've persuaded me. Clearly, this game *is* worth the candle.'

'Splendid.' Gregory beamed approvingly at me. 'I felt sure you'd see the merits of it in the end.'

And so, stifling my misgivings, I prepared to play my part in a conspiracy of which I knew all too little. Gregory was keen for me to set off immediately, but I invented reasons why I could not do so and he relented. The truth was that I distrusted everyone and everything associated with my mission. I needed time in which to unearth as much reliable information as I could. But what I succeeded in obtaining did not in the end amount to much.

Ostensibly as a peace offering following the Atkinson-White débâcle, I stood Trojan Doyle lunch at the Waldorf. He could tell me little about the scale of losses in Charnwood Investments or the identity of those suffering the losses.

'Lots of foreign money involved. Lots of secrecy. Rumour has it that the source of some of the cash wouldn't bear close scrutiny. Which might explain why the creditors are keeping so quiet. It must be galling for them. But what can they do? Charnwood's outwitted them from the grave.'

About a different subject he offered, under the influence of brandy and cigars, to see what he could discover. A chum of his was financial correspondent for one of the national dailies. *The Topical*, we both reckoned, had closed some time in the early twenties, but enough of its staff survived on other papers for it to be ascertainable whether George Duggan had ever been one of its foreign correspondents. After what Gregory had said, Duggan's ramblings did not seem quite as aimless as I had first thought, so I had decided to find out just what his vaunted Fleet Street credentials were.

I did not write to Diana about my impending visit for fear she might withdraw her invitation. This also meant I did not have to decide what reason I would advance for following her until the last possible moment. Nor did I give Chief Inspector Hornby the chance either to object to my leaving the country or to query my choice of destination. I planned to post a letter to him on the morning of my departure stating where I was going and promising to inform the British Consul of my address at all times. He would then be free to make as much or as little of it as he pleased.

*   *   *

Gregory had booked me aboard the Orient Express leaving London on Sunday the twenty-seventh of September. By Friday, I had still heard nothing from Trojan about Duggan, so I called at his club early that evening, hoping to find him on the premises. I was in luck and he emerged from the bar to sign me in. In truth, my luck did not have to be considerable: his absence at such an hour would have been a major surprise, according to the porter.

'You want to know about the *Topical* hack, I suppose,' Trojan chided me as we settled over our drinks. 'Though God knows why.'

'Our paths crossed recently. I simply wanted to check whether what he said was true.'

'Been hanging round Clapham Common late at night, have you?'

'No. What do you mean?'

'Well, it seems George Duggan *was* a foreign correspondent for *The Topical*. Before the war. A rising star, even. Then there was a sudden fall from grace. He was caught by the police on Clapham Common one night buggering a sailor. A prison sentence put paid to his career with *The Topical* and he's not been seen or heard of in Fleet Street since.'

'I see.'

'Not sure I do. Something you want to confess, is there? Something I didn't get to hear about at Winchester?'

'No, on both counts.' I forced a smile. 'But thanks for the information.'

I went down to the Embankment after leaving Trojan and walked slowly east towards Waterloo Bridge. Darkness was descending swiftly from the cloud-shrouded sky, turning the river to a wide and inky gulf. I paused by Cleopatra's Needle and stared down into the unreflecting surface of the water, reminding myself once more why common sense and self-interest dictated that I should go to Venice. My reservations were vague and insubstantial. Certainly it seemed best to ignore Duggan's allegations. I assumed they were about as reliable as his reputation. As for Max—

I spun round, suddenly convinced I was being watched from close quarters. But there was nobody there. The pavement was empty. And, if anyone had been observing me from the gardens on the other side of the road, it was too dark to know. Beyond

125

the gardens soared the night-etched outline of Adelphi Terrace, beneath which I had searched in vain for Max two weeks before. Was it him I had seen in the Strand? Was it his gaze I had just sensed resting on me? Surely not. Wherever he was hiding, it could not be close by. To have eluded the police as long as he had, he must have hidden himself well – and far from me. Yet the suspicion – the itch of a doubt I could not scratch away – persisted. Perhaps my own flight was the answer. Perhaps Venice could be my refuge from a bad conscience – or whatever it was that had dogged my footsteps in London.

'Your fault, Max,' I muttered as I turned up my coat collar and started back towards Westminster. 'Not mine.'

CHAPTER

SEVEN

'*Villa Primavera.*'

'Ah. *Buon giorno.* Could I speak to Miss Diana Charnwood, please?'

'*La Signorina Charnwood? Chi parla?*'

'Er. . . My name's Guy Horton.'

'*Signor Horton. Un attimo, per favore.*'

Rather more than a moment passed, then Diana's voice came on the line. 'Hello? Guy?'

'Yes, Diana, it's me.'

'But . . . you're so clear. I can hardly believe you're in England.'

'I'm not. I'm here in Venice.'

'In Venice? This is wonderful. I had no—'

'I decided to take up your invitation. I hope it's still open.'

'Of course it is. Where are you at the moment?'

'The Danieli. I arrived yesterday.'

'Then book out instantly. You must stay with us.'

'Well, there's really no—'

'I insist. And it's not gentlemanly to refuse a lady's request, so . . .'

'All right. I accept.'

'Come over straightaway. In fact, better still, I'll come and meet you. Quadri's in the Piazza in an hour. How would that be?'

'It would be perfect. I'll see you there.'

I put the telephone down and smiled at how easy it had been.

She had sounded genuinely pleased to hear from me and, now our re-acquaintance was imminent, I realized how much I was looking forward to seeing her again. I strolled to the window of my hotel room and opened it wide to the warm Adriatic air. Below, on the Riva degli Schiavoni, Venetians ambled between the news-stands and art-stalls, squinting in the late September sun. Gondolas bobbed at their moorings. A *vaporetto* chugged slowly away from its pontoon, heading out across the sparkling lagoon towards the Lido – and Diana. Venice at its most benign stood ready to enchant us. And I for one was happy to let it do so. Now I was here – far from England, my chequered past and troublesome present – I felt free of all the doubts and anxieties I had so long laboured under. They still existed, of course. I knew they did. But, for a little while, the illusion that they did not could be indulged.

The illusion was intact an hour later, as I sat in the sun at a table outside Quadri's Café, watching the pigeons and passers-by move and revolve in the Piazza San Marco. I stretched my legs and drew on a cigarette, wondering why coffee and tobacco seemed to taste so much better here than in London, why I seemed to feel so deliciously irresponsible. Basilicas, campaniles and associated architectural wonders generally leave me as cold as left-over stew, but there could be no doubt that some subtle brand of Venetian gaiety had crept into my soul since I had emerged from the railway station the previous afternoon and gazed about at the unchanging wonder of the Grand Canal.

I had been to Venice before, of course. Where the idle rich foregather, Max and I in our time had never been far behind. But it held no ghosts for me, no reproachful reminders of former misdeeds. The city's collective past lay treacle-thick all around. In the face of it, my memory and my conscience receded into the realms of forgetfulness.

'Hello, Guy.'

I had been expecting Diana to approach from the Piazzetta and had angled my chair in that direction. Now I started at the sound of her voice, so close to my ear she might almost have stooped to whisper into it. Whirling round, I found her smiling down at me, amused by my confusion. The smile, the sunlight, the delicate pink dress and the broad-brimmed cream hat framed a sudden glimpse of her loveliness.

'I don't always use direct routes,' she said with a laugh. 'Consider this a warning.'

I joined in her laugh and rose to kiss her. 'I'm not complaining. One surprise deserves another.'

'You mean your 'phone call?' She sat down beside me. 'It *was* a surprise. But a very welcome one.' She glanced around the Piazza and I found myself studying the play of light and shade on her neck. 'I didn't think you'd come. I didn't think you'd regard it as . . . well, I don't know, proper.' She looked back at me, her eyes clear and dark and disturbingly perceptive. 'I'm glad you did, though.'

'It didn't take more than a few wintry days in London to persuade me. I would have written, but . . . I thought you might have changed your mind.'

'Silly.'

'We men often are.' The waiter appeared beside us. Diana ordered chocolate and I another coffee. When he had gone, I lit a cigarette for her, waited a moment, then said: 'To be honest, the weather wasn't the only thing depressing me.'

'Max?'

I nodded. 'And everything he's ruined. Our friendship. Your family. People's lives.'

She looked down into her lap. 'He broke my heart, Guy. But I don't want it to heal by hardening. Aunt Vita's a dear, of course, but I've felt so . . .' She raised her head. 'I can't mourn any longer. Papa wouldn't have wanted me to. I didn't come here to forget. I came here to let go. Of all of it.'

'I suppose that's why I came too.'

'Good.' The dazzling smile returned to her lips. 'Because, until I heard your voice on the telephone this morning, I didn't think it was going to work.'

'And now?'

'I rather think it might.'

We made no early departure for the Lido. Diana suggested a stroll through the alleys and squares to the Rialto and I was happy to agree. On the way, she let me buy her a silk scarf that caught her eye as well as mine. We savoured the view from the Rialto Bridge, then retreated to a nearby restaurant for lunch. We talked of Venice and the Venetians, of Byron and Casanova, of journeys and arrivals. After lunch, we took a gondola back round the Grand

Canal to the Riva degli Schiavoni. Diana gazed at the pastel-hued *palazzi* on either side, while I pretended to do the same, but actually looked at her. Around the time we passed under the Accademia Bridge, I realized a startling truth. Given similar weather, I would have been as happy and as sensually fulfilled aboard a barge on the Manchester Ship Canal – so long as Diana was beside me.

We took tea at the Danieli. Then, while I was booking out, Diana telephoned the villa and asked for the speed-boat to be sent over to collect us. Soon, we were sitting together in its stern as it crashed back through the spraying wakes of other craft, Venice diminishing behind us into a golden horizon. The chill as of a fine chablis had entered the afternoon, herald of a perfect evening. Glancing at Diana as, hat in hand, she let her hair stream out behind her in the wind, I could not help wishing that Vita was not waiting at the villa, that only solitude – and however we might choose to fill it – lay ahead.

But Vita *was* waiting. And so was the Villa Primavera. It stood salmon-pink and creeper-clad in lush gardens beside one of the canals that thread across the Lido. An attentive staff came with the hire of the place. After they had taken my luggage away, I was ushered into a large and ornately decorated drawing-room in which Vita looked more at home than any tweedy English spinster had a right to. Diana had deserted me to bath and change and my heart sank at the prospect of spending an hour closeted with her aunt. But I need not have worried. Venice had worked its magic on her also. The bustling good cheer she had displayed aboard the *Empress of Britain* had been revived.

'I'm delighted you're here, Guy. Company of her own age – or at any rate closer to it than her decrepit old aunt – is just the tonic Diana needs. You will be staying for more than a few days, won't you?'

'Well . . . I'm not sure.'

'Do, please, if you possibly can. Take Diana out. Put a smile back on her face. Stop her brooding.'

'I'll do my best.'

'I've managed to persuade her to go to the opera on Saturday. You must have my ticket and escort her.'

'That's very kind, but—'

'Opera bores me rigid, so you'll be doing me a favour. I only arranged the evening to entertain Diana, which you can do much more readily than me.'

'In that case,' I said with a grin, 'it would be an honour.'

'Splendid. Now, before she returns . . .' She patted the cushion next to her on the sofa and I sat down obediently in the appointed place. Her voice dropped to a murmur. 'What have they been saying about poor Fabian in England?'

'Less than I think you feared. The affair seems to have passed off pretty quietly.'

'That's a mercy. And . . . your friend?'

'Still not found.'

She clicked her tongue. 'Such a dreadful business. But we must bear up.' Her bosom swelled alarmingly as she squared her shoulders against the world. 'I shall expect you to jolly us both out of any mopish tendencies while you're here. Do you think you're equal to the task?'

'I don't know. But I shall enjoy finding out.'

The next four days were ones of growing entrancement for me. Each day, the sun shone from an opalescently blue sky. In the airily baroque rooms of the Villa Primavera, or amidst the sub-tropical greenery of its garden, tranquillity seemed tangible, the senses lulled by ease and warmth, leaving space only for the pleasure I took from Diana's company – her trust, her candour, her physical closeness. A boat-trip in the lagoon, a game of tennis, lunch at one of the Lido's luxury hotels, an afternoon swim, a bath and dinner back at the villa, with Vita retiring early and Diana strolling out with me onto the verandah: it sounds idle and inconsequential, and yet it was neither. I saw in her what I suppose Max had seen in her. And she saw in me much of what she had loved in Max – till he had thrown her love away. In these echoes were signals of a danger both of us secretly relished. We held back because of them, beyond the point when we might normally have expressed what we felt and acted accordingly. We held back – and yet we went on.

In my case, a sundered friendship was not the only call to go unheeded by my conscience. There was also the small matter of the mission I had been sent to Venice to carry out. Maundy Gregory and the people hiding behind him were paying handsomely for my days in the sun and would not have been pleased to discover how little energy I was devoting to their cause. I made, in fact, no effort whatever to penetrate Charnwood's secret through his daughter. I told myself this was because there was no secret to penetrate, but that was not my real motive. The truth lay in my unwillingness to forfeit Diana's affection. I was simply not prepared to take the slightest risk with her vision of me – and what it might lead to. For the moment, losing her in exchange for a share of a fortune did not seem as attractive a proposition as, at any other time in my life, it would have.

Our night at the opera crowned the easeful days. Diana wore a gown of blue velvet, with the topaz pendant I had last seen at the party on the *Empress of Britain*. We took the speed-boat across the lagoon in the cool of late afternoon, stopped at Harry's Bar for a cocktail, then proceeded by gondola round the canals to the Fenice Theatre. The Venetians were out in force and finery, preparing to revel in some piece of tuneful nonsense by Rossini based on the story of Cinderella. Ordinarily, it would have plunged me into a coma of philistine indifference, but the gilded auditorium glowed bewitchingly in the gas-light and beside me, enraptured by the singing, sat a woman more beautiful by far than any of the painted dryads frolicking on the balcony panels around us.

During the interval, we took our champagne outside, where the chill of the evening was as refreshing as the wine, and stood on one of the bridges crossing the canal behind the theatre. The watery acoustics of Venice by night seemed to blend with the memory of the music as Diana hummed one of Cinderella's songs. Then she broke off and looked up at me so solemnly and searchingly that I yielded to the impulse of the moment and kissed her passionately for the first time. She did not resist, but clung to me as if drowning. When we drew apart, I saw there were tears in her eyes.

'What's wrong?'

'Nothing. Except. . . Have we the right to be happy . . . after all that's happened?'

'I look upon happiness as a duty, not a right. Sadness never solved anything.'

'No, but—'

I kissed her again. 'Live for the present, Diana,' I whispered. 'Live for what we have.'

'We have each other,' she said, hardly daring, it seemed, to believe her own words.

I nodded. 'Exactly.'

But our evening was not destined to end as delightfully as it had begun. We dined at a restaurant near the theatre after the performance, then strolled back to the Piazza San Marco for chocolate at Florian's, whose outdoor orchestra preserved the musical theme. It was well after midnight when we summoned the speed-boat and returned to the villa. We expected – and in my case hoped – to find that Vita had gone to bed. But, not only was she still up, she had a visitor to entertain: none other than Mr Faraday. I sensed Diana flinch as she caught her first sight of him and it was as much as I could do to force a weak smile onto my face. But Faraday's grin was as broad and oblivious as ever.

'I arrived by flying-boat this morning, *en route* to Asolo, where Sir Charles and Lady Hick-Morton have a villa scarcely less charming than this. Fearing Vita would not forgive me if I passed through Venice without paying my respects . . .'

'He's been trying to persuade me to accompany him to Asolo,' said Vita with a laugh I thought betrayed signs of strain. 'Even though the Hick-Mortons are strangers to me.'

'It was their suggestion,' said Faraday, 'when I mentioned you were here. You'd like them, I feel sure.'

'Nevertheless . . .'

'Well, think it over a little longer. I don't leave until Monday.' It was, in fact, already Sunday, but Faraday's departure still sounded horribly distant to me. I did not for a moment believe the reason he had given for his visit. I felt sure he was in Venice in order to ascertain what progress I had made. Since I had made none, the sooner he was gone the better.

Faraday was staying at the Excelsior, about half a mile away on the sea-front. When he eventually left to go back there, I offered to walk with him, ostensibly for the sake of some night air. What I really wanted, of course, was the chance of a few plain words with him in private. These I attempted to have as soon as we were clear of the villa.

'What the devil are you doing here, Faraday?'

'Trying to lend you a helping hand, actually. I thought – we thought – your chances of success would be enhanced if Vita were out of your hair for a few days.'

'I don't need a helping hand.'

'No? Do you have something to report?'

'Not yet, but—'

'In that case, I must beg to differ. We cannot wait indefinitely. Therefore, you *do* need help.'

'Not this kind. Surely you realize Vita won't rise to the bait. Who are the Hick-Mortons? Other creditors of Charnwood?'

'You needn't concern yourself with their financial circumstances. They will play their part. As you are expected to play yours.'

'I'm trying to.'

'Good. Then I suggest you apply your mind – and whatever else may be appropriate – to breaking down Diana's defences in her aunt's absence.'

'She isn't going to be absent.'

'Really? Well, as to that, we must wait and see, mustn't we?'

I left Faraday beneath the flood-lit arabesquerie of the Excelsior and walked slowly back to the villa, contemplating the folly of ever having supposed I could ignore my employers' wishes. The time had come to apply my legendary ruthlessness. But never before had I felt so reluctant to do so.

I went into the garden of the villa by the side-entrance, intending to smoke a last cigarette beneath the peach trees before turning in. It was from there, as I devised and discarded half-baked stratagems in my mind, that I glimpsed Diana through the open window of the drawing-room. I could hear her talking to Vita in anxious tones. Crushing out the cigarette against a tree-trunk, I moved carefully towards the window, until I could catch some of their words, then closer again, until I could catch all of them.

'At least you enjoyed the opera, my dear,' said Vita.

Diana laughed. 'Oh yes, I enjoyed it.'

'Did Guy?'

'I think so. In fact, I'm sure of it.' She paused, then said: 'Rossini chose a strange sub-title for *La Cenerentola*, you know. *La bontà in trionfo*. The triumph of good. Ironic, isn't it, that I should find myself glorying in music dedicated to such a proposition?'

'There's no reason why you shouldn't.'

Diana laughed again, this time with a fractured hint of bitterness. 'There are many reasons, as you know. As I fear Mr Faraday also knows.'

'He is sure of nothing.'

'Let us hope he remains so. To which end, I really think you must accept his invitation to Asolo.'

Vita sighed heavily. 'Must I? The man is so transparently inquisitive. He had the effrontery to ask me this evening whether I'd ever been to Trieste.'

'What did you say?'

'That I had, of course. That you had too. That we went together, on a whim.'

'Good. It is as we surmised, then?'

'Undoubtedly.'

'Well, I'm glad our efforts weren't wasted.'

'It certainly seems they weren't. In which case, why must I go to Asolo?'

'To keep him guessing, Aunty. Guessing wrong.'

Vita gave another heartfelt sigh. 'Very well.' A spring creaked in the sofa. 'Now, I must take myself off to bed.'

'I'll wait for Guy.'

'Good night, my dear.'

'Good night, Aunty.'

Silence followed and I knew I ought to creep away. But I lingered a moment longer and was rewarded by the sight of Diana leaning out through the window. Her eyes were closed and she was breathing deeply, savouring the coolness of the air and the nocturnal scents of the garden. I looked at her dark hair falling back from her face, at her pale breasts exposed by the low-cut gown, at the topaz pendant glittering above them, and realized with a sudden jolt that the duplicity I had just learned she was capable of made her even more desirable.

I had thought till now that she and Vita might be innocents, misjudged by Faraday and his kind in their desperation to salvage something from the wreck of Charnwood Investments. But it was I who had misjudged them. They had spoken of visiting Trieste as if it were a deliberate feint in a series of complex manoeuvres. Patently, they were hiding something.

But that only made my task easier. I had the advantage of them now and did not propose to throw it away. Besides, had Diana really encouraged Vita to go to Asolo simply in order to string Faraday along? Or had she some other reason for wanting to be left alone with me? This last thought revolved tantalizingly in my mind as she turned away from the window and I began my retreat across the garden.

*   *   *

Faraday came to lunch next day and expressed his pleasure at Vita's change of heart about the expedition to Asolo. He could not celebrate his triumph over my scepticism until the ladies left us alone in the garden, savouring coffee and cigars in wicker chairs in a sun-filled arbour of virginia creeper. And, when he did, I had to restrain myself from pointing out the pyrrhic nature of his victory.

'*O ye of little faith*,' he said with a smirk. 'It seems my intervention has been more effective than you anticipated.'

'So it does.'

'I expect to be equally successful in extending Vita's absence beyond the couple of days to which she has so far consented.'

'Good.'

'Leaving the way clear for you to make some progress here. On which point—' He leaned towards me and lowered his voice. 'I should apprise you of certain facts which have recently come to my attention concerning our charming hostesses. They left England on Thursday the seventeenth of September, but did not arrive here until Saturday the nineteenth.'

'What of it?'

'They obviously broke their journey somewhere. In Switzerland, perhaps, where the confidentiality of the banks is legendary. You might usefully apply yourself to finding out precisely where they stopped. Also why they travelled to Trieste a few days after their arrival. It may be on Italian soil now, but before the war it was part of the Austro-Hungarian Empire. Charnwood's connections in Vienna – both political and commercial – were numerous and of long standing. Trieste may have been recommended to him as a safe haven for hidden assets.'

'It may, yes.'

'Or the visit to Trieste may have been designed to deflect our attention from Switzerland. We should not suppose the ladies are lacking in subtlety.'

'I wasn't about to do so.'

Faraday's expression grew stern. 'I'm simply cautioning you against over-confidence, Horton. It will not be easy to prise the truth from the daughter of such a practised dissembler.'

'No.' I tried to shape an earnest frown. 'But I think I may be able to find a way.'

*   *   *

Diana and I accompanied Vita to the railway station the following morning. Faraday was waiting for her there with a preposterously large bunch of flowers and a clutch of smiling assurances: the Hick-Mortons' car would be waiting for them at Bassano; the drive from there to Asolo was short and picturesque; the villa was delightfully situated in the Asolean hills; their welcome would be a warm one; Vita would be in her element. She looked less than wholly convinced, but soon it did not matter. The train had borne them away and Diana and I were left behind – with only each other for company.

'Take me to the Accademia, Guy,' she said dreamily, her gaze still focused on the plume of smoke from the departing engine. 'There's a picture I want to show you.'

We went by gondola, through the Rio Nuovo. I did not ask what the picture was, nor experience my normal yawning dread of art galleries. To walk beside Diana past several centuries' worth of groaning canvas was to be reminded of the eternal superiority of flesh and blood. We came at last to the work she wanted me to see: Lotto's *Portrait of a Young Gentleman in his Study*. A pale-faced youth of the Renaissance was depicted leafing idly through a book while a discarded letter lay on the table beside him, along with some scattered rose petals and a blue scarf across which a lizard was crawling. A mandolin, a hunting horn and a deed-box, with a key on the end of a cord resting on its lid, were visible in the background.

'Do you understand the symbols, Guy?'

'I'm not sure.'

'He enjoys music as well as hunting, learning as well as risk. But he has secrets – in the box and the letters – to taint his pleasures. Some things fade, like the rose petals. Others endure, like the salamander. But which? He doesn't know the answer. You can see that in his eyes. And, four hundred years later, neither do we.'

'We know what we believe, surely.' She turned slowly to look at me, waiting for me to state my credo, waiting to judge whether it coincided with hers. 'The pleasures are always worth the risks. Without them, what is life?'

She did not reply, but stared at me for a moment in solemn contemplation, then turned and walked away. With a last glance at Lotto's questing youth, I followed.

137

* * *

We lunched at a *trattoria* on the Zattere, smiling often but saying little as we sipped champagne and let the sunlight thrown up by the Giudecca Canal warm us to the marrow. Afterwards, we strolled towards Customs House Point, Diana often moving ahead, as if determined to give me every opportunity to watch the breeze moulding her lilac dress to her body. A silence had fallen between us, turning the warmth of the afternoon to a burning pitch of expectancy. It was not yet too late to turn back, but we both knew we would not.

We reached the Point and gazed across the mouth of the Grand Canal at the campanile and the Doge's Palace. Crowds were bustling back and forth along the Molo, but, on our side, solitude seemed all about us.

'Shall we go back to the villa?' I asked, noticing Diana glance in the direction of the Lido.

'Yes,' she replied, not looking at me as she spoke. 'I think it's time we did.'

'We could find a bar and phone for the speed-boat.'

'No use. I gave Giacomo the rest of the day off. Bianca and Carlotta too.' Then she did look at me. 'There's nobody there.'

We summoned a water taxi and were at the Lido in what seemed like minutes, walking up from the villa's private landing-stage through the soundless greenery of the garden. Diana turned a key in a lock and admitted us to the empty arena she had prepared, the half-shuttered windows casting angled columns of light across the peacock-patterned rugs, the varnished wood of the balustrade, the burnished brass of the stair-rods.

We reached her bedroom, where she threw the French windows open and stood for a moment on the balcony, gazing down into the garden. Then she turned and walked back to where I was waiting. I took her in my arms and we kissed for the first time since the night of the opera.

'Stop me mourning, Guy,' she whispered. 'I can't be cold any more.'

Suddenly, all was scrambling eagerness: silk sliding across pale skin, fingers touching and exploring, lips brushing and urging. We were naked on the bed, cool linen against soft flesh, as the curtains billowed in the breeze and the sunlight splashed across us in a

138

golden flood. For a single moment, we stared into each other's eyes, confronting the needs and weaknesses the act we were about to commit would expose.

'Don't stop, Guy. Please don't stop.'

'I couldn't. Not now.'

'I'm yours.' She pressed my hand to her breast and I felt the nipple stiffen against my fingers. 'All yours.'

And so she was, her beauty magnified now every curve and crease of it was mine to caress. What I had done countless times before – with prostitutes in Salonika, with wide-eyes factory girls in Letchworth, with whimpering starlets in Los Angeles hotels – was transcended and forgotten that afternoon at the Villa Primavera. Possession and triumph fused in the pleasure we took from each other. And heightening our pleasure was the unspoken admission that what we were doing was wrong, beyond the bounds, deliriously unforgivable.

'Yes, yes,' she murmured as I thrust into her and felt her legs join behind my back. 'It's so good.'

'Better,' I panted in reply. 'Better than good.'

It was better, indeed, than either of us deserved or should have permitted, the bed creaking beneath us unnoticed, the sweat streaking our hair, the linen crumpling as we rocked and moaned. Her words in my ear and her tongue in my mouth drove me on past the point where dreams become flesh, and betrayal – of self and others, of secret wishes and blatant desires – joins in the frenzied climax.

'Yes,' proclaimed as in victory.

'For you,' declared in the teeth of the truth.

And then the slow fall back to earth, the spasm over, the flesh cooling, the bodies parting, the eyes staring in disbelief at what we had just allowed to happen.

'I never. . .never thought. . .'

'Nor me. But now. . .I see. . .'

'It had to be.'

Her head fell against my shoulder. I wrapped my arm around her, the smoothness of her skin seeping into my thoughts as something conquered, something joyously stolen – and never to be given up. Her knee nestled between my legs, the sunlight falling in dust-moted splendour across the hummock of her hip and thigh. I pulled the sheet up to cover us, kissed her lightly on the brow and closed my eyes, savouring in my memory every sensation I had experienced since entering the room, every fragment and facet of the prize I had won.

I stirred, as from a brief slumber, puzzled by a darkness across the bed, a shadow where there should not have been one. I glanced towards the window, wondering how long I had slept. And then I saw him: a motionless figure clad in black, watching us from the centre of the room. I blinked, but he did not vanish. I had seen him often enough in my dreams, but now I was not dreaming.

'Max?'

He was on us like a creature pouncing, grabbing at the sheet and pulling it off us in one movement. Diana woke instantly and rolled clear of me, a scream choking in her throat as she saw him looming above us, mouth twisted in fury, eyes blazing in hatred.

'Max, for God's—' He hit me as I made to rise, a swinging blow to the chin that jolted my head back against the brass rail behind me.

'No!' shrieked Diana.

'*Bitch!*' Max roared at her, hauling me from the bed and pushing me against the wall. 'I'll finish with you after I've dealt with my so-called friend.' His eyes were bulging, his face twitching, sweat wriggling down his temple. 'You bastard!' he bellowed. Then his knee slammed violently into my groin. Agony jolted through me with sickening intensity. He caught me as I fell forward and levered me back upright again. 'I'll make you pay for your pleasure, *old man.*'

'Max,' I said, the sound distorted by his grip on my jaw. 'Listen to me, please. Just—'

'You listen! Did you think you could deceive me? Did you really think I wouldn't realize what you'd done? That I wouldn't follow you every step of the way until I had the final proof? The proof of why you helped brand me a murderer.'

He kneed me again and the pain seared into me with blinding force. I could frame no answer to his accusations, summon no resistance to his rage. 'It was for this, wasn't it, you treacherous bastard?'

'Leave him alone,' cried Diana. She had rounded the bed and was tugging in vain at Max's shoulders. 'In God's name, Max, stop!'

'I'll stop, all right.' He let go of me for as long as it took to fling Diana back across the bed. 'I'll stop when he's had what he deserves.' His hands closed round my throat. 'How much do you know, Guy? How much has she told you?' His grasp was tightening, squeezing the breath out of me as he clearly meant to squeeze out the life. 'Not that it matters. Ignorance is no excuse for what you've done to me.' I tried to speak, but no words came. I tried to pull his hands away, but could not loosen his hold. 'I don't care about the rest. It's this I'm going to kill you for. It's this I'm going to finish before I deal with—'

A sudden splintering crash cut through his voice. His grip slackened. His mouth sagged, his gaze slipped out of focus. Diana had hit him above the left ear with the ewer from the wash-stand. I saw the china spout clasped in her hands, the shards of its smashed body falling at her feet. Then Max toppled slowly sideways onto the bed and rolled with a thud onto the floor. My momentary relief was swamped by fear. He had been told often enough – and so had I – that any blow to the left side of his head could be fatal. The bullet-wound he had suffered in Macedonia had left a patch of skull wafer-thin and permanently vulnerable. If it were ever struck—

'Max?' I knelt down beside him, one thought driving out all others. I did not want him to die like this. I did not want his last words to be ones of loathing for me – his best, oldest and least faithful friend. 'Are you all right? Max, speak to me.' But only the whites of his eyes were visible. The lids did not flicker. Nor did his lips stir. I slapped his cheek, but there was no response. 'Max?' I pressed two fingers into the soft flesh beneath his jaw-bone, searching for the pulse – but finding none.

'What's the matter?' Diana asked, crouching beside me.

'I think . . . I'm afraid . . .' I tore at his shirt, scattering buttons in all directions, and lowered my head to his chest. There was no sound in my ear, no rise and fall beneath me. 'Oh my God, he's dead.'

'He can't be. I didn't . . . couldn't have . . .'

'You hit him just about where the bullet struck.' Our eyes met, all passion drained away, with only horror to take its place. Everything we had done in that room – every breathless writhing – was corrupted and denounced by the lifeless figure beside us. 'He was warned to protect that side of his head, to be careful at all times. Like an egg-shell, the doctors told him. Easy . . . to crack.'

'Dead?' There was incredulity in her voice, a wish nearly equal to my own not to believe it was true.

I nodded and looked down at Max, his face calm now, almost peaceful. Into my mind flashed a cumulative recollection of him smiling, glass in hand, as we celebrated lucrative bets and successful swindles down the years. There were tears flowing down my cheeks. It was all I could do not to sob. Why could he not sit up and grin and offer me a cigarette? *'Good joke, eh, old man? No hard feelings.'* Why could I not retrieve and alter the last mad moments of our friendship?

Diana rose and stumbled to the door. It was standing half-open, as Max had left it. He must have followed us into the villa through the garden, I dimly supposed. He must have crept up the stairs and heard us, may even have tip-toed into the room and watched. She took a bath-robe from a hook behind the door and wrapped it round herself, shuddering as she did so.

' 'Phone the police,' I heard myself say.

'Oh Guy . . .'

'Just go and 'phone them!' My vehemence shocked her. I saw the reaction in her wide-eyed stare. 'I'm sorry. Please do it. Now. Before . . .' I could not finish the sentence – any more than I could bear to envisage what lay ahead.

Diana was gone. With shaking fingers, I closed Max's eyes and stood slowly up, struggling to order my thoughts and control my emotions. The tears had stopped, but the trembling was worse. I stepped carefully past Max and leant heavily against the brass bedstead as a wave of nausea came and went. Then I gathered up my discarded clothes and scrambled into them. From below, I heard Diana's voice on the telephone. *'La polizia? Per favore, venite subito alla Villa Primavera, Via Pasqua, Venezia Lido.'* I felt suddenly sorry for her, sorry for the guilt she must feel that was properly mine. *'È stato un incidente.'* An accident, she called it. But was it? A pure and unadulterated accident? *'Qualcuno è morto.'* Somebody was dead. Yes, somebody was. And part of me with him.

I lowered myself on to the edge of the bed and stared down at Max's body, wondering what I would say when the police arrived, how I would explain what had happened. It would all have been so different if we had never boarded the *Empress of Britain*, if I had never rushed to Vita's rescue, if Max and I had never made that foolish bargain. Then I remembered the contracts we had exchanged, the undertakings we had put our names to. They would find Max's copy when they searched him, with my signature on it.

The one secret I had managed to preserve would be uncovered. Diana would know me for the scoundrel I was. And Max's memory would be blackened still further.

He was wearing no jacket, only a shirt and trousers. Pushing my hand under his right hip, I felt the bulge of a wallet in the pocket. I tugged the button free, dragged the wallet out and opened it. There, at the back of a crumpled wad of lira notes, was the sheet of thick vellum paper I instantly recognized, folded into four. I pulled it out and clumsily transferred it to my own wallet, then forced Max's back into his hip-pocket, trying and failing to re-fasten the button. Abandoning the effort, I stood up, aware for the first time how rapidly my heart was beating, how fast and frantically I was breathing. Slowly, the panic began to subside.

I looked down at Max again, marvelling at how strangely unmarked death had left him, especially by comparison with – Then I remembered his loud denials. *'Did you think I wouldn't realize why you helped brand me a murderer?'* But he had branded himself. Surely, he could not have thought . . . could not have meant. . . But he had. He had been wrong, but he had not lied. I was not guilty, but nor was he.

'Guy?' Diana was standing in the doorway, staring anxiously at me. 'The police will be here soon.'

'Good. I . . .'

'What is it?'

'He didn't murder your father.'

'What do you mean?'

'Max. You heard him say it. He wasn't the murderer.'

'He must have been.'

'No. There was a . . . righteousness in his anger. Didn't you sense it?'

'He just felt betrayed . . . by us . . . by what you and I had done . . . that he and I had never . . .'

She was the one crying now. I put my arm around her and cradled her head protectively against my shoulder, listening to her sobs. 'There was more to it than that,' I murmured, as much to myself as to her. 'He was an innocent man. And he loved us both. And, between us, we've destroyed him.'

CHAPTER

EIGHT

The shock of Max's death left me at one remove from reality. I remember draping a sheet over his body and smoking a cigarette on the balcony with my hand shaking so badly that the ash from it sprinkled down my sleeve. I remember staring into the garden while Diana hurriedly dressed and realizing how like the hissing approach of a snake the sound of silk was as it slithered across her skin. I remember her standing beside me, her knuckles white where she clutched the rail, and saying in what was scarcely more than a whisper: 'What shall we tell them, Guy?' and I remember replying, even as the door-bell clanged below us: 'The truth. All of it.'

But such memories are more akin to historical events in which I played no part than things personally experienced. My soul had retreated to other times and places: to our first Morning Hills at Winchester, Max and I watching the mist rise from the Itchen while the Prefect of Hall called out our names and the dew on the grass soaked slowly through to our socks; to a requisitioned house in Salonika where we and four other malaria cases swapped ambitious plans for our post-war careers; to the Statue of Liberty as we gazed across at it from the slow-moving deck of the *Aquitania* and Max remarked of the New World we were about to assault, '*They don't stand a chance against a pair like us.*'

But the pairing had been sundered now. I had lost not merely a friend, but a substantial portion of my past. Like the phantom

144

limb of an amputee, it remained attached to my thoughts and reactions long after the shrouded figure on a stretcher had been carried from the villa. Max – and all he had meant to me – hovered at my elbow as the uniformed men came and went, as the questions began and the answers followed, as the particulars of death were sifted and weighed.

Within minutes of the police entering the villa, Diana and I were taken to separate rooms for questioning. If we had known how long was to pass before we would see each other again, we might have exchanged a parting word, a farewell glance or gesture. As it was, I only realized later that we were being deliberately kept apart to prevent collusion, that our explanation of what had happened was only one of several possibilities being entertained by the police.

Late in the afternoon, we were transferred in separate launches to the Questura in central Venice. I suppose it was the change in surroundings that first roused me from my trance. The room they put me in boasted one small barred window overlooking a noisy side-canal. Its furnishings comprised a rickety deal table and two hard chairs. The only decoration was a large framed photograph of Mussolini striking an heroic pose. This adorned the wall facing me, looming above the pinched face of my tireless interrogator, Vice-Questore Varsini. Towards Diana he had been scrupulously polite, not to say deferential. For me, however, he reserved a sullen scepticism that became increasingly wearing. He spoke good English, verging, indeed, on the uncomfortably meticulous. But what he was thinking emerged only in his native tongue, taking the form of gabbled asides to his colleagues in a dialect I had no hope of understanding. He blamed the language barrier for his wish to return to certain points over and over again, but from the outset I knew there was some other reason.

'Let us begin again,' he would say, as the smoke from his cigarette climbed into the glare of the single light bulb. 'What were you and *Signorina* Charnwood doing when *Signor* Wingate entered the villa?'

'We were in bed.'

'Together?'

'Yes.'

'But *Signorina* Charnwood was *Signor* Wingate's . . . fiancée?'

'They had been intending to marry, yes. But that was before her father's death.'

145

'*Sì, sì. Signor* Charnwood. Also killed by a blow on the head.'

'Yes, but—'

'You knew of the weakness in *Signor* Wingate's skull?'

'I did.'

'But *Signorina* Charnwood did not?'

'She knew he'd been shot in the head during the war, but not that the injury had weakened his skull.'

'You did not tell her so?'

'Definitely not.'

'But you cannot say *Signor* Wingate definitely did not tell her, can you?'

'Well . . . No.'

'Therefore, she might have known.'

'She had no idea. I'm certain of it. She was simply trying to stop him strangling me.' .

'And why was he trying to strangle you?'

'Because— It's obvious why, isn't it?'

'*Sì.* It is. Because he found you in bed together. *L'amico e la fidanzata.*'

'I told you. They were no longer engaged.'

'But you were still his friend.'

'Of course I was.'

'If I found a friend of mine in bed with my wife . . . I might try to strangle him. And her.'

'She wasn't his wife. Or his fiancée. He was trying to kill me and she was trying to stop him. But she only wanted to distract him long enough for him to calm down and see reason. She never meant to kill him. It was an accident.'

'That will be for the magistrate to decide, *Signor* Horton. So far, we have only a death. And many questions.'

So he did. Many, many questions. Eventually, I was invited to stay at the Questura overnight in a tone that suggested I would be forced to do so if I did not agree. The same invitation, I was informed, had been extended to *Signorina* Charnwood and she had accepted. In her aunt's absence, there was nobody to vouch for either of us. The police in Asolo had been in touch with Vita and she was expected back in the morning. Until then, Varsini signalled with a shrug, nothing could be done.

I slept little during the few hours of the night that remained when I was taken down to my cell. Like an engine I could not stop, my mind raced on regardless, hurling doubts and accusations

146

at me from the darkness into which I stared. Did Diana's account tally with mine? Was she lying awake in her cell, weeping and mourning for Max? Or was she secretly rejoicing? Was there just a chance she *had* known where on his skull any blow might prove fatal? If so—

But I was being unfair and ungrateful, the rebuke came regularly back from the rational half of my brain. She had saved my life and could never have meant to take Max's. She had grabbed at the ewer in a panic and struck without aiming or deliberating. Max's death, whatever Varsini or some unworthy part of me might like to believe, was an accident of his own creation.

And yet, and yet. . . What had he actually said in those last moments of life? '*How much do you know, Guy? How much has she told you?*' If only I could still ask him to explain. What was I supposed to know? What was she supposed to have told me? '*I don't care about the rest,*' he had shouted. But the rest of what? The treachery of his friend and his fiancée was surely bad enough. What more could there be?

Only Charnwood's murder. To that event my thoughts returned like a dog to a bone. Max was innocent. I knew that now. Somebody else had killed Charnwood. But who? And why?

Duggan could give me the answers. He had virtually offered to tell me, but I had refused to listen. Now I would listen. It was too late to save Max, but it was not too late to clear his name. As the aqueous light of a Venetian dawn stretched the shadow of the barred window across the blank wall of my cell, I swore a silent oath. I would honour Max in death as I had dishonoured him in life. I would find it in me to be a true friend at last.

But even solemn oaths must wait upon the law. Several hours of the morning had already elapsed when I was led upstairs to see the Vice-Questore again. He was in his office, a large and airy chamber overlooking the Rio di San Lorenzo. The only similarity to the room in which he had questioned me the previous night was a prominently positioned photograph of *Il Duce*. The furnishings could otherwise have been those of a well-to-do doctor's surgery. The change of venue seemed to have had an effect on Varsini, who smiled warmly as I was shown in.

'*Buon giorno, Signor Horton.* I trust you have been . . . reasonably comfortable?'

'I've no complaints.'

Two grey-suited figures rose from their chairs on my side of Varsini's desk. One was a tubby little bald-headed man with a sallow complexion and a Charlie Chaplin moustache. The other was Faraday.

'How are you feeling, Horton?' he enquired in his most syrupy tone.

'Perfectly well, thank you.'

For a second, he stared at me, pouting in what could either have been puzzlement or simply scrutiny. Then he nodded towards his companion. 'This is *Signor* Martelli, a lawyer Vita has engaged on Diana's behalf. He would be happy to advise you as well.'

'I'm grateful, but where *is* Diana?'

'She's been released. Vita's taken her back to the villa.'

'You are also free to go, *Signor* Horton,' said Varsini. 'The necessity of your overnight detention is regretted, but in the circumstances . . .' He shrugged. 'Since interviewing you yesterday, I have received a cable from the Surrey police confirming that Max Wingate was a wanted murderer capable of extreme violence. I have also received the results of the autopsy, which show that the blow to his head would not have been sufficient to cause death but for the exceptional thinness of his skull in the area struck. My preliminary conclusion is therefore that he was not intentionally killed. This appears to me to be a case of involuntary homicide, as I shall report to the investigating magistrate. He will consider the matter at a formal inquest in due course. But I am confident my findings will be upheld.'

'Death by misadventure,' murmured Faraday, cocking one eyebrow at me.

'*Mi scusi*,' said Martelli, with a faint bow in my direction. 'Perhaps I should explain that a verdict in Italian law of involuntary homicide is not an exact equivalent of the English concept of misadventure. Nevertheless . . .'

'It's close enough?'

'*Sì*. Close enough.'

'And when will the inquest be held?'

'At a date yet to be fixed,' said Varsini. 'You will be informed.'

'It's just . . . I need to leave Venice. Soon.'

Faraday's eyes narrowed, but he said nothing. Nor did he need to, as Varsini soon made clear. 'Impossible. Although I do not anticipate criminal charges being brought, you and *Signorina* Charnwood must both remain in Venice until the matter is settled.

Your passport, please.' He held out his hand. Suddenly, the affable manner had evaporated. I would not be leaving Venice until he said I could. And I had the distinct impression that, if I resisted, I would not even be leaving the Questura. I took my passport from my pocket and laid it in his palm. '*Grazie*,' he said, the smile reappearing. 'You will be staying at the Villa Primavera?'

'No.' This time, I took good care to avoid Faraday's gaze. 'I'll find a *pensione* somewhere.'

'I must have a definite address, *Signor* Horton. Otherwise . . .'

'Can I let you know later today?'

He nodded. 'So long as you do.'

'I will.'

'*Va bene*.' He rose from his chair and tugged at his lapels. 'Well, *signori*, I think our business is concluded. You must not let me detain you any longer.'

Martelli took his leave of us on the Questura steps following a flurry of handshakes and a conversation with Faraday in Italian. After he had gone, Faraday walked a few paces with me in silence, tapping his lip thoughtfully. Then he said: 'I have no reason to think you would not be welcome to stay at the villa.'

'Neither have I.'

'Then why did you tell Varsini—'

'Because I don't *wish* to stay there. Not after what's happened.'

He pulled up, obliging me to do the same. 'You don't *wish*? Perhaps I should remind you, Horton, that you're here to fulfil the requirements of your paymasters, not pander to your own whims.'

'And perhaps *I* should remind *you* that a good friend of mine died yesterday.'

'Very distressing, no doubt, but strictly irrelevant. Save in so far as the circumstances of Wingate's death do tend to suggest you have succeeded in winning Diana's confidence. She will be in an especially vulnerable state at the moment. Highly receptive to your charms, I would venture to—'

'Don't!' I snapped, grabbing at his tie and noticing the sudden outbreak of fear on his face. 'Don't venture to suggest anything. Not if you value your health.' I let go and he stepped hurriedly back, his hand jerking up to smooth the crumpled tie. 'I want no further part in this. Do you understand? I shan't be spying or prying or probing on your account – or Gregory's.'

149

He cleared his throat nervously. 'You're upset. That's understandable. But as soon as—'

'My decision's final.'

'Surely not.' The ready smile was restored to his lips, the superior tone to his voice. 'Think of the money you'd be giving up.'

'I don't care about the money.'

'Oh, but you do. Your whole life proves you do. As you'll remember once you've recovered from the shock. You'll think of what you'd be losing. And then you'll think again.'

'No.'

'Believe me, Horton, you will. But take my advice: don't delay too long. Now, excuse me, will you? I don't think we're heading in the same direction.' With that, he bustled off. I lit a cigarette and watched his receding figure until it vanished round a corner, wondering whether he might not be right after all – and praying I would prove him wrong.

I did not have to go far in search of a suitable *pensione*. La Casa di Pellicani was perched at the malodorous end of a narrow bridge about halfway between the Questura and San Marco. After agreeing terms for one of its better rooms, I walked down to Riva Schiavoni and boarded the next *vaporetto* bound for the Lido, determined to extricate myself from the Villa Primavera without delay.

Vita received me in the drawing-room, where nothing appeared to have changed – though everything had – since my arrival a week before. She was grave-faced and trembling, looking suddenly old and frail, worn down, it seemed, by one tragedy too many.

'Diana's resting. She's very tired. I imagine you must be too.'

'No. In fact . . .' My words died in the mutual incomprehension conveyed by our eyes. I wanted to apologize for abusing her hospitality, but to do so would have been to refer openly to what had happened, which her expression implied was the last thing she wanted of me. 'I'm moving to a *pensione*,' I said abruptly. 'In the circumstances, it seems . . . well, in everybody's best interests.'

'Don't feel you have to, Guy. I don't pretend to understand the morals of your generation. They are certainly not the morals of mine. Nevertheless, it's clear to me that Diana's come to care for you a great deal. And she will need the support of those she cares for in the weeks ahead. She will need it as never before.'

'And she'll have mine. It's just. . . It's difficult to explain, but I feel, for Max's sake . . . I must go.'

'Max is dead.'

'Yes. But our friendship isn't. Tell Diana—'

'Tell me yourself, Guy.' Diana was standing in the doorway, waiting to meet my gaze as I swung round. She was wearing a plain white dress and was clasping her hands together tightly as she looked at me. Her face was pale and there were shadows under her eyes. Her lips were quivering as she spoke. 'You're leaving . . . without saying goodbye?'

'No. That is—'

'One moment,' said Vita. 'I think it would be best if I left. Excuse me.' She rose and hurried across the room, pausing to lay a concerned hand to Diana's cheek before walking out through the door – and closing it behind her.

Silence leapt between us as soon as the door clicked shut. Diana took a few steps towards me, but I did not move towards her. 'I'm sorry,' I muttered, bowing my head.

'Sorry for what?'

'Everything.'

'Why are you leaving?'

'Because I can't remain. Surely you see that?'

'Because Max is dead?'

'I can't forget him.'

'Of course you can't. Neither can I. No more than I can forget what happened before he burst in. What it represented. What it signified. To me, anyway. To the police – and to Aunt Vita as well, perhaps – it may have sounded sordid and contemptible. But it wasn't, was it?'

'No. It wasn't.'

'It can't be, can it? Not if there's more than . . . physical desire.'

'Love, you mean?'

'Yes. Love.'

'Diana, I . . .' I turned away towards the window. Before I could continue, I felt her hand on my elbow. At the mere touch of her fingers through my sleeve, there burst into my mind the vision of her naked on the bed. Then I saw Max's face, stained with fury. And heard his voice in my ear. *'Did you think I wouldn't follow you?'*

'I didn't mean to kill him, Guy. Even the police believe me. Won't you?'

151

'I do believe you.'

'Then what's wrong?'

'We are. You and I. What we did drove Max to his death. Whatever the law says, we are to blame.'

'You don't mean that.'

'Yes, Diana. I do.'

Her hand fell from my elbow and I heard her move away. When she next spoke, her voice seemed to come from a greater distance than the room could contain. 'In that case, you ought to leave. And I won't try to stop you.'

I spent the rest of that day and most of the next alternately walking and drinking myself into a state of oblivion. Trapped like a fly in a bottle, I craved only the world beyond the glass, where I could seek out the truth on Max's behalf. But the glass could not be broken. Nor, until the Venetian *magistratura* gave their leisurely consent, could the cork be pulled. There was, for me, no escape.

Returning to the Casa di Pellicani late on Wednesday afternoon, I was surprised to be told that an Englishman had called in search of me and was waiting at the Oliva Nera, an unlovely local bar recommended to him by my landlady, whose brother was the proprietor. Wondering who my visitor might be, I went straight there, only to catch sight of him from some way off. He was sitting at an outside table, wearing a raincoat and trilby, peering suspiciously at a glass of fizzy beer and blending with the Venetian background about as effectively as a gondolier on the Serpentine.

'Chief Inspector Hornby?'

'Ah, Mr Horton, there you are. Take a seat. Can I buy you a beer?'

'No thanks. Just coffee.' I sat down and waited until my order had been taken, then lit a cigarette and offered Hornby one. He accepted, eagerly discarding the Italian brand he had been coughing over. 'I'm sorry I was out. If I'd known you were coming . . .'

'I hardly knew myself. But, when we heard the news. . . Well, somebody had to come over to check the details.' He flexed his shoulders. 'And I didn't travel first-class, so don't think I'm pleased to be here.' After a squint around the tiny square, he added: 'Bognor's more to my taste.'

'Couldn't you have left it to the locals? Max is dead. I should have thought that was all you wanted to know.'

152

'Not quite. There's the question of how he managed to slip out of England.'

'I can't help you there. He didn't tell me.'

'Did he tell you anything? Where he's been since the murder, for instance?'

'No.'

'Or what made him kill Charnwood?'

I wondered if I should respond by proclaiming Max's innocence. But Hornby's expression told me I would be wasting my breath. If I was to clear Max's name, it would be without assistance from the likes of a detective chief inspector who prefers Bognor to Venice. 'He said nothing.'

'Apart from accusing you and Miss Charnwood of treachery?'

I sipped my coffee and stared impassively at him. 'Apart from that.'

'I can see it must have been a real facer for him. His friend and his fiancée.' The phrase was a virtual and quite possibly deliberate echo of one used by Varsini. But, if he was trying to rile me, I was determined he would not succeed. 'Do you mind me asking . . . how long you and Miss Charnwood . . .'

'Is that really any of your business, Chief Inspector?'

'Strictly speaking, no. But it's only a matter of weeks since you were planning to stand as best man at their wedding. It doesn't look very . . . loyal, does it?'

'No. It doesn't.'

'How will you explain it to his parents? They'll be here tomorrow, you know.'

'Will they?' I had not thought about the Wingates and what I would say to them. Now, suddenly, their arrival was imminent. And I could hardly tell *them* my disloyalty to Max was none of their business.

'I expect you'll think of something, Mr Horton. You seem to be rather good at it.'

'Do I?'

'Well, you've had the last laugh on me, haven't you? I promised you at Charnwood's funeral that I'd bring Wingate to trial and see him hanged for murder. But I was wrong. The case will close without a trial. And your friend will be buried in sanctified ground. So you see, you and Miss Charnwood have done him quite a favour. Haven't you?'

*   *   *

153

According to Hornby, the Wingates were booked into the Danieli (which he pronounced to rhyme with Philippi) and were expected about midday. Shortly after six o'clock, therefore, I presented myself at the desk, sober, smartly dressed and as well-prepared as I was ever likely to be. The concièrge, who seemed to recognize me from my overnight stay the previous week but did not say so, telephoned their room. After he had given my name, there was a long and pregnant pause. Then the message came back: *Signor* Wingate would be down directly.

He looked immensely weary as he descended the staircase, his face lined and drawn. He did not smile, of course, but a mechanical shake of my hand represented a concession of sorts.

'Shall we go into the bar, sir?' I asked.

'No. I'd prefer to talk outside.'

I followed him through the revolving doors and out onto the Riva degli Schiavoni. A cloud-barred sunset was spreading its pink glow across the lagoon and the faces of the passers-by. A magical serenity offered itself freely to every stray human. But neither of us felt able to embrace it.

We started walking slowly east. Aubrey Wingate stared straight ahead, his chin raised, as if he were scanning the horizon for a sight of something – or of someone. As we reached the first bridge, I said, 'I am so very sorry about all this, sir.' He did not reply or glance towards me. 'For you and Mrs Wingate, it must have come as . . . a terrible shock. I can only express my . . . deepest regret.'

As we cleared the bridge, he veered away towards the water's edge. He stopped by a bollard and rested against it, rubbing his forehead for a few moments. Then he folded his arms and looked at me. 'I don't know what to say to you, Guy. Cecily is distraught. She still thinks of Max as a baby and feels as if her child has been snatched away from her. But I can't help thinking of what would have happened if he'd been arrested, tried and convicted. The anguish. The shame. The sheer horror of it.' He shook his head. 'Max let us down in a great many ways. But we never turned him away. The letter he wrote. . . I'm not sure I believed it. I simply had to behave as if I did. God damn it, why did you have to prove him right? Why did you have to betray him? To the police I could have understood, even approved. But with this girl?'

'I'm not sure I can explain – far less excuse – what I did.'

'She's beautiful, I'm told.'

'Yes. She is.'

'Is that the reason, then? That and nothing else?'

I sighed. 'Probably.'

'The war ruined you two. It made you greedy and selfish. But for those years in Macedonia, you'd have grown into fine young men. I'm sure of it. But as it is . . .'

'I *am* sorry.'

'And is the Charnwood girl sorry?'

'Yes.'

'It's still not good enough, though, is it? Tomorrow, they'll bury my son. Here, in a foreign land. They'll bury him and forget him. But we won't.'

'Neither will I, sir.'

He inhaled sharply and seemed to bite back some response. Then he pushed himself upright and stared out across the lagoon towards the Lido. 'I don't want her at the funeral. It would be too much for Cecily. I've sent a message to that effect via the Consulate. But they didn't seem to know your address, so . . .'

'You've been trying to contact me?'

He nodded. 'With the same message.' He turned to look at me, stiffening his jaw. 'We'll say goodbye to our son – for all his faults – in our own way. But we don't want to have to do it in the company of those who betrayed him. We don't want you there, Guy. Either of you.'

I gaped at him in disbelief. 'You're forbidding me to attend Max's funeral?'

'I can't forbid anything. I can only ask.'

'But . . . Max was my best and oldest friend.'

'So you say. But were you his?' He ground his teeth. 'I'm sorry. Perhaps I've said too much. I must go back to the hotel. We'll be leaving on Saturday. As far as I'm concerned, there's no reason for us to meet again before then.'

'No. I suppose there isn't.'

'So, I'll say goodbye, Guy.'

'Goodbye, sir.' I extended my hand towards him, but he either ignored it or failed to notice as he moved swiftly past me and marched off towards the Danieli. I did not watch him go, but turned to gaze, as he had, into the sun-gilded distance. This, I supposed, was the final humiliation my conduct had invited: to be excluded even from Max's funeral. 'Very well,' I whispered to myself – and to my forever absent friend. 'So be it. I won't be there when they

155

bury you, Max. But this isn't going to end with your funeral. I promise.'

I did not, of course, know what time next day Max would be buried. Deliberately, I made no effort to find out. But fate was determined to ensure I should not remain safe in my ignorance. I rose late and badly hungover on a brilliantly clear morning, oppressed more than ever by the knowledge that I could not leave the maze of claustrophobic alleys to which Venice had been reduced in my mind. Bursting out of the Casa di Pellicani in a violently restless mood, I made for Riva Schiavoni, hoping an aimless *vaporetto* ride might calm me down.

But even as I emerged onto the riva and glanced towards the Danieli, I realized my mistake. There, nosing out of the side-canal serving the hotel, was a black funeral launch, with the sombrely clad figures of Mr and Mrs Wingate recognizable through the window of the cabin. I watched, transfixed, as it moved slowly out into the channel and set off on its journey to the cemetery island of San Michele. As it passed the spot where I stood, I thought of the other vessel, with a coffin aboard, that would be steering for the same destination. I was not allowed to follow either. All I could do was keep my eyes trained on the gleaming black prow of the launch as it slid through the water and utter a silent prayer for—

'Faraday,' I murmured, as his smiling face came between me and the distant shape of the launch. He was standing a few yards away, patiently waiting, it seemed, for my gaze to reach him.

'Good morning, Horton. Not going to the funeral?'

'No.'

'Warned off, I take it – like poor Diana?'

'Something like that.'

He nodded. 'I thought as much. So, I don't find you busy?'

'What do you want, Faraday?'

'The information you agreed to obtain.'

'I've withdrawn my agreement.'

'It's a moot point whether you can. But, look here, I'll be satisfied for the moment by your company on a short voyage. I have to visit a yacht moored off the Zattere. There's a boat waiting for me at San Marco. Why don't you come too? The people aboard would like to meet you.'

'Who are they?'

156

'Persons of influence.'

'Like you, you mean?'

'No. Not at all like me.' He paused, then said: 'You wouldn't regret it.'

My instinct was to refuse, but I badly wanted not to be alone. It seemed inconceivable that all Faraday's acquaintances should be as odious as he was himself. 'All right,' I grudgingly said. 'Why not?'

'Excellent. Come along, then.' He led the way towards San Marco and I followed. As we crossed the Ponte della Paglia, he said: 'Heard the news from England? There's to be a general election.'

'Really?'

'You don't sound interested.'

'Can't say I am.'

'You should be. Politics are a matter of life and death. Everyone's life and death. Even yours.'

'I don't know what you're talking about.'

'No? Well, perhaps it's time you did.' He pursed his lips. 'Or perhaps not.'

We reached the jetties facing the Giardinetti Reali. Tied up at one was a small speed-boat with a tall and muscular figure waiting alongside. He nodded to Faraday and helped us aboard, casting one withering blue-eyed glance at me as he did so. His face was stern and pitted with the scars of smallpox, partially obscured by a mane of grey-blond hair. I did not like the look of him. Nor, apparently, did he like the look of me.

Faraday addressed him as Klaus and spoke to him in what sounded like German. We shoved off, manoeuvred into open water, then headed straight out past Customs House Point. As we rounded it and steered in towards the Zattere, I caught sight of an elegant three-masted schooner moored ahead.

'Is that it?' I asked, shouting to make myself heard.

'Yes,' Faraday bellowed back. 'The *Quadratrice*. Handsome, isn't she?'

I did not catch the name as he pronounced it, but, as we drew alongside, there it was, blazoned in gold copper-plate beneath the bow. *Quadratrice*. A curious word, with a French ring to it, that sounded as if it might be either an algebraic expression or a mythological creature – a quadratic equation, perhaps, or a four-headed serpent. I was about to ask what it meant when Faraday tapped me on the arm.

'The captain's waiting to welcome us aboard. You know him better as a general.'

It was Vasaritch, looking even huger than I remembered in an outfit of billowing white. He was grinning down at us from the rail like Zeus from Olympus, extending a god-sized arm to haul us up. Faraday went first, then Klaus ushered me forward as if anxious to ensure I did not turn back. Already, I was beginning to question the wisdom of accepting this invitation. But there was nothing for it now but to put on a brave face.

'Good morning, General,' I said, as my host administered a crushing handshake. 'I heard you give the eulogy at Fabian Charnwood's funeral. I didn't have the chance to speak to you then, but—'

'We speak now, eh?' He clapped me on the shoulder, knocking me off balance in the process. 'We all speak now. We and my friends.'

His friends were gathered round a table beneath the mizzen-mast: Faraday and two others. One, who would have counted as tall and burly in any other company but Vasaritch's, was a good-looking fellow of about fifty, wearing a blazer and flannels. Beside him, standing ramrod-straight, was an old man in a cream suit and white képi. His head-gear and white mutton-chop whiskers gave him a faintly Ruritanian air. Beyond the group, sun-bathing on the poop-deck, was a bronzed-limbed brunette in an abbreviated yellow swim-suit. She was spreadeagled on a towel, seemingly oblivious to her surroundings behind enormous dark glasses.

'This is the Horton you have heard so much about,' declared Vasaritch. 'Noel's latest recruit.' By *Noel* he clearly meant Faraday. With a shock, I realized I had never heard his Christian name used before. 'Well, Pierre, Karl, what do you think?'

Pierre was the younger of the two and evidently French. Karl I took definitely to be of Germanic origin. Their accents subsequently confirmed both suppositions. Pierre looked me up and down for a moment, then said: 'Looks the part. But can he act?'

'I chose him specifically for his acting abilities,' said Faraday, with a smile in my direction.

Vasaritch laughed. 'Very good. But does the leading lady approve?'

'Oh, I think so,' said Faraday.

158

'We need more than approval,' said the unsmiling Pierre. 'We need her secrets.'

'I'm sorry,' I said, tiring of the charade, 'but I'm afraid you're all labouring under some—'

'Horton's a little reluctant,' said Faraday through gritted teeth. 'He has made a new discovery in his life: scruples.'

'Are you a rich man?' asked Pierre.

'No.'

'Then you cannot afford scruples. They are more expensive than a virtuous woman. And even rarer.'

Vasaritch laughed again, but nobody joined in. Pierre looked as if he laughed only when alone, Karl as if he had set the weakness aside about fifty years ago. 'A drink for you, Horton?' said Vasaritch, encircling my arm in a manacle-like grip. 'We have everybody's poison here.'

'Er. . . No thanks.'

'Sobriety is an asset,' Pierre remarked.

'But, alas, not usually one of Horton's,' said Faraday. 'I think he must be nervous.'

'What is there to be nervous of?'

'The consequences of his newly discovered scruples.'

'When will you obtain what we want?' asked Karl, speaking for the first time.

'As I've been trying to—'

'We cannot wait beyond the end of this month.'

'Quite true, I'm afraid,' said Faraday. 'We really must have some results by then.'

'Well, you won't be getting them from me.'

'A pity,' said Pierre. 'It would be better for her if we did it this way.'

'Something soon,' Vasaritch growled in my ear. 'For the girl's sake.'

'What do you mean?'

'Ah,' said Pierre. 'A flicker of concern. Do you care about her, Horton?'

'If you mean Diana Charnwood,' I replied, glaring at Faraday, 'then, yes, I care about her. And I don't believe she's hiding anything.'

'Not good enough,' said Vasaritch.

'Well, it'll have to do, because I shall be leaving Venice soon and—'

159

'Not *very* soon,' put in Faraday. 'I happened to speak to Martelli this morning. He tells me the inquest is provisionally scheduled for the twenty-sixth.'

'The twenty-sixth? But . . . that's more than two weeks away.'

'Quite so. Two weeks in which you could extract the truth from Diana Charnwood. After all, what else is there for you to do?'

'I've already told you—'

'Tell us nothing,' said Vasaritch. 'Until you can tell us what we want to hear.'

'I happen to know she plans to visit the Isola di San Michele this afternoon,' said Faraday. 'Offering you an excellent opportunity to effect a graveside reconciliation. With a few well chosen words, you could find yourself restored as a guest at the Villa Primavera.'

'I'm not going back there.'

'Think of the girl, Horton,' said Vasaritch. He moved past us and leaned against the rail of the poop-deck, reaching out to rest his hand on the brunette's shapely rump while still looking at me. She turned her head and gave a little purr of pleasure as he tickled the soft flesh at the top of her thigh. 'Think of her and enjoy her. But strip her mind as well as her body.'

'We must know by the end of the month,' said Karl.

'And if you don't?'

'We shall use other methods,' Vasaritch replied, the geniality gone from his voice. He grabbed suddenly at the brunette's hair, yanking her head up violently. She gave a cry of pain, then another as his grip tightened. 'Other men and other methods.'

'You wouldn't like either,' said Faraday. 'Believe me.'

I did believe him. As Vasaritch released the girl, my gaze moved to Karl and Pierre, who seemed not to have noticed the incident at all, then round the deck to the accommodation ladder, where Klaus was leaning against the rail, arms folded, staring straight at me. *Other men and other methods.* Who those men might be and what methods they might employ I did not care to imagine. But the threat was genuine. My involvement in Diana's future was no longer a matter of choice. It had become a matter of necessity – for her as well as for me.

'Klaus could take you to San Michele,' said Faraday.

'I'd prefer to make my own way.'

'But you will go?' asked Pierre.

'Yes,' I replied, looking at each of them in turn, pausing to be sure they understood me. 'I will go.'

As soon as I was sure the funeral would be over – and the Wingates long gone – I walked to Fondamenta Nuove and caught the next *vaporetto* out across the sparkling lagoon to the Isola di San Michele. The cemetery was, as I had hoped, empty of all save the dead, sheltered from wind and eye by high walls and cypress trees. There, in one of the overgrown corners reserved for foreigners, Protestants and sundry apostates, was a mound of freshly dug earth and a single wreath of white lilies. *To our dear son Max*, read the card. *You strayed far and often, but never left our thoughts*. I, who had brought no flowers and sung no hymns, stood reproached by blind parental love.

How long I remained there, staring at my friend's last resting place, helpless to hold back the cavalcade of memories in my mind, I do not know. It might have been five minutes or fifty. But, suddenly, I was not alone.

'Hello, Guy.' She was dressed all in white and was staring at me with a strange and desolate intensity. 'So,' she said softly, 'you couldn't stay away either.' Stretching forward, she dropped a small wreath of blood-red roses at the foot of the grave. There was no card attached. Words, it seemed, had failed her – as they threatened to fail me.

'I'm sorry,' I began. 'Sorry they wouldn't let you attend the service.'

'It's not your fault. Nor mine, I hope, that they wouldn't let you.'

'It's nobody's fault. Not theirs. Not ours. Not Max's.'

She stood beside me in silence for a moment, head bowed. Then, glancing round at me, she said: 'How have you been, Guy – these past few days?'

'Pretty low. And you?'

'The same.'

'I didn't mean us to part as we did, Diana. I've wished a dozen times I could have those few minutes after Vita left the room over again – to use differently.' Would I be saying this, I wondered, if I had not agreed to do as Faraday asked? Did I really mean it? Or did necessity enable me to imagine I meant it?

'I've wished the same, Guy.' Our fingers entwined so instinctively it was impossible to judge whose had reached out first. 'Why

161

don't we try again? Why don't we give ourselves a little more time?'

'I'd like to.'

'We both have to stay here until the inquest. And that's more than two weeks away.'

'So Faraday told me.'

'Did he also tell you he's leaving Venice?'

'No.'

'Tomorrow, apparently. So, you wouldn't have to dread him forever popping in. If you moved back to the villa, I mean.'

Our eyes met for more than the fleeting moment we had so far risked. To look at her was to remember what we had done – and to see, reflected in her gaze, the irresistible uncertainty of all we might yet do. May God forgive me. For surely Max would not have.

'It's not going to be easy, Guy. Waiting to have our . . . immorality . . . exposed in court. But at least it might be bearable if we waited together.'

'It wasn't immoral.'

'No. But some will say it was.'

'Let them.'

'I will. If you'll give me the strength not to care what they say.'

'I'll try.'

'Then you *will* come back to the villa?'

'Unless Vita objects.'

'She never objects to anything that's good for me.'

'And am I good for you?'

'I hope we're good for each other.'

'Yes,' I said, leading her away from the grave. 'So do I.'

CHAPTER

NINE

And so I went back to the Villa Primavera. I cannot be sure now whether, left to my own devices, I would have succumbed to temptation during the weeks I had still to spend in Venice. Not that it matters. I was forced to return to the villa for Diana's sake. And once there, it was not hard to persuade myself that more or less any deception – any indulgence – was justifiable on the same grounds.

Diana had moved to a different room since Max's death. It was hardly necessary to ask why. Mercifully, though, no memory of that afternoon clung to the fabric of the villa. Max's presence had been too fleeting for any ghost to linger. When I thought of him – which was frequently – it was in other places and moods than those in which he had died. By the second night – when Diana came to me, weeping and nervous in the still small hours – I could wrap her in my arms without seeming to see Max's face hovering at my shoulder. And by the third night – when we surrendered, as I had thought we never would again, to the needs and instincts of the flesh – no scruple stayed my hand as it slid around her body.

Nor could it reasonably have been expected to. They were strange and unsettling, those days of waiting on the Lido, as autumn seeped about us in salt-tinged mists and ever colder dawns. What could we do to still our doubts and anxieties but cling to each other? I did not love her. I did not believe in the possibility of love. But she did. And every time and every way she gave

163

herself to me made the next time and the next way more irresistible still.

I gleaned her secrets without compunction. Though she did not know it, I was trying to help her, trying to save her from whatever persuasions Faraday's friends might devise. There seemed to be nothing she was not willing to tell me. Nothing except what I needed ever more urgently to discover. But for the conversation between her and Vita I had eavesdropped on that night in the garden, I would have become convinced of her innocence, convinced there really was no hidden pile of Charnwood's money. But there had to be. Otherwise, what had they meant? What else could be worth such artful concealment?

For artful they undoubtedly were. Diana opened her soul to me. There was nothing she denied me. Save one scrap of knowledge, the scrap I sought in bedroom drawers and wardrobe shelves, in purses and handbags, explored whenever chance allowed. I did not spare Vita either. Her bureau I opened, her letters I read, her pockets I searched. For time and idleness make many opportunities. And I seized them with mounting desperation. Only to be left as I had begun – empty-handed.

As the days ticked away, I reached a grim conclusion. I would have to tell them. There was no other way. I would have to make them understand the gravity of their position. Then they would volunteer the truth to save themselves. But, in the process, I would have to admit I was merely Faraday's spy, somebody more contemptible even than he was. In saving Diana, it seemed certain I would also lose her. And no amount of money could compensate me for that. Reject the concept of love as I might, I could not deny infatuation, addiction, even obsession. I was the victim of them all. And she was the cause.

Yet what could I do? What alternative was there? None, so far as I could see – except delay. The inquest was now definitely fixed for Monday the twenty-sixth. Martelli had said so during one of his several visits. He had also assured us of the outcome: a verdict of involuntary homicide and the immediate end of our confinement. We were all eager to leave Venice and planned to do so as soon as possible. What then? I did not care to wonder, for by then the end of October would be upon us. And I would have to speak. Until the inquest, I could hold my tongue – and my place in Diana's affections. But no longer.

Often, I found myself hoping for some sudden extrication from my dilemma, some *deus ex machina* to resolve my every difficulty. But it was no more than a hope – and not a very pious one either. Certainly I did not think it was fulfilled by the unexpected arrival five days before the inquest of Quincy Z. McGowan, younger brother of the late Maud Charnwood and seldom-heard-from uncle of Diana.

He was a tall barrel-chested man in his mid-forties, with a booming voice and a beaming smile, running to fat and inclining to baldness, but defiantly projecting a boyish charm. He had decided, he explained, to bring forward a business trip to England in order to give Vita and Diana any help he could in the wake of his brother-in-law's death. The news of their latest misfortune had been waiting for him at Amber Court and he had therefore proceeded to Venice immediately.

Vita and Diana both seemed overjoyed to see him and it was easy to understand why. He blew through the villa like a spring breeze, dispelling much of the unspoken dread that had settled upon us. Diana had fond memories of him as the strapping young god of her childhood, a playful uncle who had largely lapsed from her life after her mother's death. He recalled hoping the United States would declare war on Germany after the sinking of the *Lusitania* in 1915 and so give him the chance to avenge his sister. But he had had to wait until 1918 for that, in the form of a few glorious months under arms on the Western Front. His descriptions of combat did not tally with my memories, but it was impossible to resent or resist the force of his enthusiasm. I was only grateful Max and I had never crossed swords with him. The McGowans of Pittsburgh ranked not that far short of Carnegie and Frick in the American steel industry. They would have made powerful enemies. And I had enough of those already.

One of Quincy's most endearing characteristics was his modesty. 'My father made my wealth for me while I was still in diapers. And my brother Theo's made sure I've kept it. I'm just the grateful beneficiary of their acumen. Theo has the brains. And Maudie had the beauty. There was precious little left for me – except to have a lot of fun.' But he had not come to Venice in search of fun. He had come to offer a helping hand. 'If the McGowan Steel Corporation had gone bust, Fabian would have ridden to our rescue. So, it's only fair I should try to do the same.'

He proved to be as good as his word. He knew nothing of Charnwood Investments – 'Fabian always kept us at arm's length where business was concerned' – but he did know how to entertain women of any age and how to oil the wheels of any nation's legal system. He established an immediate rapport with Martelli and persuaded the American Consulate to do far more than our own had troubled to. When he was not amusing us, he was encouraging us. And when the day of the inquest finally came, his presence alongside us in the court seemed magically to guarantee a favourable outcome. Whether something more than magic was at work – such as a bribe – I had no way of knowing. But I would not have put it past him.

Certainly the inquest did go smoothly. Most of it, of course, was conducted in Italian. If the presiding magistrate expressed his distaste for the circumstances surrounding Max's death, it was not translated for our benefit. And what he said about Max's character was likewise never conveyed to us. Diana and I were questioned in English, but the convoluted process of translation had the effect of neutralizing our answers, draining them of shame as well as feeling. I could not judge how an Italian court would react to the events we described, but I felt sure it would not be with the narrow-minded sourness of a middle-class English jury. And nor was it. When the verdict came, it was calmly, almost clinically, pronounced. *Omicidio involontario*, as Martelli had predicted – and as Quincy may have taken steps to ensure.

We went to Harry's Bar afterwards, then returned to the Lido and dined at the Excelsior, buoyed up by a sense of release amounting almost to gaiety. Late in the evening, glancing around the table at my companions, I felt a sudden sense of remoteness from them, of remorse for being pleased that the book had been closed on the death as well as the life of Max Algernon Wingate. I made some excuse and went out onto the terrace to smoke a cigar, watching the white horses of the Adriatic roll in at me from the limitless night, wondering what I could have done – or not done – to avert this bitter end to our twenty years of friendship.

'You're thinking about Max, aren't you?' asked Diana, coming up silently behind me to thread her arm through mine and lean her head against my shoulder. 'I could see it in your face as you left.'

'I can't help it.'

'I don't want you to. We'll never forget him. We'll never try to.'

'None of it was his fault, you see.'

'You still think somebody else murdered Papa?'

166

'I'm not sure. I don't suppose I ever will be.' Feeling goose-pimples forming on her arm, I added: 'Shall we go back in?'

'In a moment. The sea by night is . . . so lovely.'

'Not as lovely as you.' I kissed her and saw the lights from the dining-room dance in her eyes. 'Are you looking forward to going home?'

'I think so.'

'Only think?'

'What does it mean for us, Guy – going back to England? Will we stay together?'

I should have told her then. I should have revealed my secret while I had the courage. But I knew I could delay a little longer. So all I did was kiss her again and murmur 'Of course' in her scented ear. Next day, we collected our passports from the Questura, then took the speed-boat out to San Michele, where we laid flowers on Max's grave and bade him a wordless farewell. Soon, we would be leaving Venice. But Max would be staying for ever. No blame attached to us. The court had said so. And yet he would remain, while we were free to go.

We were booked aboard the Orient Express leaving Venice on Wednesday afternoon. It was the twenty-eighth of October and time was running short. Not that there was any tension in the air as breakfast commenced at the Villa Primavera. Diana and I preserved a fictional decorum, which doubtless deceived nobody, by descending separately from our respective rooms. Accordingly, I found myself alone with Vita for ten minutes or so before Diana joined us, Quincy having gone for his regular morning tramp along the beach.

'I'm glad to have this chance of a quiet word,' said Vita. 'It's high time I asked what your intentions are towards my niece.'

I set down my coffee-cup and smiled at her. 'I'm not sure I know.'

'Then you should. She's in love with you, Guy. That's obvious to me, even if it isn't to you. So, what do you propose to do about it?'

'It's not as simple as that. You see . . .' I hesitated in the face of another opportunity to confess. And then the opportunity was gone.

'Well, hello, you two!' roared Quincy, advancing suddenly into the room, panting slightly from his walk. 'Great morning, don't you think?'

'Yes,' we chorused. 'Absolutely.'

'I met the mail-man outside. He gave me a letter for you, Vita. Leastways, I suppose it's for you.'

'What do you mean?'

'See for yourself.' He dropped an envelope in front of her, addressed by typewriter to Miss Charnwood, with no initial.

'Posted locally,' said Vita. 'How strange.'

'Aren't you going to open it?'

'It may be for Diana.'

'And it may not.'

'True, but—'

At that moment Diana appeared, smiling, at Quincy's elbow. 'Something exciting?' she asked.

'A letter for Miss Charnwood,' I said. 'The question is: which one?'

'Let me see.' Vita passed it to her. 'Well, there's no handwriting to recognize. It could be for either of us.'

'Do open it, my dear,' said Vita. 'Put us out of our misery.'

'Very well.' She slit it open with a knife from the table, pulled out a single sheet of paper and frowned at whatever message it contained. 'How extraordinary!'

'What is it?' I asked.

'I don't know. Some sort of . . . diagram. It means nothing to me. Aunty?' She handed the sheet to Vita, who peered at it for a moment, then let it fall onto the tablecloth, where we all had a clear view of it.

The sheet was blank save for a pair of concentric circles drawn in ink. They were perfect discs, the inner one about an inch in diameter, the outer about twice that. For some reason, I was reminded of the game Charnwood had played with a five-shilling piece. But this time there were two circles – and no conjurer to pluck a meaning from them.

'What do you make of it, Vita?' asked Quincy.

'Nothing,' she replied. But something caught in her throat, something suggesting dismay rather than puzzlement. Her face had lost much of its colour and, in her eyes, there was a hint of alarm. 'Some absurd prank, I suppose.'

'A mighty pointless prank, wouldn't you say – if nobody understands it?'

'I would, Quincy, yes.'

Diana picked the sheet of paper up and stared at it, then at the envelope. 'Posted yesterday, here in Venice,' she mused. 'What *can* it mean?'

'I don't know,' said Vita. 'And I don't propose to gratify whoever sent it by racking my brains trying to find out. If you'll excuse me, I have packing to attend to.' She rose hurriedly from the table, still dabbing toast-crumbs from her lips, and bustled out, leaving the rest of us to stare at each other with furrowed brows.

'Poor Aunty,' said Diana. 'This seems to have struck a nerve.'

'Anonymous letters are always distressing,' I suggested.

'But it isn't a letter,' said Quincy. 'Just a diagram. It's not abusive or threatening – so far as I can see.'

'And it wasn't necessarily even intended for Aunt Vita,' said Diana. 'It could have been for me.'

'But it means nothing to you?' I asked.

'Nothing at all.'

'Unlike Vita,' said Quincy, nodding thoughtfully.

Diana looked at him, then at me. Bafflement was turning to concern on her aunt's behalf. She replaced the sheet of paper in its envelope, clutched it pensively in both hands for a moment, then offered it to me. 'Keep this for me, Guy, would you? Just in case— Well, just in case.'

'Certainly.' I took it from her. 'But—'

'I'll go and see how she is. She may want to talk to me. Would you both excuse me?'

'What about—' But she was gone before I could finish the sentence. 'Your breakfast?' I murmured through a grimace as the door closed behind her.

'I think she's lost her appetite,' said Quincy. He grinned ruefully.

'So it seems.' I slid the envelope and its cryptic contents into my pocket. 'Or been deprived of it.'

'By an anonymous Venetian geometer? Just as well we're leaving, then.'

'Yes. I think it is. From every point of view.'

The upheaval of departure drove the subject of the strange letter – and Vita's reaction to it – out of my thoughts. By late afternoon, we were aboard the Orient Express as it pulled slowly out of Santa Lucia station. I looked through the window of my cabin at the flat expanse of the lagoon drifting past us and remembered how much

169

happier I would have felt leaving three weeks before, when Max's death had reduced my intentions to a single burning determination. Now, nothing was quite so simple. Diana and I were lovers. And her father's debts were about to be called in. A Sword of Damocles hung over us, but only I could see it. Soon, very soon, I would have to speak out – or watch helplessly as the sword descended.

As darkness fell and we neared Verona, I headed for the bar car. The ladies would be about their *toilettes* for another hour or more before dinner and the best way to forget my troubles seemed to be by downing several Manhattans while the pianist warmed his fingers to some rag-time melodies. For the moment, I desired no company but my own. Quincy McGowan, however, had other ideas.

'Great minds, Guy. A long cool drink before things get busy, eh? And a little . . . *conversazione* . . . before we leave Italy. I bet you'll be glad to cross the Swiss border.'

'I confess I will.'

'Before we do, there's something I want to talk to you about.'

'Oh yes?'

'My gorgeous niece, Diana. Since she's grown to remind me more and more of Maudie, I just can't help feeling . . . well, protective.'

'That's quite understandable.'

'It's why I came to Venice. It's why I left Pittsburgh. You see . . .' He lowered his voice to a rumble. 'My brother Theo got wind of some bad feeling among Charnwood Investments' American creditors. We made a few enquiries. Asked a few discreet questions. For anyone concerned about Diana and Vita, the answers were . . . alarming.'

Trying to appear and sound bemused, I frowned and said: 'In what way?'

He grimaced. 'Seems a lot of people – powerful people – don't believe Fabian lost as much money as reported. Seems they think it's salted away somewhere. Their money, put out of their reach by Fabian – and accessible only to his sister and daughter.'

'That's absurd.'

'Maybe. But they believe it. They feel cheated. And I guess you can't blame them.'

'What do they . . . propose to do?'

'Oh, some of it they've already done.' He paused and my growing sense of guilt invested the brief silence with vast

170

significance. 'According to Theo's informants, they've set spies on Diana and Vita.'

'Spies?'

'This Faraday Vita's told me about sounds like one.'

'Good God. Well, I never liked him, but—'

'And there are others.'

'Really?'

He nodded. 'Sure to be.'

It was becoming hard not to read double meanings into his remarks. I cleared my throat. 'But neither Diana nor Vita knows anything about Charnwood's money. If there is any hidden, they can't lead his creditors to it.'

'Oh, I agree. But we're in a minority. Fabian's clients want their money back. If they can't get it by spying, they'll try other ways. Faraday's given up and gone away, hasn't he? It seems to me the subtle approach has been abandoned. I worry they may resort to something cruder.' He left the last word hanging in the smoky air, then pointed to my glass. 'Another drink?'

'Good idea. I think I need one.' So I did. But I was also grateful for the breathing space afforded by the coming and going of the steward. The pianist played on. Conversations around us joined in a collective murmur. And the click-clack of the rails paced my thoughts through the gathering night. But I was already outrun.

'Why don't you say it before I do, Guy?'

'Say what?'

'You're one of their spies, aren't you?' Somehow, the force of his gaze seemed to preclude a denial. I did not take my eyes from his face. I was aware of no change, however slight, in my expression. But I said nothing. 'I knew before I met you. Your name, Guy. Yours and Wingate's. They crop up in the fine print of just about all the indictments Hiram and Richard Babcock are going to have to answer to next month. As directors of the Serendipity and Happenstance Investment Trust, the Blue Hills Corporation, the Tuscarora Corporation, the Wide Horizon Investment and Disbursement Company. . . Need I go on?'

'No.' Clearly, he had found all this out before travelling to England. I was a known if dubious quantity to him before we even met. 'You needn't.'

'Of course, it can't be proved you were given such lucrative positions in return for acting as the Babcocks' agents in illegal

171

deals with Canadian brewers, though what your other qualifications were I can't imagine. And it can't be proved you knew they'd been propping up their companies' share prices since the Crash by embezzling funds from the Housatonic Bank, of which Hiram was president. But I can read between the lines. You left the States to avoid being dragged down with them. Since then, I reckon you've been looking for an alternative source of income. And I reckon you've found one. I hope they paid you well for following Diana to Venice.'

'Now look—'

'Hold on!' He raised his hand. 'Let me finish. Then you can say whatever you like. You're a con-man. So was your friend. But I have no argument with how you choose to make a living. And I don't expect you to admit spying on Diana. Just don't try to deny it. It's not important, you see. She's sweet on you. That's obvious. But how do you feel about her? The same?'

I tried to inject some dignity into my reply. 'Believe it or not, Quincy, yes.'

'As I thought. So, what are you going to do? She's in danger. You must know that better than I do. How do you propose to get her out of it?'

I took a long draw on my cigarette, trying to appear calm and relaxed while my mind sifted frantically through a tangle of competing considerations. Quincy had seen through me. If I told him why I was sure Vita and Diana were hiding something, he would probably not believe me. But his faith in Vita's innocence had been tested that very morning. I had to know just how secure it really was. 'First things first,' I replied at last. 'The anonymous letter meant something to Vita. Are you sure she's not concealing vital information?'

'I have her word on it. And she vouches for Diana too. That's good enough for me. As for the diagram. . . Well, Vita may realize the seriousness of their position, which Diana obviously doesn't. She may have read some kind of threat into it. She may have been right to. If so, it's all the more urgent that we do something about it.'

'But what?' I hesitated, weighing his words carefully. I was confident now of his sincerity. And I knew him to be a wealthy man. He seemed to be preparing the ground for some kind of proposal, one that might solve all our problems. 'If, as you say,' I continued cautiously, 'Charnwood's clients won't believe what we

172

believe, that Diana and Vita are completely innocent . . .' I looked straight at him. 'Then I see no way out.'

'Oh, there's always a way out.' He grinned. 'If you have enough money.'

'What do you mean?'

'I mean that, with my stake in the McGowan Steel Corporation, I could offer some . . . compensation. A certain amount of capital, supplemented by McGowan stock, in return for the lifting of any threat to my niece and her aunt.'

It was all I could do not to laugh. This was better and more generous than I had hoped. 'You'd be willing to do that?'

'I'd be willing to negotiate a settlement. But I can't negotiate with faceless men. I need to make contact with these people. But I don't know who they are. Fabian was obsessively secretive about his clients. The most important of them – the ones who could strike a bargain on behalf of the others – are determined to remain anonymous. So, the only way I can reach them is through their agents. Through you, Guy.'

We surveyed each other, coolly and rationally, as two men of the world. If I helped Quincy, I would be in his power as well as his debt. If I refused, the sword would still tremble at the end of a fraying hair. In the final analysis, I had no choice. But first, I had to negotiate my own settlement. 'Do you intend to tell Diana – or Vita – what your suspicions are about me?'

'Not if you co-operate.'

'By arranging a meeting?'

'It's not much to ask, is it?'

'No. I suppose it isn't.' I glanced around the car, then looked back at him. 'When?'

'As soon as possible. Time is of the essence.'

'All right. When we reach London, I'll . . . make a telephone call.'

'Good. We'll have packed the girls off to Dorking by then.'

'I can't, of course, predict what the reaction to your proposal will be.'

'Leave that to me.' He leaned closer. 'And Guy, if you learn anything from Diana – anything at all – that suggests she and Vita may be misleading us . . . I want to know right away.'

'Fair enough.'

'I don't expect you to, mind, but . . .'

'I understand.' The words I had overheard in the garden floated

173

back into my memory. *'I'm glad our efforts weren't wasted. . . Keep him guessing, Aunty. Guessing wrong.'* Yes, I understood. Better than Quincy could possibly imagine. 'We all have to take . . . precautions, don't we?'

'Reckon so.' He nodded solemnly, then suddenly smiled. 'It's a deal, then?'

'Yes.'

'Good man.' He clapped me on the shoulder. 'You won't regret it.'

Would I not? It was an assurance I seemed to have heard too many times of late, too many infinitely regretful times. But every corner has to be turned in the end. Every run of bad luck has to change. As I raised my glass and glimpsed through it Quincy's smiling face, compressed as in a fair-ground mirror, I prayed that this would prove to be the moment.

So carefree was the atmosphere during dinner that it was possible to imagine my *conversazione* with Quincy had never taken place. But occasional beady-eyed glances from him assured me it had. And knowing he had the measure of me was made bearable by contemplating what I would have been forced to do but for his intervention. Instead, Diana could be left in ignorance of how divided my loyalties were. Around midnight, as I escorted her back to her cabin, a change in the sound of the train and a blast on the whistle signalled that we had entered the Simplon Tunnel into Switzerland. We were leaving Italy – and Max – behind us. She kissed me and whispered in my ear, 'We're safe now, Guy.' And I said nothing, content to let her make the most of her illusions.

'Quincy tells me he has to spend a few days in London,' Vita remarked, as we gazed from the ferry at the White Cliffs of Dover. It was the following afternoon and the sky over England was a flawless blue. According to a discarded newspaper flapping on the bench beside us, the National Government had won the general election with a huge majority and the first autumn fog had descended on the capital. 'He has some business to attend to. But I do hope – and so does Diana, I'm sure – that you'll come on to Dorking with us.'

'You're very kind, but—'

'There's plenty of room for you at Amber Court. After these

174

weeks together in Venice, we wouldn't like to think of you alone in some miserable hotel.'

'Do come, Guy,' whispered Diana, sliding her hand into mine.

'I'd like to, but I think I really ought to visit my father and sister first. I have a great deal to tell them.'

'Only right and proper,' said Vita. 'But afterwards . . .'

'I'd be delighted to accept your invitation.'

'Splendid.' She rose and sniffed the sea air. 'Now, if you young people will excuse me, I'm beginning to find it rather cold out here. I shall go below and see what's become of Quincy.'

As she waddled off, Diana kissed me on the cheek and said: 'I would like to meet your father and sister, Guy.'

'So you will. When I've prepared them for such a beautiful surprise.'

'Is that why you're going to Letchworth? To prepare them?'

'Yes. And to explain what's happened.' I smiled at her, aware of the practised ease with which I was lying, but feeling no shred of guilt. This lie had to be told – for everybody's sake. 'Don't worry. Everything will be all right.'

When Quincy and I saw Diana and Vita off from Victoria on the Dorking train later that afternoon, they assumed we were about to go our separate ways. Instead, we both booked into the Grosvenor Hotel. As soon as the porter had shown me to my room, I telephoned Gregory's office and made an appointment to see him in an hour. Quincy professed himself well pleased with the arrangement.

'What line is Gregory in?'

'The honours trade. He sells peerages, knighthoods, baronetcies and any other title he can earn commission on.'

'Titles can be bought?'

'Oh yes. Bought *and* sold.'

Quincy whistled. 'So much for the British nobility. I guess it makes my task easier. At least this fellow will be used to discussing money.'

'Used to it?' I smiled. 'Money is Maundy Gregory's mother tongue.' And mine too, as the idea taking root in my mind confirmed. If Quincy could convince Charnwood's creditors there was no hidden hoard of cash and buy them off with McGowan stock; if the whereabouts of such a hoard was the secret Diana and Vita shared, unbeknown to all except me; if my future and

175

Diana's were joined. . . Then wealth might truly beckon. '*How much has she told you, Guy?*' Max had asked. '*Nothing*,' I should have replied. '*Yet.*'

Parliament Square was shrouded in fog when we walked across it an hour later, the Palace of Westminster reduced to a blurred hulk, the face of Big Ben to a lofty glow. Through the swing-doors marked *Whitehall Gazette* we marched, past the commissionaire and the secretary and into the inner sanctum, where Gregory was waiting to receive me. But he was expecting only one visitor. Fearing he might refuse to meet Quincy, I had not mentioned I would be bringing him. And the discourtesy clearly did not please our host.

'Who is this gentleman, dear boy?' he asked, frowning ominously. As I introduced my companion and explained his relationship to the Charnwood family, the frown intensified. 'You are Fabian Charnwood's brother-in-law?' he said to Quincy when I had finished. 'Frankly, my good sir, I doubt if we have anything to say to each other.'

Quincy smiled. 'You're wrong there, Mr Gregory. I have a proposition for you. And Guy tells me you're always interested in propositions – especially when they involve large sums of money.'

At that last word Gregory's expression mellowed. 'What manner of proposition are you referring to?'

'A mutually advantageous one.'

'Which I think merits serious consideration,' I put in. 'I'm satisfied neither Diana nor her aunt can lead us to Charnwood's nest egg – for the simple reason that it doesn't exist.'

Gregory scowled. 'The question is not whether *you* are satisfied, but whether those whom Charnwood robbed are satisfied.'

And still Quincy smiled at him. 'Excuse me, but you're wrong again. The question is how much will satisfy them – whatever the source.'

Gregory stared at each of us in turn. He was not prepared for such a simplistic approach. But already he was doing his best to evaluate it. 'Perhaps,' he said slowly. 'Perhaps it is.'

'The McGowan Steel Corporation may be able to put up an equitable amount of compensation for my late brother-in-law's aggrieved clients – if the answer is a realistic one.'

'I see.'

'And, over and above that, the broker of such an agreement might expect . . . a generous fee.'

'Ah yes. The broker.' The edges of his mouth quivered. 'We must never forget him.'

'You'll get nothing from my niece or her aunt. But I don't want them to come to any harm while you find that out.'

'Laudable, I'm sure.' Now Gregory too was smiling. He was beginning to envisage how he might sell Quincy's proposition – and what commission he could charge for so doing. 'I think we may have discovered the basis for a profitable discussion, Mr McGowan.' He looked across at me. 'Would you mind leaving us, dear boy?' I guessed at once why he wanted to talk to Quincy alone. That way, I would never know for certain what terms they agreed, nor whether my share of his commission was reasonable. But I did not care. Something far more rewarding than the crumbs from Maundy Gregory's table lay within my reach. 'Wait outside, would you? While we pursue the point.'

'Certainly.' I rose and left, winking at Quincy as I passed his chair. The deal was as good as done.

And so it proved when, twenty minutes later, Gregory flung open his office door and ushered me back in. Champagne and cigars appeared as if from nowhere. A celebratory mood united with the alcohol and nicotine in an intoxicating trinity.

'I shall do my very best to persuade those I represent to accept your proposals, Mr McGowan,' he boomed, 'in the spirit of compromise which I believe should govern the conduct of all fair-minded men.'

'I can't ask you to do more,' Quincy replied, grinning surreptitiously at me.

'Faraday mentioned the end of this month as a dead-line,' I cautiously remarked.

'In abeyance, dear boy,' Gregory lisped through his cigar. 'Until we reach a settlement.'

'Which will be soon, I hope,' said Quincy.

'Indeed,' replied Gregory, consenting to remove the cigar for a moment. 'You will both be at Amber Court next week, I believe you said.'

'We will.'

'Then dine with me at the Deepdene, my hotel in Dorking, a

week tonight. I should be able to report a positive outcome to my discussions by then.'

'That suits me,' said Quincy. 'What about you, Guy?'

'Why, yes, of course.' But I had the distinct impression that my attendance would merely be a token acknowledgement of my role in bringing these two men together. They had no further need of my services. Nor, with any luck, had I any need of theirs.

Quincy and I discussed the progress we had made over a late dinner at the Grosvenor. I pointed out, as gently as I could, that Charnwood's creditors would not necessarily agree with Gregory, but Quincy was confident they would.

'For the fee I'm offering him, Gregory will do his damnedest to win them over. And I reckon he'll succeed.'

'I certainly hope so.'

'You can bet on it. We're not home and dry yet, but, hell, the harbour's mighty close.' Suddenly, his face crumpled and he pressed his hand to his forehead. He seemed to be on the verge of tears.

'What's the matter?'

'I'm sorry.' He smiled gamely. 'It's just that Diana makes me think of Maudie – more than I have in years. I suppose I want to save my niece because I failed to save my sister.'

'How could you have? Nobody was to know the Germans would sink the *Lusitania*.'

'Weren't they? The German Embassy in Washington ran an ad in the New York papers the morning she sailed warning travellers that any vessel flying the British flag would be considered a legitimate target for attack. I could have—' He stopped and chewed pensively on his cigar, then resumed in a subdued tone. 'But it's too late now for Maudie. And all the other victims. We have to think of the living.'

'When will you go down to Dorking?'

He sighed, then summoned a grin. 'Tomorrow. And you? Vita tells me you plan to see your folks first.'

'Yes. But I'll only be away a few days.'

'Preparing them for an announcement where you and Diana are concerned, maybe?'

I smiled coyly. 'Maybe.'

'Just be sure you're back before our dinner date with Gregory.'

'Don't worry. I will be.'

*   *   *

I lay awake that night reflecting on the complexity of life. If I had left Venice, as I had wanted to, immediately after Max's death, everything would have been so very different. Or would it? There was no way to know, no way to judge whether, despairing of clearing my friend's name, I would have returned to Diana in search of the consolation I had since found in her arms. For I no longer expected to achieve or discover anything that would exonerate Max. Time had eroded my faith in his innocence, time and all the other traits of my character. So, what was the point of doing even the little I had sworn to do to salvage his reputation? Why not abandon the struggle before I had embarked upon it and lose myself in the alluring future Quincy had made possible? I fell asleep very nearly convinced I should do precisely that.

But I dreamt of Max, more vividly than on any of the nights I had shared a bed with Diana at the Villa Primavera. I dreamt of him watching from the shadows as we writhed in a frenzy of lust surpassing anything we had experienced, then stepping forward, as I thrust ferociously into her, to scream even as I screamed. I woke, heart and lungs racing, my mind struggling to distinguish fear from desire. And then I knew. Even my conscience could not ignore this call. It had to be answered.

I booked out of the hotel before breakfast, leaving a note for Quincy with the concièrge. Then I collected the car from the garage near the Eccleston where I had left it before setting off for Venice and headed north. I was not going to Letchworth. Mine was a more distant destination – with a far stranger purpose.

CHAPTER

TEN

I drove north all that grey autumn day, through the supine fringes
of the fen country and the sluggish heart of the Yorkshire coalfield,
into a part of England I had always done my best to avoid: a raw
and uncongenial realm of smoking chimneys and pinched faces,
where hardship and the threat of it hung over the towns like an
invisible layer of cloud. The light failed early and I abandoned the
idea of completing my journey that evening, taking refuge at an
hotel in Durham. It was late Saturday morning before I reached
my destination, thirty bleak and empty miles beyond Newcastle:
the rough-hewn market town of Alnwick, bolt-hole of former Fleet
Street foreign correspondent George Duggan. I had waited a long
time and come a long way to hear what he had to say. Although
I expected – and half-hoped – it would amount to nothing, I felt
curiously nervous now the moment of discovery was near.

The streets were busy, but I had no difficulty finding the offices
of the *Alnwick Advertiser*: cramped first-floor premises which,
according to the sign on the door, were also the source of the
Morpeth Mercury and the *Coquetdale Clarion*. It was easy to
believe they represented the nadir of a journalist's ambition.
Certainly, the duty to inform did not appear to grip the two
yawning and scratching members of staff I discovered behind an
uneven barricade of piled back copies and paper-strewn desks.
The name of George Duggan seemed to cause them considerable
amusement.

'He was here earlier, but something urgent cropped up about eleven o'clock.'

'Yeh. The pubs opened.'

'So,' I said when their guffaws had subsided, 'where might I find him?'

'Well, you *might* find him in the Black Swan.'

'Or the Dirty Bottles.'

'But *my* money . . .' He glanced up at the clock. 'Would be on the Queen's Head.'

Their directions led me across the market place, clogged with bellowing stall-holders and their eager customers. All Northumberland and his wife seemed to have descended upon the town and the bar of the Queen's Head was invisible through a haze of smoke and a phalanx of broad-backed drinkers. Insinuating myself slowly between them, I caught the sound of a familiar cough and followed it round a head-high partition to where George Duggan was propped on a stool, swallowing rum like linctus between sucks at a clumsily rolled cigarette.

'Duggan!' I had to shout to attract his attention. Even then, his rheumy eyes surveyed me for several blank seconds before recognition glimmered. 'Guy Horton. Remember?'

'Mr Horton,' he replied. 'Well, well, well. I never expected to see *you* in Alnwick.'

'And I never expected to be here. Now I am, can we talk?'

'What about?'

'Fabian Charnwood.'

'Not sure I want to.' He tossed his head moodily.

'Then why did you give me your card? Why did you urge me to contact you if I uncovered any new information?'

'Because I thought you were helping Wingate. And because I thought Wingate could help me.'

'Max Wingate is dead.'

'I know. I read about it. He was killed by Charnwood's daughter, wasn't he? Some cock-and-bull story about him trying to strangle you and her happening to hit his head where an old war wound had weakened the skull. Do you expect me to believe that?'

'It's true.'

'And I'm Lord Beaverbrook in disguise.' He paused to cough out another lungful of smoke, then prodded me in the chest with an unsteady forefinger. 'They've bought you, haven't they, *Mr Horton*?'

181

'Nobody's bought me.'

'I thought we were on the same side. That's why I came down to London to see you. But I was wrong. You're one of them.'

'One of whom?'

'One of the bastards who—' He stopped and stared at me for a moment, then mumbled, 'I'm saying nothing.'

'You were eager enough to speak last time.'

'That was before you helped the Charnwoods get rid of Wingate.'

'Nobody got rid of him. His death was an accident.'

'It was about as accidental as this.' He tapped the Remembrance Day poppy pinned to his lapel. The war, once again, still fresh in his mind. Why? What did he mean?

I was about to ask when the landlord appeared at our end of the bar, replenished Duggan's beer and rum, then looked questioningly at me. I ordered a scotch and paid for all three drinks, but got no thanks from my companion. 'I'm certain Max didn't kill Charnwood,' I said slowly. 'I'd like to clear his name, even if it is too late to help him. I'm in nobody's pay and nobody's pocket. I've no idea what circles Charnwood moved in, but—'

'Circles!' Duggan choked on a mouthful of beer, then said between coughs: 'If you . . . really don't know . . . what it's all about . . . count yourself lucky.'

His reaction jogged my memory. I took out the anonymous letter Diana had given me for safe-keeping and showed Duggan the contents, then watched as his jaw dropped and his eyes widened. 'Sent to Charnwood's sister and daughter in Venice. A pair of concentric circles on a sheet of paper. Nothing else. No explanation. Just this . . . symbol. His sister seemed . . . alarmed by it.'

'Well she might be.'

'Why?'

He glanced around, then lowered his voice. 'Put it away, for God's sake.'

'Very well.' I slid the letter back into my jacket. 'But my question stands.'

'It'll have to. I shan't answer it.'

'Why not?'

'Because the less you know the better. Ignorance is bliss.'

'You didn't sing that song six weeks ago. You were eager to recruit any ally you could, as I recall.'

'Wingate might have been a witness. I was eager to find out

182

what he knew. You could have led me to him. Instead, you let them shut his mouth for good.'

'It wasn't like that.'

'So you say.'

'I'm telling you the truth.'

He nodded. 'Maybe you are. But I can't be sure, you see. I can't be absolutely sure.'

'Neither can I. We'll just have to trust each other, won't we?'

'Trust?' He gaped at me. 'You must be joking.'

'No. But, if you prefer to be persuaded some other way . . .'

His gaze narrowed. 'Are you threatening me, Mr Horton?'

'Only with the consequences of your own past. Does the editor of the *Advertiser* know about your spot of bother on Clapham Common seventeen years ago? Does the landlord of this pub? Or the respectable widow you no doubt lodge with? Or anybody in this tight-knit gossipy little town?'

'No,' he murmured. 'They don't.'

'Well, I'm sure you'd like to keep it that way.'

'So I would.'

'Then all you have to do is talk to me about Charnwood.'

He drew on his cigarette, suppressed a cough with evident difficulty and said: 'It's blackmail, is it?'

'Blackmailers want money, Duggan. I only want information.'

'How did you find out about Clapham Common?'

'You're still remembered in Fleet Street.'

'Am I? Well, trust my fellow journalists to get the story wrong. It was a trumped-up charge. If anybody was buggered that night, it was me. I was fitted up good and proper.' Seeing my sceptical look, he added: 'You don't believe me. But you would if you understood.'

'Make me understand.'

He ground his teeth and glared at me while smoke and drunken chatter swirled around us. Then he said: 'All right. Have it your own way. I'll talk. But not here. Not anywhere in Alnwick. Even the gutters have ears in this town.'

'I have a car. We can drive out onto the moors.'

'Make it the coast. I'll feel safer there.'

'Very well. Though I'm sure there's no real need to—'

'There's need!' He fixed me with an earnest stare. 'You'll realize that soon enough, take it from me.' In one swallow, he finished his beer. Then he clambered unsteadily from the stool and peered suspiciously through the oblivious throng. 'Let's go,' he muttered. 'Before I change my mind.'

We drove out through a narrow gate in the medieval town wall, Duggan instructing me to head east on the Alnmouth road. On a landscaped rise to our left stood a stone column, with a statue of a stiff-tailed lion glaring down from the top. Noticing me glance up at it, Duggan paused in his licking of a cigarette paper and said: 'The lion's the emblem of the Percy family – the Dukes of Northumberland. They've ruled Alnwick for six hundred years from the castle on the other side of the town. That column was paid for with subscriptions from their tenants. A token of the universal esteem in which they're held.'

'Except by you?' I asked, catching the sarcastic undertone.

'I'm not complaining. The Duke encouraged the editor of the *Advertiser* to take me on when I came out of prison after the war. No other paper would have touched me with a barge-pole.'

'That was generous of him.'

'He did it as a favour for Lord Grey.'

'Viscount Grey, you mean? The former Foreign Secretary?'

'He lives a few miles north of here, at Fallodon.' Duggan looked round at me and frowned. 'An Old Wykehamist, now I come to think of it. Like yourself.'

'Before my time. Long before.' Even so, the famous statesman's reserved reputation was known to me. He hardly seemed a likely benefactor for George Duggan, as my expression must have implied.

'Doubtful, are we, Mr Horton? Reckon I'm shooting a line?'

'Why should Lord Grey want to help you?'

'Because he realized I'd been hard done by.'

'You're saying he believed you were innocent?'

'Suspected I was, yes. Feared I was. Feared what that meant, as well, I shouldn't wonder.'

'What did it mean?'

But for answer Duggan only lit his cigarette, coughed through a few initial puffs, then said: 'We'll be in Alnmouth soon enough. There's a turning that leads down to the beach. Watch out for it.'

And so I was made to wait a little longer, till we had reached the village built on the long sandy spit at the mouth of the river Aln, driven down to the edge of the dunes and tramped out onto the beach, where a keen wind blew in from the North Sea to snatch the words from our lips and toss them up into the blue salt-scoured air, where we could be heard by no-one and where Duggan felt safe at last.

'I was a different man twenty years ago, Mr Horton. I suppose we all were. But I've changed more than most. Those who worked with me on *The Topical* could tell you that. Blame prison. And the war. For me, it was the same thing. And for the same reason.'

'What reason?'

'Charnwood.' He flicked the remnant of his cigarette out across the sand and thrust his hands deep into his pockets. 'God, how I wish I'd never even heard the bloody man's name.'

'How did you first hear of him?'

'In Vienna. On the twentieth of July, 1914. Oh yes, I remember the time and place. There's no danger of me forgetting.' He heaved a long sigh that dissolved into an expectorant cough, then pushed his shoulders back and resumed. 'I'd been with *The Topical* eight years by then. Since before Lord Northcliffe bought the paper. He tried to turn it into another *Daily Mail*, but never quite succeeded. All newspaper proprietors have a touch of megalomania, but in Northcliffe's case it was a full-blown Napoleon complex. Fortunately, I didn't see much of him. I was forever off to one European capital or another, reporting on the latest international crisis. They were flaring up like fires in a drought-stricken forest. In the Balkans worst of all. But I never doubted they'd be beaten out. None of the diplomats and politicians I interviewed over the years really wanted a war. So, why should there be one?'

'I've always understood the Germans were itching for a scrap.'

He grunted. 'Then you don't understand much. Still, why should you? It's a comforting enough thought to peddle if you're trying to account for ten million dead. Blame it all on Kaiser Bill.'

'Who would you blame it on, then?'

As he glanced at me, a strange quiver halfway between a grin and a scowl crossed his lips. Then he looked straight ahead and said: 'While you were bullying fags at Winchester, Mr Horton, Europe was arranging itself into two armed camps. Neither camp wanted to fight *or* lose face. It's a difficult trick to pull off time after time, but it could have been done. It should have been done.'

'But you're going to tell me why it wasn't?'

'Yes. I am.'

'And this has something to do with Charnwood?'

185

'Something? Yes, I reckon you could say it does. I reckon—' He shook his head irritably. 'Just listen, will you? Close your mouth and open you ears.'

It was as much as I could do not to respond in kind, but I knew insults would draw nothing from this man. He had agreed to speak. But he meant to speak on his terms, terms I was bound to accept. 'Very well,' I said softly.

'Right. This is how it was. There were more Serbs in the Austro-Hungarian Empire than there were in Serbia itself. So, Emperor Franz Josef and his advisers feared revolution within their borders – especially in Bosnia – if Serbia grew more powerful. Maybe even if Serbia simply continued to exist. But what could they do? An attack on Serbia meant war with Russia. Germany would support Austria, but then France would support Russia. And if Germany attacked France, Britain would come to her aid. Result: world war. Besides, even if they thought they'd finish on the winning side in such a war, where was the pretext to start one? Where was the just and honourable cause?

'Even you must know the answer. The assassination of Franz Josef's heir, the Archduke Franz Ferdinand, in Sarajevo on the twenty-eighth of June, 1914. I was despatched to Vienna next day to report on the funeral and its diplomatic repercussions. They seemed pretty obvious. A Serb student had fired the fatal shot. If he'd been put up to it by the Serbian government, the Emperor would have to go to war to avenge his nephew. But nothing was ever obvious in Austro-Hungarian politics. That much I knew from several previous visits. Franz Ferdinand was a difficult and widely disliked man. A lot of people were secretly relieved he was dead. And if the Serbian government could be shown to have clean hands . . .' He shrugged. 'It was a fire no bigger than several before. Containable and extinguishable. The funeral was conspicuously short of weeping and wailing. One member of the Archduke's body-guard committed suicide, ashamed, it was said, at not having died beside him in Sarajevo. But there were no other grand gestures or bloodthirsty speeches. Official reaction was calm and measured. A police investigation was underway in Sarajevo and the results were to be assessed. Meanwhile, no army units were recalled from harvest leave. The Chief of the General Staff and the Minister of War retired to their country estates for the summer. And we journalists lounged around in Viennese cafés, drinking coffee, reading anodyne hand-outs from the Foreign

186

Ministry Press Bureau and wondering what all the fuss was about. Well, on Monday the twentieth of July, I found out.

'I'd got back to my hotel the previous evening to find a note waiting for me. It was from Colonel Alexander Brosch von Aarenau, the former head of Franz Ferdinand's military chancellery. I'd first made his acquaintance during the Bosnian annexation crisis in 1908. He was the Archduke's most loyal and perceptive adviser – even after leaving his chancellery. Together, they'd drawn up far-reaching plans to reform the Empire when Franz Josef died. Brosch had all the tact and subtlety Franz Ferdinand lacked. He was especially good at manipulating the press, at using hacks like me to fly kites for his master. But you couldn't resent it. He was too much the gent for that. Besides, there was always the hope he'd drop some gem into your lap. So, a note from Brosch wasn't to be ignored. This one was an urgent scrawl asking to meet me on one of the bridges over the Danube Canal at midnight. It was completely out of character. You might find Brosch smoking a cigar and strolling around the Belvedere Palace at three in the afternoon. But skulking on bridges at midnight? Never. Or so I'd have said. But the summons was there, in his own hand. So, puzzled as I was, I went.

'He was waiting for me when I arrived, wearing mufti and looking, well, if not furtive, then certainly cautious. I'd not seen him since the funeral. He'd been more obviously upset than most of the other mourners, as you'd expect, but now . . . there was something more than grief troubling him. His manner was . . . strange, disturbing. But he wanted to talk, so, like a good reporter, I listened. He led me on a circuitous route towards St Stephen's Cathedral, using narrow empty streets I hardly knew. Even so, he kept looking over his shoulder, as if he was afraid we were being followed. At first, I thought he was being ridiculously suspicious. But only at first. Soon, I was looking over *my* shoulder too.

'Brosch started by telling me a state secret. The Joint Council of Ministers had met that afternoon and agreed the wording of an ultimatum to be delivered to Serbia on Thursday, requiring an answer within forty-eight hours. The terms of the ultimatum were intended to be unacceptable. He had no doubt Serbia would reject them. And that would mean war within a week. I could hardly believe it. He was handing me the scoop to end all scoops. And why? Because there was more to it. Much more.

' "Why are you confiding in me, Colonel?" I asked.

' "Because you are the only English journalist in Vienna I trust,"
he replied in his piping voice. "I need your help. And you need
mine. You heard of Major Köszegi's suicide?" I said I had. "A
good man. We cannot afford such losses. He came to me the day
after the funeral to confess his small part in the conspiracy. And
to repent of it."

' "What conspiracy?" I asked.

' "The Archduke's murder," he replied.

' "Köszegi was working for the Serbians?"

' "No," said Brosch. "The Serbs did not kill him, Duggan." '

' "Who did, then?"

' "A secret international organization. It calls itself the Concentric Alliance. It is run by an Englishman. That is why I have
come to you. I need to find out as much about him as I can, before
it is too late. His name is—" '

Duggan broke off and stopped, then turned slowly to look at
me. Recollection seemed to have restored a glint to his eyes, a
hint of vigour to his bearing. I knew who he was about to name.
In my pocket was a piece of paper with two concentric circles
drawn on it. In my mind were Charnwood's words as he spun a
five-shilling piece on his desk. '*A circle and a straight line may be
the same thing, depending on your point of view.*' The circle of his
power. The straight line of a bullet's flight. Here, on an empty
beach in Northumberland. And there, on a crowded street in
Sarajevo. 'I don't believe it,' I said.

'That's what I said to Brosch,' Duggan replied. ' "I don't believe
it." And that's what he'd said to Köszegi. But he changed his mind.
And so did I. Now it's your turn.'

'It can't be true.'

'But it is. True as I'm standing here, Mr Horton, and you're
standing there. True as Brosch said it. "His name is Fabian
Charnwood." '

A man throwing sticks for his dog was approaching from the village
end of the beach. Catching sight of him, Duggan turned round and
began walking hard in the opposite direction. I followed, struggling
as much to keep pace with him as to order the questions I wanted
to ask in my mind. Charnwood responsible for the assassination
in Sarajevo and hence for the Great War; for the three miserable
years Max and I had spent in Macedonia; for the shattered reason
of my brother Felix; and for the lost lives of all the men listed on

188

all the memorials in all the lands the war had touched: it was not possible, not credible, not—

'Brosch told Köszegi to pull himself together and stop talking nonsense. Where was the proof? What was the motive? Köszegi tried to answer. He'd been enlisted in the conspiracy by Brosch's successor as head of Franz Ferdinand's military chancellery, Colonel Karl von Bardolff.'

'*Karl* von Bardolff?' I interjected, recalling the old man in the white képi on Vasaritch's yacht.

'Yes. What about it?'

'It's just. . . Is he still alive?'

'Probably. Why?'

Still alive. Consorting, if he was the same man, with a Frenchman, an Englishman and a Yugoslav. Or was Vasaritch actually a Serb? '*He calls himself a Yugoslav,*' Faraday had said. '*But what does that mean?*' 'I'm sorry,' I said. 'Carry on.'

'Bardolff exploited Köszegi's doubts about Franz Ferdinand's plans for the Empire after his uncle's death. An end to Hungarian autonomy. A rooting out of Jews, Freemasons and liberals. Appeasement of the Slavic population. Since Franz Josef was well into his eighties, all this might be just around the corner. And Köszegi liked the sound of none of it, especially the assault on Hungarian rights. He put loyalty to his homeland, Hungary, above loyalty to any prince. He agreed to play his part for patriotic reasons. Bardolff was chairman of the committee responsible for security during the Sarajevo visit and explained it would be deliberately lax. Assassins would be on hand to kill the Archduke during his drive through the town. All Köszegi had to do, as a member of his body-guard, was notice nothing and prevent nothing. The assassination would be blamed on Serbia and the Empire would be spared an unthinkable future. Köszegi joined the conspiracy.'

'I don't understand. Why should Charnwood be involved in a plot to protect Hungarian rights?'

'Because they were irrelevant to the plot's true purpose. As Köszegi found out – too late. The night after the assassination, one of the other members of the body-guard got drunk and goaded Köszegi with the truth. Franz Ferdinand hadn't been killed to save Hungary. He'd been killed to spark off a world war. The conspirators had acted on behalf of an organization called the Concentric Alliance. Their motive was money. And Fabian

Charnwood was going to give them money – lots of it – out of the profits he'd make from the war they'd set in motion.'

'I still don't understand. What profits? How were they to be realized?'

'Köszegi didn't know. And he didn't want to know. He was an accessory to murder. And the ideals he thought justified the crime were a sham. For him, that was enough. The day after confessing to Brosch, he shot himself. It was only then Brosch began to take his allegations seriously. He'd always had doubts about Bardolff's integrity. And the failure of security in Sarajevo was undeniable. Could something more sinister than incompetence have been at work? He began to ask questions, to prod and probe wherever he could. He went to Sarajevo and enquired into the circumstances of the assassination. And the more he discovered, the more he came to believe what Köszegi had told him. There were seventy thousand troops camped outside the city on the twenty-eighth of June. It was their manoeuvres Franz Ferdinand had gone to Bosnia to see. The Bosnian Governor, General Potiorek, could have lined the streets with them during the Archduke's visit. That's what his predecessor had done for the Emperor's visit in 1910. He could have called in the secret police and had all dissidents and foreigners expelled from the city – as also done in 1910. But he chose to do neither. When the Archduke and his wife drove into Sarajevo with him that Sunday morning, a bomb was thrown at them, but it missed, injuring an aide-de-camp. The party went on to the Town Hall and had lunch there. The Archduke asked Potiorek if he thought any more bombs would be thrown. Potiorek said no. But what was his answer worth? He should have urged the Archduke to remain at the Town Hall until troops could be called in to protect him. But he didn't. Instead, he stuck rigidly to the programme. Or would have, but for the Archduke's wife insisting they visit the injured aide-de-camp in hospital straight after lunch. That meant a change of route. Strangely enough, though, nobody told the chauffeur. He followed the original route and pulled up sharply when Potiorek pointed out the error, exactly opposite the spot where one of the assassins, Princip, was waiting with a loaded revolver. He stepped forward and shot the Archduke, then his wife. She died instantly, the Archduke a few minutes later.'

'What did Brosch do when he found all this out?'

'He went to see Potiorek and asked him to explain his actions.

But Potiorek didn't answer. He merely drew a pair of concentric circles on a piece of paper and pushed it across his desk. He must have thought Brosch was either a member of the Concentric Alliance or well enough aware of its existence to be intimidated by the suggestion that it approved of what had happened. And he was right. Until he left Sarajevo, Brosch pretended he was one of them. He calculated that, if they were prepared to assassinate an archduke, they wouldn't hesitate to kill a colonel. Potiorek's use of their symbol had convinced him the Concentric Alliance was real – and powerful.'

'Hold on,' I protested, dragging at Duggan's elbow to slow him down. 'You're saying Potiorek was in on it too?'

'Of course.'

'But he was in the same car. The bomb could easily have killed him as well as the Archduke.'

'According to Brosch, Potiorek certainly wasn't the self-sacrificial type. His theory was that the general thought professional marksmen would be used. Young hot-heads throwing bombs must have come as a nasty shock. But, by the time he realized the dangers—'

'*Young hot-heads*. Exactly. The assassins – Princip and the rest – were genuine Bosnian nationalists, armed and trained by Serbia. Wasn't that established beyond doubt years ago?'

'Yes. It was. Under interrogation, they confessed to being agents of the Serbian secret society, the Black Hand. And the leader of the Black Hand, Colonel Dimitrievitch, was also head of the intelligence service of the Serbian General Staff. On his orders, Princip and two of the others were smuggled into Bosnia in late May, equipped with bombs, pistols and prussic acid to take if they were arrested. Four accomplices were waiting for them in Sarajevo, making seven in all. When the day came, they posted themselves along the route of the procession and waited for their chance. Six of them were arrested immediately after the assassination. Those who had prussic acid duly swallowed it. But it had no effect. Probably because they'd been given plain water instead. They were intended to live, to stand trial, to confess their loyalty to Serbia.'

'But . . . to achieve that . . . Charnwood would have had to . . .'

'Have members of the Concentric Alliance working inside the Black Hand. Yes, Mr Horton. You're beginning to grasp the scale of this conspiracy. That's what concentricity means. One closed

191

circle, surrounded by another, surrounded by yet another. And one man at their common centre.'

'Planning to provoke a world war?'

'So Brosch believed. So I've come to believe.'

'But why? Why would he do it?'

'Neither of us could imagine an adequate motive. And we didn't have time to debate the matter. You see, Brosch returned to Vienna wondering if he should trust his own suspicions. After all, whatever had happened in Sarajevo, there were no sabres rattling in Vienna. Not enough to be sure of the outcome, anyway. If there was no war, the conspiracy had failed. And he misread the signs like the rest of us. He thought compromise was in the air. Only when he learned the outcome of the Joint Council of Ministers' secret meeting on the nineteenth did he realize it wasn't.'

'So he came to you for help?'

'He had nowhere else to turn. An English journalist was about the only form of life he could be sure wasn't a party to the conspiracy. And he needed information about Charnwood. He'd met him a couple of times at Trade Ministry receptions. Knew of him vaguely as an international business-man. But he had to find out more – and quickly.'

'Through you?'

'Through *The Topical*. I told him I'd do what I could. I wasn't sure I believed him, but I knew I had to follow it up. The allegations were amazing – and frightening. If it was true, we had about a week to avert a catastrophe. If not, it was still a hell of a good story.'

'What did you do?'

Duggan stopped in his tracks and stared at me. 'Not enough, Mr Horton. It happened, didn't it? The catastrophe wasn't averted. The roof did fall in. On all of us.' He shivered. 'Let's go back to the car. It's getting cold out here. Besides, I need a fag. And I'll never light one in this wind.' We started back towards the edge of the dunes. 'I cabled *The Topical*'s London office, asking them to send me everything they had on Charnwood. While I was waiting for the reply, I tried to track down any connections he might have in Vienna. I drew a blank. The British Embassy didn't want to know. And when the answer came back from London on Tuesday, it told me precious little. Charnwood was a reputable international financier. His father had run a munitions company which Charnwood had since sold. Well, munitions suggested an interest in warfare, but even that had lapsed. There was nothing to go on.

'I met Brosch that evening. He was disappointed I'd found out so little – and even more anxious than before. The ultimatum was to be delivered to the Serbian Foreign Ministry by the Austro-Hungarian ambassador in Belgrade at 6 p.m. on Thursday. Forty-eight hours later, Austria-Hungary would be at war with Serbia. And pretty soon half of Europe would be at war with the other half. Brosch pleaded with me to do something. Anything. I suggested *The Topical* might be more helpful if I could tell them the terms of the ultimatum in advance. But Brosch said his informant in the Joint Council would be identified if that happened and so would he. They'd both be as good as dead, with nothing to show for it. Besides, he was no traitor. If war came, he'd fight for his country. But while there was a chance of averting war, we had to try, for humanity's sake, to—' Duggan stopped and shook his head, then sent up a shower of sand with a sudden violent kick. 'For humanity's sake! I ask you. He said that to me. A bloody journalist. What do I know about humanity?'

'As much as anyone, I suppose.'

He looked at me sharply, as if uncertain whether I meant it or not. Then he grunted and walked on. 'He convinced me. Or I convinced myself. It makes no difference now. I decided I had to do my bit for mankind. Charnwood held the key. And he was in England. So, I left Vienna next day and headed for home, hoping I could persuade my editor to back my judgement, hoping I could discover enough in a few short days to expose the conspiracy.

'I reached London on Thursday afternoon, with just a few hours to go before the ultimatum was delivered. I went straight to *The Topical* headquarters in Shoe Lane and got in to see the editor, Jack Glenister, at about four o'clock. He wanted to know why I'd left Vienna, so I told him. Everything. The whole story. The complete unprovable allegation. With the exception of Brosch's name. Well, I could see he didn't believe it. And sitting there, in his comfortable Fleet Street office, I couldn't blame him. I tried my damnedest to convince him. I pleaded. I cajoled. I crawled. The last seemed to make the biggest impression. He knew I was no boot-licker. So, he made me an offer. If my story about the ultimatum turned out to be true, he'd give me two juniors and a long week-end to run Charnwood to earth. It was as much as I

193

could reasonably expect. I accepted. We agreed to meet again at noon the next day, Friday the twenty-fourth of July.

'By then, news of the ultimatum had broken. It *had* been delivered at six o'clock. And its terms *were* so severe that rejection was inevitable. I went back to see Glenister. But there was a surprise waiting for me. The Chief was with him. Northcliffe. And he did all the talking.

' "You've been overdoing it, Duggan," he said. "You've been in Vienna too long. Here in London, it doesn't look the thing to start traducing patriotic Englishmen when we're on the brink of war. God knows, we'll have a hard enough job stopping the government ratting on its commitments without chasing after imaginary conspiracies."

'I told him it wasn't imaginary. I repeated the whole story. But it did no good. His other papers were bellowing for German blood and he didn't want *The Topical* stepping out of line. He grew impatient. Then downright angry.

' "Drop this, Duggan! Drop this now!" he roared. "Or I'll make sure you never work in Fleet Street again." I didn't back down. And I wasn't prepared to drop it. He left, growling darkly about my future. But everybody's future was at stake. For once, mine didn't seem so very important.

'After he'd gone, Glenister tried to placate me. "See reason, George," he said. "I had to consult the Chief. Just as well I did. For both of us. Now, he thinks – and so do I – that you're just the man to do a piece on the dispute in the Scottish coalfield. We need somebody to go up there and see whether the miners are likely to put King and country before the minimum wage."

'I was going to be got out of the way. Packed off to Scotland, about as far from Vienna as possible. The tactics were obvious. And so was the choice. Give up. Or go on. Regardless of the consequences.'

We reached the car and climbed in. Duggan stared straight ahead through the wind-screen at the wide expanse of beach and sky, fumbling with a cigarette paper and breathing hard.

'What did you do?' I prompted gently.

'Mmm?' He jerked his head round, then grimaced. 'I went on, of course. Bloody fool that I was. I told Glenister I'd forget the Charnwood story and go up to Scotland after the week-end. He was all smiles when I left. Well pleased with his day's work.' Duggan opened his tobacco-tin and transferred some of the

194

contents to the paper. 'But fooling Glenister was easy. The question was: how to go on? Without the resources of *The Topical*, I was on my own. I knew next to nothing about the business world. And absolutely nothing about Fabian Charnwood. I spent most of the rest of that day walking round the City, wondering what to do. I went to a pub near St Paul's where a bloke on the *Financial Times* I knew slightly used to drink. He was there. And happy to talk. He'd heard of Charnwood Investments and its enigmatic founder. But that was literally all. He couldn't tell me anything.' Duggan administered a practised lick to the paper and rolled it round the tobacco, picking off the surplus flakes and letting them fall back into the tin. Then he took out his matches and lit the cigarette. The predictable explosion of coughs followed. But the smoke seemed to relax him. He leant back in the seat. 'The forty-eight hours were already more than half gone. And what did I have to show for them? Sod all. That's what.

'Next morning, after tossing and turning most of the night in my hotel room, I took a train down to Dorking, determined to beard Charnwood in his lair. I'd got the address from *Who's Who*. I needn't tell you what Amber Court is like, need I? You know the place better than I do. My luck was in. In one sense, anyway. Charnwood was there. And he agreed to see me. Before I knew what was happening, I was in his study, looking at him across his desk. Such a mild, inoffensive, civilized man. I'd expected some sort of . . . monster. But he wasn't that. At least, he didn't look it.

' "A matter of desperate urgency, Mr Duggan?" he said. That was the phrase I'd used to get past the butler. "What can it be?"

'I didn't know what to say. If I was right, he wouldn't admit it. If I was wrong, he'd think I was mad. All I'd succeeded in doing was putting my head in a noose. I babbled about being a journalist who was investigating the possibility that international arms dealers might be responsible for the Sarajevo assassination. I asked him, as something of an expert, what his view of the possibility was. He said they'd have had neither means nor motive. He suggested I was over-wrought. And I might have believed him. But for the look in his eyes. He was watching me, calmly and curiously. He was almost *amused* by me. But there was nothing to laugh at. Unless . . .'

'Unless you were right and he knew you couldn't prove it?'

'Yes. That's what I thought afterwards. He should have refused to see me. Or had me thrown out. Instead, he just toyed with me.

Dangled me on a line for a few minutes. Then threw me back in the water. I left wishing I'd never gone there.'

'What did you do next?'

'Played my last card. I wasn't going to achieve anything on my own. That was obvious. And *The Topical* wasn't going to help me. So, I decided to try the Foreign Office.'

'Lord Grey, you mean?'

'Sir Edward Grey, as he was then. Foreign Secretary since Adam was a lad. A man of flexible mind but fixed habits. And those habits were well known in Fleet Street. The week-end wouldn't find him pacing his office in Whitehall. Oh no. He'd be at his cottage beside the Itchen in Hampshire, fishing for trout and savouring the bird-song. More to the point, he'd be on his own. I'd have a chance to put my case to him without being interrupted. And if I could convince *him* . . .

'The journey seemed to take for ever. Three slow trains across the Surrey and Hampshire countryside on a sweltering hot Saturday afternoon, with long waits in between at Guildford and Farnham. I finally reached Itchen Abbas at about half past four. The ticket collector at the station directed me to Grey's cottage, buried in clematis and honeysuckle down by the water-meadows, at the end of a long tree-lined lane. It really was like a picture post-card. I found him in the garden, dozing in a camp-chair as if he hadn't a care in the world. When I told him I was a journalist, he looked worried, but I assured him I wasn't there for an exclusive interview. I reckon my manner must have made that obvious. He asked me inside, made some tea and listened to everything I had to say. What he made of it I couldn't tell. He had the perfect diplomat's demeanour – patient but impenetrable.

' "You realize what this means?" I asked.

' "I appreciate its potential significance, Mr Duggan," he replied. "But you have nothing to worry about. I saw the German Ambassador, Prince Lichnowsky, before leaving London this morning and asked him to suggest to his government that Britain and Germany join in seeking an extension to the time-limit on Austria-Hungary's ultimatum so that suitable arrangements for international mediation of the dispute can be made."

' "They'll never agree."

' "Why should they not? It is a very reasonable proposal."

' "Because the Concentric Alliance has agents everywhere. They'll make sure it comes to nothing."

196

' "Oh dear me, Mr Duggan. You really must not be so suspicious. Leave this to those trained in handling such matters. They will not let you down."

'I suppose I must have seemed deranged. At the very least, deluded. An organization he'd never heard of, with fingers in every pie. Well, it's the stuff of paranoia, isn't it? But he was kind and courteous to a fault. He suggested I stay at the village inn overnight and call on him again in the morning. He expected to have good news for me by then. He saw me off with a smile and a wave of his hat.

'I did as he'd suggested. There was damn all else I could do. My best chance seemed to lie in staying close to him. But even then it wasn't much of a chance. I realized that more and more during the evening as I stared into my beer at the Plough Inn, listening to the innocent country-folk gossiping and arguing and never once mentioning Sarajevo or the ultimatum Serbia had probably already rejected.

'Early next morning, I went back to the cottage. Sir Edward looked different. More sombre. More pessimistic. "It seems my proposal was not accepted, Mr Duggan," he said. "Nor was Serbia's response to the ultimatum. Austria-Hungary has severed diplomatic relations and is believed to be mobilizing. But never fear. I have just been speaking to my permanent under-secretary on the telephone. He will be circulating a proposal to all the European powers for an ambassadors' conference in London to address the problem."

' "Another proposal?" I said, unable to conceal my bitterness.

' "It is the best we can do," he replied. "I shall be returning to London this afternoon in order to devote all my efforts to forging an agreement."

' "And the Concentric Alliance?"

' "Is not a concept I can afford to dwell upon. I am sorry, Mr Duggan, but there it is."

'I left in a daze and caught the earliest train back to London. Sir Edward wasn't on it. He was sticking to a more leisurely pace. One I couldn't see leading us out of the web Charnwood had woven. I went straight from Waterloo to Shoe Lane. It seemed the best way of finding out the latest developments. But nobody at *The Topical* knew much – beyond what Sir Edward had already told me. There was one thing, though. Somebody had telephoned several times, trying to speak to me. They hadn't left their name or any kind of message. Just a number. On the Mansion House exchange. That meant the City, which should have been dead as a dodo on a Sunday afternoon. But, when I rang, there was an answer. An anonymous male voice, speaking hardly above a murmur.

' "You've been asking about Fabian Charnwood, I understand," he said. "And not getting many answers. But I can give you some. At a price." I asked who he was. "No names. No pack-drill. But I have a lot of . . . circular knowledge. Take my meaning?" I said I did and asked if we could meet. "The bandstand on Clapham Common. Eleven o'clcok tonight. If you're interested, be there."

'So, I went. And you can guess what happened, can't you? A shadowy figure, hat pulled well down over his eyes, was waiting at the bandstand. He told me to follow him to a quiet spot. We took a path that led into some bushes. Suddenly, I was grabbed from behind and held by two men. A third man pulled my trousers down. A grinning boy appeared in front of me, stripping off a naval uniform. When he was naked, he crouched down on all fours. I was pushed on top of him. Then there were flashing torches, whistles, shouts. And the police had hold of me. But the boy ran off. They let him go. They had what they wanted.

'By the time I was brought before the magistrates next morning, Grey's proposal for an ambassadors' conference had collapsed. Nobody on the bench was interested in my protestations of innocence. I was remanded in custody and bundled off to Wandsworth Prison. And I knew better than to try and make anybody listen to me there. My case was heard the following Tuesday: the fourth of August. By then, the dominoes had begun to fall. Germany and Austria-Hungary were at war with Russia and France. And that night Britain joined in. Anybody who spoke out then wasn't just mad, but guilty of treason. Or, in my case, something even worse. And far more sordid.

'They gave me five years, Mr Horton. And I didn't get any time off for good behaviour. Probably because I didn't behave particularly well. Or perhaps because somebody had a word in a Home Office ear. Either way, I suppose I got off lightly compared with all those poor buggers mown down in Flanders. Don't you reckon?'

'I suppose you did,' I said, thinking of Felix and his vacant blinking face.

'What do you say to a drink? There's a pub in the village with

198

some quiet corners. Not that being overheard matters now. You've just about had the lot.'

The parlour-bar of the Red Lion, Alnmouth, was a warm smoke-filled haven where none of the other customers seemed even slightly interested in the doleful pair we made. Duggan looked weary beyond reviving, even after two brisk rums. I began to regret prising so much from him, began to wish I had left old wounds to heal – for my sake as well as for his. There was such a thing as too much knowledge. I understood that now. All the levity and egotism of my life had drained from my mind, leaving it clearer but bleaker than ever before. It was as if I might never laugh again.

'I came up here in the summer of 1919,' said Duggan. 'Straight after being released. Sir Edward had become Lord Grey and retired from politics to live out his remaining years at Fallodon. I wanted to ask him whether he believed I mightn't have been right after all. He didn't, of course. Or said he didn't. But he did tell me what I'd suspected at the time: that he'd thought I was out of my mind when I burst in on him at Itchen Abbas. He'd encouraged me to stay at the Plough only so he could telephone Lord Northcliffe and ask him what he should do. Northcliffe had said I was harmless but obsessed. He'd advised Grey to ignore me. And so he had. But on one point he couldn't deny I'd subsequently been vindicated. It had come out after the war that his mediation proposal hadn't been passed on by the German Foreign Ministry to Vienna until *after* the expiry of the dead-line. Somebody somewhere had been determined to ensure it came to nothing. It didn't convince Grey of the existence of the Concentric Alliance, of course. Nor did my imprisonment, which as a matter of fact he hadn't heard about. Nevertheless, there was something in it all he wasn't happy about. I think that's why he offered to help find me a job. To make amends in some way for not taking me seriously.'

'And you took him up on the offer?'

'Certainly I did. It was about the only one I was likely to get. Fleet Street wasn't going to roll out the red carpet to welcome me back. The *Alnwick Advertiser* was the best I could do. So, I buried myself here, in rural obscurity, and tried to forget. What was the point of remembering? The war had happened. Nothing could change that.'

'What about Brosch?'

'It took a lot of letters to the Austrian Embassy to find out what had happened to him. But I succeeded in the end. He'd done what he'd said he would. At the outbreak of war, he'd taken command of a field regiment on the Galician front. He was killed in action during the Battle of Rava Russka on the sixth of September, 1914. A mercifully early exit, I suppose, although I can't help wondering whether he was hit by enemy fire or . . .'

'A bullet in the back?'

'Something like that. I never named him, even to Grey, but if they *had* known . . . they'd have killed him for certain.'

'They didn't kill you.'

'Dead journalists are more difficult to explain away. If they knew I'd got to Grey, they might have thought my sudden quietus would make him think twice. A *liaison* with a sailor-boy on Clapham Common discredited the message as well as the messenger. Altogether more effective.'

'And they've left you alone ever since?'

'*I've* left *them* alone. I've kept my head down for twelve years. I've been no trouble to anyone.'

'Until now. Why take the risk of contacting me?'

'Because Charnwood's death meant I didn't have so much to fear. And because the circumstances of his death gave me a glimmer of hope that I might still be able to nail the bastards.' He stared at me defiantly, as if the rum were at last bolstering his confidence. 'Well, why not? Since the war, I've rumbled them. Why they did it. What they got out of it. Money, Mr Horton. You've seen how it flowed into the pockets of arms dealers, munitions manufacturers, military and naval suppliers. . . You've seen the war make millionaires as well as widows. Here. And all over Europe. They reaped the profit. Just as they meant to.'

'It doesn't prove they had a hand in Franz Ferdinand's assassination.'

'No. No more than it proves they killed Charnwood. But I'm certain they did.'

'Why? Why should they turn on one of their own?'

'Who knows? Because he knew too much? Because he was putting pressure on them? Maybe his financial problems had forced him to try and call in some old debts. Whatever the reason, I think he was killed by the organization he'd created, leaving your friend to take the blame. In fact, I'm sure of it.' So was I now. No other explanation made sense. But if the Concentric Alliance did exist, it was too powerful for either of us to defeat. Perhaps Charnwood's death demonstrated its ability to crush any individual, however clever, however important. If so, Max was simply an incidental victim who could never be avenged or exonerated. Just as the truth of what Charnwood had done could never be exposed. 'Got what you wanted, Mr Horton? Had all your questions answered?'

'Yes,' I murmured.

'Good. And what are you going to do now you know it all?' Duggan's stare hardened. His eyes focused on me more closely. I gazed back helplessly, unable to disguise my inadequacy – that was merely a mirror of his own. 'As I thought,' he said. 'Just like me. Not a damn thing.'

CHAPTER

ELEVEN

It was almost dark when I dropped Duggan near his lodgings in Alnwick. After all the revelations that had spilled from his lips, I think we were both eager to part. Neither of us relished the strange intimacy the sharing of such a secret gave rise to. It was too late to draw back, of course. We could not unlearn what we knew. But we could at least be rid of each other.

I left Duggan with the impression that I was starting back for London straightaway. But I required one last confirmation of what he had said before I accepted it as wholly true and accepted also my powerlessness to clear Max's name. I required the clinching word of an Old Wykehamist. So I drove north, not south. Seven miles north, through drab and ever darkening countryside to the village of Christon Bank. According to Duggan, Lord Grey lived nearby. And so he did. The postmistress told me Fallodon Hall lay half a mile further on.

There was hardly any light left when I arrived and none at all beneath the thickly planted trees surrounding the house. It was a solid unpretentious country gentleman's residence, with so few signs of life that I feared its master might be absent. But not so. The maid who answered the door said Lord Grey was at home and, when I asked if an Old Wykehamist might pay his respects, the message soon came back that he was more than welcome.

Sir Edward, Viscount Grey of Fallodon, politician, statesman, ornithologist and fly-fisherman of repute, was a lean gaunt man

202

of about seventy, who greeted me with quavering courtesy beside a roaring fire. The maid had forewarned me of his virtual blindness, which I might not otherwise have guessed at, for he hid it well. There was only a single missed button on his cardigan to give the game away.

'I have few passing visitors in this remote spot, Mr Horton,' he said after ordering tea and showing me to an armchair. 'It was good of you to think of calling. I still manage to get down to Winchester at least once a year. Do you re-visit the old place often?'

'Not as often as I should like, sir. When I was last there, I took a look at War Cloister. A most tasteful memorial. I believe you laid the foundation stone.' (Not in vain had I perused the copies of *The Wykehamist* so stubbornly sent to Max and me over the years.)

'I did, yes.'

'All too many of my contemporaries are listed there.'

'Are they? My condolences, Horton. Yours was an unfortunate generation.'

'Indeed we were. As has become apparent to me only recently.'

'*Recently*? I don't quite . . .'

'Following the death in August this year of the financier, Fabian Charnwood.'

'Charnwood, you say? I don't think I . . .'

'You remember, sir. I'm sure you do. You see, I've been speaking to George Duggan. And he's been telling me the most extraordinary story. I gather you lent him a helping hand some years ago.'

'I may have. But as to any yarn he's been spinning you, well, I'm sure you know how imaginative journalists can be.'

'Yes, sir. But I believe this particular yarn. And so, I rather think, do you.'

Grey frowned. 'If Duggan has told you what it seems he has, I confess myself surprised. I had understood his lips to be sealed on the subject.'

'Only while Charnwood lived.'

'And your interest in this matter is . . . ?'

'Personal. The man charged with Charnwood's murder – who's also since died – was a friend of mine. A Wykehamist too, by the name of Max Wingate. We fought together. In the war. As you said, ours *was* an unfortunate generation.' Grey winced, as if pained by guilty remembrance. I knew then, as he passed a hand across his face and thought perhaps of how much harder he should have striven in 1914 to stem the tide, that he would tell me as much as he could. No secrets would be allowed to stand between one Wykehamist and another.

Tea had long since come and gone by the time I finished explaining what had brought me to Lord Grey's door. He listened patiently, nodding sympathetically at intervals, with his eyes closed more often than they were open. He did not once interrupt, but sat forward in his chair, hunched in concentration. And then, before I could put to him the questions I had in mind, he answered them.

'You will want to know if Duggan's account of our meeting is accurate. Well, it is. I used the cottage at Itchen Abbas as a week-end retreat from the cares of Whitehall. It meant I could fish the Itchen, as I had at Winchester. And the reach by the cottage was . . . quite sublime. But it was not much of a retreat that week-end in July 1914. Not with Nicolson on the telephone from the office every five minutes. And then Duggan appearing in the garden. Perhaps I should have stayed in London. He would not have been able to pour out his allegations to me then. Which might have saved him from a prison sentence and me . . . well, a deal of heart-searching, shall we say? *And* I might have discovered that my mediation proposal had not been passed on to Vienna until after the expiry of their dead-line. Duggan was quite right in one sense. There was treachery everywhere. I had no idea how much. If I had understood the full extent of it, I would have. . . But what use are regrets now? I did my best. I was not to know others were doing their worst. Nevertheless, in the long cold watches of the night, I do sometimes wonder what would have happened . . . whether it might all have turned out differently . . . if I had listened to Duggan.

'You will also want to know if I think there really was a Concentric Alliance. Well, I do not know. Obviously, I did not think so at the time. But, since the war ended, so much that is ambiguous and contradictory about the events in Sarajevo has emerged that I am no longer certain of anything. I looked into the matter in some detail when I composed my memoirs a few years ago. And I came across some very disturbing facts. For instance, one of Princip's accomplices, a boy called Cabrinovitch, was known to the Sarajevo police. He had been expelled from the country in 1912. Two days before the assassination, he was seen and recognized. But the Chief of Police ordered that he be left alone. One cannot help wondering why. Then there is the question of the prussic acid. Why would the Black Hand have wanted its agents to live long enough to confess, given that Serbia could not possibly hope to win a war against Austria-Hungary – or even survive it intact? It is incomprehensible. Certainly they paid a heavy price, whatever the reason. The officer who trained Princip and Cabrinovitch and gave them their phials of unreliable poison, Major Tankositch, was killed in action in 1915. And the leader of the Black Hand, Colonel Dimitrievitch, was executed in 1917 for plotting to assassinate the Serbian Prince Regent. The evidence against him was flimsy to say the very least. Oddly enough, one of his co-defendants was a youth named Mehmedbasitch, the only one of the Sarajevo assassins who escaped. Although sentenced to twenty years' imprisonment, he was released before he had served much more than one. Treachery everywhere, Horton. Do you see what I mean? But to what end? At whose behest? I do not know. And I do not see how it would be possible to know. The most I can say is what I wrote in my memoirs. Have you by any chance read them?'

'I'm afraid not, sir.'

'No matter. I remember the exact words I used. They still seem apposite. *"The world will presumably never be told all that was behind the murder of the Archduke Franz Ferdinand. Probably there is not, and never was, any one person who knew all there was to know."* '

'Unless it was Fabian Charnwood.'

'As you say. Unless it was Fabian Charnwood. But, if so, he too has since paid the price.'

'Do you think he really was responsible for all of it?'

'To be frank, no. Not because I doubt Duggan's word. He is a well-meaning fellow and believes what he was told. Nor because the facts rule out such a possibility. Clearly, they do not.'

'Why, then?'

'Because any man clever and far-sighted enough to calculate the consequences of Franz Ferdinand's assassination could also have anticipated the horrific and destructive course the war was to take. And surely no man would have deliberately set such mayhem in motion. It would have been . . .' Words seemed to fail him for the moment. Then he composed himself and said: 'Monstrous. Diabolical. Quite simply inconceivable.'

We had talked well into the evening, and when Grey invited me to dine with him and stay the night I did not resist. He was a charming and lonely relic of a bygone age, eager to forget the painful subject I had raised and dwell instead on Winchester as he remembered it more than fifty years ago, serene and reassuring beneath the cloudless skies of his youth. And I was happy to indulge his nostalgic mood, not because he was my host, but because I too felt weighed down by my discoveries. For once, the recondite recesses of Wykehamical recollection were preferable to anything else.

I slept more soundly than I had expected and woke refreshed, the unanswerable questions and impenetrable complexities surrounding Fabian Charnwood's past refined in my mind to an extent that almost rendered them manageable. Breakfast was waiting for me downstairs, but his lordship, the maid informed me, was already out and about; he was not one to lie abed.

I found him by a pond in the grounds, seated on a bench in threadbare tweeds and a Norfolk hat, tossing bread to a quacking retinue of ducks. For all their noise, however, he heard me approach and bade me a courteous good morning.

'I must be getting off, sir,' I explained. 'It's a long way back to London.'

'Of course, of course, it's been a pleasure meeting you, Horton.' He rose and we shook hands; his was as cold as marble. 'I hope you didn't find my company last night too boring.'

'Not at all.'

'As to that other matter we discussed... Loyalty to one's friends is an admirable quality. But sometimes it is necessary to let go of the past. And to let those who are gone rest in peace. I think, if you will permit me to say so, that you have done all you can – and all you prudently should – to clear your friend's name.'

'But it hasn't been cleared, has it?'

'No. Except in your own estimation. Which is really all that matters. Take an old man's word for it.' He smiled. 'You have done enough.'

Grey's parting benison lingered in my thoughts as I drove south through the fleeting daylight of a November Sunday. Charnwood was dead. And so was Max. To condemn one was as futile as to exonerate the other. I believed every word Duggan had told me, especially when it came to the circumstances of Charnwood's death. I could not construct an adequate account of them, but that the Concentric Alliance – whatever it was, whoever its members were – had played some part in bringing him down I did not doubt. Poor Max had been their fall guy.

But to prove it was impossible. My faith in his innocence, as Grey had implied, would have to be enough. Even Diana would have to go on believing him guilty. She knew nothing of the Concentric Alliance. Her reaction to their secret symbol demonstrated that, just as Vita's reaction betrayed at least awareness of her brother's activities, if not complicity in them. But Diana was different. To vindicate Max in her eyes would be to brand her father a mass murderer. With her mother among his victims. The sinking of the *Lusitania* was one consequence of Franz Ferdinand's assassination Charnwood could not have anticipated, for if he had . . .

Enough. The choice was simple. I could go straight to Amber Court, forget what I knew and revel in the physical pleasures and material advantages Diana would be willing to bestow on me, justifying my conduct on the grounds that it was too late to help Max and therefore only sensible to help myself. Or I could pursue a hazardous campaign to expose an old but monumental crime, whose principal perpetrator was dead and whose surviving accomplices had shown themselves to be ruthless as well as powerful. In the final analysis, it was not really much of a choice at all.

But at least it could be delayed. I stopped at the George in Stamford for tea, my hopes for something stronger being dashed by a sabbatarian regulation I was too tired to dispute. There, among the potted palms and Sunday-best family gatherings, I made up my mind to head for Letchworth. My father and sister were owed an explanation of events in Venice, maybe also of my intentions towards Diana. Besides, an overnight stop in Letchworth would leave me well placed to visit Felix next day. If I could face him and hold my tongue, then I could be sure my course was set. I could be sure I was going to take the easy way out.

It was nearly nine o'clock when I reached *Gladsome Glade*. My sister greeted me with surprise and a measure of delight, my father with grim-faced indifference. I had written to them from Venice shortly after Max's death, a letter at once hasty and unforthcoming. But for my father at least that was enough. The less he knew of my doings the better he was pleased. And so, within minutes of my arrival, all thoughts of honesty and candour had drained from my mind.

'He doesn't understand you, Guy,' said Maggie when he had taken himself off to bed. 'He never has and he never will.'

'No. I don't suppose he will.'

'What are your plans – for the immediate future?'

'I'm not sure.' I should have told Maggie about Diana then. I might have won from her some form of sisterly approval for what I meant to do. But the creaking of the floorboards in my father's bedroom, the familiar pattern of the paper on the wall beside my chair and the reflections of the firelight in the photographs on the piano conspired to silence me. I belonged here and yet did not. I wanted to speak and yet could not. There, above me, where it had always hung, in a place of honour, was my mother's sampler, its words waiting to accost my gaze. *Wide is the gate, and broad is the way, that leadeth to destruction, and many there be that go in thereat.* 'I thought,' I murmured, 'I might visit Felix tomorrow.'

'Good idea.'

'How is he?'

'Much the same as ever.'

'And who's to blame for that, eh?'

'Why nobody, of course.' She frowned. 'You surely don't think Dad holds *you* responsible. It was . . . an accident of war.'

'If war can be called an accident.'

Her frown deepened. 'I don't understand. What do you mean?'

'Nothing.' I smiled dismissively and lit a cigarette. 'How are things in the teaching world?'

'They could be worse. The government generously agreed to cut our pay by only ten per cent instead of fifteen. I suppose we should be grateful.'

'What do you tell your young charges about the war?' Instantly, I regretted the question. My preoccupation with the subject was beginning to worry her. 'I'm sorry. Forget it. Let's talk about something else.'

But Maggie insisted on answering. 'I tell them it must never happen again, Guy. I tell them it *should* never have happened. What else can I say? They're too young to understand the whys and wherefores. I'm not sure I understand them myself. Do you?'

I stared into the fire for a moment, then tried to shape a carefree grin. 'Of course not. But, then again, I never give them a moment's thought. And, anyway, what would be the point? There's not a single thing I – or anyone else – can do about it now. Is there?'

I was up early enough the following morning to breakfast with Maggie. Thinking a change of scene might do us both good, I suggested we meet for lunch at the Letchworth Hall Hotel. She agreed without hesitation. Clearly, her dedication to the cause of education had been reduced along with her salary.

After a few monosyllabic exchanges with my father, I headed for St Albans. Felix's company promised to be a tonic by comparison. But a surprise awaited me at Napsbury Hospital. Contrary to what my sister believed, Felix was not much the same as ever.

'He had a funny turn over the week-end,' a nurse explained. 'Nothing to worry about. But it would be best if he stayed in the ward. You don't mind seeing him there, do you?'

I did mind, of course. The place stank of stale urine and stewed cabbage. And the patients were either comatose or manically excited, gibbering and gesticulating at the entrance of a stranger. Felix for his part looked pale and subdued, propped up in bed and staring vacantly at the ceiling. My immediate impression was that he had been drugged.

'Hello, Felix,' I said, patting his hand. 'How are you?'

He looked at me as if he could scarcely believe his eyes. 'Gewgaw! How did you get here?'

'I drove.'

'But. . . Where am I?'

'Where you've always been. Napsbury.'

'No, no. That's not true. That's what they've been telling me. But it's a lie. I've been moved. It must have happened Saturday night. They must have slipped something into my cocoa so I wouldn't wake up during the journey.'

'You haven't been on a journey.'

'Oh yes I have. I know I have. The bath gave it away. They didn't think of that. I always have one on Sundays. I suppose they didn't want to change the routine. But they made a mistake. The water, Gewgaw. The water went down the plug-hole the wrong way.' He lowered his voice to a whisper. '*Anti-clockwise.*' Then he glanced suspiciously from side to side and leaned towards me.

209

'Where am I? Australia? Argentina? I know it must be somewhere in the southern hemisphere.'

'You're in Hertfordshire.' But there was such a stricken look of betrayal in his face that I instantly repented of my words. I smiled as reassuringly as I could. 'Never mind, Felix. I know who did this to you.'

'You do?' I nodded and his eyes widened. Then he raised a quivering finger to his lips. 'Sssh! Don't tell, Gewgaw. Don't breathe a word. If you do, they'll be after you as well. And . . . I wouldn't want anything to happen . . . to my little brother, because . . .' He grinned crookedly. 'He's too young to fight.'

Poor Felix. There was no way back from the strange and troubled place the war had taken him to. And whose fault was that? Somebody whose name he had never heard. Somebody my father and sister would never have dreamt of suspecting, far less accusing. Somebody to whom fate had been altogether kinder.

I left Napsbury oppressed by the prickly proximity of madness. By the time I reached Letchworth, this sensation had transmuted itself into a pressing need for a stiff drink. With more than an hour to spare before my appointment with Maggie, I diverted to Willian, a village just south of the town, which had retained, despite absorption by the Garden City, two examples of that phenomenon most detested by the teetotal ideologues of Letchworth: the fully licensed public house. I had regularly walked the mile and a half from the Goddess factory to slake my frustration in one or other of them before returning to *Gladsome Glade*. Indeed, my happiest – or least unhappy – memories of those barren years are associated with the bars of the Fox and the Three Horseshoes. I stopped at the latter, found it as agreeably warm and quiet as I remembered and retreated to a fireside table with a triple scotch.

There I turned over in my mind the harsh realities and consoling advantages of my position. If Max were still alive, I would do all I could to help him, even if it meant confronting the unnumbered forces of the Concentric Alliance. So, at least, I told myself. But Max was dead. And so was Charnwood. I had neither friend to save nor foe to seek. There was Faraday, of course. There were Vasaritch and the sinister guests aboard his yacht. There were all the nameless people who had profited from their involvement in Charnwood's alliance of the great and the greedy. But what were they to me? The best revenge I could devise for what they had done to Max was to take my share – and Max's too – of the fortune I no longer doubted Charnwood had hidden from them. Vita knew more than she would ever tell. Perhaps Diana did too, though clearly not as much as her aunt. Their conversation at the Villa Primavera, which I had eavesdropped on, convinced me that Diana was party to some vital secret. Since her reaction to the Concentric Alliance's symbol proved she was ignorant of its meaning, that secret could only be the whereabouts of Charnwood's money, a secret she was unlikely to disclose to anyone – except her lover.

And I *was* her lover. Half-closing my eyes, I could imagine her turning to look at me as some silk garment slid from her shoulder. Reaching out, I could almost feel the tingling smoothness of her skin. Smiling to myself, I could recall every detail of . . .

I swallowed some scotch and called a halt to my deliberations. To Diana I would return. Of the Concentric Alliance I would say and pretend to know nothing. I took the letter containing their symbol from my pocket, tore it into four and threw the pieces onto the fire. If Diana ever asked for it, I would claim I had lost it. Then I remembered my contract with Max. Such an incriminating document would also have to be destroyed. I drew out my wallet, slid my copy from its pouch, unfolded it, screwed it into a ball and tossed it into the flames. Then I made to do the same with Max's copy.

But, as I unfolded it, a small piece of blue card fluttered out onto the table in front of me. Pausing, I picked it up to examine. It was a theatre ticket, the right-hand side torn, as if by an usherette. A serial number was printed along the left-hand side, with the middle occupied by the remnant of the theatre's name: *Pier The* – on one line, *Bourne* – on the next. Pier Theatre, Bournemouth, obviously. But why should Max have gone to Bournemouth?

Suddenly, a possible reason occurred to my mind. We had spent a forty-eight-hour leave there in August 1915, during initial training with the King's Royal Rifle Corps on Salisbury Plain. And a riotous time we had had, though whether it had included a visit to the Pier Theatre I could not recall. But it had been one last indulgence before a grim awakening in Macedonia, so perhaps Max had chosen it as a hide-out because of its links with our carefree past, just as he had chosen to abandon our car in Winchester because we had first met there in the long ago September of 1910.

Chief Inspector Hornby would have paid handsomely for this clue to Max's movements during the weeks following Charnwood's murder. But now, like so much else, it was irrelevant, a redundant echo of a sundered connection. I screwed up the contract and lobbed it into the fire, leaning forward to scatter the ashes with a poker, then picked up the torn ticket and decided, since it could convey nothing to anyone else, to keep it as a memento. I opened my wallet and was about to slide the ticket in when I noticed some writing on the back. I recognized the hand at once. It was Max's.

26/8/31. Where is H.L.? I stared at the words for several seconds, wondering what they meant. Charnwood had been murdered in the early hours of Saturday the twenty-second of August. The twenty-sixth was therefore the following Wednesday. Max had apparently been in Bournemouth that day, looking for somebody whose initials were H.L. But I knew no such person. Who was he? The Pier Theatre hardly struck me as a likely venue for Sir Harry Lauder. And among our ill-assorted friends and acquaintances I could not think of a single H.L. Where and who or what H.L. had been and might still be I had no way of knowing.

Yet the answer had clearly mattered to Max. Otherwise why would he have kept the ticket enfolded in his copy of our contract? It was surely more than an *aide memoire*. The place, the date and the initials all meant something. They were bound together in his mind. Or had been. Until the day of his death. I thought of the garbled accusations he had flung at me in the last few minutes of his life. '*How much do you know, Guy? How much has she told you?*' I was guilty of an obvious breach of faith, but stood condemned for something worse than seducing Diana. '*Not that it matters,*' Max had roared. '*Ignorance is no excuse.*' But ignorance of what? Not the Concentric Alliance. He had learned nothing of that, I felt certain. Nor the whereabouts of Charnwood's money. He could have had no more inkling than me about its hiding-place.

Something else, then. Something defined by the answer to the question: *Where is H.L.?* Even as I dropped my wallet back into my pocket, with the ticket secreted inside, I knew I would have to find out. At all events, I would have to try. This loose end could not be left to dangle in my thoughts. Before I saw Diana again, I would have to trace it to its beginning. Or fail in the attempt. Either way, the attempt would have to be made.

*   *   *

212

'What do you mean?' demanded Maggie, when I greeted her at the Letchworth Hall Hotel with a glass of ginger-beer and a lame apology for being unable to lunch with her. 'You said you were looking forward to it.'

'So I was. But . . . something's cropped up. I have to leave, I'm afraid. Straightaway.' I shrugged my shoulders and grinned sheepishly. 'I'll pay for your meal.'

She sighed. 'That's not the point.'

'No. I know. I'm sorry. But there it is. I must go.' I pecked her cheek and headed for the exit, only to be halted by her parting enquiry.

'How was Felix?'

'Not good. In fact. . . Not well at all.'

She glared at me suspiciously. 'Did you upset him?'

'No. Of course not. But – ' What was the use of trying to explain? My father would blame Felix's deterioration on me whatever I said. And in her present exasperated mood so would my sister. 'I *have* to go, Maggie. Sorry.'

Bournemouth Promenade five hours later extended a chill and mocking welcome. A steely rain was falling, a ghostly surf sighing on the dark deserted beach. All the worst features of an English seaside resort out of season were distilled in the bleak November night. And the pier was closed, its gates locked, its theatre absorbed within the black outline of buildings clustered at its end. Stooping in the relative shelter of a coin-in-the-slot telescope to light a cigarette, I wondered why I had been so stupid as to come to this God-forsaken spot, where the prospects of learning anything valuable were infinitessimal. I was wasting my time and energy on a fool's errand.

So it still seemed next morning when I stepped out of the Solent Cliffs Hotel and descended to the Promenade beneath a weeping sky. But there was no sense in turning back now. A hunched figure could be discerned in the booth next to the turnstile at the entrance to the pier. I tapped on the window and he slowly detached his gaze from the racing page of his newspaper.

'Is the theatre open?' I nodded towards it.

'Not till Easter, sir.'

'Would there be anybody there who could give me some information?'

'What about, sir?'

'A performance last August.'

'A performance of what, sir?'

'I don't know. That's the information I want.'

He treated me to a prolonged *I Spy Madmen* look, then said: 'Try the Entertainments Officer up at the Town Hall, sir. Mr Oates. He's your man.' And with that his eyes swivelled back to the racing page.

Mr Oates' desk stood in the dusty corner of a large office on the top floor of the Town Hall. At all events, I assumed a desk was to be found somewhere beneath the pile of disordered letters, files, notes and memoranda. But of Mr Oates there was no sign.

'He's just popped out,' announced the woman sitting behind the only occupied desk in the room. She was a pencil-thin creature of indeterminate age, with peroxide blond hair and a large gash of cherry-red lip-stick. 'He said he might be some time.'

'A pity,' I remarked, moving towards her, only to recoil as the sickly fumes emanating from a paraffin stove behind her chair rose to envelop me. 'Perhaps you . . . might be able to help.'

'It's possible, dear.' She smiled coquettishly. 'It's possible.'

'It may seem an odd question, but—'

'Oh, odd questions crop up all the time here. It's not surprising. Some of the staff are *very* odd. Especially Mr Oates.' She ostentatiously crossed her legs and waggled a spindly ankle for my inspection. 'You should be grateful you've got me instead.'

'I'm sure I should be. You, er, know about his work, do you?'

'The little there is to know, yes.'

'Well, I'm trying to find out what was performed at the Pier Theatre last August. Would you happen to—'

'Murder.'

'What?'

'Well, most of the shows Mr Oates books are murder, believe me. I've sat through a few.' Then, seeing me reach into my pocket, she added: 'Oh, I don't mind if I do.'

'Sorry?'

'You were about to offer me a cigarette, weren't you?'

'Er . . . yes. Yes, of course I was.' I had actually been about to show her the ticket. Switching to the other pocket with a sigh, I took out my cigarette case and opened it for her.

'Thanks.' She leant forward for a light and fluttered her eyelashes in what she clearly thought was a perfect imitation of

Marlene Dietrich. By the time she had fully opened them again, I was holding the ticket in front of her.

'One of yours?'

She nodded. 'Looks like it.'

'Does this mean anything to you?' I turned it over.

'The twenty-sixth of August.' She frowned. ' "Where is H.L.?" ' Then she shook her head. 'No, dear. Not a thing. Why should it?'

'I don't know. It's just—'

'Hold on. H.L.' Her frown became a smile. 'In the last week of August. Of course. It must be him.'

'Who?'

'Mr Oates booked him for the matinées that week. But he didn't turn up. Which meant Maurice Stringfellow and his dancing spoons had to stand in for him. Well, he was no substitute, believe me. To be honest, he'd be no substitute for watching nail varnish dry. I mean, *dancing spoons*. Give me a good conjurer any day.'

'Is that what H.L. is? A conjurer?'

'Well, he calls himself a presti—, prestidigi—'

'Prestidigitateur?'

'Yes. That's it. But it amounts to the same thing, doesn't it?' She chuckled. 'Silly man. But nice, all the same. You can't help liking Hildebrand Lightfoot. *When* he can be bothered to—'

'Did you say *Hildebrand*?'

'Yes. Have you heard of him?'

A phrase was echoing in my mind, growing louder by the second. A fragment of a poem by Keats, quoted by Max on the night of Charnwood's murder. '*Remember the* "dwarfish Hildebrand", *Guy*?' My thoughts scrambled back in pursuit of the memory to the pub near Dorking where we had waited for the hour of our rendezvous with Diana, to the customer who had played a conjuring trick on the barmaid and whose improbable name Max had taken for an omen of success. 'Perhaps,' I said. 'Perhaps I have.'

'Well, he let Mr Oates down badly. No apology. No explanation. He'll be lucky to get a booking next summer.'

'He was supposed to be doing matinées at the Pier Theatre during the last week of August, but failed to put in an appearance. Is that what you're saying?'

'Yes, dear. Mr Oates was livid.'

'When was he due to start?'

'On the Monday.'

'And you've not heard from him since?'

'Not a word. Mr Oates has given his agent a piece of his mind, but *he* claims he hasn't heard from him either. Well, you know these artistes. *Very* highly strung. Not that Hildebrand Lightfoot ever struck me as—'

'Who is his agent?'

'Charlie Pragnell.'

'Where can I find him?'

'London. If you really want to.'

'I really do.'

'Well, let me look up his address for you.' She rose and brushed breathlessly past me to reach a filing cabinet. After a search of several seconds, she pulled out a letter. 'Here we are. Mr Charles V. Pragnell, Pragnell-Pierce Theatrical Celebrity Agency, Bridle Street, Soho, London West One. He can tell you all you want to know about Hildebrand Lightfoot. And more, I shouldn't wonder.'

'I hope you're right.' I began to move towards the door, eager to follow the trail, to test the vague hypotheses forming in my mind. Why should Lightfoot have been in Dorking on Friday the twenty-first of August and not in Bournemouth on Monday the twenty-fourth? What had intervened? What had prevented him honouring the booking? And where—

'Are you off there now, dear?'

'Er. . . Yes.'

'Well, if you see Mr Pragnell, could you ask him to pass a message on to his good-for-nothing client?'

'Certainly.'

'Ask Mr Pragnell to tell Hildebrand that Gladys misses him. Even though he doesn't deserve it.' She blushed. 'When all's said and done, he is a sweetie.'

Dusk was settling over Soho when I arrived at the insalubrious premises of the Pragnell-Pierce Theatrical Celebrity Agency – a basement beneath a garishly decorated tattoo parlour. A telephone was ringing in the unattended outer office and I could hear somebody talking on another telephone in the next room.

'Tell him he has Charlie Pragnell's word on it,' a voice boomed. 'What more does he want?'

I pushed the door open and spotted my quarry: a rotund and evidently harassed figure in a tight chalk-stripe suit, spinning a teetotum abstractedly round his desk with one hand while clamping the receiver to his ear with the other. He winked at me to no obvious purpose.

'She doesn't touch the stuff any more. Not a drop. No. Of course it won't be Wolverhampton all over again. What do you take me for?'

I glanced round the room, blinking through the haze of cigar-smoke. The walls were lined with glossy photographs of the grinning men and heavy-lidded women I took to be Pragnell's clients. Was one of them Lightfoot? I wondered. There was no chance I would recognize him, for I had paid him scant attention the one night our paths had crossed. Max might have had a closer look, but—

'Well, just do your best. That's all I ask. Yes. Of course. Goodbye.'

Had Max been here before me? Had he asked this man the same question I was about to? Why had the answer mattered so much to him? I was on the brink either of discovery or disappointment. Close, at all events, to the end of my search.

'And good riddance,' Pragnell growled at the telephone before looking up at me. 'Now, then, what can I do for you? As long as you don't want a comedian who actually makes people laugh, I might be able to help.'

'I'm trying to find one of your clients.'

'Are you from the Inland Revenue?'

'No.'

'Pity. If you were, at least I could believe they were earning some money. Which of my glittering celebrities are you interested in?'

'Hildebrand Lightfoot.'

'Alfie Lightfoot? Well, well, he *is* popular, isn't he? More than he ever was before he performed his ultimate conjuring trick, worse luck.' Seeing my puzzled look, he added: 'Hildebrand's his middle name. He uses it on stage. Off stage, he's plain Alfred. Or was.'

'*Was?*'

'I haven't clapped eyes on him for three months or more. He's vanished like one of his white rabbits. Dropped through the bottom of his own top-hat.'

'He was due to appear in Bournemouth for the week commencing the twenty-fourth of August, I believe.'

217

Pragnell's brow furrowed. 'So he was. You're well-informed, I must say. Why exactly do you want to find him?'

'A personal matter.'

'That's what the other fellow said.'

'What other fellow?'

'You remind me of him, as a matter of fact. Out of the same drawer in life, I'd say. Not the bottom one. But not quite the top one either. He came sniffing after Alfie when the trail was a good bit fresher. End of August. Beginning of September. Some time like that. When I still thought the blighter might show up again soon. I had him booked till Michaelmas, you know. Bognor. Swanage. Ilfracombe. Weston-super-Mare. He left me with enough egg on my face to make an omelette.'

'This other fellow. Did you catch his name?'

'He didn't give it. But, then, you haven't given yours, have you?'

'Horton. Guy Horton.'

'Well, Mr Horton, I'll tell you what I told him. Alfred Hildebrand Lightfoot, conjurer, ventriloquist and mind-reader extraordinaire, gave a one-night show in Margate on the nineteenth of August and I haven't seen or heard of him since. Neither has anyone else in the business.'

'Where is he, then?'

'Your guess is as good as mine. He never was the last word in reliability. The odd missed booking, thanks to drink or women or both . . . well, it was to be expected. But weeks on end? I don't know what to make of it.'

'Is he pictured here?' I cast round at the photographs.

'*All* my celebrities are pictured here, Mr Horton.' He detached himself from his chair and waddled round to the wall beneath the frosted pavement window, signalling for me to follow. 'Even Hildebrand Lightfoot.' He pointed to one of the photographs.

It was a studio portrait of a good-looking man in evening dress, with a fine head of sleek hair and a bristling sergeant-majorish moustache. He was smiling amiably in a slightly raffish devil-may-care manner and looked as if he fancied himself as a lady-killer, possibly with good reason. But something else – some faintly disturbing glimmer in his dark eyes – also communicated itself to me. And it was at this curiously insistent quality of his features that I found myself staring most fixedly.

'Taken a few years ago, of course,' said Pragnell. 'He's a good bit greyer now.'

218

'How old is he?'

'Mid-fifties. He's never been precise on the point. Nor on any other, come to that.'

'Height?'

'About the same as you.'

I could almost see it now, almost grasp the physical reality of what I was seeking: a hint; a suggestion; a glimpse of what Max had realized before me.

'Of course, he may not have the 'tache now.'

'What?'

'Well, the theatre manager in Margate told me he turned up there clean-shaven. And almost white-haired, rather than grey. Scarcely recognizable, he said. But he was probably exaggerating. Maybe Alfie had just forgotten to apply the boot-polish. As for the 'tache . . .'

That was it. For an instant, in my mind's eye, Lightfoot's face aged ten years, shed its moustache and smiled at me in a different but familiar guise. I had him now. I could see him, as Max had seen him. Not as Alfred Hildebrand Lightfoot, conjurer, ventriloquist and mind-reader. But as Fabian Melville Charnwood, company chairman, international financier and engineer of world wars. As I stared at him, his smile seemed to broaden, his eyes to twinkle. *'A circle and a straight line may be the same thing, depending on your point of view.'*

'What's the matter, Mr Horton? You look like you've seen a ghost.'

Pragnell was right. I had seen a ghost. And I could still see him, hovering at Lightfoot's shoulder. Between Margate on the nineteenth of August and Bournemouth on the twenty-fourth, Hildebrand had had one other booking: in Dorking. He had been there to play a part – the part of a dead man. How Charnwood had tricked him I did not know. How he had lured him to his death I could not guess. But that Lightfoot's had been the body in the woods that night I did not doubt. The same height and build. Similar age and appearance. With all obvious differences battered away. It was enough to deceive the likes of me – when Charnwood's clothes covered the limbs of a corpse, when the dead man's face was a mask of gore, when his sister and daughter crouched beside him in tearful mourning. And it was more than enough to persuade the police, the pathologist and the undertaker, none of whom had ever met Charnwood *or* Lightfoot.

219

What had it taken but blood and darkness and well-told lies? And murder, of course. That small but vital component in the plot.

'Are you sure you don't know Alfie?' asked Pragnell. 'Stare at him much longer and you'll bore a hole in the photograph.'

'Where do you think he is?'

'No idea. Abroad, I shouldn't wonder. With some floozy or other. But he must be running low on spondulicks. Conjuring's all he knows.'

'He might be dead, of course.'

'Alfie? No. Fit as a fiddle.'

'Killed in an accident, perhaps.'

'I'd have heard.'

'Or murdered?'

'*Murdered?*' Pragnell frowned at me. 'Don't be so parboiled. Why would anyone do in Alfie Lightfoot?'

'I don't know.' But I did. The motive and the method had formed as cold hard certainties in my mind. Lightfoot had been paid to impersonate Charnwood. He had strengthened their resemblance by shaving off his moustache and letting the natural colour of his hair grow through. He had gone to Dorking and awaited his cue in the same wayside pub as Max and me. And later he had gone on stage – for the last time – dressed in his employer's clothes. Charnwood had killed him. And Vita and Diana had identified him. The guilt of all three was plain. As was the secret they were hiding. Not the whereabouts of Charnwood's money. But the whereabouts of Charnwood himself. 'Perhaps,' I said hesitantly, 'he was mistaken for somebody else.'

CHAPTER

TWELVE

'Bookham two five eight.'

'Good morning. Could I speak to Miss Diana Charnwood, please?'

'Who's calling?'

'Guy Horton.'

'Hold on, please, Mr Horton.'

There was a pause, then a click as Diana picked up the receiver in another room.

'Hello, Guy. I was beginning to—'

'I'm sorry not to have been in touch sooner, Diana. I've had one or two problems.'

'Is everything all right now?'

'Oh yes. Quite all right.'

'Where are you?'

'London.'

'Then why don't you come down here and tell me all about it?'

'Because I still have some – Well, I can't get away until tomorrow. Family difficulties. I'll explain everything when I arrive. Tomorrow night, some time after eight.'

'You'll join us for dinner?'

'Er. . . Yes. Thanks. Actually, I did say I'd dine with Quincy in Dorking. He's meeting a business associate at the Deepdene Hotel.'

'Is he? Well, if you'd rather—'

'No, no. I wonder if you could apologize to him for me. Say I won't be able to make it, but he's to proceed without me. Can you do that?'

'Of course. But, Guy, you're being very—'

'I'm sorry. I must dash. I'll see you tomorrow night. Cheerio till then.'

I put the telephone down and walked slowly across to the window of my hotel room. The street was a blur of grey through the rain-smeared glass, the whole of London reduced in my mind to one drab rectangle of closed doors and falling leaves. Diana would probably be gazing into the garden at Amber Court now, wondering what my abrupt and distant manner portended. But she would never guess for one moment that I had seen to the murderous heart of the plot she and her father and her aunt had hatched. Where Charnwood was hiding I did not know. But Diana and Vita knew. Tomorrow night, when Quincy was safely out of the way, I would make them tell me. Tomorrow night, I would release the anger that had been simmering within me for the past eighteen hours. It would not be easy to wait. But it would be worth it. By then, I would be even angrier than I already was.

I moved to the bedside cabinet, pulled the top drawer open and looked down at the copy of Lightfoot's photograph Pragnell had given me. I had studied it till every line and contour of his features were imprinted on my memory. I had stared at his face till it was so clearly overlaid by Charnwood's that they were almost one in my thoughts, interchangeable and indistinguishable. But not quite. Always, detaching himself from the likeness of his victim with a mocking half-smile, Fabian Charnwood emerged before me. I meant to see him soon in the flesh. And when I did, all his efforts at bribery and persuasion would be wasted. I no longer wanted his money. I no longer wanted anything he could give me. Except revenge. Not for Lightfoot or the millions of others I had never known. But for Max and Felix. For a dead friend and a lost brother. It was for them I had sworn to make him and his sister and his daughter pay. And very soon now they would pay. Dearly.

I left London late the following afternoon. By seven o'clock, I was in the saloon bar of the Wotton Hatch, the pub on the Guildford road three miles west of Dorking where Max and I had gone that fateful night and where Hildebrand Lightfoot had whiled away a spare hour before giving the last performance of his life. I did not recognize the barmaid, so there seemed no point in showing her Lightfoot's photograph. Instead, I sat quietly in my corner, drinking whisky with no discernible effect, until eight o'clock struck and it was time to go.

There were fireworks streaking into the sky above Dorking as I drew the car to a halt in the driveway of Amber Court and climbed out into the cold gunpowder-scented air. I had forgotten till now that it was Guy Fawkes' Night. Everywhere, stuffed and grinning effigies of my hapless namesake were being burnt to celebrate the defeat of a conspiracy which seemed quite trivial compared with the one I was determined to expose. Would some future generation, I wondered, commemorate the Concentric Alliance in fire and song? Or would they never have heard of it at all?

I pressed the bell and waited, remembering how Diana had led me back from the woods that night, fooling me so completely with her orchestrated display of grief and shock that even now, when I knew the truth, it seemed as if she must have been in earnest. So much pretence, so much deception, then and later. But no longer.

The maid opened the door and ushered me in with a smile. I was expected. I was welcome. She led me down the hall and into the drawing-room. 'Mr Horton, miss,' I heard her say as I lingered out of sight. 'Thank you, Susan,' Diana replied. I stepped forward, the maid retreating past me. And there they were, sipping their pre-prandial sherries by the fire: Vita huge and benevolent in mauve and pink, Diana dark and enigmatic in a blue and gold dress, with the topaz pendant glittering as ever at her throat. They turned in unison to greet me and Diana began to rise from her chair. 'Guy, it's so—' But then they saw the expression on my face. And perhaps, in that instant, they both guessed what it meant.

'What's the matter, Guy?' Diana asked, pulling up and staring at me. 'What's wrong?'

'I'd like to speak to you alone.'

My tone forbade argument. After only a moment's thought, she said: 'Very well. Would you excuse us, Aunty? We'll use the morning-room.'

'No, no, my dear. You stay here. I want to have a word with Cook. Besides, I'm sure it's nothing . . .' But Vita's confidence died as she looked at me. She rose with a graceful display of effort and walked slowly from the room, casting me a concerned glance

– in which some stern hint of warning seemed also implicit – as I held the door open for her. Then she was gone.

For a moment, I thought Diana might try to dispel her foreboding by laughing or trying to kiss me. But she could see I meant to remain aloof. She took a slow circular route back to her chair, retrieved her cigarette from its ashtray and gazed curiously at me as she drew on it. Then she said: 'Well, Guy? What is it?'

I walked towards her, slipping Lightfoot's photograph from my pocket as I crossed the room and slapping it down in front of her on the coffee-table. For several seconds, she stared at it, a frown of false puzzlement creasing her brow. Awareness of her beauty – of the infinite desirability of her body beneath the caressing lines of her dress – prised its way into my thoughts. Then anger blotted it out. 'Are you going to pretend you don't know who he is?'

She looked straight at me. 'I don't.'

'Alfred Hildebrand Lightfoot.'

'Who?'

'Doesn't the name mean anything to you?'

'Not a single thing.'

'Well, perhaps you never bothered to find it out. A tedious detail you could leave dear Papa to deal with. But the face. You know the face, don't you?'

'No.'

'Imagine it a few years older, with greyer hair, no moustache . . . and a great gaping wound where half of it ought to be.'

She permitted herself a grimace of distaste. 'I don't know what you mean.'

'This is the poor bastard you identified that night. This is what's rotting to dust in your father's grave.'

'Guy, for God's—'

'I'll spell it out, shall I?' I was shouting now. I could hear my voice cracking, see my hand trembling. But to remain calm was impossible. To speak of it at all was to rage against the trick they had played. 'You and your wouldn't-hurt-a-fly aunt helped your father fake his own death. I'm not sure yet why he needed to disappear so conclusively, but I expect money's the answer. This way, he can welsh on his debts *and* spend his ill-gotten gains. You needed two unsuspecting souls to pull it off and you found them in Max Wingate and Hildebrand Lightfoot. Max to be your despairing suitor with a motive for murder. And Lightfoot to be his victim. Your father lured Lightfoot up into those woods on the

224

basis of some spurious commission to impersonate him. Then he beat the man's brains out, leaving you to claim the corpse as his own and Max to carry the can. It was clever, wasn't it? Bloody clever, if you'll pardon the pun. The police never thought to question his identity. Why should they when his sister and daughter were weeping so copiously over the body? The pathologist and the undertaker didn't know him from Adam. And his valet had conveniently been dispensed with, so there was no danger of him quibbling about whether it was his master or not. You even coped with me turning up unexpectedly. Like everybody else, I never thought for a moment you'd be lying, so, naturally, I didn't examine the body too closely. After all, it wasn't a pretty sight. But, then, it wasn't meant to be, was it?'

Her eyes had been fixed on me throughout, as if the sheer intensity of her gaze could beat back my accusations. Her lips were compressed in a thin line, her hands held rigidly at her sides. She must have realized there was no point in denying it. But she could at least refuse to admit it.

'Even before you met us aboard the *Empress of Britain*, you were planning it, weren't you? You and Vita were on the look-out for somebody with few friends or relatives to turn to if he found himself fleeing for his life from a murder charge. Who better than one of two expatriates returning to England after a lengthy absence? Hence Vita's generous invitation for us to attend your party. I suppose I should be grateful Max arrived before I did. Otherwise, I might have been chosen. Or perhaps you'd have judged him to be more suitable anyway. Quicker to succumb to your advances. Readier to believe your lies. And they were lies, weren't they? Right from the start. Every single honey-toned endearment. The engagement was a fraud. And the elopement was a trap. I sprang it, of course, by obligingly taking your father's bribe. But Max was the one caught in its jaws. It would have worked perfectly if he'd been arrested soon afterwards. Or even if he'd never been seen again. But luck turned against you there, I'm afraid. It always does in the end.'

'I don't know what you're talking about,' she said with icy stubbornness.

'Then let me enlighten you. Lightfoot arrived early for his appointment. So did Max. And he took me with him. We all ended up waiting in the same pub on the Guildford road. The Wotton Hatch. And Lightfoot introduced himself to the barmaid, using his

225

Christian name, which we happened to hear. Hildebrand. Unusual, you see. Easy to remember. As Max did, a few days later, when he passed through Bournemouth and saw it on a hoarding at the pier. He must have thought it an odd coincidence and gone along to the matinée out of curiosity. Or perhaps a darkened theatre struck him as a good place to hide. Either way, he soon had more than coincidence to contend with. Lightfoot's performance was cancelled. Nobody knew why. He simply hadn't shown up. But when Max contacted Lightfoot's agent and saw this photograph, *he* knew. He knew, for the first time, what you'd done to him. And then he came after you. Did you realize? Did you sense he was on your trail? Is that why you started giving me the glad eye? In the hope he'd see us together and jump to the wrong conclusion?' I stepped closer and, slowly reaching out, cupped her chin in my hand. 'Well, was it, Diana? Was all that heat and passion just a diversionary tactic?'

Her skin was cool and soft. I slid my fingers up over her jaw till they were touching her pursed lips. Then, goaded by her silence, I grasped her mouth and squeezed it open, till I could see the clenched white teeth within and feel the nervous breath fanning my knuckles.

'You treacherous bitch! You let him find us together. You let him believe we'd both betrayed him. And then, when you were afraid he was about to tell me what had happened, you killed him. Not to save me. But to save yourself. You hit him exactly where he'd unwittingly told you to. Hard enough to be sure he'd never speak again. You murdered him, Diana. Just like your father murdered Lightfoot. But Lightfoot wasn't my friend. Max was.'

Her head was tilting back as my grip tightened, her eyes widening. Suddenly, with an oath, I whipped my hand away. She cried out and stumbled to the sofa, leaning against it for support, raising one arm as if to shield herself from me.

'Aren't you going to deny it? Aren't you going to try to talk me round? Or persuade me in your own inimitable way? It wouldn't work, of course. It's too late for all of that. But I'd be disappointed if you didn't even make the attempt. It would be uncharacteristic of you to admit defeat so easily. And unworthy of your father. Don't you think?'

'You're wrong,' she panted. 'This is all . . . all madness.'

'Yes. It is madness. But it's what you did. Why, Diana? That's what I can't understand. Why do so much for such a man? For

God's sake! Look at your mother's picture, there on the wall. Her blood's on his hands. Hers and the blood of every one of those poor bastards we'll be keeping a two-minute silence for next week. From an Austrian archduke through to a second-rate conjurer. All of them. Dead because of your father.'

She turned to look at me. There was a difference now in her expression, a hint of something genuine. 'What . . . what has my mother to do with . . .'

'The Concentric Alliance! I know about that too, darling mine. Don't think for an instant your *sang froid* when their letter was delivered to you in Venice is going to count for anything now. Just because you managed to carry it off better than your aunt, I'm not about to—'

'That's enough!' declared Vita, bursting into the room red-faced and quivering with what could as easily have been fear as rage. 'That's quite enough!' She halted in front of me and tried for a moment to stare me down. Then, seeing I was not to be cowed, she moved past me and threaded her arm protectively through Diana's. 'How dare you talk to my niece in such a fashion? What's the meaning of it?'

'Ears burning, were they, Vita? Or just one of them, from being pressed to the keyhole? I hope you found it easier than craning over the guard-rail on the *Empress of Britain*.'

'Your . . . ranting . . . could be heard all over the house, young man. And I repeat: what's the meaning of it?'

'Crystal-clear, I should have thought. I'm accusing you and Diana of being accessories to murder. Of perjuring yourselves. Of lying through your teeth. Of weeping to order and grieving on cue. Of aiding and abetting Fabian Charnwood in his attempts to evade justice. And by association of complicity in all his damnable works.'

Vita's grip on Diana's arm tightened. She swelled with what she no doubt believed would be an impressive show of outraged innocence. 'Absurd! Preposterous! And deeply offensive!'

'To anyone with a shred of decency, yes. But not to you two. I'll tell you what hits you so hard. It's truth. An unfamiliar commodity in your world. An unwelcome and inconvenient intruder. Well, it's here now. Out in the open. And it's not going away.'

'I think that's exactly what you should do after such a torrent of hurtful nonsense,' Vita asserted. 'Go away and let us *try* to forget what you've said.'

227

'Oh no. You're not going to be allowed to forget a single thing. When I leave here, I'll be going to the police. They'll listen to me. And they'll believe me, Vita. I'll make them. So, don't think you can disregard my words. They'll be ringing in your ears from now till the day your brother is dragged out of hiding. Till all three of you are forced to answer for what you've done.'

'The police won't listen to you. They have more sense. Besides, there's not a shred of—' Vita stopped abruptly and stared at me above clamped lips. Proof was the word she had been about to use. But to have done so would have represented an admission that there was something to prove after all, that my allegations were not as groundless as she had claimed.

'We'll see,' I said slowly. 'I think I can persuade Hornby to order an exhumation. What will it reveal, do you suppose? I'd say it was odds on there being something – some minor overlooked detail – to prove who the occupant of that grave really is. Your brother. Or somebody of similar build and appearance. Somebody like him but not quite the same. Which way would you lay your money? There'd be a great deal at stake, remember. You couldn't afford to lose. If you did, you'd have more than the police to worry about. There'd be Faraday and all the merciless people he represents. The people you've helped your brother cheat. His accomplices in a seventeen-year-old conspiracy.'

'What conspiracy?' put in Diana, the urgency of her tone implying she really did not understand.

'It's too late to play the innocent,' I replied. 'Your father must have told you about the Concentric Alliance. Probably a long time ago. After all, the money for your education, your dresses, your whole pampered existence, came from the profits he made out of the war. A pity your mother had to die in the process. But perhaps you offset that against the advantages as easily as he did.'

'Don't pay any attention,' hissed Vita. 'Your mother has nothing to do with this.' But in Diana's eyes, as she looked round at her aunt, was a glimmer of doubt. And, for the first time, I began to think she really might not know all of it.

'Hold on, Vita,' I said, stepping closer. 'Have you and your brother been keeping something from Diana?'

'Of course not.'

'That's it, isn't it? She doesn't know about the Concentric Alliance. She really doesn't.'

'Neither of us does. We have no idea what you mean by—'

'Their symbol struck a chill into your heart. But it didn't affect Diana. I thought she was just a better actress. Now, I'm not so—'

'I don't know what you're—'

'The concentric circles, you lying old bitch! We all saw them. But only you reacted as if you'd also seen a ghost.' I turned towards Diana and there, written clearly in her face, was confirmation. She had helped her father escape. But she had not understood what she was helping him escape from. 'Listen to me carefully, Diana. What you're about to hear is the gospel truth.'

'I want you out of here now!' shrieked Vita, breaking away and bustling to the door. 'This very minute.' She pulled the door open and stood imperiously beside it, but I did not react. I kept looking directly at Diana, holding her gaze with mine, commanding her to listen.

'The Concentric Alliance is a secret international organization of which your father is or was the head. Seventeen years ago, they arranged the assassination in Sarajevo that sparked off the Great War. They made huge profits from subsequent sales of arms and munitions and from other investments they were able to time precisely thanks to knowing when the war would break out – because *they* brought it about. It was your father's idea. It was his brain-child. A greedy infant, as it turned out. One that gobbled millions of lives. Including your mother's. Your father killed her as surely as if he'd fired the torpedo himself. As surely as if he'd held her beneath the waves until he was certain she'd drowned.'

'No,' she murmured. 'It can't be so.'

'But it is. You know it is. You can recognize truth when you hear it. Perhaps it explains all sorts of odd little mysteries you've puzzled over. From the day they told you your mother was dead. To the day you watched Vita blanch at the sight of a pair of concentric circles drawn on a sheet of paper.'

'Aunty?' said Diana numbly, staring past me. But Vita did not answer. Even her fund of denials was exhausted.

'Now you know how they feel,' I persisted. 'The millions of widows and orphans your father made along with his millions of pounds. Now you have some inkling of the grief and destruction he happily sowed in order to reap . . . to reap the privileges you've enjoyed. Adequate compensation for a motherless adolescence, were they? I don't suppose so. But maybe they helped your father persuade you to love him – and to come to his aid in his hour of need. What did he tell you? What lie did he invent to cover his tracks?'

'I didn't need to be *persuaded* to love my father,' she retorted, her eyes blazing with sudden anger. 'Or to help him when—' And so we arrived, in the jagged hush of imminent admission, at the end of all pretences. She would not say it aloud. Not yet. But it had been acknowledged between us and could not be renounced. Charnwood's guilt, reverberating in Vita's silence. And Diana's, echoing in the hollowness of the love he had nurtured in her – and of the life he had built for her.

'Where is he, Diana? Tell me. For Max's sake. And your mother's. Tell me where he's hiding. I have a right to know. And you have a duty to tell me.'

'Duty?'

'You can't shelter him any longer. You can't believe you should.'

'Can't I?'

'No. Not now. You know too much. Give it up. Give *him* up.'

'Diana, you shouldn't—' But a single glare ended Vita's intervention. Diana turned slowly to look up at her mother's portrait, then slowly back to confront her aunt.

'Papa always confided in you,' she said with surprising mildness. 'Always you and never me.'

'You were too young to—'

'To understand?'

Vita closed the door and leant back against it, her knuckles white where they clasped the handle. 'Surely, my dear, you see that . . . none of this should be discussed . . . with a third party present. It. . . It would be. . .unwise.'

Diana stared at Vita for several long cold seconds. Then she looked at me and said in a voice devoid of all emotion: 'Please wait for me in the library, Guy. I want to speak to my aunt in private. I won't keep you longer than necessary.'

'I'm not leaving until I have what I came for.'

'You've made your position quite clear. Now, please, leave us. I'm not going to run away. And you won't have to come looking for me.'

'Be sure I don't.'

'You won't. Believe me.' She glanced down as she added: 'In this if in nothing else.'

*   *   *

230

And so, reluctantly but obediently, I went to the library and waited, as I had on the night of the murder. Then, I had waited to be questioned, puzzling over the preponderance of Great War literature on Charnwood's shelves as I did so. Now, I was expecting answers. And his choice of books made horribly good sense. His preoccupation with the subject was that of a designer with his greatest project. Here, meticulously recorded, were the battles and campaigns he had secretly initiated, the toll of dead men and dismantled nations he had to his credit. The well-stocked library of a civilized man of letters or the bulging ossuary of a vicarious wager of war: they were, in Charnwood's case, the same thing.

What Diana and Vita were saying to each other I could only imagine. Recriminations and reproaches might be flying thick and fast. Indeed, I hoped they were. They were likely to suit my purpose better than anything else. For, contrary to what I had told Vita, I was not at all confident of being able to prove the allegations I had made. The police might not listen to me. An exhumation, even if they agreed to one, might fail to yield conclusive results. But Diana's horror at my revelations concerning the Concentric Alliance had strengthened my hand. It was just the tool I needed to prise her and Vita apart. And from their distrust might flow my victory. *Divide et impera*. It was a fitting strategy to use against Fabian Charnwood, the arch-divider. But would it be a successful one?

I had waited nearly an hour to find out when the door opened and Diana entered the room. She was grave and calm and pale as marble. And the topaz pendant no longer hung around her neck. But what its absence signified I could not judge.

She closed the door, took a few steps, then stopped and looked straight at me. In her eyes burned neither defiance nor guilt. It was as if she had resolved some struggle with her conscience to her complete satisfaction, rendering my accusations unimportant by comparison. It was as if the time for feminine pretences and subtle evasions was gone, enabling the real Diana Charnwood to show herself at last.

'Well?' I began. 'Are you going to tell me where he is?'

'The world believes my father to be buried in Dorking Cemetery. I don't think you'll find it easy to shake that belief.'

'You leave me no choice, then.'

'But to go to the police?'

'Exactly.'

231

'It would be a mistake, I assure you. They wouldn't take your word against ours. The word of a known scoundrel against that of a respected man's sister and daughter.'

'My God, you have a—'

She held up a hand to silence me. 'And, even if they did, even if they discovered what you claim they would discover, then it would end badly for you.'

'Why?'

'Because I would say you were part of the plot. I would say you had helped us at every stage – until a lovers' quarrel had made you turn against me. And that I think they *would* believe.'

She meant it. There was no doubt of her sincerity. And, in my own mind, little doubt either of Hornby's eagerness to swallow such a story. It would, after all, make better sense of the circumstances of Max's death than the only account I could give.

'I didn't murder Max, Guy. It truly was an accident. I had no idea he was even in Venice. What happened at the villa that afternoon was . . . from the heart. I don't expect you to believe me. But understand this. If you turn what we did and what it led to into one kind of lie, I'll turn it into another. And, since you seem to think I'm an accomplished liar, you should be in no doubt of how much more persuasive than you the police will find me.'

'Persuasiveness won't save you.'

'No. But it might save my father. If I said you had murdered him and set out to saddle Max with the blame, then Lightfoot's part in it might seem simply to be a device you had invented to incriminate me while exonerating yourself. Lightfoot may or may not be missing, but where is the proof he died in place of my father? The results of an exhumation are unpredictable. As you pointed out to Aunt Vita, there would be a great deal at stake.'

So there would. But I could hardly believe Diana was prepared to sacrifice herself to save Charnwood. Not after all I had told her. 'Don't the crimes he committed against humanity mean anything to you, Diana? Doesn't your mother's memory matter to you? Don't you understand? He isn't worth saving.'

'Don't *you* understand, Guy? I love my father. I trust—' She broke off and glanced away. 'I trusted him.'

'But he didn't trust you.'

'So you say. And so Aunt Vita more or less admitted, when I forced her to.' Her chin dropped, but my hopes soared. They *were* divided. 'But I want to hear the truth from his own lips before . . .

before I . . .' She shook her head. 'I won't condemn him without a hearing. It's as simple as that.'

'For God's sake!'

'Besides, if everything you say is true, justice isn't what would greet him on his emergence from hiding. The Concentric Alliance would pre-empt any police inquiry. They would find him – and impose their own punishment. I can't let that happen.'

'Why not? Are you going to tell me he doesn't deserve to be punished?'

'No. But that isn't the point.' She raised her head and stared at me. 'If the Concentric Alliance was responsible for my mother's death, then *all* its members should be made to answer for it, not just one of them.'

'Of course. But we can't—'

'Yes we can. I've thought of a way, you see.' Some of the calmness had left her now and been replaced by a strange and contagious excitement. 'A way to bring them all down. Wouldn't you like to do that, Guy?'

'How?'

'Papa kept some documents in a safe in his study. He took them with him when he left. I didn't know what they were. But Aunt Vita knew. And she's just told me in return for my promise to do everything I can to stop you going to the police. They're the full records of the Concentric Alliance, past *and* present. Financial transactions. Letters to and from other members. Minutes of secret meetings at which their activities were discussed. Quarterly accounts showing who was paid how much and what for. The names of the guilty men, complete with the evidence against them. The truth, not just about the war, but about every single thing they've ever done.'

It shimmered before me in her description: as complete a victory as I could possibly imagine. Was this what she was offering? If so, how did she propose to save Charnwood from the wreck? What was her price? 'Your father has all this with him?'

'Of course. He'd never part with it.'

'Then what—'

'Unless he was forced to. I can lead you to him, Guy. And I can persuade him to hand the records over to you. You could give them to the press. You could even sell them to the press if you wanted to. I think they'd pay handsomely for such a sensational story, don't you? It would be on every front page around

233

the world. And the people my father made rich would be ruined overnight. Don't you see? You can have your revenge – and your reward too, if you like.' She paused momentarily. 'On one condition.'

'What condition?'

'Allow Papa to remain in hiding. That's the only way I can make him agree to surrender the records. You tell the press we found them among his papers. You let the world believe he really is dead.'

'You want him to get away with it?'

'He's only one man, Guy.'

'He's also their leader. The worst of them by far.'

'Their leader, yes. At least initially. In recent years, probably not. Otherwise, his financial problems would never have become so acute. As to his being the worst, well, if Faraday's a fair sample, how can you be sure?'

'Still a murderer many times over. And you want to spare him.'

She gazed at me in silence for a moment, then said: 'It's my price. And it's non-negotiable. Take it or leave it.'

'If I leave it?'

'Then I've already spelt out the consequences.'

'And what about Max? What about *his* reputation? *His* memory?'

'After this comes out, nobody will believe he murdered my father. Faraday and the people hiding behind him will take the blame. As in a sense they should.'

'But it's not the truth, is it?'

'It's more of the truth than you'll ever succeed in dragging into the open.'

Diana was right. I had set out to exploit her exclusion from the secret her father and aunt had shared and I had succeeded. But it was success at a price. Instead of capitulation, she had presented me with a choice. The Concentric Alliance or Fabian Charnwood. I could not have both. And, without her help, it was questionable if I could have either. 'Where is he?' I said levelly.

'Do you accept my terms?'

'Just tell me where he is.'

'Not until we reach an agreement.'

'Yes, then, damn it. I accept your terms. But does Vita?'

'She accepts this is the only way to stop you going to the police.'

'Good.' I raised my eyebrows expectantly. 'Well?'

'He's in Dublin.'

'*Dublin?*'

'Yes. Not Zürich or Trieste or anywhere else likely to have crossed his creditors' minds. But somewhere sufficiently anti-British to ensure a degree of official obstructiveness if the Surrey Constabulary – or anyone else in this country – starts making enquiries.'

'Where in Dublin?'

'I don't know. Neither does Aunt Vita. We have a post office box number we can write to in emergencies. He checks it daily. My proposal is this. You and I travel to Dublin. We deliver a letter asking him to meet me as a matter of extreme urgency. At that meeting, I tell him what you want, making it clear that, unless he co-operates, you'll go to Faraday and set the forces of the Concentric Alliance on his trail. As I see it, they pose a far greater threat to him than the police. He'll have to agree. He'll have no alternative.'

Nor any alternative, I realized, but to tell his daughter the whole truth at last. She meant to demand a long overdue explanation of why her mother had died. And he would have to give her one. He would have to give both of us what we wanted.

'Why are you hesitating, Guy? Isn't this better than what you came here for?'

'Perhaps.'

'A chance to set history right. An opportunity just for once to make the guilty suffer more than the innocent. A way to make them pay.'

'They'll stop us if they can.'

'They won't have the chance. They won't realize the threat we pose to them until it's too late.'

And afterwards? I wanted to ask. Would there not come a time when we too were made to pay? I knew what she would say. I heard the answer in my own head, in one of the phrases she had used. *Just for once.* How alluring such a prospect was. To bring the roof down around their heads. To name the false captains and the fraudulent kings. To bring them all to book. Just for once, to rise above fear and frailty. Just for once, to act without counting the cost or reckoning the gain.

'What do you say, Guy?'

'I say: when do we leave?'

The ghost of a smile flickered at the edges of her lips. 'As soon as possible. Here . . .' She pulled a copy of *Bradshaw* from a nearby shelf, placed it on the table behind us, thumbed through the index, then turned up the appropriate page. 'Let's see. There's a train from Euston to Holyhead at eight thirty in the morning, connecting with a ferry to Kingstown. We can be in Dublin by six o'clock. And we can have a letter in the post office, awaiting my father's collection, first thing the following morning.'

'Tomorrow, then?'

'Yes. And I think we should leave this house immediately. I don't want to be here when Quincy returns. Let Aunt Vita tell him we've gone to visit your family. Let her tell him whatever she likes. You can be sure it won't be the truth.'

I was sure, given how fondly Quincy had spoken of his sister. But mention of his name reminded me that he was, even as we talked, negotiating with Gregory on Diana and Vita's behalf. Should I alert him to what I meant to do? No. The fewer who knew the better. Besides, I would have what I wanted long before he parted with any money. And then he would not need to part with a single cent.

'Very well,' I said. 'It's agreed.'

'Good.' Diana moved towards the door. 'In that case, I'll go and—'

'Before you do!' I grasped her forearm and turned her slowly back to face me. 'One thing, Diana. One point I want clearly understood. This is an alliance of necessity. And a temporary one at that. If you try to double-cross me, I *will* go to the police. The fact that we were once lovers won't stop me.'

'I never thought it would.'

'And in case you were thinking of trying to—' I stopped, regretting the gibe before I had even uttered it. She widened her eyes, daring me to continue. But she must have known I would not. Any claim to moral superiority on my part deserved to be scorned.

'We don't have to admire or respect each other to do this, Guy,' she said coolly. 'We just have to observe a truce. Once it's served its purpose . . .'

'Yes?' I wondered how far her foresight stretched. As far as the possibility that I might wait until the whole world knew about the Concentric Alliance – *then* reveal Charnwood's hiding-place? Or further – into some fresh treachery of her own? 'What happens then, Diana?'

But she did not answer. Slowly, she detached my hand from her arm and pushed back a strand of hair from her brow. 'I must pack a bag,' she said in a matter-of-fact tone. 'There's no time to be lost.'

CHAPTER

THIRTEEN

Diana said nothing during the drive to London and I did not press her to. For the moment, it seemed, we had both said enough. In the darkness and the silence, Max rode with us like a tangible memory, my mind sowing his face among the reflections thrown back from the wind-screen and his words among the notes of the engine. *'You reckoned I was mad to do it, Guy, didn't you? And maybe I was. But no madder than you are to do this. Watch her, old man. Watch her like a hawk. She did for me with her smiles and her blushes and her soft words. Don't let her do for you as well.'* I glanced round at her and pondered the warning. She was staring straight ahead, thinking perhaps of her mother as I thought of my friend. We had a truce. We had a shared purpose. There was nothing to worry about. And yet . . . *'I thought the same, old man. Nothing to worry about. But there was, wasn't there? There always is.'*

We spent the night at the Euston Hotel, breakfasted early and left aboard the Irish Mail at half past eight. We were calmer now, less angry with ourselves and each other. A truce was after all a truce. While it lasted, I would have to trust her and she would have to trust me. But for that to be possible, she would first have to tell me the whole truth about the conspiracy her father had conceived – the conspiracy in which she and Vita had played their willing parts. As the train slid out of Euston station and it became apparent there would be nobody else in our compartment, I lowered the corridor blinds and sat down opposite her.

However drab the setting, however damning the evidence, however much I loathed her, Diana Charnwood was still the most beautiful woman I had ever known. The fur collar gathered at her throat made her look like some Russian princess. The cool directness of her gaze suggested she might, if she chose, explain everything – yet apologize for nothing. She should have begged for my forgiveness. But, if anything was certain, it was that she never would.

'Well?' I said, leaning forward to light her cigarette. 'No second thoughts? No misgivings about what we're going to do?'

'None. Once I take a decision, it's taken for good.'

'Or ill?'

She did not answer, but drew on her cigarette and returned my sarcastic smile with icy faintness.

'Your father must have been grateful for your decisiveness when you agreed to help him fake his death.' Still she said nothing. 'When was that, by the way? When did he first put the idea to you?'

'Does it matter?'

'It matters to me. I'd like to understand every step that led to Max's death. We've a long journey ahead of us. So, there's plenty of time for you to make me understand. Isn't there?'

'Yes. There is.' She looked out of the window, half-closing her eyes, though whether in resignation or concentration I could not tell. 'If you're sure you want to know.'

'I'm sure.'

'Very well.' She took one more draw on her cigarette. 'By the beginning of this year, it was obvious to Papa that Charnwood Investments wasn't going to survive. It came as a shock when he told us. I'd always taken our prosperity for granted. Suddenly, my whole pampered existence – as you described it – was under threat. To make matters worse, Papa was afraid some of his clients would take drastic steps if they lost their money. He said they were dangerous people who'd stop at nothing. I didn't entirely believe him. I thought what he really feared was the shame and disgrace of bankruptcy. Now, I realize he was quite right. Maybe Aunt Vita realized that from the start. But I can't claim to have done so. There are no extenuating circumstances in my case. I wanted what I'd always had – fast cars, fine wine, fashionable clothes, luxury

239

hotels and handsome men; the best of everything. Well, according to Papa, I would soon have to accustom myself to a very different life, one of penny-pinching and making-do. It made me angry just to think of it, as I suppose he knew it would. It made me grab the chance of avoiding such a future when he offered it to me. It made *me* willing to stop at nothing. ˙

'Papa's scheme was to divert as much capital as remained in Charnwood Investments into secret accounts held under an assumed name; vanish in the most effective manner possible by appearing to be murdered; lie low until the fuss caused by his insolvency had died down; then establish a new life in South America or the Far East, where in due course Aunt Vita and I could join him. When I asked how such a scheme could actually be put into effect, he had the answer ready. He'd been planning it for some time. He'd seen the crisis coming and had prepared for it.' She shrugged. 'The art of good business, I suppose you could say.'

'Had he already found Lightfoot then?'

'Oh yes. *I* had, in a sense. Aunt Vita took me to a variety show in Eastbourne as a treat for my sixteenth birthday, just after Easter, 1919. Hildebrand Lightfoot was on the bill. His resemblance to my father was astonishing, as I told Papa when we got home. He showed little interest and, twelve years later, I'd forgotten all about it. But he hadn't. He'd traced Lightfoot and seen the resemblance for himself. They weren't identical, of course, but the similarity was close enough for what Papa had in mind. Lightfoot led an itinerant existence, moving from one seaside lodging-house to another. He had no family. And he was pressed for cash. He was ideal in every way. Papa put it to him that, in his line of business, he occasionally needed an alibi. Would Lightfoot be willing to supply such an alibi by exploiting their physical likeness – for a substantial fee, of course? Naturally, Lightfoot agreed.

'When Papa explained how we could make the world believe he was dead by killing Lightfoot in his place, I felt sure it would work. Why not, after all? What was there to go wrong? Nothing, so far as I could see. As for Lightfoot, I tried to think of him less as a person than an anonymous stranger whose extinction was a regrettable necessity.' She paused. 'Disgusted, are you, Guy?'

Determined neither to condemn nor excuse till I had heard it all, I said nothing, merely raised my eyebrows in a silent invitation for her to continue.

She cleared her throat. 'I still believe nothing would have gone wrong but for Papa's insistence that we had to supply a murderer as well as a victim, that his creditors wouldn't be deceived by a motiveless killing. But he knew them better than I did. And it was bound to be easier for Aunt Vita and me if the police had an obvious culprit to pursue. So, I agreed. I even suggested how to find one.'

'By exploiting your legendary ability to attract and fascinate men?'

'Yes,' she replied with complete seriousness. 'Exactly.'

'Like you did with the fiancé who killed himself?'

'Peter was a fool. But men are, you know.' She paused. 'Present company excepted, of course.'

'Did the trip to America have *any* other purpose?'

'No. An Atlantic crossing struck me as the quickest and surest method of finding the right sort of man. But the voyage out was a disappointment. It wasn't until we came back that I chanced on just the type I was looking for. And since you *did* ask, I'd have chosen Max ahead of you every time. Beneath the cynical exterior, I could detect a romantic heart yearning to be lost and possibly broken. Beneath yours, there was a heart rather too much like my own. Besides, Max looked as if he *could* commit murder if driven to it, whereas you . . .'

'Yes, Diana? Whereas I what?'

She looked away. 'It doesn't matter. Max fell for me. More completely than I'd dared to hope. He said he'd been waiting for me all his life without realizing it. He said I was his salvation. Instead of which, he was mine.'

'And no more to you than that? No more than a pawn for your father to sacrifice?'

'His devotion flattered me. Sometimes, it even moved me. But it didn't stop me doing what needed to be done.' She paused, as if waiting for me to react. But my anger was well under control now. Even my expression gave nothing away. 'You were my only reservation,' she continued. 'I was afraid your friendship with Max might complicate matters. But Papa soon put my mind at rest. He regarded you as a positive asset, especially when he made enquiries and found out just how dubious a past you and Max had shared.'

'Why should our past have been an asset?'

'Because it suggested you could easily be recruited as Papa's informant. And because we knew that, if Max refused to be bought

241

off, it could only be because he really was infatuated with me and wouldn't hesitate when *you* suggested we elope. I was to tell the police after the event that Papa had admitted being alerted to our plans by you – in exchange for a large amount of money. It would have satisfied them on every point and had the additional advantage of making Max distrust any help or advice you offered after his arrest.'

'What stopped you?'

'Your presence in Dorking that night. It hardly seemed consistent with what I'd intended to say.'

'Human nature isn't always consistent.'

'No. I suppose that's why so many things went wrong. Because of human nature. Papa had told Lightfoot he would be needed in the early hours of the morning to deliver a bribe to a tax inspector, while Papa would actually be hundreds of miles away at a week-end house party in Yorkshire, thus supplying a perfect alibi should the tax inspector turn out to be trying to trap him. Lightfoot had accepted the explanation readily enough. Given how much he was being paid, he wasn't likely to quibble. I met him at the front gate shortly after one o'clock, made sure he left his car well down the road, handed him the envelope containing the bribe and escorted him up through the woods towards the point where he was supposed to meet the man. Dressed as he was and clean-shaven, he really did look like my father, at least by torch-light. And I could hear him practising Papa's tone of voice under his breath as we went along. That upset me, believe it or not. Knowing he would never need to speak the lines he'd carefully learnt.

'Papa was waiting in the woods just short of the stile. He hit him from behind, knocking him unconscious. We emptied his pockets, re-filling them with Papa's wallet, watch, handkerchief and so on. Then . . .' For the first time, something that might have been remorse caught in her throat. But she soon conquered it. 'Then I retreated down the path while Papa delivered the fatal blows. It didn't take long, but . . . there was a great deal of blood. He was shaking like a leaf afterwards. I don't think either of us expected it to be so horrible.'

'The first time your father had killed with his own hands, I suppose.'

A fleeting glare was her only response. She continued as if I had not interrupted. 'We parted there. Papa went round to the

242

front gate and left in Lightfoot's car – which, as a matter of fact, he'd paid for. I went back to the house, collected Aunt Vita and set off again at a quarter past two. I thought Max would already have fled by then, having discovered the body, taken it for my father and realized he'd be accused of murdering him. But human nature intervened again. The love I'd so successfully inspired must have made him press on towards the house, then hide when he heard us approaching, not knowing who we might be.

'Aunt Vita was flagging and I stopped to let her recover her breath. That's when I said a stupid thing. "Stay here if you like, Aunty. I'll take a look at the body, then come back." "No, no," she replied. "We should behave as if we don't know what we're going to find." We hardly spoke above whispers. Neither of us thought for a moment there would be anybody close enough to hear. And we were nervous. I suppose that's why Aunt Vita couldn't help asking, "Where do you suppose Max is?" "Long gone," I answered. And then she said, "I almost feel sorry for him, you know. Betrayed by his friend as well as his fiancée." Those were her very words. They must have struck Max like a dagger to the heart. He burst out of the undergrowth just ahead of us and fled back along the path. We called after him, but he didn't stop. He'd heard enough to know we were all against him. Even you.'

'So, that's why he took the car without waiting for me. Why he wrote to his father, accusing you and me of betraying him. Why finding us together in Venice must have seemed the final confirmation of his very worst suspicions.'

'Yes, Guy. I'm afraid so.'

If I had taken the right path that night. . . If I had followed Max, instead of the sound of Vita's voice. . . If I had never left the car at all. . . There were so many ways the sequence of events could have been altered. But not the result. That remained the same, however I approached it; the same for ever.

'Then you appeared. Another surprise, adding to our confusion. But we coped rather well, don't you think?'

'Oh yes,' I said, the bitterness of what Max must have thought of me infecting my words. 'It was a virtuoso performance.'

'Aunt Vita redeemed herself by persuading you to escort me back to the house. Once we'd lured you away from the body, we were safe. Papa had sacked his valet, Barker, months before and none of the other servants were likely to stir. Even if they had, they'd have been taken in as easily as you were. It *was* convincing. Especially to the creditors of Charnwood Investments. As far as they were concerned, my father was dead.'

'Perhaps you should have had him cremated.'

'We considered it. But Papa thought it might arouse suspicion. I didn't realize until later, of course, just how suspicious some of his investors were, even before the murder. They must have got wind of his financial difficulties. Papa had warned Aunt Vita that Faraday was working for them – and hence for the Concentric Alliance. Naturally, she couldn't tell me why we had to tread so carefully, why we had to avoid offending him at all costs. I thought our troubles were over after the funeral and the inquest. But they weren't, were they? They were really only just beginning. And Venice wasn't far enough away to put them behind us. Even there, we were watched. By you, among others.' She smiled at me. 'Are you going to deny it, Guy? Are you going to pretend you weren't paid to come after us, that you didn't start an affair with me in order to find out how much I knew?'

'Two can play at that game. Can *you* pretend you didn't encourage me for the same reason?'

'Perhaps I did.'

'Or because you were afraid Max had also come after you?'

'No. That isn't true.' She stared at me and I at her. She sounded sincere, but so she had all too often before. There was no way to be certain. I wanted to believe her, if only because it made it easier to sustain our truce. If she had set out to trap Max by seducing me, why go on with our affair after his death? Why, unless, buried within the coils of our similar natures, there was some stubborn affinity we could never disown? 'You must believe me, Guy. I never meant to kill him.'

'You meant to see him tried for murder – and possibly hanged.'

'I'd have spoken up for him in court. I'd have said what a terrible provocation finding my father waiting for him rather than me must have been. I wouldn't have let them hang him.'

'Just rot in gaol for the rest of his life?'

'I hoped he'd never be caught. I hoped he'd have the good sense to run and keep on running. Hurting Max was never my intention.'

'Merely a regrettable necessity, like standing by while your father murdered Lightfoot?'

'Well? Haven't you done some things that don't bear much

244

scrutiny? Fraud. Theft. Blackmail. Papa told me all about you, Guy. You're in no position to preach.'

'I never aided and abetted murder.'

'No. But the Concentric Alliance did. It aided and abetted millions of murders. They're why we're going to Dublin. Remember that.'

'I'm not about to forget.' The bargain we had struck remained a good one. The truce we had concluded remained valid. *Watch her, old man. Watch her like a hawk.* Yes, Max. I intended to. But I also intended to do what we had set out to do. She and I were together in this – for the moment.

Suddenly, the door slid open and the ticket-collector entered, swathed in the humility he no doubt reserved for first-class carriages. 'Good morning, sir. Good morning, madam. Tickets, please.' I handed them over and, as he clipped them, he smiled and said, 'Going through to Dublin, sir?'

'Yes.'

'Have a pleasant trip.'

As the door slid shut behind him, Diana's eyes met mine. 'It won't be a pleasant trip,' she murmured. 'But let's hope it's a successful one.'

I had the vague impression that the Irish Free State was still racked by civil war, as it had been in the early twenties, but Diana assured me peace and civic order had long since prevailed. Charnwood had chosen a placid looking-glass version of England in which to hide, a backwater where none would think to find him – save those who knew he was there.

It was already dark when the ferry docked at Kingstown – or Dun Laoghaire, as it had apparently been re-named since independence. I saw little of the port, or of Dublin, come to that, through the gas-lit drizzle. We went straight from Westland Row station to the Shelbourne Hotel, where we booked in as Miss Wood and Mr Morton, travellers from London. When we met again, over dinner in the sparsely populated restaurant, Diana showed me her letter to her father. It was as short and sweet a lie as she could ever have put her name to. But it seemed just what was required to draw Charnwood out. There was no need for me to suggest the slightest amendment. In the arts of deception, she knew no peer.

245

Shelbourne Hotel,
St Stephen's Green,
DUBLIN.

6th November 1931

Dear Papa,
I must see you as soon as possible. I am in the most
dreadful difficulties and need your advice as never before.
Do not worry. Nobody knows I have come to Dublin.
Please telephone or write to me at this address – where I
am registered under the name of Wood – without delay,
saying where and when we can meet. I will come anywhere
you choose at any time you choose. But I *must* see you.

Your ever loving daughter,
Diana.

The city was grey and quiet when we left the hotel early the
following morning and walked up to the General Post Office in
O'Connell Street. I recognized its pillared frontage from newspaper photographs at the time of the Easter Rising, when it had
served as the rebels' headquarters. It seemed surpassingly odd to
enter and find, instead of a sand-bagged nest of Fenians, patient
Dubliners queuing at polished counters beneath a roof echoing
not to gun-fire but the staccato impact of date-stamps on ink-pads
and pass-books.

'We'd like this to reach the box-holder today if possible,' said
Diana, handing the letter to a clerk at one of the windows.

He glanced at the envelope, which bore the magical number but
no name, then said: 'It'll go to the sorting office today right enough,
madam, but I can't say when the holder will collect it, now can I?'

'Where is the sorting office?' I put in.

'The main one's in Sheriff Street, sir. But there are boxes at all
the sub-offices as well.'

'Surely you can tell from the number which office it'll go to.'

'Indeed I can, sir. But I can't tell you. Strictly confidential, do
you see? That's the object of the exercise.'

'Why on earth did you ask him such a question?' hissed Diana as
we left. 'Were you *trying* to make him suspicious?'

'Of course not.'

246

'I told you. Papa checks the box daily. We'll have a reply soon enough.'

'What if we don't?' A possible answer was already forming in my mind. There had been a twinkle in the clerk's eye suggesting even strictly confidential information could be obtained – at a price.

'We will,' declared Diana. 'I know my father. He won't let me down.' As we emerged onto the pavement, she turned right and began walking fast in the direction of the hotel.

'He already has,' I murmured. But she did not hear. Nor did I intend her to. For I shared her confidence that she would hear from Charnwood. Whether she meant to tell me when she did so was, however, quite another matter. And I was determined to be prepared for every eventuality.

It was possible, we both admitted over a late breakfast back at the Shelbourne, that the letter would not reach the appropriate sorting office in time to be collected by Charnwood that day. It was Saturday and the onset of the week-end was against us. The only certain reward for our promptness was to know it definitely would be waiting for him on Monday. But Monday, with so much resting on his response, seemed an agonizingly long way off.

'Have you really no idea where he is?' I asked in my frustration.

'None,' Diana replied. 'He said he would contact us when the time was ripe. Until then, the less we knew, the less likely we were to let something slip.'

'What about the bank accounts he siphoned the money into? Are they here?'

'Presumably. But I'm only guessing. We were to suggest they might be in Switzerland if we thought we needed to.'

'To draw attention away from Ireland?'

'I suppose so. But, wherever they are, they'll be well hidden.'

'Like the man himself.'

'Yes. But Guy—' She reached across the table and fleetingly touched my hand. It was no more than the lightest of pats, but carried with it a sort of electric memory of the pleasure her slender fingers had given – and taken. 'He will respond. I have no doubt of it.'

'And meanwhile?'

'We wait. As best we can.'

* * *

247

The week-end slowly elapsed. We accompanied each other on aimless walks round the mist-wrapped city, never going far from the Shelbourne in case a message arrived. We took meals together in the hotel restaurant, maintaining an outward show of ease and harmony, while in the secrecy of our own thoughts. . . But our relationship was false on too many levels for certainty about what we felt. Platonic friends; breathless lovers; venomous foes; dispassionate allies: we had played every part and lost ourselves in none of them. What was there left, then, but the recognition of two dissemblers? What was there left but the blankness beneath the masks?

Yet, still and all, we were united in our attempt to topple the Concentric Alliance. When I told Diana all I had learned from Duggan – when I listed the evidence and led her along the long-extinguished powder-trail from the guns of August to her father's door – I saw in her eyes the certainty growing that what he had done was unforgivable.

The Shelbourne stood on the northern side of a broad square, the centre of which comprised a public park. There, among the falling leaves, the laughing family groups and the ducks begging for bread, Diana turned to me as Sunday afternoon was wearing towards dusk and said without preamble: 'He's ruined both of us, hasn't he, Guy? But for the war, we might have become admirable people. Instead, what are we?' She gave a resigned smile. 'A confidence trickster and a spoilt bitch.'

'They're not the descriptions I'd choose,' I protested.

'But accurate?'

'Perhaps. The war probably changed as many people as it killed. To find that one man may have been responsible for so much . . .'

'And that man is my father.'

'Yes. He is.'

'When Mama died,' she said, looking into the distance, 'I was twelve years old. I held the whole world responsible, not just the Germans. And I resolved to make the world pay. By taking everything I could from it and giving nothing back. By breaking other people's hearts just as mine had been broken. By proving I couldn't be made to care as much for anyone or anything ever again. Except—' She broke off and I sensed we were close to the truth about herself, or part of it. 'Except my father,' she resumed. 'I turned to him for love and shelter. And he gave them – unstintingly. But the irony can't have escaped him, can it? Just as it can't escape me now. I blamed everybody. Except the one who was truly responsible.'

'What will you do . . . when you meet him?'

'What I've said I'll do.'

'I mean . . . about your mother.'

'I don't know,' she replied, glancing round at me. 'I honestly don't know.'

'Would it help if I came with you?'

'No. He might see us together before showing himself. And then he never would. Besides . . .'

'Yes?'

'This is between my father and me.' Her jaw stiffened. 'Between us and nobody else.'

Monday came, but with it no word from Charnwood. '*Watch her, old man. Watch her like a hawk.*' And so I did, Max. But her calmness – and the words she had uttered in the park – sowed suspicion in my mind. She had a telephone in her room. There were porters galore to bring a letter to her at any hour of the day or night. How could I be sure he had not already communicated with her? And how could I be sure what she intended to do when they met? '*Between us and nobody else,*' she had said. But what had she meant?

I had to know. Too much was at stake to leave to chance – or to a daughter's desire for revenge. I had to find a way into her thoughts. And that was why – so I told myself – I behaved as I did on Monday evening.

After dinner, I escorted her up to her room. On the three previous nights, I had left her at the door. But not tonight.

'May I come in?'

'Of course. But . . .'

The door clicked shut behind us. She was standing very close to me, breathing with nervous shallowness. So beautiful, swathed in an inky blue dress. So desirable. And I had the perfect excuse. 'All those times in Venice,' I said, looking into her dark inviting eyes. 'Each one better than the last. I can't forget them, can you? The things we did. The ways we loved.'

'*Loved?* Is that what we did?'

'Wasn't it?'

'I don't know. Perhaps the word doesn't matter.'

'But the act?'

249

'Oh yes, Guy.' She took my hand, raised it to her breast and pressed my palm against her nipple. 'The act matters. The act is everything.'

Everything? No. But close to it. Close to something precious – something I could no more forget than regret – as I slid the clothes from her body and took her, oh so slowly, in the Dublin night. Again. And yet again.

'I've wanted us to do this so badly.'

'Why?'

'To prove I was right. I didn't choose you, Guy, because I was afraid you'd come to matter too much to me.'

'Another lie?'

'No. Not this time. Not a lie. The truth.'

The truth? Maybe. Or maybe the truth was the one intimacy withheld, the eighth veil she would never drop. After the shock of finding we both wanted so much – and could both have it – there was still doubt waiting for the ecstasy to fade.

Next morning, while she was bathing, I searched her belongings for a letter from Charnwood. There was none. Instead, there was something far worse, something cold and hard, waiting to meet my grasp beneath a silk peignoir in the bottom drawer of a tallboy. There was a gun: an evidently brand-new derringer. And it was loaded.

I complained of a headache over breakfast and retreated to my own room, claiming a few hours' rest would see me right. Diana was solicitous but, so far as I could tell, unsuspecting. As soon after she left me as seemed safe, I slipped out of the hotel, using the service lift and the side-entrance in Kildare Street. Then I headed for the GPO.

There was no sign of the clerk we had spoken to on Saturday and the one who dealt with me turned out to be an embodiment of Hibernian rectitude. My pleas of desperate life-or-death urgency left him unmoved. The names and addresses of box-holders were a sacred trust. He would never part with them. My hints at bribery only made matters worse. In the end, I did well to escape without the police being called.

I decided to try my luck at the Sheriff Street sorting office, to which a passer-by gave me directions. It lay half a mile east, behind Amiens Street railway station. I struck out across O'Connell Street, pausing between the tracks in the centre to let a tram rattle by.

Did she really mean to kill him? I wondered. Did she really mean to make him answer so finally for her mother's death? If so—

'Begging your pardon, sir!' A boy's high-pitched voice was followed by a twitch at my sleeve.

'What the devil do you want?' I snapped. Seeing his ragged clothes and importunate face, the answer seemed obvious. But I was wrong.

'This is for you, sir.' He pushed a blank white envelope into my hand. 'From the gentleman yonder.'

'What gentleman?'

'The old fellow outside the Metropole.' He pointed back at the hotel adjacent to the GPO, then scratched his head. 'Well, sure, he was there a moment ago.'

'Old, you say?'

'White-haired. And British, like yourself.'

I raced across to the hotel and looked in both directions, then tried the side-streets to south and north. Nothing. No sign. No trace. I launched back into the GPO. He was not there. Nor in the palm-fringed foyer of the Metropole, where I sank into a chair and, with shaking fingers, opened the envelope.

Dublin,
10th November 1931

My dear Horton,
Congratulations on your persistence. It has quite confounded me. I have, of course, received my daughter's letter. But you should know that I have also received a letter from my sister, forewarning me as to your intentions. Naturally, I have no choice but to yield to your demands. But Vita's intervention enables me to impose one small condition. I will meet you to surrender the documents. But only you, Horton. Not Diana. If she accompanies you – or I see her nearby – I will not show myself. I hope to deliver this letter to you in circumstances that will enable you to withhold its contents from her. Certainly, I think it would be wise to do so. And also wise not to alert her to our meeting. I suggest the Wellington Monument in Phoenix Park at eight o'clock tomorrow morning, early enough for you to leave the Shelbourne without Diana noticing and for there to be few if any witnesses to our encounter. Pray excuse the lack of a signature. I think you will agree it is a sensible precaution. Until tomorrow.

251

*   *   *

It took me as far as O'Connell Bridge to decide what to do. There I screwed up Charnwood's note and dropped it over the parapet into the Liffey. Then I walked swiftly back to the Shelbourne, pausing at the taxi rank just short of it to tip a cabby ten shillings in return for his guarantee that he would be there at half past seven the following morning, ready to drive me out to Phoenix Park.

I had hoped to gain the safety of my room undetected and so postpone facing Diana for as long as possible. But luck was against me. As I entered the hotel and made for the stairs, the lift doors slid open and she stepped out, frowning in surprise at the sight of me.

'Guy! I thought you were resting.'

'Er . . . I was. But then I . . . decided to see what a breath of air would do for my head.'

'And what did it do?'

'Cleared it. Very effectively.'

'Good. I was going to take a stroll in the park. Would you care to accompany me?'

'Certainly.'

We went out, crossed the road and entered the park by the nearest gate. Neither of us spoke and the silence stretched itself into something tense and expectant. We followed a curving path along the edge of a pond, walking slowly, each waiting for the other to say something, anything. Then I realized what I should already have asked and blurted out the question in sudden haste.

'Have you heard from your father?'

'No. I confess . . . I'm beginning to worry. Surely I should have done by now.'

'He probably didn't receive your letter until yesterday. He might even have gone away for a few days. We'll have to be patient.'

She frowned at me once more. 'You *have* changed your tune.'

'I'm only trying to be realistic.'

'*Realistic?*' She stopped and stared at me. In seeking to cover my tracks, I had gone a long way towards arousing her suspicions. 'Is that what you were being last night, Guy – realistic?'

'Last night has nothing to do with it.'

'Hasn't it?'

'Of course not.'

'You've been to the GPO, haven't you?'

252

'What?'

'You've tried to wheedle Papa's address out of them – or buy it.'

'No.'

'The headache. The sudden desire for fresh air. Do you think I'm a fool?'

'As I told you, I—'

'You've been gone nearly an hour.'

'No, no. Nothing like as long.'

'I telephoned your room. To see how you were. You *might* have slept through the bell. But I don't think you did, do you?'

'Er. . . No.' My brain raced in pursuit of a convincing lie. In my desperation, I remembered an old maxim: alter the truth as little as possible. 'You're right. I thought I could bribe one of the clerks into supplying your father's address.'

'What happened?'

'I came away empty-handed. As no doubt you could have told me I would.'

'Yes. I could.' Her expression lightened. Her sense of superiority was appeased – and hence deceived.

'It was a stupid thing to do. I—'

'It was worse than stupid!' She was angry with me but no longer suspicious: I had escaped. 'Papa's quite capable of having an informant on the staff ready to alert him to just such an attempt.'

'Don't worry. I never specified which box-number I was in-terested in. The clerk we saw on Saturday wasn't on duty.'

'We must be grateful for small mercies. What I can't understand is . . . why you did it.'

'Perhaps last night *was* the reason. Perhaps I wanted to get what we came here for . . . before our truce turned into something else.'

'You think it might?'

'Let's say I'm afraid it might. I can't forget Max, you see. I—'

'Guilt? Is that it, Guy? Is that what you woke up with this morning? Not a headache, but a bad attack of conscience?'

'I suppose it was.'

'I thought we'd accepted each other for what we really are. But it seems I was wrong.'

I faced the contempt in her gaze and nodded. 'Yes. It seems you were.'

'Then let's hope we hear from my father very soon. Before our truce disturbs your re-discovered conscience any further.' At which she turned on her heel and strode back towards the hotel, leaving me to follow some paces behind, with my pride dented but my secret intact.

It was still intact that evening, when I escorted Diana to her room after a dinner during which we had exchanged barely a word. So was her contempt. But that, it seemed to me, was a small price to pay for the prize I would shortly claim.

'Perhaps something will happen tomorrow,' I disingenuously remarked as she slid the key into the lock.

'It well might,' she replied, pushing the door open and stepping across the threshold. 'My father has always had an impeccable sense of timing.' Glancing round, she caught my nonplussed look and added: 'Tomorrow is Armistice Day.'

'Ah, yes,' I said, marvelling at my ability to have overlooked such an obvious point – as I felt sure Charnwood had not. 'Of course. It had—' But before I could finish the sentence, Diana had closed the door in my face. A second later, I heard the bolt slide home. 'Until tomorrow,' I said to myself as I turned away. 'Until the truce is over, darling mine.'

CHAPTER

FOURTEEN

It was barely light when I left the Shelbourne, a still black night giving way reluctantly to a still grey day. The cabby was waiting as promised, lured back by my generous tip of the previous morning.

'Phoenix Park, wasn't it, sir?'

'Yes. Near the Wellington Monument.'

'Right you are, sir. The Iron Duke's Needle it is. Sure, he was born in Dublin. Did you know that?'

'I don't believe I did.'

'Oh yes. But, like many a sensible man, he didn't stay to die here.'

There was to be more, in a similar vein, as we headed west. I said little, but it made no difference. The fellow's chatter was self-sustaining. I sat back in my seat and smoked a cigarette and wondered just what I would find waiting for me. Charnwood had no choice but to do as he was asked. He had said so himself. And yet . . .

I must have lost track of time, for suddenly, it seemed, we were there, turning into the park through open gates hung from pillars topped with lanterns still lit against the faltering darkness. Ahead stretched an arrow-straight tree-lined avenue, while to the left, through the bare branches and the slowly lifting dusk, loomed a tall stone obelisk.

'Is that the monument?'

'It is, sir.'

'Then stop here. I'll walk the rest of the way.'

'Just as you like, sir.'

I paid him off and checked my watch. It was ten minutes to eight. I had wanted to arrive a little early, for Charnwood, I felt sure, would not be late. I started along the avenue, trees, bushes and a wrought-iron fence denying me a complete view of the monument for some way until abruptly they ceased and there it stood, stark and steepling, at the centre of a wide lawn.

I crossed the lawn to the foot of the monument and gazed up at it. It must have been all of two hundred feet high, a tapering stone pillar with a pyramidal top, resting on a vast square plinth, from the base of which radiated a dozen or so sloping steps that ran down to where I stood. A tarmacadammed path linked it to a road, screened by trees, that turned off the main avenue from which I had approached. Absolute silence reigned in the gathering brightness. And when I looked at my watch I saw it was now only a few minutes to eight.

I began to walk round the monument, glancing up at the bronze reliefs of Wellington's victories that adorned the plinth. Then, as I neared the south-western corner, a flight of rooks rose cawing from the trees at the far end of the path and a figure appeared, heading slowly towards me along it. A slim erect figure in hat and overcoat, carrying a Gladstone bag in his right hand, moving with the faint stiffness of an old but agile man. Fabian Charnwood, beyond doubt and question. And somewhere far off, a clock was striking eight.

We met where the path joined the pavement surrounding the monument. We met and eyed each other from a few feet apart, as wary as we were disbelieving. He had acquired a Vandyke beard, grey where his hair was white, but was otherwise unaltered, recognizable but inconspicuous beneath the camouflage of his own obituary.

'I have what you asked for,' he said quietly, holding out the bag. 'It's all in here.'

I took the bag from him, placed it on the ground and pulled it open. Inside was a bundle of documents tied with string, wedged between two fat leather-bound books.

'The accounts and minute books,' he said. 'Along with the more sensitive correspondence I accumulated over the years.'

I closed the bag and stood up with it in my hand. 'How do I know everything's here?'

'You don't. But nor do you need to. You have enough there to destroy a great many famous and respectable people. Isn't that what you want?'

'Is it enough to destroy the Concentric Alliance?'

'I have already destroyed it, Horton, in the only significant sense. I have taken their money, you see. Such of it as they entrusted to me, which was a great deal. And I have deprived them of their. . . Well, leader is too strong a word. But, without me, they have no common centre. No common purpose, indeed, but the desire to recover what they think I stole from them.'

'And didn't you?'

'Yes. If one can be said to steal anything from those who have already stolen it.'

'With your help, surely. You were – you are – the biggest thief of them all.'

'I suppose I was. Or am, for the moment.' He glanced to right and left. 'But moments may be all there is at our disposal. We should not fritter them away.'

'You needn't worry. Nobody knows we're here.'

'Do they not? As to that—' He gave a little mirthless chuckle. 'What will you do with the records, Horton? Tell me. You may as well. There's nothing *I* can do to stop you.'

'I shall take them to the press.'

'Or sell them to the press?'

'I'm not doing this for money, Charnwood.'

'No. I don't think you are. It must be a novel experience for you. A sudden conversion to the cause of truth.'

'It is. And you can take the credit for it. I never thought truth was worth fighting for . . . until I discovered the scale of the lie you'd inflicted on humanity.'

'Ah, the war,' he said, deliberately echoing a phrase he had used once before. 'Always there is the war.'

'Thanks to you, yes.'

'There would have been a war anyway, you know. There would have been some other pretext, even if I had not supplied one.'

'Why did you supply it, then?'

'Because the key to profit is timing. It took me several years to recruit the soldiers, politicians and financiers who comprised the Concentric Alliance. The plan I put to them was to sink a vast

257

sum, much of it borrowed, into gold, insurance and stock likely to rise on the outbreak of war, while short-selling stock likely to fall, then net an even vaster profit when war came, as the state of affairs in Europe rendered inevitable. It depended for its success on determining in advance when that would happen. It was obvious the Balkans represented the likeliest flash-point, but I came to realize that the only way to be certain – the only way to know exactly when to take out the investments – was to create the flash ourselves. When I learned of Franz Ferdinand's intention to visit Bosnia, I knew our chance had come. We had already infiltrated both the Black Hand and Franz Ferdinand's military chancellery. Between them, his death was rendered a certainty. And it was certainty we required.'

'Never mind the consequences?'

'They were necessarily unpredictable. Grievously so, in the case of my dear wife. Her death was . . . difficult to come to terms with.'

'It still is for Diana.'

'Of course.' He bowed his head. 'It was bound to be. Difficult, if not impossible. That is why I did not tell her about the Concentric Alliance.'

'And why you hadn't the courage to face her as well as me?'

He looked up. 'Not exactly. There were other considerations.'

'Such as?'

'Such as that car.' He pointed towards the main avenue. Looking round, I saw a black limousine driving slowly past. As my eyes followed it, it turned left and drew to a halt beyond the trees near the end of the path. 'Are you absolutely sure nobody knows we're here, Horton?'

'Nobody could.'

'Yet I fear they do.'

Three figures climbed from the car and started along the path towards us. As they cleared the trees, they separated, one coming straight on while the other two took diagonal courses across the lawn. It looked horribly like an outflanking manoeuvre. For a few seconds, I told myself I was mistaken. Then I recognized the figure on the path as Faraday. And the man on our right as Vasaritch's boatman in Venice – the huge and menacing Klaus.

'Climb to the top of the steps with me,' said Charnwood.

'Why? There's no—'

'Quickly!'

He moved past me and I followed, up the broad sloping steps

to the foot of the plinth. We turned in unison to find Faraday halfway along the path, with Klaus and the other man keeping pace with him about fifteen yards to either side.

'We haven't much time,' whispered Charnwood. 'I have a letter here for Diana.' He took an envelope from his pocket and handed it to me. 'Will you deliver it for me?'

'Yes. But—'

'Put it away!'

I slid it into my jacket, staring at him incredulously. 'You knew this was going to happen, didn't you?'

'I thought it likely. The organization I created is a formidable one. Nobody knows that better than I do.'

'What do they want?'

'Something they cannot have.' He smiled, for the very first time I could ever recall. 'Just like you and me, Horton.'

Faraday stopped as he reached the end of the path and peered up at us from beneath the brim of his homburg. Klaus took up position at the north-western point of the pavement surrounding the memorial, the other man at the south-western point. He was less massively built than Klaus, but equally forbidding in appearance, hook-nosed and flint-eyed, a black hat propped well back on his head and a long raincoat hanging unbuttoned round his gaunt frame. Klaus's black greatcoat was also unbuttoned, but Faraday was swaddled in scarf and gloves, with the collar of his coat pulled well up. He rubbed his hands together as if to keep warm, then said: 'Good morning to you both. This is an unexpected pleasure.'

'Unexpected perhaps,' said Charnwood. 'But scarcely a pleasure. What do you want, Noel?'

'The contents of the bag Horton is holding. And your company when we drive away from here.'

'You know what the contents are?'

'I know they include material you promised to destroy long ago.'

'Did I?'

'You have broken faith with too many people, Fabian. This is no time for bluster.'

'I agree. But what is it a time for?'

'Harsh realities. Klaus you both know. Let me assure you that O'Reilly here is as good a marksman – and just as ruthless.' As if on cue, the two men drew revolvers from within their coats. 'Our requirements are simple. Surrender the bag, Horton, and you

259

may be on your way. What happens after that need not concern you.'

'How did you know we were here?' I countered.

'We followed you from the Shelbourne. Just as we did yesterday, when Fabian also followed you and arranged this meeting. O'Connell Street was no place for a confrontation. But this . . .' He glanced around. 'This is altogether more suitable.'

'But how did you know I was in Dublin?'

Faraday smiled. 'The lovely Diana. She has struck terms with us. Partly for a share of however much money we recover. Partly to avenge her mother. Sharper than a serpent's tooth, eh, Fabian?'

So, she had done for both of us, just as she had planned. The show of reluctance; the suggestion of sincerity; the hint of murderous intent: they all amounted to her victory and my defeat. I swore under my breath and looked at Charnwood, expecting to see him reeling before the blow. But there was no sign of the slightest reaction. His voice was unwavering as he spoke. 'It seems you have us at a disadvantage, Noel.'

'Indeed we do. Put the bag down, Horton, and walk away.'

'You will never reach the road,' said Charnwood from the corner of his mouth. 'They do not mean to let you live.'

Charnwood was probably right. But what choice did I have? In compliance lay my only hope. I was gripping the handle of the bag so tightly all feeling was draining from my hand. My heart was racing, my breath coming in shallow gulps. Sweat was forming beneath the band of my hat. Klaus and O'Reilly were watching me like two wolves who had cornered a rabbit. And Faraday was smiling. 'You have a chance to extricate yourself from this, Horton. I suggest you take it. I really do.'

'And . . . if I don't?'

'Neither of these men will hesitate to fire if I give the word. And they won't miss. They never do.' Slowly, Klaus raised his gun and pointed it straight at me. 'Give it up, Horton. Follow Diana's example.'

'I—'

'One moment,' put in Charnwood.

'No more moments,' retorted Faraday. 'We must—'

'Listen to me!' Charnwood's raised voice silenced Faraday, as if neither had quite shed the instincts born of whatever their relationship had previously been. 'I have wedged beneath my tongue a phial containing not plain water, I assure you, but prussic acid in sufficient concentration to cause certain death should I bite into the phial and swallow the contents. As I will, unless Horton is allowed to leave here with the bag and every single document in it. Once I am dead, Noel, you will not find so much as a farthing of your masters' money. So, what is it to be? Their money or my life?'

He was bluffing. Surely he had to be. If not, he had foreseen this turn of events and guarded against it. And, what was more, he wanted me to escape with the records I had just extorted from him. Why? Looking down, I saw Faraday frown. He too was perplexed by the apparent contradiction.

'An answer, if you please,' said Charnwood.

Faraday clenched his teeth. 'Very well,' he replied. 'Horton may go.' Klaus looked sharply at him, but lowered his gun without protest. 'With the bag.'

'Good,' said Charnwood. 'Give him the keys to your car, would you? I do not want you going in hot pursuit of him.' When Faraday hesitated, he added: 'Remember the money.'

'All right. The car also. Give Horton the keys, O'Reilly.'

'They're in the ignition, sir.'

'Ready and waiting for you, it seems, Horton.' Did Faraday's sarcasm disguise a trick? I could not tell.

'We shall see,' said Charnwood. He looked round at me. 'Well, Horton, what are you waiting for? Walk to the car and drive away. The quickest way out of the park is straight ahead, then left. That'll bring you to Islandbridge Gate.'

'But—'

'Go! Now!'

I obeyed, my legs threatening to buckle beneath me as I descended the steps. Faraday smiled as I passed him and murmured, 'Until we meet again,' his eyes heliographing the additional words *very soon*. Then he was behind me and only the empty path and the screen of trees lay between me and the car. Resisting the temptation to run, or even look back, I began walking steadily, my thoughts consumed by the overpowering desire to escape. The craving for flight blotted out all analysis of what was happening and why.

'Stop!' Faraday's voice, raised in a peremptory shout, halted me in my tracks when I was only a few yards from the trees. I looked over my shoulder to see him, Klaus and O'Reilly closing on me. 'Stand exactly where you are.'

261

'What are you doing?' cried Charnwood, hurrying down from the monument and coming after them.

'Calling your bluff,' Faraday replied, looking back at him.

'But the money!'

'Was not quite bait enough. I have just seen through the ploy, Fabian. If you want Horton to leave with the records, it can only be because you want them to be published. And that can only be because you do not intend to face the consequences of publication. They represent your suicide note, don't they? In which case, you will be unable to lead us to the money. But perhaps the records can. Perhaps that is why you are so anxious to put them out of our reach. If so, we may as well have them without further ado. Don't you agree?'

'You're wrong. I swear I—'

'Put the bag down, Horton!' said Faraday, rounding on me. 'Now!' He stopped and signalled for Klaus and O'Reilly to do the same. The two men raised their guns and trained them on me. They were about ten yards away, their arms outstretched, hard and steady as their faces. I saw their index fingers curl round the triggers, saw their eyes narrow as they took aim.

'All right,' I blurted out, dropping the bag. It thumped to the ground at my feet. 'You can have all of it.'

'Indeed we can,' said Faraday. 'We can even have a guarantee against the possibility that you have already perused the documents. A necessary if regrettable guarantee, I think you will agree.'

'What. . . What do you mean?'

'I mean you have to die, Horton. Here and now. I'm sorry, but there it is. O'Reilly—'

When I heard the report of the gun, I thought it was the last sound that would ever reach my ears. My brain shaped a banal notion of death's bewildering unexpectedness and braced itself against pain as severe as it seemed likely to be brief. But suddenly it was O'Reilly falling, not me, blood bursting from the back of his head. And Charnwood was holding the only gun that had fired and was shouting, 'Run, Horton! Run!' And I was stooping to grab the bag and turning away even as Klaus was whirling round to fire. And Charnwood, hit square in the chest, was toppling backwards. And I was bursting through the trees, twigs and branches tearing at my face, my lungs straining for air, and hurling myself across the pavement and round to the driver's side of the car.

The key *was* in the ignition. Hope flared: the hope that I might actually survive the next few seconds, never mind the next few minutes. I whipped the door open, flung the bag across the seat and bundled in after it, aware that a bullet had just whined over the roof of the car. Swearing and praying simultaneously, I turned the key, pulled the starter and heard the engine burst into well-tuned life. I forced it into gear, pushed the accelerator towards the floor and felt my left foot begin to shudder violently as it raised the clutch. Then, with a squeal from the tyres, the car surged forward. A bullet splintered the rear nearside window. The door flew wide open, bouncing back far enough from its hinges for me to grab the handle and slam it shut. Another bullet pinged off the bonnet. As I careered round a bend in the road, I glanced up at the rear-view mirror and saw, through a gap in the trees, two crumpled figures lying motionless on the grass. Then they were out of my sight.

'Concentrate!' I shouted to myself. 'Straight ahead. Then left.' There was the turning, as Charnwood had promised. I took it on what felt like only two wheels, saw the gate, narrower than the one I had entered the park by, drove through and swerved left onto the road beyond. Had I been thinking clearly, I might have taken the right-hand turning a short distance ahead and so put the park behind me as swiftly as possible. Instead, I sped past it and found the boundary wall of the park tracking my route, with the Wellington Monument visible beyond the trees. And suddenly Klaus, who must have calculated I would make just such a mistake, appeared in front of me, scrambling over the wall and jumping down onto the pavement. I would have been past him in the second it took him to rise, but that too he judged exactly. Still crouching, he steadied the gun in both hands, took aim and—

I wrenched the wheel to the right, bending and flinching as the tyres shrieked and the wind-screen shattered. Glass was showering over me, my vision distorting as the car skidded. I saw something vertical in my path and stamped on the brake. But too late. With a smashing of yet more glass and a grinding of metal, the car struck a lamp-post on the other side of the road, lurched, juddered and slewed to a halt.

Suddenly, the only sound was a hissing from the fractured radiator. As the car had rotated to rest round the lamp-post, I had fallen across the seat and now found myself propped against Charnwood's bag, my brain adjusting all too slowly to the little I

263

could see from such an angle: a steam-blurred patch of Dublin sky, framed by the jagged remnants of the wind-screen; a twisted section of bonnet, the steam condensing into beads and rivulets on its polished black surface; and the nearside wing-mirror, miraculously unbroken, in which the reflection of Klaus was growing larger and larger as he strode towards me, gun in hand. I glanced down at my own hand, blood trickling from a wound at the base of the thumb. A tiny triangle of glass, imbedded in the flesh, winked back at me. And I knew this was to be the end: stupid, undignified and brutal, before the blood on my hand had even begun to thicken. Before I had learned even one of the names of those who had ordained my death.

Then I saw it. On the floor in front of me, where it had been thrown from the glove compartment. A revolver. They had left a gun in the car. Loaded? If not, it made no difference. If it was – His shadow fell across me. He reached for the door-handle as I rolled forward, grasped the gun and rolled back, feeling the triangle of glass bite as I stretched my finger towards the trigger. The window slid across my sight as he yanked at the door. My arm straightened as I turned. His face loomed above me. A smile of satisfaction turned to a grimace of horror. Then I squeezed the trigger and learned the truth. The gun *was* loaded.

I lay there for several seconds, hearing nothing but the panting of my own breath. Then I sat up, clambered from the car and looked down at him. He lay supine in the road, blood draining from a hole above the bridge of his nose to form a dark and spreading pool beneath his right ear. His mouth was half-open. His eyes were staring blindly up at me. And the gun was still clasped in his hand. On the other side of the road, gaping at me, stood a fat man leaning on a bicycle. A cigarette dropped from his sagging lower lip as he stared, scattering ash down the bib of his overalls. I was beginning to tremble, beginning to lose control. But I still had to escape. I grabbed the bag and began to run, back the way I had driven, towards the turning I had not taken, away from the park, away from three deaths and my own so very near extinction. Where Faraday was I did not know. Nor could I stop to find out.

As I rounded the bend, I remembered the gun waggling in my hand, and paused to shove it into the bag. Then I ran on, down and over a stone bridge across the river, then up again past what looked like army barracks. I was aware of people staring at me and pointing, of one or two shouts in my wake. I reached a railway bridge and a busy cross-roads. An east-bound tram was picking up passengers to my left. I ran towards it and leapt onto the platform just as it was pulling away.

'Saints preserve us,' said the conductor as I cannoned into him. 'Aren't you in a tearing hurry to be somewhere else?'

I was. But where? Where exactly was I to go? Klaus and O'Reilly were surely not Faraday's only assistants. Others might be waiting for me at the Shelbourne. Yet I had no other refuge in this alien city. I was a fugitive with nowhere to hide. Except in England, of course. Except in the country I knew. I had a start on them, a precious start I was determined not to waste. And in my pocket I had a first-class return ticket to London. 'Kingstown,' I said abruptly. 'I must get to Kingstown. Dun Laoghaire, I mean.'

'Call it what you like, sir, I can't help you there. We only go to Eden Quay.'

'I *must* get to Dun Laoghaire,' I said, grabbing his arm for emphasis.

'Then calm yourself. A stroll over the bridge from Eden Quay will bring you to Tara Street station. You can get a train to Dun Laoghaire from there every half hour at least.'

'Thanks,' I let go of him. 'I'm sorry.'

'No need for your apologies, sir. Just your fare will make me a happy man.'

The tram clanked and swayed on its agonizing crawl through Dublin's crowded streets. Watched suspiciously by other passengers, I bound my bleeding hand in a handkerchief and mopped the sweat off my face, glimpsing reflections of myself, wild-eyed and dishevelled, in the windows opposite. I held the bag in my lap, never once letting go of the handle, and tried desperately to order my thoughts.

How and when had Diana communicated with Faraday? It could scarcely have been before we left Dorking, unless it was during the hour I had waited for her in the library. But perhaps she had not needed to. Perhaps Vita had done it for her. In which case her letter to Charnwood had been *intended* to make him see me alone, sparing Diana the painful necessity of explaining her treachery to us and leaving the way clear for Faraday to surprise us.

265

Not that he *had* surprised Charnwood. The gun and the phial of prussic acid – if it existed – proved he had expected to be betrayed. And that proved Faraday right about the records of the Concentric Alliance. They *were* Charnwood's suicide note. They were his farewell to the world. And it was up to me to ensure the world received his farewell.

Speed was of the essence. The longer I delayed, the likelier it was I would fail. The Concentric Alliance was everywhere. But such an extensive organization might react slowly to events. If I could contact Duggan and exploit his Fleet Street connections, it was possible – just possible – that we might pre-empt them. But first I would have to reach England.

I was in luck at Tara Street, racing up the steps just in time to catch a late-running train to Dun Laoghaire. But the emptiness of the train should have forewarned me of the disappointment lying in wait at the other end.

'The Holyhead ferry left more than half an hour ago, sir,' announced the ticket-collector at Dun Laoghaire station.

'When's the next one?'

'In just a little over ten hours, sir.'

'*What?*'

'It'll give you plenty of time to see the town. A bit more than most folk would think it warranted, to be perfectly honest.'

'Is there no other way I can get to England?'

'To be sure there is, sir. Go back into Dublin. If memory serves, there's a ferry to Holyhead from North Wall Quay about one o'clock.'

Back into Dublin, with more than three hours to wait? No. It was not to be countenanced. Faraday was quite capable of studying a timetable and calculating my options. He would come for me long before any ferry did. 'There has to be some other way,' I insisted.

The ticket-collector scratched his head. 'Well, now, you could go down to Rosslare, I suppose, and cross from there to Fishguard. But that's an evening sailing too. And more than three hours later than from here. No, no, you'd be much better off going from North Wall.'

'Nevertheless, when *is* the next train to Rosslare?'

'Well, if you took the ten o'clock down to Bray, you could catch the ten thirty-five from there to Wexford and be at Rosslare

Harbour by . . . let me see . . .' He thumbed through a dog-eared booklet. 'Twenty past three.'

With six or seven hours to wait for the Fishguard ferry. But what did that matter? If it was the least logical choice, it was also the choice Faraday was least likely to think I might make. Rosslare it would have to be.

The shock of all that had happened can be the only excuse for my stupidity. It was another hour or so before my brain began to function properly. With a compartment to myself aboard the Wexford train, I reckoned it was time to examine the documents I had very nearly died for and for which three other men *had* died.

My mouth dropped open when I looked down at the bag and realized the enormity of my mistake. Faraday had only to travel to Dun Laoghaire and describe me to the ticket-collector – '*Englishman in a hurry with Gladstone bag*' – to be given a detailed itinerary of my future movements. The straight line of my flight had suddenly become the circular despair of a rat caught in a trap.

To my left, the Irish Sea stretched away, grey and tantalizingly smooth, towards the homeland I seemed destined never to reach. How far was the Welsh coast? Fifty miles? Sixty? It might as well have been a thousand for all the difference it made. But self-pity would not give me wings to fly with. I could not go on and I could not go back. There was therefore only one thing to do. At the next stop, I got off the train.

Though no doubt assured of a warm place in the hearts of its true-born sons, Wicklow struck me that chill November morning as just about the grimmest and least welcoming place I could have chosen to take refuge in. Old men in threadbare clothes leaned on every other door-post, sucking at pipes. Barefoot children crouched in the gutters, playing dibs. And huge-girthed women gathered at shop windows to gossip and gripe. Only the dogs paid me any heed, perhaps recognizing in the passing stranger some of their own furtiveness. The rest of the population of Wicklow seemed unaware of my existence. And that, I reminded myself, was just as well.

I made my way to the harbour, sat up on the wall, lit a cigarette and anxiously considered what I should do next. A wind started to get up and toss stray spots of rain in my direction. The barnacled assembly of coasters and fishing smacks began to bob at their moorings. And an idea took tentative shape in my mind. I lit another cigarette, and by the time I had finished it the idea had become a plan of action.

Docherty's Bar, hard by the quay, seemed as good a place as any to try my luck. The cavernous interior smelt like smoked mackerel soaked in Guinness and most of the customers looked old enough to be able to remember the Great Famine. But the barman seemed an amiable soul, one who might be willing to aid a romantic cause. And he evidently approved of my choice of whiskey.

'It's a pleasure to serve a gentleman of discernment,' he remarked, casting a scornful glance at his other patrons.

'Perhaps you'd be willing to give me some advice, then,' I ventured.

'What advice would you be after, sir?'

'I was wondering if you knew of somebody with a boat who might be willing . . .' I lowered my voice. 'To run a gentleman of discernment over to the Welsh coast.'

He squinted at me for a moment, then nodded thoughtfully. 'I might, sir. But, now, why wouldn't you be taking the ferry from Dun Laoghaire . . . if you don't mind me asking?'

I smiled. 'An affair of the heart is the problem. I have a certain young Dublin lady's retinue of muscular brothers on my trail. They'd be waiting for me in Dun Laoghaire.'

'Would they, though?' He too smiled. 'I see your difficulty.'

'But can you see any way out of it?'

'Maybe I can, sir. Maybe I know just the man for what you have in mind. He'll be in later. I'll have a word.'

'Thank you. I'd be obliged. Meanwhile . . .' I drained my glass. 'I'll have another tot of your excellent whiskey. And perhaps you'd care for one yourself.'

Nearly an hour had passed, and I had retreated to a corner table, the bag stowed beneath it at my feet, when a short wiry man with a face like a monkey left a conversation with the barman to join me. Before he had said a word, his stained guernsey, woollen hat and weather-beaten complexion raised my hopes.

'Mick tells me you want to take a private cruise to Wales.'

'I do, yes.'

'I might be able to help you there. I keep a boat in the harbour.

Pretty little thing. The *Leitrim Lassie*. Sturdy as they come. I take fishing parties out in her in the summer. Week-enders from Dublin and such.'

'And at this time of the year?'

'Oh, I tend to my lobster-pots in her. She's kept in trim, don't you worry.'

'So, she might be . . . for hire?'

'She might. At the right price.'

'And what would that be?' I had sufficient cash about me to cater for most contingencies. But I knew he would expect me to haggle.

He looked me up and down, grinned and said without hint of irony: 'Twenty pounds, sir. A bargain, I think you'll agree.'

I laughed. 'Out of the question.'

'It's a three or four hour trip. Eight or more for me to see home again. And I can take you to Pwllheli. That's on the railway, which you'll be wanting, won't you?'

'Er . . . Yes.'

'But not the Holyhead line. So, no danger of running into those brothers Mick mentioned.'

'Even so . . .'

'Desmond Rafferty may not come cheap.' He winked. 'But he comes awful quiet.'

'Does he?'

'Oh yes, sir. As the grave.'

'I'll pay you ten.'

'Fifteen.'

'All right. Fifteen pounds.'

'Guineas.'

I sighed. 'Guineas it is.'

'Then you have your private cruise.' He extended his hand. 'Would a four o'clock sailing suit you?'

Rafferty had business to attend to before we left and so had I. Wicklow Public Library was not likely to be mistaken for the British Museum, but it did possess a current *Bradshaw*, which contained both bad news and good. Whenever we reached Pwllheli, it would be too late for the last train with onward connections to London. But at least I could be sure of catching the first train in the morning. Then, connections permitting, I would be in London by half past two. I left the library, went straight to the nearest post office and despatched a telegram to George Duggan, care of the *Alnwick Advertiser*.

> Have evidence we need to expose them. Meet me London
> tomorrow. Rose and Crown, Warwick Street, six o'clock.
>   HORTON.

By choosing the pub I had taken him to in September and allocating three and a half hours to possible delays on obscure Welsh branch lines, it seemed to me that I had been as cautious as I needed to be. Duggan would go to the North Pole in search of what I was carrying. He at least would not let me down. Nor would I let him down. We needed each other. As never before.

The weather had deteriorated by four o'clock, rain sheeting across the harbour in a stiff westerly. And the *Leitrim Lassie* looked to my land-lubber's eye like the kind of craft that should never venture beyond an estuary. But needs must. And Rafferty, resplendent in flapping oilskins, was nothing daunted.

'Sure, it's nought but a squall. It'll blow itself out like one of my wife's tempers. Settle yourself in the cabin and enjoy the trip.'

The cabin was aft, separated from the wheel-house by a stretch of deck. As soon as we were under way, I retreated to its relative privacy, took the documents from the bag and laid them out on the small chart table. Several hours of solitude lay before me, with Rafferty busy at the wheel. This was the chance I had been waiting for all day to find out just how much knowledge – how much power – Charnwood had placed in my hands. As we cleared the harbour wall and set out on our voyage, I lit the hurricane-lamp, hung it from a beam above the table, and commenced another voyage – into the innermost circles of the Concentric Alliance.

CHAPTER

FIFTEEN

So now I knew. All the actions. All the names. All the steps along
the path. Charnwood's secrets were mine, in committee-man's
prose, accountant's columns and carbon-copied correspondence:
worse than I had imagined, because they contained only cunning
and logic, where I had expected to find evil and madness. But
megalomania featured nowhere in what the Concentric Alliance
had done. It had been shaped in Charnwood's likeness: calm,
cautious and calculating, yet always remorseless in its pursuit of
profit, and – when necessary – utterly ruthless.

Its origins lay in Charnwood's mind and in a committee of his
leading clients he established in the spring of 1909 to sanction
unorthodox investments on their behalf. So far as I could judge
from its minutes and resolutions, Charnwood invited its members
to take advantage of the political and military connections he had
made across Europe during the years he had spent selling
weaponry for his father's firm, Moss Charnwood. He believed
Austria-Hungary's annexation of Bosnia the previous autumn
would lead to a world war within five years. And he maintained
that his wealth of contacts would enable him to predict its outbreak
to the very month. By accumulating large stock-holdings in the
shipbuilders, munitions manufacturers and military suppliers of
every affected country, buying gold whenever the price dipped,
taking out war insurance however punitive the premium and short-
selling war-sensitive shares when the time came, he anticipated

that they could all in due course reap not simply a vast profit, but a fortune for life. To achieve this, however, they would have to borrow enormous sums to finance investment on the necessary scale. And they would have to be patient.

Charnwood's clients needed little persuading. Most of them had probably already been won over in private conversations. They agreed to his proposals – and to the need for secrecy and forbearance. Charnwood was entrusted with the records of their transactions and assured of their complete confidence. Capital was borrowed and spent. Other members were co-opted. Sub-committees were established in France, Italy, Germany, Russia, Spain, Switzerland and Austria, presided over by Charnwood. What he had initially called the Special Investments Committee became one of several Concentric Committees, as he dubbed them. And then, some time in 1912, he made his first reference to the Concentric Alliance, a secret triplet of the two armed alliances into which the European powers had divided.

It was early in 1913, perhaps reflecting the ambitiousness of this new title, that discussion began of something euphemistically described as precipitation. Every financial resource of every member had been called upon to take advantage of the crisis arising from the invasion of Turkey's Balkan provinces by Serbia, Bulgaria, Greece and Montenegro in October 1912. Charnwood's contacts in Vienna had convinced him Austria-Hungary would not tolerate an enlarged Serbia and that war would therefore result from her expansion into Macedonia. But it had not followed. Emperor Franz Josef, supported by his nephew and heir, the Archduke Franz Ferdinand, had held out for peace. So, as their debts mounted and their earlier confidence began to evaporate, the members of the Concentric Alliance started wondering if they could precipitate events rather than wait upon them.

And now the maggot entered the fruit of their greed. Precipitation was only a last resort, Charnwood said, only a sensible precaution. But the maggot grew. And pierced the skin. In September 1913, Franz Ferdinand announced his intention of visiting Bosnia the following June in his capacity as Inspector-General of the Army. Charnwood's contacts spoke of the dangers of such a visit. If Franz Ferdinand were to be assassinated, a peaceful voice would be silenced and Franz Josef would have no choice but to avenge his nephew. War must then inevitably follow. Of course, if he were not assassinated. . . But why not make sure he was? It lay within the Concentric Alliance's power to do so. Their agents were in effective control of security in Sarajevo. They had penetrated the Black Hand, whose leader, Colonel Dimitrievitch, could be fooled into thinking Austria-Hungary would merely demand expulsion of the ruling Serbian dynasty – something Dimitrievitch himself was eager to bring about – if the Archduke died. And they could place their own marksmen in Sarajevo to guarantee – whatever happened – that he did die.

At every stage of the plan's development, it was dutifully stated that something was bound to happen to render its implementation unnecessary. As a formula for the suppression of misgivings, this may have served its purpose. But nothing did happen. And the plan *was* implemented. On twenty-eight June 1914, with every last loan drawn upon and every last investment taken out, '*events*,' Charnwood dryly reported, '*were satisfactorily precipitated.*' Within little more than a month, they had what they wanted. And the world had war. The threat posed by Colonel Brosch and an unnamed journalist was acknowledged and dealt with in unspecified fashion. No other threat appeared to exist. The Concentric Alliance had covered its tracks.

I scoured the records of the years that followed for some sign of remorse, some hint of collective guilt. But there was none. Some members must have lost their sons. And Charnwood, I knew, had lost his wife. But, if they regretted what they had done, they stifled such sentiments in the face of the profits which flowed into their accounts, fulfilling, indeed surpassing, all their founder had promised. They never again needed to take a direct hand in history. With what they earned from the war – from every Dreadnought built and sunk, from every army contract for the supply of bully beef and boots, from every shell fired and every gas canister emptied – they could grow fat and wealthier still for the rest of their days. And so they did. Or so, at any rate, they must have thought they would.

But their trust in Charnwood's astuteness grew into a vulnerable complacency. And his astuteness began to fail. Nothing so simple as an assassination could cure the Great Depression. From October 1929 until they petered out in August 1931, the accounts told a consistent story of vanishing capital and diminishing assets. The scale and speed of the losses were as breathtaking as those of the profits. How much Charnwood's clients knew of this was unclear. His letters and reports to meetings reflected only a blithe

273

optimism which he cannot have felt. Why he allowed matters to deteriorate so rapidly was equally obscure. What of his fabled foresight, his legion of expert contacts? It was not as if nobody warned him how questionable his investments had become. The failure of the Credit-Anstalt, for instance, had been predicted more than a month before in a letter from a senior official in the Austrian Ministry of Finance. But Charnwood's only response was to increase his deposits with the bank. He seemed determined to turn a crisis into a catastrophe, a perverse and self-destructive inversion of what he had done in 1914.

No wonder the members of the Concentric Alliance found his posthumous insolvency so hard to believe. Where had all the money gone? Some into the funds he meant to draw on after fabricating his own death, presumably. But the rest? Surely there was too much for poor judgement alone to have devoured. Yet seemingly it had. I had no way of judging the state of these people's finances beyond Charnwood's orbit, but nobody, however rich, could be indifferent to such staggering losses. And they *were* rich. Rich and powerful. I had heard of most of them. I had read about them over the years – their honours and appointments, their good works and grand reputations.

And now I knew on what foundations their glittering careers had been built. Falsehood and fraud were only to be expected. They were the lingua franca Charnwood's clients had spoken and understood. They were the current in which I had also swum. But the war – the commissioning of one murder and the *precipitation* of ten million others – was something else. The war was too high a price to pay. I had paid less than most of its victims, yet still the resentment seethed within me as I studied their records and gaped at their profits. They were all as guilty as each other. And I held the proof of their guilt in my hands. Charnwood had given me the means to destroy them. So destroy them I would.

The engine had stopped. How long ago the *Leitrim Lassie* had ceased to press forward through the high wind and heaving sea I could not tell, but now, certainly, she had abandoned the struggle. Above the creaking of her timbers and the roaring of the waves, I could hear Rafferty moving about on deck. Then there came a rumble of ratcheting metal. He was lowering the anchor. Shading my eyes from the glare of the hurricane-lamp, I peered out through the port-hole. There were a few flickering lights ahead. Could we be off Pwllheli already? I glanced at my watch. It was nearly half past seven. More than three hours had passed since our departure from Wicklow. But storm-tossed though they had presumably been, I could recollect nothing of them. For all that time, I had dwelt in a world apart – the hidden world of the Concentric Alliance. I looked down at the documents detailing their every secret, sliding back and forth across the chart table, and I knew I had gleaned enough. Re-tying the string about them, I bundled them back into the bag.

Almost at the same moment, Rafferty lurched through the door, breathing heavily, with water streaming off him. 'Holy Mother of God,' he declared, staring at me. 'You're a calm one and no mistake. I expected to find you sick as a dog and scared out of your skin, not fastening your bag like some doctor who's just called on a wealthy patient.'

'Are we there?' I demanded.

'We're off the Welsh coast, sure enough.'

'Good.'

'About fifteen miles west of Pwllheli.' He smiled weakly. 'I've anchored in Aberdaron Bay.'

'Why?'

'Because there's a gale blowing, in case you hadn't noticed. And because the engine's losing power. Water in the fuel-line, I shouldn't wonder. What with that and a strong tide, we were lucky to clear Bardsey Sound.'

'But we did clear it. So, why not carry on?'

'Eager to meet your maker, are you? Look at this.' He pulled a bundle of charts out of a locker, spread one of them across the table and pointed to the outline of the Welsh coast. 'We're south of the Lleyn Peninsula in a stiff westerly. Between Aberdaron Bay and Pwllheli is this hungry customer.' His finger traced the shape of a wide inlet between two sharply defined headlands to the east of us. 'Hell's Mouth, they call it. And it wouldn't mind gobbling us for supper, believe you me.'

'It looks harmless enough.'

He rolled his eyes. 'What would you know?'

'I know you agreed to take me to Pwllheli.'

'And so I will, when the tide turns and the wind eases.'

'When will that be?'

'A few hours, no more. Better late in this world than early in the next, as my sainted mother used to say.'

'I have to be in Pwllheli by half past five tomorrow morning.'

'And you will be, sir. Trust Desmond Rafferty to set your feet safely ashore well before then. Why, you can dock my wages if I don't. Can I say fairer than that?'

I wondered for a moment if I should ask to be put ashore straightaway. But I had no idea how to get to Pwllheli from Aberdaron on a wet and windy night. It promised to be substantially more difficult than trusting to Rafferty's seamanship. 'Very well,' I said. 'Have it your way.'

'And to ease your impatience, I have a bottle of Bushmills aboard. Why don't we ride out the storm over a few drams?' He glanced curiously at the bag I was still holding tightly in my hand. 'I'm thinking you needn't be afeared of those brothers bobbing up in Aberdaron Bay. If it's them you *are* afeared of.'

The lure of good whiskey was strong at that moment. I needed something to burn away the horrors of the day – the horrors of all I had done and learned. I dropped the bag and pushed it under the table with my foot, then summoned a casual smile. 'What else should I be frightened of?'

'Nothing, sir.' Rafferty grinned. 'Not even shipwreck – when I'm here to ease your passage.'

And so, as the boat pitched and rolled at anchor while the gale blew itself out beyond the shelter of the bay, Rafferty and I sat on narrow bunks either side of the cabin and made steady inroads into his Bushmills. Rafferty reminisced about the days of sail and his wartime experiences in the Royal Navy. These had ended with his being picked up by the Germans after abandoning a sinking destroyer during the Battle of Jutland. 'Two and a half years in a POW camp in Bavaria, sir, then home to find the IRA and the Black and Tans going at each other like fighting cocks, leaving the likes of me to play piggy-in-the-middle. Don't talk to me about the good old days.' Even the carefree Desmond Rafferty, it seemed, had had his life altered by a war of other men's making. Was there anyone it had not touched? I wondered. Was there anyone not entitled to the revenge I had it in my power to wreak?

I lay back on the bunk and slipped irresistibly into a dream-laden sleep. Diana was waiting for me, warm and pliant, tempting and treacherous. But Klaus was also waiting. He sat up as I stooped over him in the road, grinned crazily and reached out to close his

276

hands around my throat. And then came velvety oblivion, like a hood over a condemned man's face.

I woke in broad daylight, a pallid sun winking at me through the port-hole. The boat was apparently still at anchor, stirring only gently. The storm had passed. I propped myself up, aware of a leaden ache in my head and looked instinctively at my watch. It was half past eleven. I stared at the hands disbelievingly. Half past eleven in the morning! I had slept for more than fifteen hours. It was impossible. And yet it was true. As true as it was potentially disastrous.

'Good morning to you, sir,' said Rafferty from the cabin doorway. 'Strong tea to start the day?' He held out a chipped enamel mug.

'Why the devil didn't you wake me earlier?' I snapped, jumping to my feet.

'It would have been easier to wake the dead.'

'You knew I had to be in Pwllheli by half past five.'

'And so you were, sir, so you were.' He set the mug down and shook his head. 'I owe you an apology, though. Your whiskey last night. I slipped something into it to make you sleep like a log.'

'*What?*'

'I bought an *Evening Herald* before we left Wicklow. There was a report in it of a shoot-out in Phoenix Park early yesterday morning. Three men killed. And a well-dressed fellow seen running away with a Gladstone bag in his hand.'

Angry at my own stupidity as much as Rafferty's hang-dog air of mockery, I grabbed him by the collar of his oilskins and pushed him back against the door-post. 'What have you done, you interfering bloody fool?'

'I've been an interfering bloody fool, as you say, sir. I reckoned there must be money in the bag. A falling-out among thieves. Something like that. So, I told you we had engine trouble, anchored in Aberdaron Bay and slipped you a Mickey Finn. Then I took a look in the bag. I'd planned to put you ashore at Abersoch while you were still drowsy and head home with a sight more than fifteen guineas to show for my trouble. But . . . my plans changed when I found out what you had.'

'You've seen the documents?'

'Every last one, sir.'

'And you realize what they are?'

277

'I've a fair idea, sir. It's only because of them I didn't drop you at Abersoch. They . . . set me thinking.'

'I have to get them to London. I have to make sure the world learns what they contain.'

'Is that why you killed those fellows in Phoenix Park?'

'I didn't kill all of them. But one of those who died was Fabian Charnwood.'

'They're after you, then? They're hot on your trail?'

'What do you think?'

'I think you'll be needing these, sir.' He reached into his pocket and pulled out five bullets. 'I took them out of your gun in case you turned nasty.' I let go of him and, with a crumpled smile, he dropped the bullets into my hand. 'I don't exactly know what all this is about, but I can read and understand as well as the next man. It's the war, isn't it? You're after hanging all that dead meat round those grand people's necks.'

'I am, yes.'

'Then good luck to you.'

'I'll need it, won't I, now you've delayed me?'

'You'll only be a few hours late reaching London.'

'Yes. A few hours. When every second counts.'

'I'm sorry, sir. But I wasn't to know, was I?'

'Get out of my way.' I pushed past him onto the deck. The *Leitrim Lassie* was moored between two other boats of similar size in a neat enclosed harbour. Gulls were wheeling and shrieking overhead, with sunlight flickering on the water and warming the huddled house-fronts of Pwllheli. Ahead, silhouetted against the sky on an embankment bordering the harbour, I could see the statue of a soldier in helmet and battle-dress. Even tiny Pwllheli had its fallen to remember.

'The railway station's just across the way, sir,' said Rafferty. 'I'll give you a hand up. You'll not be forgetting this, will you?' To my astonishment, I saw he was holding the bag. I grabbed it from him with a scowl, then opened it and began to leaf through the contents. 'It's all there, sir. I promise.'

'It had better be.'

'Sure, what would I be wanting with it? Worse than carrying dynamite in your hip pocket.'

'You think so?'

'I think it'll never see the light of day. But if it does . . . I'll be proud to have helped.'

'Hindered, more like.' Satisfied on the point, I closed the bag and looked straight at him. 'You haven't asked for your fifteen guineas yet.'

'I wasn't sure you'd think I'd earned it, sir.'

'I don't reckon you have.' But something in his eyes softened me. He could have dropped me at Abersoch while I was still insensible. He could have pushed me and the records of the Concentric Alliance overboard. He could even have handed me over to the police. Instead, he had done his best to make amends. 'But have it anyway,' I said, reaching for my wallet.

'You're a gentleman, sir. A real gentleman.'

I might have been considerably less of a gentleman had I appreciated the dire consequences of Rafferty's intervention. But they did not dawn on me until I reached the railway station booking office.

'The next train's at twelve forty-five, sir,' the clerk informed me. 'For London, change at Barmouth and Ruabon.'

'When will I arrive?'

'The connecting train for Ruabon is the four o'clock from Liverpool, due into Paddington at . . . a quarter to midnight.'

I stared at him in stupefaction. 'A quarter to midnight? That's ridiculous.'

'Ridiculous or not, sir, it's the best the Great Western Railway can do for you at this time of the year. Do you want a ticket?'

'Yes,' I replied levelly. 'But tell me, where will I be at six o'clock?'

'Six o'clock? Let's see.' He ran his thumb down a timetable column. 'Approaching Shrewsbury, sir. You're due there at twelve minutes past.'

'Thank you so much,' I said through gritted teeth.

'Not at all, sir. Is it to be a single or a return?'

'Single.' I could not now hope to reach the Rose and Crown until after midnight. By then, Duggan would have given me up for lost. Somehow, I had to prevent that happening. Somehow, I had to speak to him before his patience ran out. 'First class. To Shrewsbury.'

'Shrewsbury, sir? Not London?'

'No. Not London. I've changed my mind.'

* * *

279

A man in a hurry finds dawdling even more agonizing than standing still. So it was for me as ramshackle trains hauled by labouring locomotives took me slowly round the north-east corner of Cardigan Bay, then up across the Cambrian mountains and down the Dee Valley to Ruabon. There were precious few travelling the same route, so I was left alone in my compartment to chafe at the lack of progress and search through the bundle of newspapers I had bought at Pwllheli.

Reports of the shootings in Phoenix Park and descriptions of the man seen running away were what interested me. But there were none to be found. The British press evidently regarded gunfights in Dublin as commonplace. And for their insularity I was duly grateful. They were welcome to keep their blinkers on until I chose the moment to remove them. Meanwhile, the less attention paid to a lone wayfarer with a Gladstone bag the better.

Many times, none the less, as the train steamed and stuttered through the wastes of Merionethshire, I relived in my mind those fleeting moments of violence. I saw the gun once more in O'Reilly's hand, heard again the twin reports and watched anew as Charnwood toppled slowly to the ground. And I remembered also my dream of Klaus's eyes opening and his hands encircling my throat. I shuddered and looked nervously round to be sure I was still alone. As I always was – except in my thoughts.

For there Diana's taunting smile of triumph could not be evaded. She had punished me as well as her father. I should have realized she could never be out-deceived. A truce with her was a pact with the Devil. She would never stop lying, never stop manoeuvring for her own advantage. She would never fail to be at least one step ahead. I fingered the letter for her Charnwood had entrusted to me and considered opening it. But something stopped me. Respect for what had turned out to be a dying man's last wish? Perhaps. Or perhaps it was the prospect of handing it to her one day with the seal unbroken, of taunting *her* in the only way I could.

But Diana, I told myself, no longer really mattered. My quarrel was with the Concentric Alliance. Mine and Max's and Felix's – and all our generation. There was something more than the desire to avenge them driving me on, of course. There was the realization that I knew too much to strike any kind of deal. Faraday and the people he served would kill me if they could. My only hope was to render killing me pointless – by shouting Charnwood's secrets from the roof-tops. I was on the side of truth and justice because I had no alternative. They had become the key to my survival.

My survival also depended on George Duggan, the only other outsider who understood what the Concentric Alliance was all about. If I could deliver their records to him, he would know how best to broadcast them to the world. But first I had to contact him. Thanks to Rafferty and the Great Western Railway, that did not promise to be easy. Yet it was not impossible.

The London train left Ruabon at half past five and reached Shrewsbury forty minutes later. I got off, hurried out to the taxi rank and instructed a cabby to take me to the best hotel in town. This, according to him, was the Lion, an old coaching inn turned Trust House where my every want would be catered for.

My only want, in fact, was a room with a private telephone and the services of the hotel operator to put a call through to the Rose and Crown, Warwick Street, London. Within ten minutes, she had found the number and connected me. It was not yet a quarter to seven and I was confident Duggan would still be waiting for me.

'Rose n' Crown,' answered a gruff male voice.

'Good evening. I wonder if I might speak to one of your customers.'

'That depends, dunnit? Which one?'

'George Duggan.'

'Never 'eard of 'im.'

'I'm sure he's there. Would you mind asking? It's very important.'

'I'll bet it is. 'Old on.' I heard him move away from the telephone and shout: '*Mr Duggan wanted on the blower! Mr Duggan!*' Then he came back. 'No Duggan 'ere, mate.'

'There must be.'

'And I'm telling you there ain't. I've got better things to do than – 'Ang on a minute.' He moved away again. '*You Duggan? Why didn't you say so sooner? There's the 'phone. Don't be all night. Mary Pickford promised to call me abaht now.*' He loosed a rasping laugh. As it died away, I heard the receiver being picked up. But only silence followed.

'Duggan?'

There was a pause, then a horribly familiar voice said: 'Where are you, Horton?' It was Faraday; Faraday where he should not

281

be, knowing what he should not know. 'Why aren't you here? You told Duggan you would be.'

'Where. . . Where is he?'

'In Alnwick, of course. Spending what we paid him on cheap rum and sour beer.' It could not be true. Surely he would not have betrayed me. But how else could Faraday have learned of our appointment? 'He did the sensible thing, Horton. Why don't you do the same? Come here now and meet me. Give me the records and you'll have nothing to fear. We could even discuss a price.'

No. He was lying. My head was the only price they meant to pay. If I had reached the Rose and Crown on time, they would have been waiting for me with something far more conclusive than money. How could Duggan have done it? He had betrayed his own past as well as my future. He had sold his soul along with his secret. Unless. . . Had he been working for them from the start? Had he lied to me at every stage?

'Give it up, Horton. Give it up while you still have the chance. You were lucky in Dublin. You won't be so lucky again.'

'Go to hell.' I slammed the telephone down and pulled my hand away as if it were burning, as if Faraday's thoughts could trace me down the miles of cable to my hiding-place. I stood up, sweating in the chill of the room, and stared at my reflection in the mirror above the fire-place. Where was I to go now? Who was there left to turn to? 'Damn you, Duggan,' I murmured. 'Damn you for a traitor and a coward.'

I picked up the telephone again and told the operator I wanted to call the Queen's Head, Alnwick. That was where he would be. There, or in one of his other soaking-holes, drinking away any guilt he might feel for what he had done. So, if I could not accuse him to his face, at least I could shout the words in his ears. '*How much did they pay you, Judas? How much did you turn out to be worth?*'

For several minutes I stood there, rehearsing the bitter things I would say to him. Then the operator rang back. She had found the number and was putting me through.

'Queen's Head.'

'Is George Duggan there?'

'George? No. . . Who's asking?'

'A friend of his.'

'Well, if you're a friend, I'm surprised you haven't heard. George was murdered last night.'

'*Murdered?*'

'He left the Black Swan at closing time, but never got to his lodgings. They found his body in Bow Alley this morning. Knifed to death. And robbed, seemingly. Though what anybody would want to steal from poor old George I can't—'

My right hand was trembling as I reached down to cut him off. I replaced the telephone in its cradle and sat down on the edge of the bed. Duggan was dead. He had not betrayed me. In a sense *I* had betrayed *him*. For why, after all, had they killed him? Why, after letting him live so long? Because Diana had named him as my informant and Faraday had decided his lips should be sealed for good. That was why. There could be no other reason. In my eagerness to convince Diana of her father's guilt, I had signed George Duggan's death-warrant.

And I had very nearly signed my own into the bargain. Finding my telegram in Duggan's pocket must have struck Faraday as an extraordinary stroke of luck. But in one respect at least he was wrong. My luck had not run out in Dublin. Desmond Rafferty's devious mind and the GWR's winter timetable had been my unlikely saviours. But for them, I would have walked into a trap. Instead, I still had a chance of winning. Less of one, without Duggan to help me. But a chance none the less. And I had something else as well: another name to add to the long list of those I might still be able to avenge.

'As long as they haven't caught you,' I said, rising from the bed, 'you can still catch them.' Then, hurrying to forestall fear and doubt, I threw on my hat and coat, grabbed the bag and rushed from the room.

'Dining with us this evening, sir?' enquired the head waiter as I passed him in the foyer.

'Yes. Book me a table for half past eight, would you? I have a spot of business to attend to first.'

'Certainly, sir. Look forward to seeing you then.'

He would not be seeing me, of course. Nor would Trust Houses Ltd be seeing the colour of any of my money. I was leaving the Lion Hotel for the first and last time.

I walked back to the railway station and bought a ticket to London. The next train did not leave until ten o'clock. I spent the hours between in the bar of the nearby Raven Hotel, drinking enough scotch to ensure I slept on the journey. I would need my

283

wits about me in the morning. I would need to be more alert than I had ever been before. And, even then, I might not be alert enough. It was no good trusting to luck. From now on it was a question of nerve and judgement: my nerve and Faraday's judgement. Which, I wondered, was in better repair?

CHAPTER

SIXTEEN

The overnight train from Shrewsbury was due in London at half past five on Friday morning, the thirteenth of November. It promised to be truly a Black Friday for the Concentric Alliance. Or for me, of course.

I had always told myself I was not superstitious. But I began the day as I meant to continue it: cautiously. At the last stop before Paddington, I got off. After ninety frozen minutes in the waiting-room at Reading, I caught a workmen's train to Ealing, then took to the Underground, emerging at Oxford Circus into the comforting melée of a fog-bound rush hour.

I found a barber in Bond Street to make me look respectable, then walked down to Jermyn Street for breakfast at Cox's Hotel. Their telegraphic address – *Anonymous, London* – had long stuck in my mind. And this morning anonymity was what I needed. I could not think of any reason why Faraday should know where I banked, but I still made several trial passes of the entrance before going in to withdraw a substantial amount of money from my account – and to lodge a Gladstone bag in one of their more commodious safe-deposit boxes. With Charnwood's documents off my hands and the gun inconspicuously stowed in the poacher's pocket of my overcoat, I was as well prepared for what lay ahead as I could be. I set off for Holborn with a degree of confidence that surprised me. It should not have, however. Lack of alternatives doth make heroes of us all.

*　*　*

'I've come to ask you a favour, Trojan.'

'They're scarcely my stock-in-trade, Guy.'

'Max is dead. Did you know?'

'I heard. Some bedroom brawl in Venice. In which you played a less than glorious part.'

'I'm trying to make up for that now. Wouldn't you like to help me? For Max's sake?'

'Can't say I would. But tell me what the favour is anyway.'

'I want to meet the journalist who gave you the information about George Duggan.'

'Piers Caversham, you mean? Why?'

'I can't explain. It's very important, though. More important than . . . well, anything.'

'You sound as if you've turned religious. You haven't, have you?'

'I've certainly had my eyes opened. And I need to talk to a journalist about what I've seen.'

'Piers doesn't stray beyond the Square Mile for subject matter. He'd only be interested if—'

'Money's at the heart of it, Trojan. He *will* be interested.'

'Well . . . I suppose I could see if he's free for lunch. You'll be paying, I take it?'

'I was hoping we could meet at your club. The venue needs to be . . . discreet.'

'So, *I'll* be paying?'

'If you can persuade Caversham to come, I'll give you whatever you think the bill will amount to in cash here and now.'

'You *have* turned religious. See a bright light on the road to Dover, did you?'

'Not exactly. Are you going to 'phone Caversham?'

'Yes, yes. I'm going to 'phone him. But there's no need to hurry. I've never known Piers refuse a meal.'

'Maybe not. But believe me, Trojan, I *do* need to hurry.'

As predicted, Piers Caversham rose readily to the bait of a free lunch. Three hours later, I made his acquaintance in the bar of Trojan's club in Pall Mall. He was a lean languid bright-eyed fellow, whose mixture of cynicism and perceptiveness immediately raised my hopes. We adjourned to the dining-room and discussed journalism, politics, Winchester and his own *alma mater*,

286

Charterhouse, over roast beef and burgundy. Eventually, when I was sure those occupants of nearby tables who were not deaf as posts were at least drunk as lords, I mentioned the war. Caversham had served several years of it in Flanders and admitted, under pressure from Trojan, to earning an MC. But even brandy could not warm his memory of the Trenches. 'An awful time,' he muttered into his glass. 'Bloody awful.'

At which point, apparently as a flight of speculative fancy, I suggested the entire conflict could have been engineered by an international cartel of business-men. Caversham found the theory entertaining and listened while I explained what they might have done and why. I could sense him thinking at one point it could almost be true. And then, when Trojan's notorious bladder obliged him to leave us for a few minutes, I told him it was. True *and* attestable.

'But I thought. . . Sureiy you were just . . . flying a kite.'

'I have documentary evidence of their responsibility for Franz Ferdinand's assassination. What I want to know is: would your newspaper publish it?'

'You're joking.'

'No. I can prove every word of what I've said. And, more than that, I can identify the guilty men. They sit on the boards of the most reputable companies, here and abroad. They're powerful, influential and highly respected. Every door is open to them. They're bowed to and waited on wherever they go. They rule the roost in half a dozen countries. Including this one.'

'I don't believe it.'

'I don't blame you. Neither did I. Until I saw the proof.'

'Proof you have – and want to see published?'

'Yes.'

'And the names?'

'Especially the names.'

'But—'

'What about this story you had for Piers, Guy?' roared Trojan as he rejoined us. 'Leaving it a bit late, aren't you?'

'I've just told him all about it.'

'While I was splashing my boots? I call that damned unsociable.'

'You didn't miss much,' said Caversham, looking across at me. 'It was something and nothing.'

'I might have guessed.' Trojan fell into his chair and grinned in my direction. 'As a partnership, Horton and Wingate always had a reputation for not coming up with the goods.'

'Wingate?' queried Caversham. 'Haven't I heard of him in connection with—'

'The Charnwood murder,' growled Trojan.

'Ah, yes. Of course. Charnwood. That's the name. Or should I say one of them?'

'Perhaps you should,' I murmured.

'What?' bellowed Trojan.

'I'm afraid I must be going,' said Caversham abruptly, rising to his feet. 'Dead-lines and all that.' He smiled. 'Thanks for lunch, Trojan. We must do it again soon. At *my* club.' His restraining hand ended Trojan's token effort to stand up. 'Sit there and finish your brandy, old chap. Horton will see me out.'

We set off east along Pall Mall, neither of us remarking on the fact that I had not turned back at the doorway of the club. At first, Caversham seemed lost in thought. Then, after a few paces, he said: 'Do you know, I was as drunk as Trojan until you said your story was true. Now, I've never felt more sober.'

'It *is* true.'

'And Charnwood was one of them?'

'Their leader.'

'Murdered by your friend Wingate?'

'No. Not by Max. By them. To prevent his documents falling into my possession.'

'But fall they did?'

'Yes.'

'Complete with all their names?'

'Every one.'

'And will I have heard of . . . every one?'

'Most of them, certainly.'

'Tell me, then. Tell me the names I'll know.'

So I did, as we descended by Carlton House Terrace to The Mall and circled slowly round the Admiralty into Whitehall. From there we walked south, guided by instinct, towards the Cenotaph, on which the Remembrance Day wreaths still lay, blood-red beacons in the murk. I had finished long before we reached them.

Caversham made no immediate reply. He turned down Horse Guards Avenue and I followed. There, between the blind flank of the War Office and the heedless façade of the Board of Trade, he

288

stopped to light a cigarette. Then he looked at me with the sort of shocked intensity he might last have experienced in Flanders and said: 'You can prove these people were involved?'

'Yes. And I can deliver the proof to your editor before the day is out.'

'You mean it, don't you? You really mean it.'

'Of course. It's them or me.'

His eyes narrowed. 'You feel . . . threatened?'

'I'm a hunted man, Caversham. And the hunt can only end when they recover those documents – or the world receives them.'

'Through the columns of my newspaper?'

'Exactly.'

We started walking again. 'You were the friend of Trojan's who wanted to know what had become of George Duggan, weren't you?'

'Yes.'

'Did you get some of this . . . proof . . . from him?'

'He pointed me in the right direction, certainly.'

'I see.' Caversham paused, then said: 'Trojan told me you were once mixed up with Horatio Bottomley. Is that true?'

'You shouldn't believe everything Trojan says. Especially in his cups.'

'Only they let Bottomley out of prison a few years ago. We see quite a lot of him in Fleet Street. He's always trying to peddle some bizarre story. Usually about him being the victim of a high-level political conspiracy. It's nonsense, of course. He's a broken man in body *and* mind.'

'Are you trying to tell me you think I've imagined all this?'

'I might have done. But for a strange item I picked up on the wire yesterday. The *Alnwick Advertiser* seemed to think former colleagues might want to be informed of the sudden demise of one of their employees.' Caversham turned to face me. 'George Duggan has been murdered.'

I shrugged. 'Apparently so.'

'That's why you said "them or me", wasn't it?'

'Yes.'

'Only now, it would be them or *us*, wouldn't it?'

'Not once the news was out. It would be too late for them to do anything about it then.'

'Too late? Yes. It certainly would be.'

We reached the end of Horse Guards Avenue and crossed over

289

to the Embankment. There I stopped to gaze down at the fast-flowing Thames. Caversham looked south, towards the fog-wreathed bulk of Parliament. But the clock-face of Big Ben was invisible. The time was out of sight.

'You're a lucky, man, Horton. I might have been in their pay. If so, I'd have promised to arrange a meeting with my editor. As it is . . .'

'Yes?'

'I'm a husband and a father and a relatively contented man. Ten years ago, I might have helped you take them on.'

'But not now?'

'Now, I've more sense than to try. You're fighting against hopeless odds. If you can prove what you've told me – and I don't doubt you can – then you can prove more than our cosy scheme of things could possibly bear. It would tear too much apart. Don't you see? Even the innocent won't let that happen.'

'Are you refusing to help me?'

'I'm refusing your offer of a suicide pact, yes. I had enough of self-sacrifice in the war. Enough to last me for the rest of my life, which I hope will be long and uneventful.'

'I'll find another paper to take the story if you don't want it.'

'You won't. You won't find anyone to touch it. Even if you did, this . . . alliance, as you call it . . . is influential enough to ensure the story could never be published. The people you've named control half the commercial life of this city. Together they're unchallengeable. And we know from George Duggan's example what happens to those who are crazy enough to defy them.' He flicked the remains of his cigarette into the river. 'Goodbye, Horton. I'll do my best to forget everything you've said. I suggest you do the same.'

As he moved past me, I grabbed at his elbow. 'Caversham! For God's sake—'

'Let go of me!' He shook my hand off and I saw he was trembling. He glanced from side to side, as if worried we were being watched. 'Leave me alone, dammit. I don't want to hear any more. Do you understand?'

'Oh yes. I understand. You're afraid of them.'

'Yes. I am. And so should you be. You can't destroy such people. Nobody can.'

'If I can't, they'll destroy me.'

'I know,' he said, with a faintly apologetic shake of the head. 'I know they will.' Then he stared straight at me and added: 'In fact, I'm certain they will.'

With that, he strode off towards Hungerford Bridge. I watched him go, wondering if he would look back. But he did not. Already, he was glad to have seen the last of me. And so, I realized, would be anyone else I told. No-one would want any part of what I was trying to do. No-one would be foolish enough to come to my aid. I had become the man who knew too much. And I could forget none of it.

I started walking in the opposite direction, with no particular destination in mind. An hour or so later, as dusk began to close about me, I reached the Royal Hospital and wandered in through its courtyards, nodding respectfully to the Chelsea Pensioners who shuffled across my path. I stopped by the statue of Charles the Second to smoke a cigarette and wondered if these proud old soldiers would welcome the knowledge I possessed.

Not that it mattered. I seemed unlikely to have the chance to share my secret with anyone. Out there, somewhere, as solid and invisible as the fog had made every landmark of London, stood the Concentric Alliance, barring the door to my future. I could not blame Caversham for walking away. I would have done the same in his shoes. But no such choice was open to me. Walk or run or crawl, I still could not hope to escape.

Suddenly, fear boiled into anger. I rushed out of the Hospital and hailed the first east-bound cab.

'Where to, guv'?'

'Euston Hotel. And step on it.'

Collecting the car from the hotel garage entailed some risk, since Diana knew I had left it there. But even the Concentric Alliance could not be everywhere. With the car, I could be in Dorking by early evening. And, with the gun, I could make Diana pay the same penalty as she had wished on me. If I could not escape, then why should she? They meant to kill me. I had no doubt of it. And they were beyond my reach. But she was not. And it would give me some satisfaction to study her face as she realized as much. I could not beat them. I knew that now. But at least I could fix the terms of my defeat.

Nobody was lying in wait for me at the Euston Hotel. I filled the Talbot with petrol and let the engine rip as soon as I was past

291

Putney. Speed was what I craved above all: the speed to outrun them. But no matter how fast I went, I knew they could travel faster – and reach further.

I pulled off the road south of Leatherhead and confronted the futility of my journey over a cigarette. Diana might not be at Amber Court. Even if she were, could I really kill her in cold blood? And even if I could, might I not simply be doing the Concentric Alliance's work for them? Perhaps, if I simply created enough of a disturbance to be arrested, I could tell Hornby the whole story and hand him the evidence. But did I seriously think he would ever be allowed to use it? *'You can't destroy such people,'* Caversham had said. And he was right. *'If I can't, they'll destroy me,'* I had replied. And I too was right.

I drove slowly up the lanes towards the house, the headlamps funnelling before me into the night. Some way short of the entrance, I stowed the car beneath some trees and continued on foot. Surrey was pitch black and silent after the glare and bustle of London, the squelching of my shoes on the leaf-mush of the verge and the crack of the occasional twig beneath my heel amplified in my mind till I could believe the whole world knew where I was – and what I was about.

I reached the entrance and found the gate closed, as I had never known it to be. And padlocked into the bargain. It was reassuring to know somebody else might also be frightened. Was Diana living in fear, I wondered – fear of my coming by night, armed and desperate, to make her pay for what she had done? She must have hoped they would kill me in Dublin. She must have laid her plans on the assumption that it would end there. But it had not. For both of us, the end remained uncertain.

I was about to climb over the gate when I heard a car approaching, then saw the glimmer of its headlamps. There was just time for me to scuttle into the undergrowth before it appeared, growling up the lane and braking to a halt as it turned into the entrance. I shrank back and watched as a figure clambered out and walked up to the gate: the burly unmistakable figure of Quincy Z. McGowan.

Quincy! Of course. I should have thought of him sooner. Only someone with a personal grudge against the Concentric Alliance would be foolhardy enough to help me. And Quincy *would* have such a grudge, once he knew of their indirect responsibility for Maud Charnwood's death. His love for his sister had been

292

complete and unconditional. He had tried to avenge her by fighting the Germans in 1918. And he would not hesitate to do so again by fighting the true culprits in 1931. Here at last was the ally I needed.

As he fumbled with the padlock, I stepped forward and spoke his name.

'Who's there?' he barked, whirling round.

'Guy Horton.'

'Guy!'

'For God's sake keep your voice down. I must speak to you. It's a matter of life and death.'

'Well, I've been wanting to speak with you since you didn't show up for our dinner with Maundy Gregory last week. But I didn't reckon on getting my chance like this. Why don't we go up to the house?'

'Is Diana there?'

'Hell, no. But you must know that. Isn't she with you?'

'No. What about Vita?'

'Oh, she's at home. Has been ever since you and Diana left. This damned padlock's on her account. She's been twitchier than a cat with fleas. Lord knows why.'

'I know why.'

'You do?'

'Can we go somewhere quiet? Not the house. Not anywhere we'll be seen. I'll explain everything. Believe me, you'll want to hear what I have to say. It concerns your sister.'

'Maudie?'

'You were fond of her, weren't you?'

'I worship her memory. But what—'

'Wouldn't you like to know who killed her?'

'A German U-boat commander called Schwieger killed her. Her and twelve hundred other souls aboard the *Lusitania*.'

'There's more to it than that.'

'What do you mean? What are you driving at?'

'The truth, Quincy. The whole truth. I can tell it to you – if you're willing to listen.'

I heard him take a long thoughtful breath. Then he said: 'Where do you want to go?'

The car we drove away in was, ironically, Charnwood's Bentley. It had stood neglected in the garage at Amber Court till Quincy's decision to commandeer it. He took me up to Box Hill and stopped on the crest, with the lights of Dorking winking at us from below. In one of the black voids between the lights was Dorking Cemetery – and the grave of Fabian Charnwood. But his body was not to be found there. As for his spirit, perhaps that hovered about me as I spoke, clinging to the leather upholstery he had so often sat on, watching me in the mirror that had reflected his face so many more times than mine.

I told Quincy everything, from start to finish. Every step I had taken since our last meeting. Every secret I had learned. From the murder of Hildebrand Lightfoot, back through the annals of the Concentric Alliance to the assassination in Sarajevo. What had happened on and since the night I was supposed to dine with him and Gregory at the Deepdene Hotel. How his brother-in-law had really met his death. And why, when everything else was stripped away, his sister had met hers.

At first, he was incredulous. Surely Diana and Vita could not have done what I alleged. Surely they could not have deceived him so completely. He was angry with me for saying such things, unwilling to entertain the possibility that they might be true.

But they *were* true. As his anger abated, he began to recall and acknowledge the contradictions and inconsistencies that proved them so: the mystery of the missing money; of Max's journey to Venice; of Diana's abrupt departure from Amber Court; of Vita's subsequent anxiety; and of the letter delivered to the Villa Primavera containing the Concentric Alliance's secret symbol. To that above all he reverted. To that and the past it hinted at. It seemed to strike some stubborn chord in his mind, to convince him where nothing else could.

By the time I had finished, his mood had changed. He was no longer either sceptical or outraged. He had become glum and thoughtful, picking his way through the tangled threads I had laid before him.

'Fabian's documents fix responsibility for the war squarely on the organization he set up?'

'Yes. They're proof positive. Of what was done. And who did it.'

'And the documents are in your possession?'

'They're safely hidden.'

'Waiting for you to find someone willing to help you nail these bastards?'

'If I ever do.'

'Oh, you just have, Guy. You just have.' He drew a hip-flask from his pocket, took a swig from it, then offered it to me. 'Bourbon. I reckon we both need a shot, don't you?'

I felt immensely grateful as the first mouthful seeped into my senses. With the second came a lessening of the tension. I had given him what I had promised: the truth. The next move was his to choose. Knowing that was to have a great weight lifted from my shoulders.

'They're not going to get away with this, Guy. None of them are. My own niece, for God's sake. How could she make a deal with these people? How could she bear to do it?'

'I'd like to be able to ask her.'

'Where's she hiding?'

'I don't know.'

'Does Vita, do you think?'

'Maybe.'

'I'll wring it out of her if I have to. She's sat in that house for the past week nursing her secret like some old witch cradling a dead child. She's only been out once. Into Dorking, last Friday. We know why now, don't we? To mail a letter to a dead man. Whose side is she really on?'

'I'm not sure. Does it matter?'

Quincy sighed. 'I reckon not. Not when you boil it down. The lies all come to one thing in the end. The god-damn war. And Maudie's death. To think I was on the point of paying good money to her murderers. And why? To save the necks of a pair of conniving cold-hearted . . .' As his words petered out, I saw his right hand wrap itself round the steering-wheel and squeeze tightly. 'Diana's always looked like her mother. I've let that make me think she almost *is* her mother. But no. She has her father's nature. Maudie's image. But Fabian Charnwood's soul. May it rot in Hell.'

I was glad to hear him speak so bitterly. The truth had turned his avuncular concern for Diana and her aunt to a sudden hatred of the Charnwoods and all their works. I could only hope it was sufficient to blind him to the dangers involved in an attack on the Concentric Alliance.

'I'll bet you weren't sure I'd believe you,' he said, releasing the steering-wheel.

'How could I be? It is . . . difficult to believe.'

'Not for me, Guy. It makes sense, you see. It tallies.'

295

'With what?'

'Maudie's trip home in the spring of fifteen. There was something on her mind. Something she wanted to share. About Fabian, she said. An affair, I thought at first. Better discussed with her mother than her kid brother. But she kept hinting it was about business. Well, I didn't want to know about that. She was always . . . morally fastidious. A few strokes our old man pulled would have set her back on her heels. So, whether Fabian was kicking over the marital traces or cutting some commercial corners . . . it seemed best for her to forget it, whatever it was. And I told her so.'

'Was she never more specific?'

'Not until the day the *Lusitania* sailed for England. May first, 1915. Graven in my memory. Graven deep. I'd travelled with her from Pittsburgh to see her off. Mother hadn't been well enough to come with us. Father and Theo had been . . . too busy. So, I was the family representative. The last one to see her alive, as it turned out. She seemed preoccupied that morning. Gloomy and distracted. I went aboard with her and opened a bottle of champagne in her cabin. It didn't brighten her mood. Sorry to be saying goodbye, I supposed. But that wasn't it. She'd never been one for tearful farewells. Anyhow, she wasn't upset. She was . . . weighed down. "What do you do, Quincy," she asked, "when you find out someone you love has done something truly terrible?" Well, I didn't think she meant *truly* terrible. I still thought she was over-reacting. But now . . .'

'You think she *knew*?'

'She'd found out something. It has to have been about the Concentric Alliance, doesn't it? Someone she loved. And something truly terrible. She'd come home for advice. But she was leaving without it.'

'What answer did you give her?'

'A useless one, Guy. A smart young man's fat-headed piece of champagne wisdom. "You forget it, Maudie," I said. "You forget all about it. You let it blow over." She looked at me so . . . pityingly. She must have realized then there was no-one she could turn to. No-one to share the burden with.'

'You can't be sure what she meant.'

'No. I can't be *absolutely* sure. But I can wonder. What she'd decided to do when she got back to England. What she *would* have done, but for that torpedo off the Irish coast.'

It was as if he was beginning to think Charnwood had deliberately engineered Maud's death. Surely I could hear the suspicion forming in his voice. Nothing in the documents suggested anything of the kind. But he did not know that. Nor was there any reason for me to force the knowledge on him. 'Whether directly or indirectly I can't say, Quincy, but the Concentric Alliance was certainly responsible for your sister's death. And for every other casualty of the war.'

'And even if Fabian's dead, there are plenty of his co-conspirators living high on the proceeds to this day?'

'Yes. There are.'

'Then we'll have them, Guy. By God, we'll have them.'

'But how? According to Caversham, no newspaper would dare to—'

'No *British* newspaper, maybe. But what about the American press? From what you've said, the Concentric Alliance doesn't have any American connections.'

'Not as far as I—'

'There's your answer, then. We'll take the story to the *New York Times*. Or the *Washington Post*. We'll give *them* the proof. And I can guarantee they'll want to use it. More than a hundred thousand Americans died in the war. And hundreds of thousands more couldn't understand why they had to. Well, now they will, won't they?'

He was right. The Concentric Alliance did not wield enough influence in the United States to prevent the truth about it being told. And once told there, it would echo round the world. There was a way out for me after all. And Quincy McGowan was pointing me towards it.

'Together, we can pull this off, Guy. We'll have the power and wealth of the McGowan Steel Corporation at our backs. We'll have everything we need to bring these people to book. Are you willing to give it a try?'

'Of course I am.' The decision was a simple one, because there was simply no alternative.

'The Babcock business may catch up with you in the States. You realize that?'

'It doesn't matter.' It seemed indeed scarcely significant, a trivial appendage of a forgotten existence.

'Good. In that case, we must get you – and the documents – across the Atlantic as soon as possible.'

297

'How? I can't just—'

'Oh, but you can. Listen. I'll go up to London first thing tomorrow morning and buy us a couple of tickets for the next sailing to New York. When the time comes, I'll tell Vita I have to visit some foundries in the north on business. Instead, I'll meet you in Southampton and we'll slip away with the documents. A week later, we can have them sitting on the desk of whichever newspaper editor we choose.'

It sounded easy. And why should it not be? Faraday was looking for me, not following Quincy. I had only to lie low until sailing day, recover the bag from the bank and present myself in Southampton. Quincy would do the rest.

'So long as we're careful, nothing can go wrong. After I've bought the tickets, I'll drive out to the Anglo-American Club at Iver. Call me there tomorrow afternoon. Let's say three o'clock. I'll make sure I'm in the lounge, where they can easily page me. Then I'll be able to tell you when we're leaving. The day before we sail, I'll take the train to London, double-back to Southampton and stay overnight at the hotel near the docks.'

'The South Western?'

'That's the one. Meet me there two hours before sailing. We'll go aboard at the last moment. *Don't* use the boat-train.'

It was going to happen. Soon, very soon, I would be free. 'Quincy, I—'

'If you're going to thank me, Guy, don't bother. I'm doing this for Maudie.'

'I know. But even so . . .'

'Save it till we're at sea, eh?' He plucked the hip-flask from my grasp and held it up to his lips. 'Here's to the torpedo *we're* going to fire.'

'So long as we're careful,' Quincy had said, *'nothing can go wrong.'* And I was determined to ensure it did not. I drove back as far as Wimbledon that night, left the car on the Common, walked down to the station and took the Tube to South Kensington. The area boasted plenty of obscure hotels. I booked into one more obscure than most – the Bute Court in Queen's Gate – and vanished from sight. The following afternoon, promptly at three o'clock, I rang the Anglo-American Club from a call-box near the Albert Hall, praying Quincy would come to the telephone before my money ran out. My prayer was answered.

298

'I'll keep this short and sweet, Guy. We're booked aboard the *Leviathan*. She sails Tuesday at noon. Can you be in Southampton by ten o'clock that morning?'

'Yes.'

'Good. Till then, keep your head down.'

'Don't worry. I will.'

I walked out across Hyde Park, feeling safe among the nannies wheeling their charges by the Serpentine. A Salvation Army band was playing hymn music with righteous gusto in Kensington Gardens. Weak sunlight was breaking through the clouds to gild the drifts of fallen leaves. Ducks were squabbling over breadcrumbs, dogs chasing sticks, children kicking footballs. The mundane clockwork of England was ticking serenely on. But not for much longer. For I was about to serve my complacent fellow-countrymen an unpalatable dish: the truth. After that, nothing would ever taste the same again.

CHAPTER

SEVENTEEN

By Tuesday, I was grateful to have done with lying low. I left the Bute Court before dawn, my only luggage comprising the Gladstone bag I had collected from the bank the previous afternoon. I was relying on the stewards of the *Leviathan* to smarten me up once we were at sea. Until then, my fellow-travellers would have to take me as they found me.

I took a cab to Clapham Junction and boarded a stopping train to Southampton, burying myself behind a newspaper in a third-class compartment. A bleak grey morning made its lethargic appearance as the train wheezed and rattled through Surrey and Hampshire. We reached Winchester, where I did my best to ignore the name-board and its associations. What Max required of me was resolution, not regret. The train drew out and I left memory behind.

But not caution. The South Western Hotel adjoined Southampton Town station, where the train terminated. Suspicious of anything so simple, I got off at a workmen's halt a mile or so short of my destination and walked the rest of the way through a maze of back-streets, heading always towards the wailing of the gulls and the salty tar-laden smell of the docks.

There were several liners in. I could see their funnels between the cranes and gantries visible beyond the shipping offices and warehouses of Canute Road. One massive triple set, painted red, white and blue, already had steam up. It was the *Leviathan*, waiting to bear me and my secret away.

300

On the boat-train to London four months before, Millington the toping Jeremiah had told me the time-ball on the roof of the South Western Hotel operated at ten o'clock every morning. I sat in the park on the other side of the road, smoking a cigarette and waiting for the hour to be signalled. At five to ten by my watch, the ball was run up the mast. As soon as it dropped, I picked up the bag and walked smartly across to the hotel entrance.

The lobby was almost empty, stray murmurs echoing in its marble heights. The tumult of summer was long gone. Only the stubborn and the desperate were taking ship for the New World. I was directed to Quincy's suite on the first floor. 'Ah yes,' the concièrge remarked. 'Mr McGowan said he was expecting a visitor. Do go straight up.'

I found him lounging in a smoking-jacket amidst the debris of a large breakfast. He greeted me warmly, gesturing towards the same view of the *Leviathan* I had already savoured, framed now by one of the tall curving windows of his sitting-room. 'There she is, Guy. Ready and waiting. I sailed home on her at the end of the war, you know, from Liverpool. She was a dazzle-painted troopship then. *Levi Nathan*, the men called her. It'll be strange to go aboard thirteen years later on account of the same war – and what your bagful of secrets says about it.'

He pointed to the bag, which I had placed on a side-table. 'Do you want to look at the contents?' I asked, pulling it open.

'No, no,' he replied, stepping across to run his fingers over the bundle of books and papers. 'There'll be time enough for that once we're under way. So long as it's all here – and proves what you say it proves.'

'It is. And it does.'

'That's good enough for me. In a—'

There was a knock at the door and a call of '*Room service*'. Quincy grinned. 'I ordered some champagne. Reckoned we should wish ourselves *bon voyage*.'

'Splendid idea.'

'Well, why not? We do have something to celebrate.' He walked to the door and pulled it wide open, then said: 'Come on in, gentlemen.'

What happened next was so fast and unexpected that I had been seized and my right arm pinned behind my back before I could do more than blink. I heard the door close, saw Faraday and Vasaritch standing in front of me and felt the cold touch of a gun

301

barrel against my temple. Then pain jagged through my shoulder as my arm was twisted towards breaking point. I cried out, only for a large hand to be clapped over my mouth.

'Be quiet!' hissed Vasaritch. 'We want no noise. The gun has a silencer. And I will use this—' He raised his other hand for me to see, clenched but apparently empty. Then, at a twitch of his thumb, a four-inch blade sliced out of its stock. 'If I have to.' He said something in a Slavic tongue and the hold on my arm slackened. 'You understand?' I nodded. 'Good.' He took his hand from my mouth and began frisking me, swiftly finding and removing the revolver. 'What is stolen is taken back,' he growled. Then, stepping away, he turned to Quincy and said: 'The records?'

'They're in the bag on the table.'

'We should examine them here,' said Faraday, glancing at me before he added: 'In case anything's missing.'

'Yes,' replied Vasaritch. 'We should. Milan—' Milan was apparently the name of the huge ox-limbed creature holding me. After a burst of instructions in what I took to be Serbo-Croat, he frog-marched me into the bedroom and pushed me down onto the chair by the dressing-table. Vasaritch relieved him of the gun while he took out lengths of rope clearly brought for the purpose, twisted my arms behind the back of the chair and tied them together round the base of the splat. Then he forced a cloth between my teeth and bound it there as a gag before fastening my ankles to the stave. The knots were tight and the rope thin enough to cut while strong enough to withstand any amount of struggling. I was hog-tied and helpless.

'No tricks this time, Horton,' said Faraday from the doorway. 'Your lucky streak is at an end.'

'Enough,' said Vasaritch. 'The records are all that matters.' There was the hint of a rebuke in his tone.

'Of course,' said Faraday, smiling humbly. 'Let's have a look at them.' He retreated into the sitting-room and Vasaritch followed, muttering something to Milan as he left.

Milan waited a moment, then began checking the knots. He need not have bothered, for he had done his work well. My thigh muscles were beginning to ache and blood was trickling from one corner of my mouth, where the rope had cut into it. At length, he stood up, grunted in evident satisfaction and strode from the room.

For several minutes I was left alone. I could see none of them through the doorway, only hear the rustling of paper and turning

302

of pages. If they meant to kill me, what were they waiting for? Goaded by fear, anger and self-reproach, I strained at the ropes, trying to wrench myself free. The chair gave a few creaks, but remained firm. The certainty that I was wasting my energy washed over me, but what else was I to do? I had walked into a trap. Surely there was some alternative to waiting till the trapper returned to finish me off.

But there was not. Unless it was to brood on how I had been deceived. Quincy must have been playing a devious game of double bluff from the moment he arrived in Venice. His shock and rage on hearing my story had merely been the devices of an accomplished actor. He had known it all before I breathed a word. Because he was one of them. And who, I asked myself, was not? Just a few vainglorious fools. Like me.

Then, just as I was thinking of him, Quincy ambled into the room, closing the door softly behind him. 'Sorry about this, Guy,' he said, stooping over me to dab at the blood on my chin with his handkerchief. 'The man mountain doesn't know his own strength. But, then, who does? His own strength – or his own weakness?' He looked me in the eye and must have been able to read there the accusations I would have flung at him had I been able to. 'Well, maybe we do now, you and I.'

He moved past me to the bed and flopped down onto it, fixing me with his gaze in the dressing-table mirror. 'Faraday and Vasaritch are going to be quite a while sorting through those papers. So, I thought we'd have a talk. Well, I'll talk. You just listen.' He took out a cigar, lit it and leaned back against the pillows. 'Sorry I can't offer you one, but . . .' He shrugged. 'In case you're wondering, my motives in this aren't completely mercenary, just substantially so. You see, my father left his entire fortune – including his controlling block of shares in the McGowan Steel Corporation – to my brother Theo. Oh, Theo pays me well for what I do, which he'd tell you isn't much, but I'm *dependent* on him, that's the hell of it. Dependent on his generosity, his approval, his . . . opinion. It comes hard at my age, let me tell you. Damned hard.' He sighed and took a puff at his cigar. 'So, when Faraday came to me a couple of months ago with a lucrative proposition, I jumped at it. You bet I did. He said he was acting on behalf of Fabian's aggrieved clients. They wanted their money back. He'd already put you on the same trail. But he'd decided to hedge his bets. He thought a member of the family – a favourite uncle, to

303

be precise – might be able to wheedle the truth out of Diana where a skirt-chaser like you couldn't. I agreed to try – for a fee sufficient to buy me freedom from brother Theo. Cash on delivery, you understand. And I've just delivered. As soon as Faraday's run his expert eye over those accounts, I'll be paid what's due to me.'

My eyes widened, but he did not seem to notice. His share of Charnwood's money was all he could think of. He did not know – as Faraday shortly would – that the money no longer existed. I had not mentioned the point during our counsel of war on Box Hill because it had not seemed important. The Concentric Alliance's responsibility for the war had eclipsed all thought of what Charnwood had done with the proceeds. But not in Quincy's mind. In his mind, it was the only thing that mattered.

'When I got to Venice, I saw things weren't as simple as Faraday supposed. It was clear to me Vita and Diana knew you were spying on them. So, why were they letting you? Because they had nothing to hide? Or because they knew you were looking for the wrong thing in the wrong place? Well, it had to be the latter. They *were* hiding something, no question. But not what we thought.

'I'm not sure when the suspicion first formed in my mind. It grew slowly, as I watched and studied them and tried to figure out why Wingate should have followed Diana to Venice after murdering her father. Little niggles of doubt. Little irritating unanswered questions. And then the blinding realization. Fabian wasn't dead. It was him they were hiding, not his money. I called a meeting with Faraday aboard Vasaritch's yacht and put my theory to him. He agreed it fitted the facts. But he wanted hard evidence. He said he'd send a letter to the villa, addressed to Miss Charnwood – without specifying which one – containing nothing but a piece of paper on which he'd draw a pair of concentric circles. He said neither Vita nor Diana should recognize the symbol. If one or both did, it meant Fabian had told them secrets only a man expecting to die – or hoping to be thought dead – would part with. He wouldn't explain what the symbol meant. Said it was better for me not to know. And I reckon your experiences bear him out on that point, don't you?

'Well, Vita's reaction to the letter supported my theory. I was convinced Fabian was alive. And that he had the money. But where was he? Vita definitely knew. Diana probably did too. And, sooner or later, I was sure they'd let the information slip. If I stuck to them long enough, they'd be bound to give him away. Patience was the key – as Faraday agreed. My negotiations with Gregory were a put-up job, designed to explain the lifting of the dead-line without alerting you to the change of strategy. We just couldn't be certain where your loyalties lay by then, you see. Besides, the further you were off the scent, the better it suited me. I didn't want you getting any of the credit. So, naturally, I encouraged Faraday to think your allegiances had become questionable.

'And so they had, hadn't they? But, as for the scent, well, it seems you had a better nose for that than me all along. When I got back to Amber Court the night you whisked Diana away, I found Vita too worried and distraught even to lie plausibly about where you'd gone. Fearing you'd stolen a march on me, I applied some . . . pressure . . . to dear Vita. It didn't take much to loosen her tongue. In the end, she was glad of a shoulder to cry on. She realized the game was up when I made it clear I knew Fabian was still alive. After that, she admitted everything. And everything included the Concentric Alliance.

'It shook me to the core, I won't deny. A world war, engineered by my brother-in-law and the people who'd hired me to find his money. At first, I couldn't believe it. Then it began to make sense. Not just because of what Maudie had said aboard the *Lusitania*. There was the symbolism as well. The concentric circles Faraday had drawn. And the name of Vasaritch's yacht. *Quadratrice*. A geometrical term meaning a circle used to square other circles.' He chuckled. 'And to think the old man used to say the money spent on my education could just as usefully have been thrown into the Ohio river!' His chuckle became a guffaw.

'Don't look so sombre, Guy. Maybe you've no choice with a gag on, but I have good news for you, believe me. I'm saving you from yourself. You and Diana. When Vita told me what the two of you were planning, I knew you'd never get away with it. Not just because of Faraday and his masters, but because this is a story the world doesn't want to hear. The war was Germany's fault. The politicians have been telling us that for thirteen years, so it's got to be true. Do you seriously think they'd let you put the record straight? Do you seriously imagine you'd ever be allowed to? This was a fool's crusade from the start, Guy. You were never going to get to Jerusalem.

'As for Diana. . . Well, a daughter's love runs deeper than a brother's, I guess. Deep enough to blind her to everything except the desire for revenge. She didn't betray you, Guy. Not in Dublin, anyhow. Faraday named her as his source to deflect attention from me. And to goad Fabian, I suppose. That would have pleased him more than a little. Vita sent Fabian the letter at my direction. It was the only way I could think of to make him insist on meeting you alone, the only way to prevent Diana getting hurt or taking matters into her own hands. You were expendable, but Diana . . . She's my niece, for God's sake. I owe it to Maudie to see she comes to no harm. That's what I meant about my motives. Sentiment featured on the list. Low down, I admit. But it featured.'

He scrambled to the end of the bed and sat leaning against the rail, close enough to lay a consoling hand on my shoulder. I longed to throw it off, to leap from the chair and stuff his expensive cigar – along with his expansive words – down his throat. But all I could do was squirm.

'I was angry when I heard what had happened in Phoenix Park. Not because they'd killed Fabian. I told Vita he'd be safe once he handed over the records, but I'm not sure even she believed that. Anyhow, he had it coming. Nor because of the threat to my fee. Faraday hadn't found it difficult to track you down in Dublin, so I didn't reckon you'd be able to stay on the run for long. No, you weren't the real worry. Diana was.

'When the Irish police began investigating the killings in Phoenix Park, they found a cab driver whose description of a fare he took out to the park from a rank near the Shelbourne Hotel matched that of a man seen running away after the shooting. At the Shelbourne, they discovered the description also fitted an Englishman staying there called Morton, not seen since the night before. They were told Mr Morton had been the constant companion of another guest from England, Miss Wood, who was still in the hotel. So they took Miss Wood in for questioning. She claimed Morton was just an acquaintance whose affairs she knew nothing about. Eventually, they decided to show her the three bodies in case she recognized them. But no. She said she'd never seen any of them before.'

Poor Diana. I felt for her then, waiting all day for me to return, wondering where I could have gone. Then the police, full of questions she dare not answer. And Charnwood's corpse on a mortuary slab: a dead father she dared not claim.

'It must have been hard for her, Guy, don't you reckon, to stand there in that morgue and disown him? But she is hard, of course. Hard as a diamond. And determined. They gave up questioning

306

her in the end and let her go. Just about the time last Friday night when you surprised me at the gate of Amber Court. Did I say surprised? Answered my prayers would be nearer the mark. I had you. Where Faraday had failed not once but twice, *I* had succeeded. Enough to justify a bonus, I reckon. Well, we'll have to see about that.

'I had to think quickly, of course, but that's something I've always been good at. Quick to get into trouble and quick to get out of it, the old man used to say. Anyhow, I had you, but I didn't have the records. Not quite. Still, you swallowed my line about going to the American papers, so laying hold of the records only meant waiting for this little subterfuge to run its course. Not bad, eh? And don't feel too sore about it, because it really was the best thing you could have done. The very best.

'Diana reached Dorking while I was in London on Saturday. Vita didn't tell her about the letter she'd sent to Fabian for fear of how she might react. And she didn't tell her about my involvement for the same reason. Diana's nerves were stretched taut by not knowing where you were or what you were up to or what she ought to do for the best. When I got back from Iver, I could see the state she was in and I reckoned there was only one way to get her off the hook without showing my hand. Vita agreed to back me up. I said you'd contacted me, told me everything and proposed we all decamp to the States with the records. I couldn't explain why you'd gone to meet Fabian alone, of course, without mentioning Vita's letter, so you'll have to dream up something to account for that. Be sure it's credible. We don't want—'

He broke off, noticing my confused expression in the mirror. Then he smiled broadly. 'You haven't got it yet, Guy, have you? We're all getting out. You, me, Diana and Vita, in exchange for the records. They're the terms Faraday and Vasaritch have agreed to, negotiated by my good and generous self. Diana's waiting in her cabin on the *Leviathan*. According to me, you said she was to go aboard early; you'd make contact once you were safely at sea; Vita and I would follow on the *Olympic* tomorrow to avoid a suspicious simultaneous departure; and we'd all meet up in New York next week to drop our bombshell on an unsuspecting world. Well, that's not quite how it's going to turn out. There'll be no bombshell, because there'll be no records. They stay here. You tell Diana you sold them to Faraday. You tell her you did what comes naturally to any con-man: you took the money and ran.' He grinned and blew a self-congratulatory pair of smoke-rings towards the ceiling. They rose, dissolving as they did so in a mirage of concentricity.

'Yes, Quincy,' I wanted to say. '*Very clever. But money is the rock on which your plan founders. There isn't any, you see. No doubt you're about to offer me some condescending fraction of your eagerly anticipated fee for selling this lie to Diana. But you needn't bother. Because you won't be paid anything. Not a penny. Not a cent.*'

'She has to be convinced it's all over, Guy,' he said, lowering his voice. 'If you just vanish along with the records, she'll go on pursuing the faint possibility of avenging her mother, especially now she has her father to avenge as well. She'll go on and on till they're forced to silence her. No, she has to believe you've sold out. She has to be persuaded her only ally is a man of straw. And she has to leave England. There are too many reminders here, too many reasons to go on chasing after the truth. She'll snap out of it in the States, believe me. I'll make sure she does. Oh, you can leave that side of things to me. I'm an old hand at it. All you have to do is tell her you've betrayed her, then walk out of her life. I'll even pay you to do it. Fabian died still owing you a thousand pounds, didn't he? So, why not let me write you out a check for that amount? One that won't bounce. By the way, I don't expect you to stay aboard till the ship reaches New York. Not with the Babcock trial still rumbling on. No, no. I'm a reasonable man. The *Leviathan* calls at Cherbourg this evening. Get off there. Go wherever you like. You'll have some spending money in your pocket. More than enough to use as seed-corn in a poker school. Or to snare some rich widow in Monte Carlo. You'll come out of this better than you could reasonably have expected to. Thanks to me.'

'*You think so, Quincy? You really think so?*'

'I'll tell you a secret, Guy. Strictly between ourselves. Diana wanted to believe you were still honouring your bargain with her. She wanted to believe it so much I didn't really have to work very hard at fooling her. Oh, it sounded good, I know. The freedom-loving American press; the transatlantic dash into their welcoming arms; victory against the odds. I spin a convincing yarn when I need to, no question. But there was more to it than that. I think she might feel something for you. *Really* feel, I mean. If I'm right, it makes you damn near unique among men. Just a pity we'll never find out, isn't it?'

Was he right? I wondered. Between the genuine doubts and false hopes, between passion and perversity, was there still something drawing us together? What was her mood as she waited aboard the *Leviathan*? What did she expect to happen when we met? Was I to be more than an ally of last resort? Was *she*?

'I'll tell you another secret, too. The last thing Maudie said to me when I saw her off on the *Lusitania*. Nothing about the Concentric Alliance. But about the voyage. She had some premonition she might not survive it. Made me promise, if she didn't, to look after Diana. She was worried Fabian would become too dominating an influence on the girl if she was no longer around. And she was worried about what kind of an influence he'd be. With good reason, as it turns out. I didn't take her seriously at the time. But I *did* promise. And it's good to keep a promise, don't you reckon? Even if you wait sixteen years to do it.'

He let himself fall back onto the bed, bouncing slowly to rest on the mattress, and stared up at the ceiling. His voice took on a wistful tone, as if even his cynicism had its limits. 'I should have listened to her, Guy. I should have dragged her off that ship by her hair. Then none of this might have. . . But I didn't. The *Lusitania* sailed with Maudie aboard. And at Penn station an hour later, waiting for the Pittsburgh train, I bought a *New York Times* and read the German Embassy's ad. "*Travellers intending to embark for an Atlantic voyage are reminded that a state of war exists between Germany and Great Britain. The war-zone includes the waters adjacent to the British Isles. Vessels flying the British flag in the war-zone are therefore liable to destruction and travellers sailing in them do so at—*" '

The door flew abruptly open and Vasaritch strode in, followed by Faraday. The general's face was flushed and twitching with suppressed fury. Quincy sat slowly up and stared at him uncomprehendingly. He did not yet know why his employer should be upset. But I did. Only too well.

'What's the matter with—'

'Shut your mouth!' roared Vasaritch. 'It is this man—' He stooped over me, knife in hand, flicked out the blade, prised at the rope holding the gag in place, then ripped through it and pulled the cloth from between my teeth. 'It is this man I want to hear. Where is the money, Horton? Where is it?'

'I haven't—'

A stinging blow caught me round the chin. There was blood on Vasaritch's knuckles as he pulled away and more of it clogging my mouth as he bellowed at me. 'Do not say *haven't* or *can't* or *don't* or *won't!* Just tell me where it is before I kill you!'

'Hey!' put in Quincy. 'What's the problem? You have the accounts, don't you?'

'We have them,' said Faraday, his voice icily calm. 'But they reveal nothing. Charnwood recorded an incredible series of capital losses, presumably to cover his tracks. What he really did with the money is unexplained.'

'No it isn't,' I protested. 'The losses *are* the explanation.'

'Absurd. Charnwood was a skilled financier. He could never have made such mistakes, one after another. It is simply not possible.'

'Where is it?' repeated Vasaritch.

'I've no idea.'

'*Where?*'

'I tell you I—'

Vasaritch had swept back his arm to hit me again when Faraday laid a restraining hand on his elbow. 'If he knows,' he said softly, 'he will have some record of it. We have examined every piece of paper in the bag. But he may already have removed the vital piece.'

'Very well,' growled Vasaritch, lowering his arm. 'Search him.'

Faraday squatted in front of me and smiled. 'Which pocket is it in, Horton? I don't want to have to turn them all out.'

'I've removed nothing from the bag.'

'Perhaps not. But in Phoenix Park, while you and Charnwood were waiting for us on the monument, didn't I see him hand you something? A letter of some kind? Or a note of where he hid the money?'

Of course. Charnwood's letter to Diana. Was that what it contained? Not a father's fond farewell, but the number of a Swiss bank account? It was possible, quite possible. And I had been planning to deliver it unopened! 'Inside pocket of my jacket,' I said, nodding to my left.

'Thank you.' I shuddered as Faraday slid his questing fingers in to find the envelope, an involuntary reaction that seemed to amuse him. 'Don't worry, Horton. This is all I want.' He stood up, flourishing the letter. 'Here we are.'

310

'He asked me to give it to Diana,' I explained. 'A message from him to his daughter.'

'Saying what?'

'I don't know.'

Faraday squinted at the seal. 'You haven't opened it?'

'No.'

'Why not?'

I shrugged. 'You wouldn't understand.'

Faraday raised one eyebrow, as if in reluctant agreement, then tore the flap of the envelope open, drew out a sheet of writing paper and unfolded it. 'Charnwood's hand, unquestionably,' he murmured. 'No address. Just a date. The tenth of November. The day before—'

'What does it say?' Vasaritch broke in.

'I'll read it, shall I?' Faraday replied in a soothing tone. 'No doubt it contains what we want amidst the other patrimonial blessings. "*My dear Diana, Tomorrow I am to meet Horton in Phoenix Park to surrender the records of the Concentric Alliance. When you learn this, you will probably assume I insisted on meeting him rather than you in order to avoid accounting to you in person for the things I have done. But I am not quite so craven. My real reason is to keep you out of danger, of which there may be a great deal. Whatever happens tomorrow – and I fear the worst – you should know that I loved your mother very much. Alas, I also brought about her death. Unintentionally, it is true. Indirectly, as one of the unpredictable consequences of war. But it was a war set in motion by an organization I created and controlled. Thus I cannot evade the charge. It has long hung heavy around my neck. A few weeks ago, I travelled to County Cork and stood on the Old Head of Kinsale, gazing out at the stretch of ocean where the* Lusitania *sank and your mother's body may still lie. I confessed to her then what I must admit to you now. Why I—*" '

'The money!' shouted Vasaritch suddenly, shattering the strange spell Charnwood's words had cast on the room. 'What does he say about the money? I do not want to hear about Old Heads of Kinsale.'

Faraday looked at him with the merest flicker of contempt, then sighed and said: 'I believe we're coming to the point. Shall I continue?' Met only by a glare, he looked back at the letter and resumed. ' "*Why I did it. Why I conceived and executed a plan to precipitate a European war. For profit, as my co-conspirators*

311

believed? Not fundamentally. To see if it could be done, I suppose. To discover whether, by one calculated intervention in the course of events, I could alter history and determine the future. Your mother's death was my answer. I altered many things. I changed the lives of millions. But I determined nothing. I precipitated my own wife's destruction. And what was my reward? To watch a pack of greedy—" ' Faraday cleared his throat. ' "*To watch a pack of greedy fools grow rich,*" ' he read expressionlessly.

'He calls us fools?' spluttered Vasaritch.

'Sticks and stones,' Faraday replied. 'There isn't much more. It must hold the key. "*I gave them wealth and power; too much of both. I watched them abuse my gifts. And I saw their avarice – which was only a mirror of mine – reflected in you. That was the hardest to bear. That was what finally persuaded me to take back what I had given. Losing money is as easy as making it, if you know how. For the past two years, I have systematically wasted as much money as they would entrust to me on worthless assets and doomed investments. I have thrown most of their wealth away . . .*" ' Faraday's voice faltered. ' "*And much of their power with it. . . The Great Depression . . . has been the means . . . to my end.*" '

Silence fell, filled by our mutual disbelief. Charnwood had neither lost the money nor hidden it. He had destroyed it. He had fed it, pound by pound, into the hungry jaws of universal insolvency. And all that remained was a confetti-cloud of waste-paper shares and bankrupt stock.

Several seconds passed, then the letter slipped from Faraday's fingers and fluttered to the floor. He leaned slowly back against the wall behind him, sighed heavily and closed his eyes. 'Gone,' he murmured. 'All gone.'

'It can't be,' said Vasaritch, his deep voice tolling like a bell.

'But it can,' Faraday responded. 'I thought those accounts were . . . doctored, concocted. Now I see . . . they are deadly accurate.'

'He kept some. I know it. I know how he thought.'

'It seems you didn't.'

With an oath, Vasaritch snatched up the letter. 'There must be more,' he growled. But his eyes, as they scanned the page, told a different story. With another oath, he screwed the letter into a ball, staring ahead as if he could see Charnwood's face before him, then let it fall at his feet. 'Why did he do it? Why?'

'He's told us why.'

'What is there to be done?'

'Nothing.' Faraday pushed himself upright and tugged at the lapels of his coat. 'We must go.'

'Go?'

'We have the records. There is nothing else. Anonymity is our only consolation.'

'Hold on,' put in Quincy, rising from the bed. 'What about my fee?'

'Commission,' corrected Faraday. 'No principal; no percentage.'

'That's not what we agreed. There wasn't any mention of—'

'Settle for it, Mr McGowan,' said Faraday, laying a cautionary hand on his shoulder. 'Be grateful for it.'

'Grateful? I'll be damned if—'

'Damned is better than dead. If we *had* found the money, we could not have allowed either you or Horton to remain alive.'

'What?'

'Rich people attract blackmailers. One fee would never have been enough for you.'

'We should kill them anyway,' snarled Vasaritch. 'They know too many names.' He turned and shouted for Milan. A second later, he appeared in the doorway, his huge shadow stretching towards us.

'No,' said Faraday. 'This is not Ireland. This is a first-class hotel we have been seen entering in a country where I am widely known and you, General, are highly conspicuous.'

'I do not care!'

'But I do. The risks would have been worth taking for what we hoped to find. But we have found nothing. And nothing is what these two gentlemen will remember of our dealings. Isn't it, Horton? No names. No facts. No fantasies of re-writing history.'

'None at all,' I replied, looking at Faraday and Vasaritch in turn to underline my sincerity.

'McGowan?'

A second or two passed during which it seemed Quincy might contest the point. Then he caught my eye and said: 'The same goes for me.'

'Good. Should you ever change your minds, the sort of back-alley misadventure that befell Duggan might well befall you. He made the mistake of failing to forget what he knew. Don't make the same mistake, will you?'

'No,' I said emphatically. 'We won't.'

Quincy flopped back down onto the bed and shook his head

313

dolefully. Faraday nodded and turned away. But Vasaritch was not satisfied. He stepped forward, closed his right hand round Quincy's chin and jerked it painfully up, then brought his left hand down onto the crown of his head like the opposing jaw of a vice. 'I did not say you could sit down, *Mr* McGowan,' he rasped.

'I . . . I'm sorry. I didn't mean—'

'What will *you* remember?'

'Nothing. Not. . . Not a god-damn thing.'

Vasaritch held him for several more breathless seconds, then said: 'There is cowardice in your eyes, *Mr* McGowan. The cowardice of a fat Bulgar peasant.' I saw Quincy flinch as Vasaritch spat into his face. Then he was thrown flat across the bed like a discarded fish as the general turned on his heel and strode from the room, Milan stepping hurriedly aside to make way for him. 'We go,' he bellowed over his shoulder.

'Excuse us, gentlemen,' said Faraday, following at a slower pace. 'Let us hope we never meet again.'

A second later, I heard the outer door close. Silence briefly possessed the room. Then a ship's hooter sounded through the window, rattling the sash. And Quincy rose unsteadily to his feet, manipulating his jaw as if afraid it were broken.

'Untie me, for God's sake!'

'Oh . . . OK. Of course.' He crouched behind me and began fumbling with the knots. For several minutes, neither of us spoke. Neither of us, indeed, seemed to want to speak. What, after all, was there to say? The records had gone. The proof had vanished. And the money did not exist. While we, somewhat to my surprise, were still alive.

At last, my hands were free. Shooing Quincy impatiently away, I bent forward and set to work on my ankles. He rose and lurched towards the door, then noticed the letter, lying in a crumpled ball on the floor. He sat down glumly beside it with his back against the wall, slowly flattened the letter out, then read it, his lips miming the words as he did so.

'Is there anything Faraday didn't read out?' I asked, as I tugged through the last twists of the knot.

'See for yourself,' said Quincy distractedly. He passed it across to me and my eye went instantly in search of the last phrase I had heard. '*The Great Depression has been the means to my end.*' There it was. With just one paragraph beneath.

'*What of the diverted capital I told you we were to live off? It is*

314

gone, all gone. There was always less of it than I led you and Vita to believe. And now there is none. The little that remained in August I have since disposed of. Why? Because sitting here to gloat over the discomfiture of my enemies has afforded me none of the satisfaction I had hoped for. And because I cannot allow the arrogance of youth to feed on the cowardice of old age any longer. I have shaped you too much in my own likeness, Diana. I have made you a party to one murder and quite possibly the perpetrator of another. I do not know if you meant to kill Wingate. His death may truly have been an accident. Only you can say. But I cannot take the chance, do you see? I cannot risk you becoming worse than me. I owe your mother that at least. If you killed Wingate for the sake of a privileged future, then I must ensure that you killed him in vain. I must see to it that you do not profit by following the example I set. I must end what I began. Thus your future, if it is to be privileged, will not be so because of any bequest from me. My only gift to you is priceless: a new beginning, untrammelled by my tainted wealth. Use it wisely, my child. And may God bless you. I remain, Your ever loving father.'

'Cold comfort for all of us, eh?' said Quincy as I looked up. 'No nest egg for Diana and Vita to peck at. No way out of servitude to brother Theo for me.'

I stared coldly at him, folded the letter as best I could, then slipped it into my pocket and began rubbing some life back into my shins and ankles.

'I bet you think I've been a damned fool.'

'So you have. And worse.' I stood up, stamping away the pins and needles. 'But what does it matter now?'

'Not a whole lot, I suppose.' He stayed where he was, slumped against the wall, frowning at the failure of his hopes and schemes, a figure at once abject and contemptible. He seemed almost to be on the verge of tears, the billowing confidence I had put my trust in crushed into lumpen self-pity.

I wanted to be out of his sight and hearing, as far as possible from this cigar-stale scene of his disappointment and my defeat. I was sorry and angry and bitter. But most of all, somewhere so deep it dragged down every other emotion, somewhere shamefully close to the core of my being, I was relieved it was over. 'Where's my ticket?' I asked abruptly.

'Mmm?' said Quincy, speaking as if from a great distance.

'My ticket.'

'Oh. . . In the drawer of the, er, bedside cabinet.'

I stumbled to the cabinet and slid the drawer open. There it was, wedged beneath a United States passport. One first-class berth in my name on the *S.S. Leviathan*, bought when Quincy thought he could afford to be extravagant. I stuffed it into my pocket behind Charnwood's letter and glanced at my watch. It was all right. There was time enough. I was not going to be left behind.

'You're . . . still going, then?'

'Why not?'

'No reason, I suppose. But . . . what will you say . . . to Diana?'

'What do you think?'

'I . . . I don't . . .' He gazed pleadingly up at me. 'I can't pay you now, of course, but . . . why inflict the truth on her? Why not tell her what we agreed? You're never going to see her again. Whereas Vita and me. . . There's no sense muddying the water, is there?'

'We agreed nothing. You dictated terms. Those terms no longer apply. As to what I'll tell Diana . . .' I stood by the door, looking down at him. 'I haven't made up my mind. You and Vita can while away your days aboard the *Olympic* wondering what I've said. I hope the uncertainty agrees with you.' I turned to go, then pulled up. There was one last thing that needed saying, one final condemnation he did not deserve to be spared. 'Do you know the worst of it, Quincy? I think your plan might have worked. I think we might actually have got away with it. But you threw the chance away. And it'll never come again. Cheating me was no big deal. But you managed to betray – how many did you say it was? – more than a hundred thousand Americans. Mull that over back in Pittsburgh. Remember it, whenever you're tempted to tell brother Theo what to do with his job. Because you won't tell him. You'll never tell him. Vasaritch was right. There *is* cowardice in your eyes. And it'll always be there.'

CHAPTER

EIGHTEEN

I stood on the boat deck as the *Leviathan* backed slowly out of Ocean Dock and turned to head down Southampton Water. The sky was one low unbroken dome of grey, the sea dark and oily, the gulls strangely silent as they swooped and hovered in the fitful breeze. The vast ship was more than three quarters empty according to the purser, but seemed wholly so to me, desolate and despairing as the tugs nudged it on its way. There were no fanfares, no crowds, no streamers. This was a chill and furtive leave-taking, late November in spirit as well as fact.

Worse lay in wait along the Itchen Quays, sliding into view as we passed the mouth of the river. The *Empress of Britain* was in port, pale as a remembered ghost, solid as the rails I leant against. Summer was long gone. And so was the friend I had stood beside half a world and four months away.

'*Well, that tears it, doesn't it?*' he seemed to say once more.

'We knew it was coming,' I murmured in reply. 'Or, rather, we should have known.'

My mood had not changed since leaving Quincy's suite at the South Western. It had merely intensified. I was free and I was alive. It should have been enough to make a man like me happy, let alone content. But I had held history in my hands and seen it snatched away. I had been tempted by a fleeting touch of God-like power. Comfort and wealth seemed now the pettiest of ambitions. It would not last. I knew that. Guy Horton would soon be

317

reclaimed by his true self. But, for the moment, he felt the loneliest man in the world. On the emptiest ship. And the widest sea.

Waiting below, in her cabin, was Diana. We had met for the first time sailing towards this port. We would meet for the last sailing away from it. The circle was very nearly closed. But what would seal its circumference? The truth? Or yet more of the lies we had chased around its rim? I paced the deck, smoking one cigarette after another, waiting for the last of England to fade greyly astern, waiting till a choice had to be made – or offered. A truth for a truth. Or a lie for a lie. In the end, as we passed the Nab Tower and headed out into the Channel, I realized only she could decide.

Was she really there? I wondered, as I stood at the door of her cabin and raised my hand to knock. Perhaps I would have preferred her not to be, would have been grateful to find she had seen through Quincy's ploy and slipped ashore at the last moment. But she had not. Before my knuckles could touch the door a second time, she opened it.

There were no words at first. A nod, a flicker of the eyes, a quiver of the lips. Then she stepped back and I entered. She was wearing the black suit I had last seen as I drove away from Amber Court after the inquest. False mourning had met secret grief. One pretence had begotten another. She would want to know who had killed him. She would want to understand. But could I allow her to?

'You haven't brought the records with you?' she asked, frowning at me.

'No. I. . . We have to be careful.' I looked away. 'Did Quincy tell you what happened in Phoenix Park?'

'Yes. But not why you met Papa alone. Nor why you left me to . . . learn of his death as I did.'

'I went alone because your father insisted I should. And I didn't come back for you afterwards because Faraday said you were acting as his agent.'

'He was lying.'

'Yes. I realize that now.'

'And how did Papa know you were in Dublin in the first place?'

'I . . . I'm not sure.' Her frown deepened. 'Perhaps he kept watch on the Shelbourne. Perhaps . . .' Irritated by the inadequacy of my words, I whipped out the letter and handed it to her. 'He asked

318

me to give you this. I'm sorry it's so. . . It couldn't be helped.'

She sank down onto a chair and flattened the letter out on her lap. For as long as it took her to read her father's message, she was oblivious to my existence. I moved to the plate-glass window and peered out towards the grey horizon. Minutes passed. Then some awareness – fainter than any specific movement – told me she had finished. I turned round to find her looking straight at me. 'You've read this?' she said, her eyes narrowing as incredulity gave way to suspicion.

'Yes. I have.'

'There's no money left?'

'None at all, it seems.'

'But . . .' She stared down at the letter. 'Why?'

'You know why, Diana. You just don't want to believe it.'

'That's not true. I—' Her gaze swung back to me. 'Tell me now. Who betrayed him? How did they know he was in Dublin?'

'Tell *me* something first. Answer the question your father poses in his letter. Did you mean to kill Max?'

'Of course not. I've—'

'Don't toss a thoughtless lie at me,' I shouted, growing suddenly angry. 'Think what you're saying. Did you set out to kill him?'

'It seems you believe I did, Guy. So, what difference does it make what I say?'

'The difference is that I want to know the truth.'

'I've already told you the truth.'

'Have you?'

'Several times. I'm just not sure you were listening.'

'What does that mean? Yes or no?'

'It means I'm tired of defending my past actions.' She flushed. 'Especially to you.'

'*Yes or no?*'

She stood up, dropping the letter onto a table beside the chair, and ran her hand down over her hip. Her eyes met mine, then moved away, then met them again. There was no answer. There never would be. She was breathing rapidly as her mind raced to outwit me. But it was racing in the wrong direction. 'Where are the records?' she asked abruptly. 'I have a right to see them.' And so the issue was decided. It was to be a lie for a lie. I silently wished her well of the fraudulent future she had chosen. 'I want to see them now.'

'But some things you want you can't have.' I smiled. 'I sold the records to Faraday. They're gone. Lost for ever. Like your father's money.'

'What?'

'I sold them. I struck a deal. I turned a profit. Well, there was none to be made out of honouring our bargain, was there? As soon as I read the letter, I realized that. It's why I screwed it up in disgust. I had to look elsewhere, Diana. Surely you can see I had to.' A strange sense of satisfaction flooded over me as I embroidered the lie. Why should I not let her hate me and trust Quincy? She had deceived Max often and completely enough to deserve this. She had forfeited her right to the truth. And mine with it. 'I did what you should have expected me to do. I named my price. And Faraday paid it.'

'My father laid down his life to help you escape with those records,' she said slowly. 'And you simply sold them.'

'Correct.'

'I see.' She moved uncertainly to the bedroom doorway and leant back against the frame, keeping her eyes fixed upon me. 'I see it all. Now.'

'Do you?'

'*You* betrayed him, didn't you? *You* led them to him.'

'Maybe.' I shrugged, happy to let her invent part of the fiction herself. 'I didn't owe your father anything.'

'And they paid better, of course. Better than he or I could.'

'Exactly. Money outlasts truth and beauty. It grows, while they fade.'

'Bastard,' she murmured.

'Call me what you like. But you can't call me a murderer, can you? You can't call me anything worse than you already are.'

'You killed him, didn't you?'

'Did I?'

'Answer me.'

'No. I won't.' I shook my head and smiled. 'I'm tired of defending my past actions. *Especially to you.*'

Suddenly, spurred by the echo of her own words, she lunged into the bedroom and out of my sight. I reached the doorway just in time to see her bending over her clutch bag where it lay on the bedside cabinet. Then she whirled round to face me, raising the derringer in her right hand as she did so. I had forgotten about it amidst the press of events. But Diana had not. And she was pointing it straight at me.

320

'No! For God's sake! I was ly—'

She squeezed the trigger, her expression fixed and determined. But there was only a click. And, as she squeezed again, only another. She glanced down at the barrel and grimaced in rage. I could see her thinking what I too was thinking. Quincy or Vita had discovered the gun and removed the bullets. No doubt they had acted to save her from herself. But they had only succeeded in saving me.

I walked slowly across the room, prised the gun from her grasp and slipped it into the pocket of my jacket. She was breathing even more rapidly than me, shocked, it seemed, by her misjudgement, bewildered by two things her life had left her ill-prepared to meet: failure and frustration. 'That was lucky,' I said, as calmly as I could. 'For both of us.'

'Get out of here,' she said, in a subdued but imperious tone.

'Gladly.'

'And stay away from me for the rest of the voyage.'

'Don't worry. I'm jumping ship at Cherbourg. You'll soon be rid of me. For good.'

She looked at me for the first time since trying to kill me. The fit had passed. The wish was no longer strong enough to act on. But the hatred remained, mingling with the first stirrings of something much less simple. 'Just now,' she said slowly, 'you were going to tell me you'd been lying, weren't you?'

'Yes.'

'But that wouldn't have been true, would it?'

'Of course not.' She wanted to believe me. She needed to believe me. But there was doubt in her eyes, a faint suspicion that I had somehow misled her. And a creeping realization that she would never know for certain. 'How could it have been?'

She broke away and moved to the window, clasped her hands together in front of her and stared fixedly out. I could tell by the very set of her shoulders that she meant to do so for as long as I remained, that she would not look round until she was sure I had gone. This was the end between us. Neither of us had won. But neither of us had admitted defeat. Other than to ourselves.

'What else,' I added, as I turned towards the door, 'could you possibly imagine?'

I went back on deck and tossed the derringer over the aft rail into the foaming wake. Then I took several slow circuits of the deserted

321

promenade, wishing the journey was already over and Diana and I had more than doors and companion-ways between us.

Confident though I was that she would not leave her cabin until I had disembarked, I decided to take refuge in the male preserve of the smoking-room, commanding as its wide windows did a view of the bow – and hence of Cherbourg, as soon as it came in sight. I had the room to myself at first and, though the cocktail list offered in deference to the Volstead Act only such delicacies as sarsaparilla and lemon soda, the steward supplied Manhattans as strong and frequently as I required.

I had just started the third of these when a tubby and ominously amiable American flopped into the chair beside me. 'A fellow passenger,' he proclaimed. 'You're a rare and welcome sight, sir. I've been rattling round that lounge they call a social hall downstairs like a pea in a drum.'

'Have you really?'

'I have. And *social* isn't the word for it.'

'No?'

'You're British, right?' He squinted at me.

'Yes,' I replied cautiously.

'And well educated by the sound of it. The Classics. Greek Mythology. All that stuff.'

'Well . . . I suppose . . .'

'You may be able to help me, then. I was looking at the paintings round the wall of the *un*-social hall.' He laughed and waited in vain for me to join in, then continued undaunted. 'Four of them. Depicting the Pandora story, so I was told. You know? Pandora's Box.'

'I know.'

'Well, what I was wondering was—' He broke off at the approach of the steward and went up in my estimation by demanding a large Jack Daniels. 'What I was wondering was this. She got curious and opened the box, right?'

'More or less.' Like Charnwood, I suddenly thought. Simple curiosity was what had made him do it. The wish to know what lay beneath the lid of the jar labelled WAR.

'And out flew . . . everything bad in the world?'

'All the Spites of mankind, yes. Old age. Illness. Insanity. Lust. Greed. Jealousy. And the rest.'

'Which mankind had been free of till then?'

'Yes.'

322

'So . . . what would have happened . . . if she hadn't?'

'Hadn't released them?'

'Right.'

'Well, we wouldn't be plagued by them, would we?'

'We wouldn't know what it's like to be those things you said? Old, sick, mad, greedy and so forth?'

'Exactly.'

'Life would be . . . perfect?'

'Yes. Except . . .' Suddenly, it came to me. Charnwood had seen the world standing on the brink of war and had pushed it over. But, if he had stayed his hand, the world would not have retreated from the brink. In the end, it would still have fallen. 'Except,' I resumed, 'that, if Pandora hadn't opened the box, somebody else would have.'

'There was never any hope it could remain sealed for ever?'

'Not really.' I smiled, reflecting on the inadvertent irony of his words. 'You see, Hope was one of the Spites imprisoned in the box.'

My companion frowned. 'Why did Hope have to be shut away?'

'Because it always lied. And, true to form, after its release, it deceived mankind into believing the other Spites could be overcome. They couldn't, of course, but thinking they could at least made them seem bearable.'

'So Hope did some good after all?'

'I suppose it did.' As the steward returned, I gazed past him at the featureless sky beyond the window. It was as grey and wide and empty as my future seemed. And yet . . . 'I suppose we prove the point, we sorely afflicted but stubbornly optimistic mortals.'

'We do?'

'Well, even when the worst happens . . . we continue to hope for the best.'

'I'll certainly drink to that.' He smiled and raised his glass, inviting me to share his toast. Which I did. More in hope, of course, than expectation.

Four hours later, I was standing in the stern of the Cherbourg tender as it pulled away from the *Leviathan*. The liner's vast black flank soared above me in the night, its porthole-lights watching my departure like a hundred unblinking eyes. Was Diana standing in one of those glimmering circles of gold, I wondered, looking down as I left? I could not tell. Nor could she, if she were, discern one muffled figure looking up from the puny craft that bore him away. What either of us felt or saw or believed was as obscure to the other as the day we met. And it was too late now for it ever to be otherwise. I would board the next train to Paris, while she carried on to New York. And the tangents of our separate destinies would diverge at an ever greater pace. Never to meet again.

EPILOGUE

The weeks that followed my flight from England were nomadic and aimless, while the truth they revealed was as unwelcome as it was predictable. My long partnership with Max – and our cosy arrangement with the Babcocks – had sapped my appetite for the self-sufficient life of the wandering con-man. My instincts were sound, but my reactions were suspect. Loneliness and fallibility nibbled at my nerves. My finances dwindled. My prospects deteriorated. My confidence declined.

Then memory began to exert a power over me it never had before, drawing me back to Venice, to an empty villa on the Lido and a neglected grave on the Isola di San Michele. The turn of the year found me lingering in the fog-shrouded city, riding the *vaporetti* by day and trying my failing luck in the Casino by night. I knew I should leave, but I had nowhere to go. And to desert Max in death seemed somehow more difficult than to betray him in life.

It was in the middle of January that my sojourn in Venice was transformed by an encounter at the Casino with Francesco Contanari, wealthy dealer in Byzantine antiquities. He was, of course, no more a scion of Venetian nobility than I was a gentleman of independent means. When the pretence and artifice were stripped away, we were beasts of the same stripe: Francesco's antiquities were as inauthentic as his blood-line. He was eager to recruit an assistant, to collect his *objets d'art ancien* from their

325

place of dubious manufacture in Istanbul and to pose as a knowledgeable collector whenever a client needed the spur of a rival bid to turn his interest in a thirteenth-century icon into an offer of hard cash. I was equally eager to be recruited. And so began an association which, if it did not banish my regrets, at least paid off my debts.

It was not, however, destined to be as long as it was lucrative. A telegram from Francesco's mistress-cum-secretary – whose charms I had myself on one occasion failed to resist – reached me in Istanbul at the end of April, warning me that Francesco had been arrested in Rome, after selling a scabbard supposedly worn by Emperor Andronicus Comnenus to a personal friend of Mussolini; I was on no account to return to Venice.

But where was I to go instead? Drifting up through Bulgaria and Yugoslavia with money in my pocket but no destination in mind, I stopped for a few days in Sarajevo, serene and pre-posterously pretty in a bowl of green hills filled with plum blossom and spring sunshine. I visited the reception room at the Town Hall where Archduke Franz Ferdinand and his wife had been enter-tained to lunch on Sunday the twenty-eighth of June, 1914. I walked along the Appelkai to the exact spot where they had been shot dead that afternoon with their lunches still undigested: the wrong turning which had become Fabian Charnwood's apotheosis. And I met an old man in a café who recalled for me the events of that day with greater acuteness than he could have known. *'Nothing was said. Nobody was told. But we knew he was going to die. There were more assassins than guards waiting for him in Sarajevo.'* Yes. And behind the assassins the Concentric Alliance had also been waiting, to count the ripples as they radiated from one precipitated event into an ever wider future, as far as May 1932 – and well beyond.

A few days later, on the train from Belgrade to Vienna, I found myself involved in a poker game with several well-heeled pas-sengers, one of whom so resembled Faraday in manner and appearance that I could not resist cheating him out of most of his winnings in a single hand of red dog. It was a petty act of vicarious vengeance, but it yielded an unexpected result. A hearty but watchful Australian who had just about broken even during the game caught up with me at the Süd-Bahnhof in Vienna and insisted I dine with him and his wife at their hotel that evening. There he revealed himself as Donald Beaumont, millionaire bookmaker and owner of a chain of betting shops reaching from Perth to Parramatta. He was about to diversify into the casino business and needed staff who knew the tricks of the trade. Who better to keep an eye on the customers than a debonair Englishman with a flair for dealing from a stacked deck? He was, in short, offering me a job. And the salary sounded distinctly attractive. He gave me twenty-four hours to think it over.

That night, I tried to retrace the route followed by Duggan and Colonel Brosch after their rendezvous by the Danube Canal on the twentieth of July, 1914. But it was hopeless. Their footsteps had faded along with their secrets. It was easier – and safer – to pretend they had never spoken, to each other or to me. The time had come to abandon the trail in spirit as well as deed, to start again in a country where I knew nobody and nobody knew me. Next morning, I accepted Beaumont's offer.

And so, in circumstances I could never have envisaged, I returned to England. I was booked aboard the *S.S. Orama*, sailing for Brisbane from London on Saturday the twenty-fifth of June. I reached London on Thursday the sixteenth, with barely a week in which to bid my family an overdue farewell. A Christmas card from Venice – with no address to write back to – represented the total of my efforts to keep in touch since abandoning Maggie at the Letchworth Hall Hotel seven months before. As ever, my explanations promised to be no more acceptable than my apologies. Perhaps that was why I decided to visit Felix first. He at least would be pleased to see me.

But, to my astonishment, when I took the train up to Napsbury the following day, I found he was no longer in residence at the hospital.

'He was discharged in January,' the matron informed me.

'*Discharged?*'

'Well, transferred, actually, to the Brabazon Clinic.'

'The what?'

'It's a private hospital in London. Very highly thought of. They do excellent work there. Of course, if we could give the patients here as much attention as they'd receive at the Brabazon, then I'm sure—'

'The Brabazon is private, you say?'

'Certainly. And extremely expensive. The fees are astronomic. But worth every penny, I should think. If you can afford it.'

327

*   *   *

But neither my father nor my sister *could* afford it. There was the mystery. I took a taxi to Hatfield and caught the next train to Letchworth. It was nearly half past three when I arrived, so I headed across the common towards Norton School, preferring to meet Maggie at the gate rather than face my father alone at *Gladsome Glade*. The afternoon was hot and Letchworth at its most stultifyingly placid, the Garden City in full and earnest leaf.

Some of its infant citizens were already streaming out, serge-shorted and summer-frocked, when I reached the school. Spotting Maggie's car in the yard, I propped myself against the bonnet, lit a cigarette and waited for her to emerge. Which she did, ten minutes later, weighed down by an armful of exercise books and a week's load of pedagogic cares. But of surprise at seeing me there was curiously little sign.

'I saw you from the staff-room, Guy,' she explained, giving me a sisterly peck on the cheek. 'Since you only ever turn up unannounced, it didn't take me long to recover from the shock. The deputy head took you for my beau.'

'And do you have a beau . . . for me to be mistaken for?'

She wagged her finger at me censoriously. 'Don't think you can distract me like that. Where have you been all these months?'

'Didn't you get my card from Venice?'

'Yes. For all the use it was. I wrote to the British Consulate, but they had no idea where you were.'

'Why were you so anxious to contact me? Was it about Felix?'

'Oh!' Now she did look surprised. 'You know about that, do you?'

'I've just come from Napsbury.'

'Ah. I see.'

'Well I don't. Care to explain?'

'Of course.' She smiled. 'Tell you what. Last time we met, for lunch at Letchworth Hall, you stood me up. Treat me to tea there and I'll tell you the whole story.'

'Can't you just tell me now?'

'Oh no, Guy.' Her smile acquired a mischievous edge. 'I'm not going to risk you walking out on me a second time.'

*   *   *

328

As we drove down through the town, past the Goddess factory and numberless other milestones of my discarded youth, Maggie sang the praises of the Brabazon Clinic and cheered me with her descriptions of the progress Felix had made there. But of the reasons for his transfer from Napsbury and of the means by which his fees were being paid she said nothing – until we were seated in the lounge of the Letchworth Hall Hotel, with tea and scones safely ordered. There, amidst the white napery and antimacassared leather, where silver spoons tinkled demurely in fine china saucers and sunlight glimmered respectfully through thick lace curtains, I made my last – and least expected – discovery.

'The reason we've been able to secure the best care for Felix money can buy is a simple one, Guy. You see, Felix is now a wealthy man. His money's held in trust, of course. I'm one of the trustees, along with his benefactor's solicitor and—'

'I don't understand. What money? What benefactor?'

'Somebody he served under during the war, apparently. It seems he only found out about Felix's illness quite recently. As soon as he did, he put thirty thousand pounds into a trust to fund his treatment.'

'*Thirty thousand pounds?*' It was the price of a peerage. I had that on no less an authority than – 'Who? Who is he?'

'We don't know. It was a condition of the gift that he remain anonymous. His solicitor, Mr Grogan, was sworn to secrecy. I've tried questioning him, but he gives nothing away. I've even contacted Felix's old CO in the Hertfordshires. He can't recall any officer rich enough – or fond enough of Felix – to have done such a thing.'

'When did you first hear about this?'

'Last November. A couple of weeks after you did your disappearing act. Mr Grogan wrote to us from Dublin. Completely out of the blue.'

'*Dublin?*'

'Yes. What of it?'

I stared past her towards the window. There had not seemed to be a breath of wind outside, but the curtain was moving, as if stirred by the faintest of breezes. What had Charnwood asked, when we lunched together at the Ambassador Club? And what had I replied?

'*If you could change one thing, just one, that the past has placed beyond your reach, what would it be?*'

'*I would give my brother Felix back his sanity. He lost it in the war.*'

'*Ah, the war. Always there is the war.*'

'Are you all right, Guy?' asked Maggie, reaching across to lay a concerned hand on my elbow. 'You look as if somebody's just walked over your grave.'

Maggie drove me down to the Brabazon Clinic in Roehampton the following afternoon. My father stayed in Letchworth, ostensibly because of a bowls fixture. And perhaps it was true. Over breakfast, he had remarked with evident relief that at least he did not have the Rector of Stiffkey for a son. Since, according to his newspaper, the good rector was shortly to stand trial in the Consistory Court for immoral behaviour with teen-age girls, it was not much of a compliment. None the less, I had the impression that news of my salaried employment in Australia – when I finally announced it – might win from him some grudging form of approval.

As for Felix, he was clearly less troubled – if no saner – than he had been for years, responding better than I had dared hope to the régime of the Brabazon, which was as restfully attentive – and as obviously expensive – as Maggie had led me to expect. We took tea with him on the lawn, in an atmosphere more reminiscent of a five-star hotel than a lunatic asylum. And, though there were trees all around us, he never once mentioned glimpsing the enemy hiding among them.

'He really is coming along splendidly,' Maggie remarked as we drove away afterwards through the sun-grained air of early evening. 'The doctors are delighted with his progress.'

'So they should be.'

'It's funny about his benefactor, though.' She had asked Felix if he could remember anybody he had served under during the war who might have felt indebted to him; naturally, he had not been able to. 'Do you think we'll *ever* find out who he is?'

I shrugged. 'Your guess is as good as mine. But, whoever he is, he's done more for Felix than we could. If anonymity's all he wants in return, perhaps we should let him have it.'

'I suppose so. It's just. . . Well, you can't help being curious, can you?'

The setting sun flashed up at me from the river as we crossed

330

Putney Bridge. And the memory of a stroll along the Bishop's Walk with Diana came into my mind as if it were some half-recalled fragment of a life I had led in a previous incarnation. 'Can't you?' I said. 'I think I can.' Then the bridge was behind us. And the memory was gone.